Madge Vertner

Madge Vertner

Mattie Griffith

Introduction by Holly Kent

Hastings College Press | Hastings, Nebraska

Production Editor and Proofreader
Emilie Barnes

ISBN-10: 1942885148
ISBN-13: 978-1-942885-14-6

This edition of *Madge Vertner* was produced with the assistance of Accessible Archives (accessible-archives.com).

Manufactured in the United States of America

Text is printed on acid-free, chlorine-free paper with 30% postconsumer recycled content. Cover is printed on 100% recycled paper.

Contents

Introduction

Holly Kent

Every time Mattie Griffith told the story of how she became an
abolitionist, she told it slightly differently. The basic facts of Griffith's
life, and her work as an antislavery advocate, are clear. Griffith was
born into a slave-owning family in Kentucky in 1825 and, as a young
woman, inherited six enslaved people, whom she emancipated after
leaving the South and joining the antislavery movement. Over the
course of her abolitionist career, she wrote two novels, *Autobiography
of a Female Slave* (1856) and *Madge Vertner* (1859–1860), which failed
to make the kind of national splash she had hoped they might but
which nonetheless earned considerable praise and positive attention in
antislavery circles.

It is the specifics of how Griffith went from slave-owning
daughter of the South to radical antislavery activist in the North that
remain slightly obscure. Sometimes Griffith asserted that she became an
abolitionist at the age of five, after she witnessed one of the men whom
her family owned, "Uncle Dick," being sold away from his family.
"She cried herself to sleep that night," an 1857 *National Anti-Slavery
Standard* profile of Griffith noted, "but ever after she was the friend and
champion of the slave."[1] At other times, Griffith dated her conversion
to abolitionism to hearing of the vicious attack on antislavery Senator
Charles Sumner by a proslavery assailant.[2] Whatever the trigger for
Griffith's conversion to abolitionism, her fierce dedication to the
antislavery cause is evident. The moment Griffith set pen to paper to

---

[1] *The National Anti-Slavery Standard* XVIII: 10 (July 25, 1857), *Accessible
Archives.* <http://www.accessible-archives.com/>.

[2] For more on Griffith's encounter with Sumner's work, please see Joe Lockard,
Autobiography of a Female Slave (Jackson: University Press of Mississippi, 2010),
405.

denounce the "peculiar institution" of slavery, she irrevocably severed all of the ties that bound her to her Kentucky friends and family and made it impossible for her to ever return to the region where she had been born and raised.

Apart from taking the direct step of emancipating the enslaved people whom she owned, Griffith was initially unsure about how she could best contribute to abolitionism. Writing to prominent members of the Boston Female Anti-Slavery Society Anne Weston and Caroline Weston in December 1857, Griffith declared "I am only too happy to serve the Anti-Slavery cause in any manner no matter how humble or how great *only use me*.... This I know I owe to the slaves for Circumstance, Accident, and Condition cast my life among them, and through my very *blood* … I have helped wrong them."[3] Obligated by her own complicity in the slave system and the myriad ways in which she had personally benefited from the slave economy to become an abolitionist, Griffith was eager to dedicate her energies to the antislavery movement. But how and where could those energies best be put to use?

One significant way to contribute to the battle against slavery during the 1850s was to write abolitionist texts. After all, Griffith came of activist age in a post–*Uncle Tom's Cabin* world, in which the power of literature to raise awareness about the evils of slavery had been dazzlingly demonstrated by that bestselling novel. Serialized between 1851 and 1852 in the antislavery newspaper the *National Era* and published in book form in 1852, Harriet Beecher Stowe's book was remarkably popular, selling 300,000 copies domestically and 1.5 million copies internationally in its first year alone.[4] In the wake of this incredible success, new space opened up in the literary marketplace for fiction focused on slavery. While none of the anti- (or pro-)slavery novels published in the wake of *Uncle Tom's Cabin* achieved anything resembling its success, the 1850s was notable for its unprecedented

---

[3]   This letter is cited in Larry Ceplair's ground-breaking article about Griffith and her life and work, "Mattie Griffith Browne: A Kentucky Abolitionist" *The Filson Club History Quarterly* 68 (1994), 224.

[4]   For more on reception of Uncle Tom's Cabin, please see Joan Hendrick, *Harriet Beecher Stowe: A Life* (New York: Oxford University Press, 1995), 218–233.

receptivity to antislavery fiction and for eagerness on the part of abolitionists to (at least seek to) recreate *Uncle Tom's* popularity.

The *National Anti-Slavery Standard's* article about Griffith claimed that it was Stowe's novel that had inspired her to write antislavery fiction as her primary means of contributing to the abolitionist cause. "Just about this time, while she was in vain endeavoring to find a way to accomplish her purpose," the paper recounted, "the first volume of 'Uncle Tom's Cabin' was put into her hands, and then she determined to write a book, for she felt as if she knew more of the subject than Mrs. Stowe."[5] Unlike the Connecticut-born Stowe, Kentucky-native Griffith could write about slave-owning society from the inside, as a woman who had herself been a slave owner and had seen the evils of slavery first-hand during her childhood and adolescence. A significant part of Griffith's power as an antislavery novelist came from, as abolitionist newspaper the *Liberator* phrased it, this status as "a Southern witness."[6]

Griffith's first novel, *Autobiography of a Female Slave*, was published in 1856. As the book's title suggests, the story purports to be the first-hand account of an enslaved woman, Ann, about the horrors of her experiences in slavery and her efforts to emancipate herself. When she was mistaken for a formerly enslaved author in the antislavery press, however, Griffith hastened to correct this misapprehension, making her real identity known to the abolitionist community.[7]

By initially presenting her work as though it were slave narrative, Griffith risked providing ammunition to proslavery advocates, who insisted that all first-person accounts of slavery were, in actuality, abolitionist fictions. Responding to these concerns, abolitionists who reviewed *Autobiography* stressed that the text, although fictional, was nonetheless rooted in first-hand knowledge of slavery. Griffith was, as the *Liberator* noted, "a lady born, bred and educated at the South"

---

[5]   *The National Anti-Slavery Standard* XVIII: 10 (July 25, 1857), *Accessible Archives*. <http://www.accessible-archives.com/>.

[6]   "Autobiography of a Female Slave" *The Liberator* XXVII: 2 (January 9, 1857), *Accessible Archives*. <http://www.accessible-archives.com/>.

[7]   For more on Griffith's decision to reveal her real identity to abolitionists, please see Joe Lockard's excellent afterword to his edition of *Autobiography of a Female Slave* (Jackson: University Press of Mississippi, 2010), 408.

who had for many years been "a close and inevitable observer of the institution whose workings she portrays."[8]

Autobiography, while not a popular success, nonetheless attracted a great deal of favorable notice from abolitionist periodicals and advocates. Antislavery activist Lydia Maria Child was typical in praising the novel (which featured numerous, graphic scenes of the physical and emotional abuses suffered by the enslaved) for being "painful in its power."[9] Noting that the book was not entirely polished in its prose style, the antislavery press nonetheless praised the book for painting a visceral portrait of what enslaved people endured within slavery.

Griffith's second (and, as it transpired, her last) full-length fictional work about slavery, *Madge Vertner*, unlike *Autobiography*, centered on a heroine who was the pampered daughter of a wealthy slave owner. The novel began serialization in the *National Anti-Slavery Standard* in July 1859. "Many of our readers," editor Lydia Maria Child declared, "will be glad to find in our present issue the beginning of a new Story, by Miss MATTIE GRIFFITH, author of 'The *Autobiography of a Female Slave*,' and whose previous contributions have added much to the interest of our columns."[10] Much as reviewers had done in their discussions of *Autobiography*, Child underlined Griffith's status as a white Southern woman, who had extensive personal knowledge of slavery. "Having spent the greater part of her life in Kentucky, her native State," Child wrote, "she is perfectly familiar with all the social and domestic influences of slavery, and therefore able to enlighten the people of the North as to its effects upon both the masters and the slaves."[11]

Throughout *Madge Vertner*'s serialization, Child emphasized the novel's popularity with *Standard* readers. As she noted in January

---

[8]   "Autobiography of a Female Slave," *The Liberator* XXVII: 2 (January 9, 1857), *Accessible Archives*. <http://www.accessible-archives.com/>.

[9]   Lydia Maria Child, "How a Kentucky Girl Became an Abolitionist," *The Independent* (March 27, 1862): 6–7.

[10]   Lydia Maria Child, "A New Story by Miss Griffith," *The National Anti-Slavery Standard* XX: 11 (July 30, 1859). *Accessible Archives*. < http://www. accessible-archives.com/>.

[11]   Ibid.

1860, the novel was being "read by many persons with eager interest."[12] Perhaps as an effort to address previous criticisms of Griffith's work as lacking in polish, Child also quoted an (unnamed) "gentleman of cultivated literary taste and wide experience" who asserted, "The style of the story is an improvement upon the past (which, in my judgment, was never bad and always indicated high promise)."[13] In addition to noting the ways in which *Madge* was artistically superior to *Autobiography*, Child asserted that there was definite interest on the part of *Standard* readers in seeing *Madge* appear as a book. "We are frequently asked," she wrote, "if the story will be published in book form. We can only say that we think it worthy to be issued in that shape; and as we know that some valued friends of the cause are of the same opinion, we hope it may find a publisher able to appreciate its merits."[14]

As Child offers no further excerpts from *Standard* readers praising *Madge Vertner*, it is difficult to assess her claims about the novel's popularity. That Child chose to serialize the novel from beginning to end may have been because *Standard* readers were indeed eager to see the entire book, because of Child's desire to support Griffith in her abolitionist literary work, or some combination of the two. Given the lack of additional evidence, it is impossible to get a definitive sense of how *Madge* was received by the *Standard*'s audience. What is certain is that the novel did not (despite Child's and, likely, Griffith's hopes) ever appear in book form, until the edition you are reading now. If *Madge* was, indeed, as popular with abolitionist readers as Child claimed, why was it not published in book form until 2015?

The answer may well be the timing of *Madge*'s serialization. By 1859 and 1860, the antislavery literature bubble that had developed in the wake of *Uncle Tom's Cabin*'s publication had largely burst. Stowe's second antislavery novel, 1856's *Dred; A Tale of the Great Dismal Swamp*, while also a bestseller, failed to achieve the same dramatic level of success which *Uncle Tom's Cabin* had. After 1856, antislavery

---

[12] Lydia Maria Child, "The Story of Madge Vertner," *The National Anti-Slavery Standard* XX: 35 (January 14, 1860). *Accessible Archives.* < http://www. accessible-archives.com/>.

[13] Ibid.

[14] Ibid.

novels were consequently published in smaller numbers by both mainstream and abolitionist presses.[15] The late 1850s and early 1860s were also notably fraught years in the history of American slavery and abolitionism, with the antislavery and (broader American) press and public preoccupied by John Brown's failed slave insurrection at Harper's Ferry and subsequent execution for treason, the pending, already contentious 1860 presidential election, and increasingly acrimonious debates about secession. With the abolitionist and popular media so much absorbed by presidential politics and Brown's trial and execution, there may well have been little room for an antislavery novel like *Madge* (which focused on the domestic, rather than on the political side of slavery) to find a publisher, let alone widespread success. Given its relative obscurity during its own era, why, then, is *Madge Vertner* a significant novel for contemporary readers to consider?

While it did not find a large audience upon its initial publication, the novel provides a fascinating lens into debates about slavery, abolition, race, and gender at this vitally important moment in American history. From *Madge Vertner*, we can learn more about discussions within the antislavery movement about how slavery could best be brought to an end, gain insights into how racial hierarchies and categories were constructed during this era, and delve deeper into conceptions of women's rights in the pre–Civil War era. The novel also raises questions that remain significant (and unresolved) in contemporary America, about how to best combat racial inequality, how the social construction of race shapes individuals' lives and broader societal structures, how whites can be (and fail to be) effective allies to people of color in struggles for civil rights, and the ways in which gender and race shape (and limit) women's access to bodily autonomy and public power.

One of Griffith's chief preoccupations in *Madge Vertner* is demonstrating the hypocrisy that lies at the heart of proslavery ideology. Throughout her novel, Griffith deconstructs proslavery advocates'

---

[15]   For more on antislavery fiction and its publication in the late 1850s and early 1860s, please see Holly M. Kent, "Femininity, Authority, and the Politics of Authorship in Women's Antislavery Fiction, 1821–1861" (Ph.D. diss., Lehigh University, 2010).

insistence that slavery was a "positive good" for the enslaved—was an institution in which "childlike" enslaved people were loved and protected by benevolent, paternalistic masters. Slavery, Griffith emphasized, was driven and sustained solely by slave owners' desire to become rich by exploiting enslaved people's bodies and labor, and any claims to the contrary were pure fiction. Throughout *Madge Vertner*, Griffith gives the most sentimental proslavery rhetoric to one of the novel's most villainous characters, the heroine's father, Colonel Vertner. The Colonel is well aware of why he (and his friends and neighbors) are slave owners: because slave-owning has made them rich. When the naïve Madge insists that her friend Helen's new, theoretically abolitionist husband will liberate their slaves after their marriage, the Colonel cynically (and, as it transpires, accurately) asserts that "she will learn, so will my little Madge, that a man don't lightly throw away forty thousand dollars."[16] For Helen's husband, the Colonel, and (by implication) all slave-owning men, enslaved people are not people, but are rather living, breathing dollars and cents.

The Colonel, therefore, knows perfectly well what slavery really is: a brutal economic system in which enormous profits are generated for slave owners by the uncompensated labor of the people whom they own. This does not prevent him, however, from paying lip service to proslavery platitudes about the supposed value of slavery for the enslaved. As the Colonel tells Madge's suitor Mr. Butler, "It really makes a master happy and proud to see so many poor dependent beings around him, looking up to him as their benefactor and the dispenser of all their comfort and happiness."[17] By giving such declarations to the Colonel, who throughout the novel dispassionately treats enslaved people as exploitable property, Griffith highlights the hypocrisy of proslavery rhetoric. Men like the Colonel would rhapsodize about their paternal love for the enslaved one moment, Griffith demonstrates, and heartlessly sell enslaved families down the river the next.

In her novel, Griffith also deconstructs proslavery ideology by dismantling proslavery advocates' willful misreadings of enslaved

---

[16]   Mattie Griffith, *Madge Vertner* (Hastings, Ne.: Hastings College Press, 2015), 206.

[17]   Ibid 159.

people's behavior to support their arguments. In one of *Madge's* notable passages, Griffith creates a scene that, at least initially, seems as though it could have come straight out of a proslavery novel. In this scene, a group of enslaved people hold a joyful dance in the middle of their master's plantation. Such tableaus pervade proslavery fiction, with the gleeful dancing of the enslaved intended to demonstrate both African-American people's ostensibly innate, "animalistic" sensuality and their ecstatic contentment within the confines of slavery.

Griffith's representation of enslaved people seizing this brief moment of happiness takes a sharp turn away from typical proslavery representations of such events, however. Her narrator concludes her description of this dance by noting that "scenes of animal life and enjoyment such as these—little gleams of sunshine and pleasure in a world of blight—form the basis upon which certain wiseacres build up a wondrous superstructure of argument in favor of slavery."[18] The fact that enslaved people seize what opportunities they can for joy is not an argument for the justness of slavery, Griffith contends. It is, rather, a testament to the resilience of enslaved people, who find small moments to celebrate and affirm their humanity within a fundamentally vicious, dehumanizing institution.[19]

As incisively as she questions proslavery ideology in *Madge Vertner*, there are nonetheless moments in the text where Griffith problematically echoes proslavery ideas, without fully questioning or undermining them. Even as Griffith insists that slavery is an economic, rather than familial, relationship, she creates emotional bonds between her enslaved and white characters that would not have been out of place in a proslavery text. After Madge's friend Helen dies, for example, the one person who remains inconsolable and refuses to leave her grave is the elderly, enslaved woman who had cared for Helen since she was an

---

[18]   Ibid 54.

[19]   As scholars such as Stephanie Camp have noted, these types of everyday resistance were systematically engaged in by enslaved people during the antebellum era, as they used social gatherings as a means of claiming alternative space on their master's plantations. Please see Stephanie M. H. Camp, *Closer to Freedom: Enslaved Women and Everyday Resistance in the Plantation South* (Chapel Hill: University of North Carolina Press, 2004).

infant. "'I knows all 'bout dis dear baby dat sleeps in dis grave,'" this unnamed woman declares, "'I was her nurse, her mammy, and I knowed her well as my own chile.'"[20] Whether Helen's "mammy" actually had her own children or not goes notably unremarked upon. What is certain is that her love for Helen was the primary emotional relationship of her life, and that Helen's death is a devastating blow from which she will never recover.

Griffith may have included this character to further indict the ways in which slave-owning society encouraged white, elite women to relate to their children. (It is certainly noteworthy that all of the slave-owning mothers in *Madge Vertner* are cold, distant figures who show little interest in, and play minimal roles in the lives of, their daughters.) She may have created the character to praise enslaved women for their emotional generosity in loving and caring for the (often neglected) children of the families who owned them.

The presence of a selfless mammy figure who seemingly has no life or concerns outside of her mistress is nonetheless deeply troubling. It powerfully echoes proslavery ideology's insistence that enslaved people wanted nothing more than to care for their master's families, which negated the existence of their own families entirely. A strong statement about the fundamental falseness of proslavery ideology, *Madge Vertner* nonetheless sometimes fails to sufficiently problematize the proslavery notion that enslaved people's primary interest in life was their beloved owners, rather than their own lives, homes, and families.

In addition to considering proslavery ideology, in *Madge Vertner* Griffith also devotes considerable time to discussing the most effective way forward for the abolitionist movement. Given the deep entrenchment of slavery within the South (and within the United States as a whole), how could the emancipation of the enslaved and the destruction of slavery be most efficiently achieved? *Madge* holds out little hope that enslaved people themselves will be able to take any meaningful steps toward their own liberation. In the novel, almost all of the enslaved characters who seek freedom end up failing, dying, or both in the attempt. One enslaved character, Daniel, is able to escape from

---

[20]   Griffith, *Madge Vertner,* 251.

slavery and (notably, only because of Madge's assistance) build a new life for himself in Canada. The fates of the other enslaved characters who seek to emancipate themselves, however, are not so happy, ending in capture, imprisonment, corporal punishment, sale away from their families, alcoholism, and death. In *Madge Vertner*, enslaved people consistently resist their enslavement, but these efforts almost always fail in the face of the tremendous social, legal, and political power of slave-owning men.

Griffith is similarly pessimistic about white Southern women's ability to make any meaningful contributions to abolitionism. The novel's two strongest antislavery voices, Madge and her friend Helen, both die with their dreams of emancipation entirely unrealized. Lacking the economic, legal, and political power possessed by their fiancés, husbands, and fathers, Helen and Madge are blocked from translating their passionately held antislavery values into any kind of effective action.

Unfortunately for the abolitionist cause (and for the novel's enslaved characters), by the end of *Madge Vertner*, Madge and Helen are both dead, and the men they love have proven completely unwilling to honor their dying wishes by emancipating their families' slaves. Rather than liberating the enslaved on his plantation, Helen's widower Mr. Norton "continued to keep and add to the number which his wife had left him."[21] Rather than living up to "his promise to his daughter of liberating his slaves," Colonel Vertner yielded to "self-interest, love of worldly possessions and a profound belief that holding slaves was an unerring mark of respectability," and broke the abolitionist vow that he had made to Madge on her deathbed.[22]

Madge Vertner thus takes a rather grim view of abolitionism's future, with enslaved and antislavery white female characters suffering, failing, and (in many cases) dying in their fruitless struggles for emancipation and abolition. If there is some hope for the enslaved and for the abolitionist cause in the novel, it comes from a rather unexpected source. After detailing Mr. Norton and Colonel Vertner's refusal to emancipate their families' slaves, Griffith concludes her

---

[21]   Ibid 321.
[22]   Ibid 320.

novel by declaring to her readers "Let all such as condemn these two men remember to do their part to lessen such unjust power by fighting a good fight, and casting a true vote in 1860."[23] Two weeks after this declaration appeared in the *National Anti-Slavery Standard*, the (antislavery, though by no means abolitionist) Republican Party nominated its candidate, Abraham Lincoln, for the forthcoming presidential election. *Madge Vertner*'s conclusion implies that voting an antislavery man like Lincoln into the White House could be a productive (perhaps, the only productive) step forward in the fight against slavery.

This conclusion is in many ways a jarring one, as it pins the primary hopes of the abolitionist movement on voters—voters in 1860, of course, almost invariably being white men. And throughout *Madge Vertner*, white male characters are consistently villains who lack any kind of moral compass and who systematically support and sustain slavery. The novel therefore troublingly indicates that the future of slavery will be determined by a population who consistently prioritize worldly power and economic gain over moral imperatives. As Griffith writes, lamenting the political clout of evil slave trader John Sharpe, "he is a voter—one of the Democratic sovereigns—and his existence cannot be quietly wiped out or overlooked, as though he were a woman."[24]

Here, perhaps, we have a suggestion of the kind of radical social change that Griffith felt would be necessary if the abolitionist cause were ever to truly move forward. As long as morally corrupt white men like Sharpe had political power and virtuous, antislavery white women like Madge and Helen did not, the future of abolitionism was in severe jeopardy. The implied solution to this quandary is to ensure that the voices of right-thinking women like Madge and Helen not be "wiped out," but rather be heard within American politics. A member of the woman's rights movement during the Civil War and a leader in the National Woman's Suffrage Association after it, Griffith indicates in

---

23   Ibid 321.
24   Ibid 67.

Madge Vertner that white female enfranchisement would be necessary to moving forward politically on emancipation and civil rights.[25]

In *Madge Vertner*, Griffith also explores how racial and gender hierarchies impact the lives of free and enslaved African Americans and white women in the South. In Southern society, Griffith argues, even the most privileged white women have notably little power over their lives. At the beginning of *Madge Vertner*, its titular heroine appears to wield considerable influence over her wealthy, powerful planter father. However, while Colonel Vertner is happy to give his beloved daughter whatever she wishes for materially, as soon as she asks him to emancipate the Vertners' enslaved population, the Colonel makes it clear how limited the scope of her power truly is. "'You are a very young girl, Madge,'" the Colonel tells her sternly, "'and can't understand business affairs. I'll buy you as many ponies, dogs, dresses or pianos as you want, but I will positively not listen to you when you urge such a foolish request.'"[26] Madge can expect to be materially indulged by her father (provided, of course, that she continues to please him), but not to have any say over the "business affairs" of the Vertner plantation. Warned by her father that her requests to emancipate the enslaved are "'going far beyond your privilege,'" Madge indignantly exclaims "'My *privilege*! Why, papa, what that is in your power should limit *my* privilege?'"[27] Madge goes to her grave not understanding that the power that her father has to determine the extent of her privilege is absolute.

Circumstances for free women of color and enslaved women are, of course, infinitely more dire than they are for the (ostensibly) white, wealthy Madge.[28] Because of their race, gender, and condition of servitude, enslaved women constantly live with the threat (and, all too often, with the reality) of rape and sexual exploitation at the hands of white men. The pervasive sexual violence and abuse that enslaved

---

[25] For more on Griffith's Civil War and Reconstruction political life, please see Lockard, *Autobiography*, 414–416.

[26] Griffith, *Madge Vertner*, 67.

[27] Ibid 68.

[28] As will be discussed later in this introduction, Madge believes herself to be both white and her father's legitimate heir, but was in fact born out of wedlock and is part African American.

women suffer in slavery permeates *Madge Vertner*, with enslaved
parents helplessly worrying about white men's prurient interest in their
preadolescent daughters, enslaved women dying after having been
"seduced" by their white masters, Madge decrying the "fancy trade"
of light-skinned enslaved women being sold into sexual servitude,
and enslaved character Maria explaining that she fled from slavery
specifically to obtain "the right to her own body."[29]

Although not legally property, free women of color in the South
fare little better in *Madge Vertner*. Seduced from freedom in the North
to live as the Colonel's secret mistress in the South, free character Rachel
notes bitterly (and correctly) that "There is nothing or no one to protect
a free woman of color" in Southern society.[30] Although technically
free, Rachel has no means of effectively protecting herself from the
unwelcome sexual advances of John Sharpe, or from the severe public
flogging she receives after attempting to help the enslaved Maria flee
slavery. Throughout her novel, Griffith highlights both free and enslaved
African-American women's inability to maintain bodily integrity, protect
themselves from sexual exploitation and abuse, or have any meaningful
control over their own lives.

Stressing the severe injustice and inequality that racial slavery
(and a more broadly racist society) subjected enslaved and free people of
color to, in *Madge Vertner* Griffith also nods to both the power (and the
arbitrariness) of the racial categories that dominated Southern society.
Towards the end of the novel, Madge is revealed to be the mixed-race
daughter of her white father and a "quadroon" mother. As soon as
this information is revealed, Madge loses her fiancé, her status as her
father's heir, and, ultimately, her life, as her African-American heritage
renders her "unmarriageable," illegitimate, and unable to live within
the parameters of respectable, white Southern society. As Rachel tells
her (after revealing the truth of Madge's parentage to her), Madge has
been cursed by "'the one drop which, in the eye of whites, corrupts your
blood and puts you beyond the pale of refined sympathy.'"[31] The "one
drop rule" instantaneously transforms Madge from white to African

---

[29]   Ibid 31.
[30]   Ibid 165.
[31]   Ibid 298.

American, and as such, from being privileged and powerful to being a social outcast.

While noting the seeming ambiguity of racial categories, Griffith also expresses a powerful belief in the biological reality of racial difference. Like many white abolitionist writers of the antebellum era, Griffith strongly associates the qualities of independence and intelligence with whiteness. In the novel, the most intellectually gifted, freedom-minded African-American characters are those with the highest "percentage" of white ancestry. Free African-American Rachel's "high and indomitable spirit" is consistently linked to her white heritage, and the talented, fiercely independent enslaved character Stephen (as Colonel Vertner asserts) "should not have been a slave; there was too large an infusion of Caucasian blood in his veins."[32]

Linking whiteness to intellect and independence, in *Madge Vertner* Griffith conflates blackness with a strong emotional receptivity and an innate, powerful connection to the natural world. In the text, the narrator notes the supposed "emotion, sensibility, and tenderness of the negroes," and claims that members of "wild, poetic Negro race" inevitably possess a "susceptible temperament."[33] Madge's (previously mysterious) incapability of conforming to the expectations of white ladyhood (specifically, her inability to take an interest in abstract ideas or books, and her status as "a child of nature") is seemingly "explained" in the novel by her status as a partly African-American woman.[34] Associating her African-American and mixed-race characters with "wildness," the natural world, and emotion rather than reason, Griffith echoes dominant nineteenth-century ideologies that depicted African-American people as fundamentally unsuited for full social, political, and civic equality with whites. According to these ideologies, African Americans were to be admired for their supposed, potent emotionality and their powerful connections to nature, but were also rendered unfit for full citizenship precisely because of these "irrational" characteristics.

Madge Vertner thus raises questions about the kind of post-emancipation society Griffith hoped for. Insistent that slavery was a

---

[32] Ibid 126; Ibid 266.

[33] Ibid 156; Ibid 189; Ibid 189.

[34] Ibid 73.

national evil that needed to end, Griffith does not seem to have foreseen an equal role for newly freed African Americans in a post-slavery world. In the novel, the one African-American character who finds freedom does so in Canada, rather than in America, and the novel's primary African-American and mixed-race characters (Madge, Rachel, Stephen, and Madge's mother Alice) are all dead by the story's end. As was true for many white, antebellum antislavery activists, Griffith is much clearer in calling for abolition than she is in envisioning a fully racially egalitarian, post-emancipation society.

Less than a year after the final chapter of *Madge Vertner* was published, the Civil War began. And fewer than five years after that final chapter appeared, the Thirteenth Amendment was ratified, and slavery was abolished in the United States. In 1860, Griffith despaired of ever seeing slavery brought to an end. A decade later, the Fifteenth Amendment had been passed, African-American men had been enfranchised, and the first Southern African-American men had been elected to the U.S. Senate.

The Thirteenth and Fifteenth Amendments (at least partially) answered some of the questions *Madge Vertner* raised, about how, when, and whether slavery would be brought to end, and the status that newly emancipated African Americans would have under American law. This legislation, however, left the majority of the novel's questions unresolved. How would America grapple with the terrible legacy of racial slavery? What would true racial equality look like, and how could it best be achieved? How would race and gender continue to shape women's and men's access to public space, public power, and a public voice? *Madge Vertner* raises all of these complex, difficult questions, leaving Americans in the twenty-first century to continue to seek the complex, difficult answers.

....

Dr. Holly Kent is Assistant Professor of History at the University of Illinois-Springfield, where she teaches classes in U.S. women's history, nineteenth-century U.S. history, fashion history, and the history of slavery and abolitionism. Her document project "How Did Women's Antislavery Fiction Contribute to Debates About Gender, Slavery, and Abolition, 1828–1856?" is available through Alexander Street Press' *Women and Social Movements* database. Her article on women's mourning clothing during the Civil War is forthcoming in the *Women's History Review,* and she has articles and book chapters on feminist and queer pedagogies forthcoming in the *Seneca Falls Dialogues Journal* and *Safe Zone: Creating and Facilitating Allies of LGBTQ Young Adults.* She is currently assembling an edited volume on teaching fashion studies in interdisciplinary university classrooms.

Notes on the Text

Several factors make *Madge Vertner* a difficult text to produce. Because the novel was serialized weekly over 10 months and because it contains a variety of dialects, there are many editorial inconsistencies that become obvious once the chapters are compiled and placed side by side. We have tried to maintain Griffith's attempts to differentiate between dialects, but we have also corrected some inconsistencies and incidentals that might be distracting to readers. In addition to modernizing punctuation (e.g., closing up spaces around dashes or quotation marks), we have made the following changes.

Corrections to Inconsistencies

Some words or phrases are spelled inconsistently throughout the original text and do not follow any pattern or rule. In those cases, we have chosen the most frequently used variant or specified for clarity.

- "I'se" rather than "Ise"
- "good-bye" rather than "goodbye"
- "'kase" rather than "kase"
- "pony" rather than "poney"
- "riding-whip" rather than "riding whip"
- "Alec" rather than "Aleck"
- "Madgy" rather than "Madgey"
- "&c." rather than "etc."
- "t'oder" rather than "toder" (Note that this variation occurs only in Chapter 8, used by Uncle Peter and Aunt Polly. "t'other is used by all other characters who speak in dialect.)
- "its" (possessive pronoun) and "it's" (for "it is") are used incorrectly in many places. We have corrected for clarity.
- "Agin" is used in dialect to mean both "again" and "against." We have clarified: agin = again; agin' = against.

Unchanged Inconsistencies

- Some character names are spelled inconsistently, depending on which character is speaking. We have changed only those instances where there seemed to be an actual error. If a variation seemed to be an affectionate or familiar nickname (e.g., "Madgy" or "Rove") or was in keeping with a character's dialect, we did not change it.
- Mrs. Vertner introduces Madge to a novel by Charles Reade called "Never Too Late to Mend." The actual title is "It Is Never Too Late to Mend" (1856), but we did not correct it in the text.
- Madge's wet-nurse is referred to as "Luce" or "Lucy" by several characters, but Mrs. Vertner refers to her as "old Susy" (Chapter XXVIII). Based on the plot, this may not be inaccurate.
- The variants "sempstress" and "seamstress" are both used in the novel to describe Rachel. The word "sempstress" is used only in Chapter XIX, between Madge and her father. The variation could be intentional, so we did not correct it.

I

All travelers who passed Col. Vertner's place were struck by its remarkable beauty and neatness. It was scarcely large enough to be styled a plantation, and altogether too respectable for a farm; so they compromised the matter, and called it The Place. It consisted of about four hundred acres of flat, low land, in the swampy, tobacco producing part of Kentucky. Everything about it bore the mark of thorough care and labor. Unlike its neighbors, it had no broken gates or loose fences; perfect order and exact neatness were strictly observed. All the out-buildings, cow-houses, stables, &c., were in scrupulously neat style.

The Colonel being something of a jockey, his horses were cared for as though they were members of his family. Each stall was numbered, and the troughs of white oak were washed and scrubbed until they bore a polish. Once a week, Col. Vertner inspected the stables, and woe to the ostlers if anything was discovered out of order. True, there was rarely an occasion for complaint, as the servants shared with their master in care for the stock. Once a year they sent up a representation to the Agricultural Fair, which was held at L——, and Col. Vertner's grays generally bore off the first prizes. To have lost the prize, or come off "second best," would have been little less than disgrace to Pompey and Jake, as we all know how strong is the feeling of competition with the negro.

If the out-buildings were in order, the mansion itself was a bijou of taste. A winding avenue, lined with stately elms, led up to a large white house, that seemed planted amid blossoming shrubs and wild creeper vines. Passing the piazza, we entered a wide, airy hall, at the end of which wound upward a spiral stairway. At the left, a door led into the parlor, a room pleasantly and tastefully fitted up. It was evident that an artistic eye and a tasteful hand had been at work here. You found nothing gorgeous or incongruous; no inharmonious combination of color, but a cool, low tone that soothed and subdued the eye. The carpet and chairs were green, harmonizing well with the fluttering white lace curtains and the rich old pictures that hung on the walls.

In a large arm-chair, near a side window, sits a lady of middle age, engaged with a book. Let us look at her, as she reads. The face seems a peculiar one; it is not strong, but every feature denotes precision; the eyebrow is as immobile as stone, and the small gray eye is resolute, though slow; the mouth small and tight; lips that may possibly part into a smile, but never break forth into a free laugh. She is just the person of whom you would never feel like asking a favor, for you are sure that there is no generous movement of life there, and we see that her pulse beats as regularly and slowly as the ticking of the old clock on the library mantel; the very folds of that brown silk skirt denote the minute precision of the wearer's character. If she is interested in that book, we only know it by the constant fixture of the eye upon the printed page, for there is no play of countenance, no change of color to show that she sympathizes with the author.

But over by the opposite window is an entirely different looking person. Madge Vertner was a wild, sprite-like girl of sixteen, tall and slight of figure, with light-waving brown hair, and large blue-gray eyes. Though the face was free, happy, and unwritten by care, an earnest observer might have detected a peculiar and sobered light that sometimes stole out from those usually full and happy eyes, betokening a mind and heart that only waited to be aroused to purpose and action. Watch her now, as she gracefully swings her little form out of that window, calling gleefully to her dog.

"Down, Rover, down; what, sir, do you try to leap in when I forbid you? down, I say, down this moment; here, catch my hat, bring it to me"; and away she tossed her straw hat, with its blue ribbons and gauzy veil fluttering in the wind. The dog started after it, and brought it back to his mistress. "Thank you, sir—now, that will do; I am tired of playing with you—go to your kennel. Here, Pomp, come take Rover off and put him to bed."

At this summons, a little black fellow, apparently about nine years old, emerged from the corner of the building. This boy was a peculiar looking child; as black as the ace of spades, with round, pop eyes that were kept in a perpetual roll. As he now bowed and grinned, he displayed a regular row of polished white teeth, that might have excited the envy of many a higher and better born lad.

"Laws, Miss Madge, Rover's not gwine to let me put him in the kennel jist yit. Why, him's wantin' to set up and bark at de moon for good whiles longer."

"How do you know, Pomp? I expect you have not been very particular in seeing to Rover lately, and so don't know his habits." Then, turning to the dog, she said, "What, poor fellow, does he love to sit up and look at the moon? So does his mistress. 'Like mistress, like dog.' Well, Pomp, leave him alone, for he whines now at the thought of being caged and housed up. There, away, Rover—away—and prowl about the lawn as much as you please. I shan't have you controlled. Be as free as you please. I never liked control."

Turning away from the window, she walked to a centre-table and began toying with a pile of uncut magazines.

"I wish I loved to read," she sighed forth; "it seems to me there must be a world of joy lying in these packed-up pages, yet I could never extract it; books are blunders to me—I am never in company with them. History is gloomy, and romance trite. I better like the woods, my pony and my dog. I always feel as if the earth had a soul—ay, and a tongue; but these books are speechless organs to me. Still, they must have voice and charm, for you, mother, have been reading steadily all day. Now, won't you tell me what that book is about?" And she flung herself gracefully upon a low ottoman at her mother's feet.

"Don't interrupt me, Madge," said the mother, "for I am at the most exciting part of this truly wonderful book." Mrs. Vertner said this without ever lifting her eyes from the page.

"Oh, but mother, you are wearing out your eyes; you might stop long enough to tell me about it; now do, dear;" and she passed her little white hand down the page. "Don't, child—don't; when I have finished it, you shall read it."

"Oh, no, mother, I could not read a book through, I haven't patience for it; but now I am tired, have been out in the woods all day, and, before I go to bed, I want you to talk awhile with me. Tell me of this book. See, 'tis too late for you to read without a lamp, and here in the moonlight let us sit, while you tell me of what you have been reading."

Madge laid her young head on her mother's lap, while the long brown curls fell back from the face and head, and the sweet moonlight shone softly over her. Mrs. Vertner laid aside the book, and looked down at the beautiful face of her daughter, as it laid there, baptized in a flood of moonlight. She smiled as she gazed, and, passing her fingers through those silken curls, said:

"I have been reading a very touching story, called 'Never Too Late to Mend.'"

"'Never Too Late to Mend'?" repeated Madge, slowly; "what a strange title!"

"Yes, it is strange, but I dare say the ingenious author intends it shall signify something."

"Well, tell me about it, mother—for the name puzzles me so."

"Well," replied the mother, "it begins with a young girl whose lover is poor."

"Oh, mother, stop just here, please, for that is the way they all begin, and that's why I can't read your books. I don't understand or sympathize with these love affairs; they make me sleepy. You needn't talk any more about it; I'll just let my head lie here, and look up at the moon."

"The book also tells," continued Mrs. Vertner, "of a Mr. Eden, a kind, eccentric minister, who felt called upon to live in the prison and attend the convicts. He went there, and the troubles and sorrows which he witnessed are related with frightful accuracy. A poor man by the name of Robinson, who had been imprisoned on a charge of theft, went through the most terrible tortures; he so pined for the sunlight and the society of his fellow-prisoners that once, during the Sunday morning service, he (in violation of prison rules) spoke to one of the convicts, and was, in consequence, condemned to be locked up six hours in the dungeon. This so acted upon his nervous system and his imagination that, when taken out, he could scarcely walk; his limbs failed him, and he groped along the galleries and corridors of the prison, like a crawling child; the poor wretch trembled if you spoke to him; 'twas as if the nerves had been laid bare by the surgeon's knife, and quivered to the action of the air. He went into the dungeon, the 'black keep,' a man; he came out a dotard, a child. For days afterwards, he raved in the delirium of fever; then he told how he had once seen a poor boy tied up in the prison jacket, and dashed with cold water, until sense itself was lost; then, as a little child, he wandered back to the scenes of his early childhood, prattled of his mother, his sister and one other tenderer name—his Mary. During this time, when not utterly alone, he was watched over by brutal keepers, who laughed and derided these touching agonies; and when the doctor pronounced his fever broken, and recommended a liberal diet, the fiendish keeper, out of excess of brutality, diminished his usual rations, and so kept him weak and feeble. He even denied him the use of the infirmary beds, and the poor wretch, weak in body, broken in nerve, and as helpless as a three months' babe, was set to work upon a heavy crank. The picture which Mr. Reade draws of him, as he tried to work—for he was a ready and a willing hand—is pitiful. The wretch failed in his work for want of strength, and so was put into the jacket and showered—until he gasped away!"

"Oh, mother, where was Mr. Eden then? Didn't he remonstrate? Was nothing done, and the poor helpless wretch left to those fiends, to be murdered as they pleased?"

Madge had risen from her mother's lap, her hair was thrown away from the face, and those great solemn eyes were glaring in the moonlight. With lips white and parted, she leaned forward and drank in every word of that most wonderful story; then, clutching Mrs. Vertner's dress with her quivering hands, she cried out—

"Oh, tell me more of this, for, though it cuts my heart like a blade, I must hear it"; and then, giving way to her feelings, she laid her head again upon her mother's lap and sobbed as a babe.

"Why, Madge, dear," said Mrs. Vertner, "a moment ago you called the story stupid, and asked me not to tell you of it. Now you are crying over one of the most naked facts of the book. I have stripped it of its marvellous beauty. You ought to read it as the author tells it, not take my lifeless account."

"But, mother, do you think it is true? Had he facts upon which to go, or is it merely what Mr.——(what's the author's name?) imagined?"

"Mr. Reade wrote the book, and I think, dear, he must have had a groundwork of fact; you feel that in reading it. I dare say there is great mismanagement in the prisons, and a great deal of cruelty allowed; 'tis horrible to think of; I shan't recover from the effects of this book for weeks."

"Why, mother!" exclaimed Madge, lifting up her head, "if it indeed be true, we should never recover from the effects of it until the evil be removed."

"But, child, it is the English prison system he has attacked. I don't know that we are so bad in America."

"But are not the English people human beings? and if there is wrong done there, and human suffering follows, are we not bound to speak, to testify against it? It is the human race that we vindicate, not simply our townsmen, countrymen, and family, whom we should protect. Shouldn't we speak against wrong wherever and whenever we see it?"

"Why, I suppose so, Madge; but don't be so impetuous, so terribly in earnest; it may be only true in part. Charles Reade is a great writer, and a simple fact, when worked upon by his magic pen, may assume all the strong effects of tragedy. It is not worth while, at any rate, to fire up so, child; we can do nothing. Only see how wildly your eyes flash, and you tremble like a leaf! Calm yourself, and to-morrow read the book. I shall be glad if this 'Never Too Late to Mend' introduces you to books; take it, read it; and if you like it, I shall get you all of Reade's books."

Shortly after this, Madge went to her room, but her thoughts were still in that prison, of which her mother had told her. Her chamber was a little curiosity in its way. It had been fitted up by Madge herself. There was no carpet—she would not have one in her room—but the floor had been painted with odd, fantastic Indian figures, and the walls also represented various pictures of Indian warfare, and scenes from the lives of the pioneer settlers of her beloved State. There was a portrait of Boone, in his dress of wild skins, attended by his faithful dog, which her father had had copied from the original portrait which decorates

the walls of the Capitol at Frankfort. There was also a portrait (perhaps
executed from fancy) of that young eagle-eyed Kenton, whose wild,
romantic history has given additional interest to the early Kentucky
legends. A tomahawk, with a brace of silver-mounted pistols, hung on
the mantel, while a true Kentucky rifle was suspended over the door; for
Madge was a good markswoman, and loved the wild sports of forest-life.
A small cabinet of shells stood in a corner opposite to a large stuffed
reindeer, whose glass eyes seemed to watch and guard the quaintly
furnished apartment. The only civilized things were the bed (which
abounded in frills, laces and ruffles), a looking-glass, and a vase of fresh
flowers; but it was remarkable that there was no book or writing-desk
there.

Now, as Madge entered, the moonlight, gleaming through
opposite windows, made everything seem weird and doubly quaint.
She paused in the centre of the apartment, and glanced around her;
then went to the window and looked out upon the moonlight as it
quivered over the yard and the cabins. For the first time in her life,
Madge was sad; the feeling was so new, so strange, that she could not
call it unpleasant. She loitered only a moment at the window, when she
thought of Robinson in the jail.

"Well, I must know more of him," she said, and, drawing the
blinds, she lighted a little stained glass lamp and opened the first volume
of the book. She tried to read the commencement, but could not
appreciate the love-scenes; then laying it down, she said:

"I'll not read it—'twill tire me; mother will tell me about it to-
morrow." She rose and began to prepare for sleep; but as her little fingers
fumbled the pins and knots, her eyes kept wandering over towards
the book, and, throwing a long white wrapper over her shoulders, she
sighed out—

"It's no use—that story charms me, whether I will or no. I'll try it
again."

This time she skipped several hundred pages, and began where
the reader is introduced to ——— prison. Before she had gone over ten
pages, her eyes began to start, her brows to knit, her lips to part, and
great beads of perspiration to break out over her face. See how low she
bends her head, how her eyes glue to the page and how thickly comes
her breath!

So she read for hours; and, as she read, her frame seemed to swell and to glow. Thus a young, true soul for the first time took its life-lesson from the hand of a great master. This girl, who hitherto had only loved the free air, the woods, and field sports, and turned with infinite disgust from books, now sat the night through, poring over a touching story told by a true artist. Madge read on and on, or, rather, she did not read, she actually seemed to live in that prison, to suffer with Robinson and with Josephs. A tight cord bound her brow and a gathering chill crept over her flesh; the nerves were all at their utmost tension. This fine, healthy girl, who had never before known such feelings, was stepping into closer communion with her own sympathies; she was learning of the sorrows and troubles that so often darken human life. At length, feeling as if she could not read another word, almost maddened by it, she laid the book down and rested her head upon the table, when suddenly she heard a buzz of whispering voices just below her window. She had never known fear, but now her nerves were in such a state of excitement that she could scarcely resist a scream. In a moment or so, however, she collected herself, listened again, and again heard the voices. She then extinguished her lamp and stole gently to the window, under which she heard whispers. Kneeling down there, she listened attentively.

"Now, Milly," said the voice of a negro man, "if we can only pass farmer Jones's place without the dogs betrayin' of us, we can soon git to the river and cross; thar we'll be met by friends; and after we's crossed, we is safe enuff. Only jist keep up yer sperits."

"But, Jack, I thinks we'd better wait till to-morrow night; I'm feard; s'pose we is found out, then 'twill be harder with us. Massa'll sell us shure, to a trader."

"But we is not gwine to be found out, if you'll only keep up yer sperits. I am gwine to-night. I doesn't want to be a slave another day, and doesn't yer know that the other lot is awaitin' fur us? Now do come along—we can cross safe enuff at—"

Then the voice died away, and Madge turned the "Venetian," and saw the two dusky figures moving slowly, cautiously away—now hiding behind a bush, now emerging, but always keeping as near in the shadow as possible.

"So, so, Jack and Milly are for running off, are they? Luckily I overheard them. I'll go instantly and rouse papa, and have the runaways caught; 'twas well that they came under my window to hold their council. But I'll defeat them—they'll be brought back in short time." As she turned to gather up a crimson dressing-gown, which hung upon a chair near her bed, her eye suddenly fell upon something that gleamed in the moonlight. She stopped, looking at it strangely; her bosom began to heave, and her eye to dilate; 'twas the open book, which she had been reading. How whitely it glistened! She bent forward toward it, her dressing-gown fell from her hand close at her feet, her eye gleamed! From that book she saw the figure of poor Josephs, with outstretched arms, calling to her for mercy. There was Robinson, too, supplicating for freedom. She saw the heavy-grated dungeon, she heard the cries of stricken souls, she saw the worn faces of those whom unjust power had made martyrs, and, pressing her hands to her eyes, she murmured inwardly—

"No, go and be free, poor wretches! I am no turnkey, no Hawes, to exult over your suffering. Robinson and Josephs speak to me through those two fugitives that I was about to arrest"; and, with this, she flung herself upon the bed and was soon sleeping soundly.

II

The next morning, Madge rose refreshed, and went out, as usual, for her morning walk upon the lawn, where she met Rover. "Come, old playfellow," she cried; "come, now, off and away for a scamper"; and she and the dog started for an animated foot race. They ran up and down and around the lawn. Madge's hat fell from her head and swung upon her shoulders, while the brown curls blew and sported about in the cool morning breeze.

"Now, sir, come off—let us take a race through the quarter"; and they started off in the direction of the cabins.

As this bright young creature came bounding by, in the excitement of a morning romp, her white dress floating in the wind, the blue ribbons of her hat streaming out, and her curls fluttering, she presented a strange contrast to the odd-looking figures grouped about "the yard." The slaves gazed at her with undisguised admiration. "Ain't she pretty?" "Looks fur all de world like de angel of de Lord"; "She's de heavenly lamb." Such were the plaudits which were shouted forth as she passed.

"Her's jist as wild as a fawn."

"An' jist as full of romp as dat ar' young colt in de stable; her's allers gwine, never still a minit," said an old gray negro, who sat smoking a pipe in front of his little cabin. "Puts me in mind of dem shiny spirits I sometimes sees when I has de fever, an’ shuts my eyes, an’ seems to go off to heaven like.”

These words were addressed to his old wife, who stood in the doorway of the cabin.

“Now, Peter, you allers talks dat ar’ way ’bout Miss Madge, but afore goodness I does t’ink long’r missus dat ’twould be a sight better if Miss Madge didn’t romp ’bout an’ tear round so. ’Pears to me she ain’t nuff of lady for one raised into her sarcumstances.”

“Now, you jist hush long’r yer pride, Poll; Miss Madge knows what her’s ’about. Now, for all she tears ’bout so, play long her dog, I notices she never talks long’r poor whites. She jist holds her head as high as missus when any trash comes ’long.”

“She daresn’t look at any of ’em sort, for missus take de very skin offen her if she was to.”

“Well, now, Poll, I am agwine to tell you ’bout de time when mas’er was little boy. You know, Poll, you didn’t allers ’long to the Vartners; you isn’t one of de ole stock.” Peter uttered this with an air of conscious superiority, which the better-born, the self-elected class always assume toward the humbler.

“What’s you allers a tellin’ me that for, Pete? I doesn’t care if I was one of de bought ones; I’se lived long nuff in dis family to have de right to be considered one of um.”

“No, no, Poll, you’s a good ’ooman, an’ my wife, but it doesn’t make you one of de ole stock for all dat.” He took the pipe from his mouth, looked kindly, condescendingly at his wife, reseated himself upon the stool, and smiled a self-conscious smile of Brahminical satisfaction.

“Good morning, Uncle Peter and Aunt Polly; why, how sleepy and dumpsy you look,” cried a young, gay voice; and Madge Vertner stood in front of them.

“Good mornin’, Miss Madge,” exclaimed the two old negroes, and Uncle Peter rose, dashed his pipe away, and remained standing in the presence of his young mistress.

“Sit down, Uncle Peter,” said Madge.

“No, please, missy, not when you is ’bout.”

"Sit down, I say," repeated Madge, and Uncle Peter, with a politeness something akin to that of the Earl De Stair, obeyed the command of majesty.

"Aunt Polly, you look cross; has he" (pointing to Uncle Peter) "been scolding you?"

"Bless yer, Miss Madge, Peter's allers a hurtin' of my feelin's and throwin' up to me dat I am not one of de reg'lar family sarvants—dat I come 'long wid a bought lot. Now, I'se bin a good bit of time in dis family—plenty long for um to quit dat sort of talk."

"I think so, too, Aunt Polly; and if he married you, he ought not to trouble you in this way. Why, Uncle Peter, a man's wife is as good as himself, isn't she?"

"Yes, Miss Madge, Polly is nuff better 'an me, an' she is my ole 'ooman, an' a good un into the bargain; but fur all of 'at, she didn't come of as high a family. I an' my pappy, an' his pappy, an' his pappy's pappy afore um, 'longed to the Vartners, an' dar wan't no better breed saved from de ark dan de Vartners."

Madge smiled, her eyes sparkled queenly, and a dash of red stained her cheek and brow. The blood of the Vertners acknowledged the compliment of the veteran slave.

"But, Uncle Peter, hasn't she been living in the family long enough to become one of them? Why, we have a good number of servants, papa says, who do not belong to the original stock."

"'Tain't no use a-talkin' 'bout it, young missy, 'kase yer kant make a body of de ole family stock. They's got to be born to it."

Madge smiled, and did not seek further to convince him. Perhaps she believed his doctrine sound, at least when applied to people of a different complexion from herself.

"Oh, laws, Uncle Pete, has you hearn the new?" cried a hearty-looking negro girl, as she rushed up, half breathless, to the cabin; "beg pardon, Miss Madge, didn't see you at fust"; and she dropped an odd, graceless, but polite curtsy to the young mistress.

"What's the matter, Ruth?"

"Laws, Miss Madge, some of our folks has done run 'way last night—orful."

"Who?" inquired Madge, without any effort to seem surprised.

"It's orful mean of um to run way—I wouldn't do sich a thing" (she was then debating in her mind the safest method of escape). "Hopes they'll be kotched. They desarves to be even sold to de rice-fields, too—hope mas'er won't let 'em stay here."

The old negro man slowly, steadily eyed the speaker, then took another whiff of his pipe, and, as the girl began another harangue, said:

"Hush, Ruth, yer says a sight more 'an yer believes."

"Laws, Uncle Peter, I doesn't, 'pon my soul I doesn't."

"Off now, Ruth, an' don't be swarin' in front of my cabin. I tells you yer has mighty little soul to swar by."

Our heroine had watched Uncle Peter's face closely during this conversation. She had read but few books, and had never known society or life in cities; she turned away from poetry, romance, and social pleasure; but a human face, in the rough, was a book full of interest to her. This one of the old negro's, however, puzzled her. There was an untranslatable *something* in his manner that went home to her, but his countenance was moveless and heavy.

Aunt Polly joined in with Ruth in strong denunciation of "the *on*-grateful niggers that left the most *splendidest* of homes." Madge and Uncle Peter alone expressed no contempt. The blowing of the horn broke off the talk, and Ruth and Aunt Polly were obliged to hasten to their daily labor. Uncle Peter, being a very old family servant and a great sufferer from rheumatism, was placed, by the kindness of his master, on the "free list"; so he sat smoking his pipe while the other slaves went to work.

Madge listened. "Uncle Peter!"—she spoke slowly and with more than her wonted caution—"is it easy to catch runaways? If they had five hours' start, don't you think they might have the best of the race?"

There was something in the tone of her voice which surprised the old negro. He threw down his pipe, picked it up again, eyed her with an inquisitive regard, but said nothing. The question was repeated—this time with increased interest.

"I doesn't know nothin' 'tall 'bout it, missy, but I 'spect they's putty sartin to be kotch."

Madge still listened, but did not continue the conversation; then, whistling to Rover, she bounded on, apparently as free, careless and light-thoughted as ever.

Passing the front of the mansion, she saw her mother upon the verandah, pulling honeysuckles. "Good morning, mamma; how soon you are up! Isn't it nice to snuff this fine air? and those coral honeysuckles, how sweet they are!—throw me one."

"Madge, dear, how long have you been up, and where have you been racing?"

"All round the lawn and through the quarter. I feel so strong and well, mamma, I do believe you would be better if you rose as early as I do." And the girl seated herself on the step of the verandah, close to the place where her mother was standing. Laying aside her hat, she leaned her head against a column, and rested it amid the honey suckle vines, until the sweet scented coral blossoms mingled with her curls and played over her soft face.

"What a sweet pillow of flowers, and how delicious is this air! Oh, mother, I feel better in the early morning—isn't it splendid?"

"I think it's nice for a morning nap."

"Why, mamma, I couldn't sleep after the sun was up; it seems a shame to waste such hours."

"They are not wasted, dear, in healthful sleep; besides, you are younger than I am, and go to bed much earlier, so you can afford to get up earlier."

"Yes, but I sat up very late last night, yet I am up at the usual hour this morning."

"And pray, dear, what kept you up last night?"

"I was reading *that* book." A change came over the girl's face.

"Oh, 'Never Too Late to Mend.' How much did you read?"

"I finished the first volume."

"Didn't you like it?"

"'Tis dreadful—don't speak to me of it. I had forgotten it in this beautiful time, but now it comes over me, and I get sick."

"Oh, well, we will not talk of it. You must not think too keenly of it—'twas only a romance."

"But it *might* be true. Ah, there's papa"; and she bounded down the lawn to meet Col. Vertner.

This person, who is designed to be an important character in our story, merits a somewhat minute description. Imagine, then, a tall, athletic man—square, heavy shoulders, prominent chest, face full of fixed determination, with strong Roman features, an inflexible mouth, dark, blueish-gray eyes, quick and concentrated in glance—broad brow, over which a few sparse iron-gray locks floated—and you have a sketch of Col. Vertner.

"Good morning, daughter"; and he wound his arm round the waist of Madge. "Well, Rover, you are always with your pretty mistress"; and he stooped to pat the friendly dog, who had been licking his hand. To see a man thus warmly caressed by a young, affectionate girl, and his hand licked by a faithful dog, we should conclude that he was a person of tender and gentle nature; but women sometimes love (with household affection) the rudest and sternest creatures, and dogs are not always sagacious of their master's faults.

"Isn't it a splendid morning, papa?"

"Yes, dear, but the summer is wearing on, and I have not yet taken you on a pleasure jaunt. Where would you like to go?—to the Springs?"

"Oh, no, papa; it's too gay and stupid!"

"Why, what a paradox! Gay and stupid!"

"It don't make any difference what kind of a dox—it is true."

"Ah, well, I don't mean to take you to the Springs; but how would you like a trip to the Cave?"

"*The Mammoth Cave?* Oh, delightful! Shall we go?"

"Yes, if you wish it; but what will your mamma say?"

Madge hesitated a moment.

"Oh, I suppose she'll not like to go there. I am sure she will prefer the Springs, but, papa—"

"Well, say it out, dear."

"I cannot go to D—— or E—— Springs. I should suffocate there. I don't dance, don't like company, and why should *I* go to the Springs?"

"Your mamma says it's time you were introduced to society. Why, child, you are sixteen; after awhile you'll be wanting a beau."

"A what, papa?" Madge looked quizzical.

"A lover, dear."

"Oh, I've plenty of them."

"Have you? who and where are they?"

"You, Rover, my birds, my pony, and the little squirrel I am trying to tame."

"But there is another sort to come."

"Well, let him come. *I* shan't seek him; and when he arrives, I'll let him see that I am no game."

"But, Madgy, all young ladies have beaux."

"I am no young lady, papa—only your wild, romping Madge. Please don't talk to me about things I can't understand."

"I won't, and, to say the truth, I am glad to have you feel thus. There's your poor cousin Mary, who was married the year she quitted school, and a wretched life she has had."

By this time they had reached the verandah. Mrs. Vertner stepped out in front, holding a bunch of honeysuckles and roses in her hand.

"How pretty!" cried Madge; "give it to me, mother."

"How selfish, child! You always take the flowers, as though you had exclusive right."

"And I feel so, mother. I never scruple to pull a flower, no matter where I see it growing, and no matter who has planted it."

"But, my dear," exclaimed her father, "you would not rob a neighbor's garden."

"Not *rob* his garden, father; but I would pull his flowers without his leave, and never think I had robbed. Flowers seem to naturally belong to me. I plucked those exquisite dahlias and tube-roses of Mrs. Goodhill's, the other day, and I afterwards heard that she was much distressed."

"Why, Madge, this is theft, injustice, which I did not expect from you. Mrs. Goodhill is so fond of flowers! She planted them herself, and surely is entitled to the work of her own hands. I am sorry for this."

Col. Vertner looked really hurt, but Madge shook her head distrustingly.

As the family party were about entering the breakfast-room, which opened on the verandah, a stout negro man came round the angle of the building, and approached Col. Vertner. Taking off his hat, he halted, as if expecting permission to speak.

"Well, Alec, what is it?" asked Col. Vertner.

"Please, master, there's some little trouble this morning."

"What is it?"

"Well, sir, I blowed the horn at the usual hour, to call the hands to work, and, as I counted um over, there was two a missin'.'"

"Did you examine the cabins? have they been well hunted?"

"Yes, sar, I sarched well 'fore comin' to you."

"D—n it, this is ugly business. Excuse me, my dear! I'd forgot you were present," he added, as he turned to his wife.

Alec remained standing, holding his slouched hat and playing with its torn rim. At length he said, as his eyes were fixed upon the ground—

"I am sorry fur this, master—it's the fust thing of the sort that's happen sense I was 'pointed overseer."

"Well, Alec, I don't blame you, for you are a faithful servant; but we must not idle now. Saddle the horse, ride hard to the village, and get Tom Hynes and his men. No, stay—saddle my horse also; I must go in and have these d—d vagabonds (excuse me, my dear) advertised, and see to the engagement of Tom Hynes's men myself. This is a devilish piece of busines. Excuse me, my dear. Go, hurry, Alec."

And the negro was off like a streak of lightning, well pleased that his master had not blamed him.

"Now, come, my dear, and take your breakfast, before you start off on this exciting business." And his wife laid her hand gently on his shoulder.

"Oh, yes; but, Lucy, I must be quick about it; there is no way of knowing how long these negroes have been off. I must ride into town and have the pursuers off as soon as possible. But, excuse me, my dear, this is no fit subject for your ears; how a man lets business affairs plague him, when he can so forget the presence of his wife. But come in, we will take a cup of coffee together."

He drew her hand within his arm, and they passed into the breakfast-room, where a handsomely-laid table awaited them. Bouquets, arranged upon the mantel and sideboard, gave to the room the air and fragrance of a garden; and the meal itself was the very ideal of a breakfast, consisting of sandwiches, tea, coffee, and iced fruits. When they sat down to the table, Mr. and Mrs. Vertner were too well bred to allude to that which was troubling both their minds. Conversation flowed as freely and pleasantly as though nothing had disturbed their domestic or household arrangements. No surprise was even traced in the yellow face of Daniel, as he moved around the table. Everything went on as usual.

When Madge came in, she did not ask questions or betray anxiety on the subject of the fugitives, but ate her breakfast with apparent heartiness and gusto.

"Daniel," said she, at the conclusion of the cheerful meal, "tell Pomp to saddle my pony and bring him round."

"What, daughter are you for an early scamper?"

"Yes, papa, I am going to take my usual ride. I see your horse at the door; are you going out?"

"Yes, to the village."

"Well, suppose I accompany you?"

"I am sorry to decline your pleasant company, daughter; but I am going on business, and shall, perhaps, be detained for several hours."

"That will make no difference. I can ride into the village with you, and return alone. It is so long since we have had a sociable ride, I *must* go."

"Well, there is no resisting your *must*; but be very swift in getting ready, for I cannot lose many moments."

Madge fled from the room, and soon returned, looking beautiful, in her dark-green habit, black hat and ostrich feathers.

Mrs. Vertner watched her daughter and husband as they mounted their horses and galloped swiftly down the avenue, in the direction of L——.

"Poor Madge! how wild and thoughtless, to be sure," she sighed, as, turning from the verandah, she entered the parlor, and seated herself at the window, where she was soon lost in the perusal of the second volume of "Never Too Late to Mend."

III

The fresh morning air and the excitement of a swift gallop acted favorably upon Madge's animal spirits. Everything she saw drew forth warm expressions of admiration; her father looked upon her with more than his wonted pride, as she distanced him upon her swift-footed pony, and called laughingly back—

"Come on, laggard papa—you were in *such* a hurry, and yet I out-ride you"; then pausing until he overtook her, she touched the whip to the silken neck of her pony and dashed on like an arrow, while her gay, ringing laugh mocked him with its silver cadence.

"Dear girl," exclaimed her father, as he overtook her suddenly and placed his hand upon her bridle, "will you ever be more than a child?—you are so frolicsome! am I never to have a word of talk with you?"

Madge laughed heartily, but made no other reply.

"Your mother told me last night that you wanted to read a book—some novel of Reade's—what was it called? I am glad that something has turned your attention to books. You are getting old enough, dear, to give over, to a certain extent, these boyish sports."

Madge looked up, her eyes sparkling from under her hat.

"But, dear papa, I do not like books, and I love nature. Why should I read, if I have no taste for it?"

"Because, my child, I wish you to be informed."

"Informed of what? I once tried to read History, as you wished me, but I felt no interest in those old dead kings; and all the time I sat thumbing the pages, my heart was heavy; I wanted to be running with my dog or riding through the woods. The very atmosphere of your library was musty and sickening to me. Papa, it doesn't do *me* any good to know of those ugly old past times, but I am sorry that neither you nor mamma are satisfied with me. Last night I read that curious book, "Never Too Late to Mend," and it made me feel fifty years old. 'Tis a dreadful thing—my blood grows cold now, as I remember it."

"Did you read it last night?"

"Yes, I sat up until a late hour, poring over it, and it seemed as if my brain were on fire. Papa, are people so very bad, so cruel? If they are, I don't wish to know anything of the world."

"Oh, no, my child; you must not learn life from novels. I don't want you to have any such unhealthy views. The world is a very good place, and people quite good enough."

As they neared the village, they were met by two negro men, carrying baskets. They took off their hats to the fine gentleman and his daughter. Col. Vertner greeted them with the customary "Well, my boys," and Madge nodded her head.

"Negroes are always at work, papa."

"Yes, my child, they were made for it."

"How glad I am that I was not born a negro. Papa, should not you hate to be one?"

"Yes, my child, with my present knowledge; but if I had been born a negro, I dare say a merciful Providence would have given me their satisfied feeling."

"They *do* seem happy; don't they?"

"Yes, the happiest people in the world."

"Yet they sometimes run off." Madge looked at her father earnestly.

"That's because they yield to a momentary discontent, and, like children who run away from school, they regret it instantly."

"Then why don't they return? Aunt Candie, who ran away from Dr. Lacy, never came back, and yet she had a letter written to the Doctor, saying how happy she was in Canada. Last night, when I heard Jack and Milly talking under my window, I was tempted to call you and tell on them; then I thought perhaps they would be happier, and I should not disturb you."

Col. Vertner checked his horse suddenly.

"Madge, did you know of these runaways?"

"Yes, I heard them whispering under my window."

"And did not tell me of it!"

"I did not like to. It would not have been right. I should have given you time to track them."

"Madge!" Col. Vertner's voice was stern.

"Papa!" the girl's tone was surprised, but affectionate. Simultaneously they turned their horses head to head, and the father and daughter looked inquiringly into each other's faces. There was a pause of a few seconds, which Madge broke by saying frankly—

"Papa, I had been reading of the terrible cruelties in an English prison, and my heart was softened. I thought perhaps these slaves were unhappy—were fleeing away in the hope of bettering themselves. I couldn't, I dared not step between them and the object of their flight. If I have done wrong, and given you trouble, I am sorry."

"My child, you have acted very foolishly, but naturally for a girl that was excited by a novel and could not discriminate; but how could you run the parallel between my place and an English prison? You have not seen any cruelties at home."

"No, sir, but something, I don't know what, forbade my speaking. Once, at school, when I saw Katherine Livers steal a quire of paper, and I was asked about it, I refused to give evidence; and though I knew Jack and Milly were stealing, I couldn't inform on them."

"Yet you took Mrs. Goodhill's flowers." Her father smiled.

"But I felt that they were mine!"

By this time they had entered the village, and were passing through its centre and main street. Everybody bowed to Col. Vertner, and looked admiringly at his young daughter, as they rode quickly by.

"Now, papa, adieu. I'll return home by the new road—come home as soon as you can"; and, striking her pony, Madge dashed down a side street.

Col. Vertner rode on, until he came to a long, narrow building, of dirty frame—the public house of the town—in front of which were seated several men, smoking cigars, chewing tobacco and discussing politics.

"Good mornin', Colonel; a fine day."

"Good morning," replied the Colonel, and, dismounting, he walked up to a rough, red-faced man, who had on a red flannel shirt, a straw hat, and was smoking a cigar.

"Tom, I'd like a word with you."

"At your sarvice, Colonel."

The gentleman retired with the loafer to a more quiet spot, at the end of the long building.

"I have a little matter of business I wish you to attend to," said the Colonel. The loafer's face brightened. Business had been dull—a negro-catcher is generally a loafer—a man of permanent business habits could never be induced to turn out on such expeditions; for, besides being seldom lucrative, they are never respectable; so the riff-raff, or "poor white trash," as the negroes style them, generally take this office.

"Any niggers bin slippin' off, Colonel?"

"Yes, two—a man and his wife—and here" (handing him a paper) "is a written description of them and an offer of reward if taken in or out of the State—dead or alive—which you are to post in the most conspicuous places."

The man bowed as he received the paper, and, in a tone of professional boasting, replied—

"If they ain't faster 'an deers, I'll have um shortly—fur my dogs is sure on a scent."

Col. Vertner turned away without further words. Business once arranged, the lordly gentleman and slaveholder dared not condescend to speak further with a contemptible slave-catcher.

Nodding carelessly to the group, he remounted his horse and rode rapidly away.

....

There was a cloud upon the Colonel's brow; and when he was fairly beyond the precincts of the village, he turned his horse into an obscure path, and rode briskly along, the cloud deepening on his brow, and his cheek growing constantly paler. A dread secret locked in the soul is worse than a Spartan fox in its torturing bite upon the vitals.

We shall follow this gentleman of the world, in his seemingly retired ride, through woods. Up hills and down green valleys, he kept his course until, in the very thickest of the forest, in front of a rude cabin, his horse suddenly checked its course, as if accustomed to this as a stopping-place.

We have said the cottage was rude, but, if rough, it had about it the marks of a refined taste; flowers bloomed around, wild vines clambered over the rough walls and latticed the windows. The grass plot in front was green and fresh, the rose bushes were neatly trimmed, the path swept. You knew, at once, that taste and neatness kept watch.

Col. Vertner dismounted, and, throwing his bridle-rein carelessly over his horse's neck, left him to browse on the grass.

At the cabin door he was met by a tall mulatto woman, apparently about thirty years of age. She received him politely, kindly, almost affectionately—not as a slave, but as a friend, a lady.

And she *was* one of nature's crowned queens. Tall and graceful of limb, with a smooth throat, erect head and drooping shoulders, she moved as gracefully as a swimming swan. Her features were regular and comparatively small, with large, mournful black eyes, that seemed to enshrine in their melancholy depths the genius of her wronged and unhappy race. About her rather small and fine mouth there was a look of pain, evinced in a deep contraction of the corners. The wrapper of spotless white cambric, which was fastened at the throat by a knot of scarlet ribbon, set off finely her rich olive complexion. After speaking to her, Col. Vertner entered the cabin and flung himself hastily into a chair. The woman stood gazing timidly at him. At length she ventured to speak.

"Has anything gone wrong with you?"

"No, no, no." At the conclusion of each of these monosyllables, he drew a faint sigh; and while the woman stands gazing, with her heart in her eye, upon the man who has betrayed her, let us look around upon the cabin.

Though everything is simple and homely, there is an air of refined taste in the selection and arrangement of furniture, which half redeems the cabin from the charge of poverty. The uncarpeted floor is white, fresh and polished, from constant use of the scrubbing-brush, and a few rather pretty prints, without frames, are pinned upon the walls. Flowers and green branches festoon the rafters. A table in the centre of the room, upon which is placed a work-basket, and beside which is a small red cushioned rocking chair, complete the furniture of this little rustic home. Within a small inner room, the door of which is ajar, stands a bed, with its cool white drapery blowing and fluttering about in the morning breeze.

Col. Vertner looked around with a nervous stare, then smiled a bitter, forced smile, and, holding out his hand, invited the woman to his side.

"Rachel, it is suspected in the village that you have harbored runaway slaves here." His eye seemed to penetrate her. She crouched down to his side, and, taking his outstretched hand, began to plait the fingers, while she kept her eyes bent upon the floor, without making any reply.

"If you have done this, Rachel, you *must* leave this place at once. I have no power nor will to protect you."

He attempted to withdraw his hand, but she held it firmly; her lips quivered slightly, and here was a barely perceptible moisture about the eyelids. Then an attempt at articulation, a hard and violent swallow, as if words were choking her, and she said—

"Who accuses me?"

"No one as yet, but I suspect you."

"And would you hint at such a thing? would you *dare* to expose me to the terrible penalties of your law?"

She spoke rapidly, and with emotion, while her swarthy cheek glowed with crimson and her black eye glittered like a serpent's. For a moment the man was awed; he put out his hand and laid it upon her head, but she recoiled from the touch. Rising from her lowly position, she walked to the window, pressed her long, sallow fingers to her eyes, wiped away a few hot tears, then turned, as if made strong to express the thoughts that were crystalizing at her heart.

"Andrew Vertner, I am not now and never was a slave. Did society do me justice, I should be openly recognized as your cousin, for I am your uncle's child; and had he lived, I do believe he would have owned me as such in the face of the world. I wish I had staid in the North, where he sent me; and so I might, had you not decoyed me here with vain and foolish promises. I did not quarrel with you because you failed to keep those promises. For years I have lived only to be near you, and now to cast me off and refuse me that protection which natural and human right gives me!"

Col. Vertner was silent. These words had fallen upon his heart as truths. There are moments when even the most worldly and calculating men feel the bite of self-consciousness; glimpses of truth flash over them, when, seeing their lives as they are, they detest themselves. Rachel saw the moment and seized it.

"I do not say that I have or have not harbored runaway slaves. Certainly none of yours have been here. But I do say that I would not refuse lodging and food to a poor wretched outcast, flying from tyranny to liberty. If for this I am to be driven out of your State, why, drive me when and whither you please. I have some secrets which I shall use, if I am goaded too far."

Col. Vertner turned pale as he looked upon the woman's glittering eye, and listened to her determined tone, and, trying to smile, he said:

"Well, Rachel, don't be angry; we will not talk further about it now. Only don't let me hear complaints of you on this score. To be sure, I can't blame you for giving a cup of cold water or a crust of bread to a poor famishing wretch at your door; only be particular, and don't bring me and yourself into trouble."

She knelt down beside him and wound her long, graceful arms about his neck, and laid her soft olive cheek close to his.

"Do you know, Andrew, that this day, two years ago, I put away a little box of treasures, saying that in twenty-four months I would open it. Do you want to see it?" The voice was thick and husky, and the woman's form trembled, as she leaned still closer to the breast of Col. Vertner.

"No, Rachel, do not open that box. I know well enough what you have locked away; 'twill only trouble you, and can give me no pleasure."

The woman remained silent for some moments, with her eyes fixed attentively upon him, while he seemed lost in the maze of a half-troubled dream.

"Your daughter, Andrew, where and how is she?"

"Ah, Madge? I parted from her an hour or so ago. She is at home, I hope, and is as well and bright as a summer butterfly."

"I never saw her but once, and then I did not think she looked like you. A sort of strange, truant-looking child, and yet I liked her face. Is she much to you?"

"The very apple of my eye." The father's face brightened as he spoke.

"And my poor child"—Rachel's voice was low and reproachful—"never knew the love of a father, but my affection for her was all the more intense. How strange it is that, of all my children, not one has lived to bless my life! I am so lonesome at times that I feel like taking my own life, and would were I not such a coward."

Again the wily man plied the disappointed and half broken-hearted woman with oily words and specious promises; and when, after a visit of an hour, he rose to leave, she was softened, soothed and deluded.

IV

When Madge left her father, she rode directly homewards, thinking but little of the proceedings of the previous night; for she was a happy spirit, no shadow having fallen upon her young life. Nothing had ever occurred to call forth her sympathies, and she believed that everybody was happy because she was so herself. 'Tis pleasant to meet with such characters—pleasant to know that there are those for whom even thought has no sadness! Pretty butterflies, with gilded wings, flitting safely along dangerous paths!

Madge forgot the book which had struck so powerfully upon her heart-strings—forgot the poor fugitives, and only rioted in a full sense of enjoyment. Her course lay through a beautiful wood, and along the track of a winding stream. She was quiet, and rode slowly along, taking in, by spiritual draughts, the deep beauty of the scene! Nature has a voice and a charm for such simple, loving children, which she refuses to the too curious and impertinent. Madge did not seek to pry into strange secrets; she only listened, waited and admired; and so the charm worked well. Insensibly, she was growing, and learning of nature. The quiet woods, the bird melody-whispering winds, and sweetly-blowing flowers were weaving a charm for this child, who brought to their companionship a willing and a happy spirit. She grew like them, by the force and beauty of her own nature, taking no lessons of art, but living simply and naturally. She revolved in her mind the prospect of the promised trip to the Mammoth Cave, and determined to press the matter upon her mother's consideration.

As she reached a little swell in the road, which commanded a fine prospect, she halted and gazed around with a delighted eye. Far away in the distance were long slopes of verdure-covered earth, a variety of hill and dale, dotted here and there with a white farm-house, and at broken intervals she caught glances of the picturesque Green river which wound through the landscape like a strand of emerald and diamond.

"How lovely this is!" cried Madge, as she bent forward to pat and caress her pony. "This scene really inspires me. Only see it, Silk; why, how you prick your ears, as though you *smelt* the beauty. I see it with my eyes."

Madge was in the habit of talking to Silk and Rover as though they were fully capable of understanding her.

"Why, what is the matter with you, Silk? how you prick up your ears! Come, what is it?" and the young lady looked round inquiringly, as if to satisfy herself. "I am sure I see nothing in the direction of that thicket, and yet, Silk, you keep your eyes and ears turned there. Come, let's be off for home"; and, touching her riding-whip to the neck of her pony, she galloped on.

Just then there was a motion of the grass and a haggard-looking thing—could it be a human head?—was lifted from the screen of brushwood, and a pair of wild, fearful eyes glared around, with an expression of curious wonder; then as suddenly withdrew itself to the friendly hiding-place.

Let us look into that dingle, and see who or what is hidden there. Step this way with me, obliging reader, and, as I pass the tangled brush-wood, divide the thick-growing leaves, and peer down into the long, damp grass, tell me what you see. What is that strange, haggard, half-clothed looking thing? Is it a wild beast, or has it the appearance of a human creature? Look again—closer—and tell me if it is not a woman. Forget your prejudice against a black complexion—forget those misshapen African features—overlook that worn and torn dress—and ask the wild, weird, witch-like thing what brings her here.

She will tell you that, for four days, she has not tasted food, save a few wild, half-poisonous berries, which she clutched at in her hurried flight through the woods. Look at those bruised and briar-torn limbs; see that nervous quiver and gasping breath at every uncertain sound in the forest. Ask her why she is here, and she will tell you that she is seeking liberty at the risk of starvation and death; that she was sold away from her husband, and all that was left her was such speed as laid in her limbs, and such ingenuity as belonged to her brain. Look at her as she crouches there under cover of the thicket, trembling at every sound, humble, poor, degraded, asking for no foot of ground, leaving you your money, your friends and your home; only begging for the right to her own body. Tell me, will you turn away and join hands with the agents of the law, drag this wretched woman from her hiding-place, and give her back to the man who dares to call her a slave? No, I am sure you will not. Were you even born a slaveholder and a believer in slave-owning, you would renounce the traditions and teachings of your life, forget sectional pride, false education, and say with me, "God speed the fugitive."

....

When Madge arrived at home, she was met at the gate of the avenue by Pomp, whose broad white teeth shone in a wide grin of welcome to his young mistress. He had some wonderful story to tell her of Rover. Madge listened with apparent interest, laughing at the funny parts, and expressing amazement at that which was meant to be marvellous.

"I tells yer, Miss Madge, as I went 'long through the big road, Rover he jist follow right arter me, an' he scream out jist like a boy ever time he see one of 'em critters."

"You didn't let him do anything cruel or ugly, Pomp, did you?"

"Oh, no, Miss—he never wants to; but he's a good dog at a fight; if any other dog makes at him, he is sure to pluck up an give him a good fight."

"I don't object to that, and want him to have pluck."

"Yes, I knows, Miss Madge, dat yer never likes him to be beat. Yer wants him to whip."

"To be sure I do"; and, drawing her rein, she galloped up the avenue, leaped off the pony, and throwing the bridle to a groom, rushed into the house.

"Madge," said Mrs. Vertner, "where did you part from your father?"

"Ah, mamma, are you still poring over that book? I've had such a splendid ride! The air was so delicious, and, about a mile and a half from here, there is a glorious prospect; you ought to see it mamma."

"You have not yet answered my question."

"What was it, mamma?"

"I asked you where you left your papa."

"Oh, I parted from him at the village. You know he had some business to attend to; perhaps he will not return early."

"He expected to see the negro-catcher and have the runaways advertised; but surely, that would not require much time. I hope he will soon return, for I wish him to join us in our afternoon drive. It is outrageous for those negroes to give us so much trouble. I do hope your papa will conclude to sell them if they are caught."

"Do you think he will, mamma?" inquired Madge, as she laid aside her riding-hat.

"I shall persuade him to, for they will only give more trouble if they remain upon the place. Moreover, the effect of their example will be very bad upon the others."

Madge did not reply at once, she moved about the room, in a half-doubtful mood. At length, turning sharply round, facing her mother, she said:

"If the runaways are found, I shall ask papa not to sell them, but to forgive them, and allow them to remain at home."

"Why will you do this, Madge?" asked Mrs. Vertner, in the same quiet tone of voice.

"Because I heard Milly say, last night, under my window, that she was afraid if they should be caught that papa would sell them down the river."

"You—heard—Milly—say—this—under—your—window—last—night?" Mrs. Vertner spoke slower than usual, making a pause at each word.

"Yes, mamma, that's what I said." Madge spoke carelessly.

"I can't believe the evidence of my ears! *You* heard this, Madge Vertner?"

"Certainly, mamma; Milly and Jack were speaking under my window at a late hour last night, planning their flight. I heard every word, and could have reported them."

"And why didn't you?" This time Mrs. Vertner spoke sharply.

"Because I didn't want to. I had been reading about Robinson and Josephs. My heart was touched, and I resolved not to be wicked and expose these poor runaways."

"Madge Vertner! have you been reading 'Uncle Tom's Cabin,' and has it driven you mad?"

"No, mamma, I have not read 'Uncle Tom's Cabin,' nor am I mad."

"Come, child, sit down beside me?"

Madge took the chair near her mother, and looked inquiringly in her face.

"My dear, do you know that you have been guilty of a very great wrong?"

The girl shook her head.

"You might have saved your father a great deal of money, which will have to be spent in order to get these slaves back."

"I hope they will not be caught, and papa need not spend his money unless he pursues them."

"But he *will* pursue them."

"Why?"

"For several reasons. In the first place, they are worth several thousand dollars, and he will desire to make them an example to others. If these succeed in getting off, the others will make the same attempt, and we should have a slave stampede, right off, in the neighborhood."

"Mamma, you said you would have let Josephs out of that prison jacket if it had cost you your life; my sympathy went a little farther. I couldn't do Josephs or Robinson service, so I showed mercy to Milly and Jack."

"The cases, my dear, are very dissimilar—Josephs and Robinson were ill-used, brutally-treated prisoners, while our slaves are kindly treated. Of course, my dear, you believe slavery to be right."

"Certainly, mamma, because the Bible teaches it; at least our minister says so"—answered Madge, with the sweetest naiveté.

"And our servants are all well and kindly treated."

"Yes, mamma, I believe they are."

"Then why did you hesitate to expose Milly and Jack?"

"I don't know, dear mamma. I see fully the truth of your reasoning; yet, if the matter were to do over again, I am sure I should act the same way."

Mrs. Vertner looked pityingly upon her child, then, kissing the fair young brow, said,

"Madge, read your Bible and pray over this; then you will see it in the right light."

The library door stood ajar, and had Mrs. Vertner looked out into the hall, she might have seen Daniel's yellow face pressed close to the open door. He had been listening, aye, swallowing every word of that conversation. How his great eyes gleamed with wonder as he listened, and what an angel did "Miss Madge" seem to his simple heart! As she swept by him with the long train of her riding-habit dragging on the floor, and her plumed hat in her hand, he gazed after her with something like reverence; and the lips so true to the pulse of the heart broke out in a cordial, almost fervent, "Miss Madge." She looked round, surprised and not displeased at the tone, and, smiling kindly, passed on to her room.

V

We must ask the reader to return with us, for a short time, to Rachel's cottage.

After Col. Vertner left, she remained a few moments, looking after him, straining her eyes and ears until the last sight had faded and the last sound had died away; then, turning into the solitary room, she set about some customary avocation.

After a while, she went into the inner room, and, opening the drawer of an old worm-eaten bureau, took out a little box, carefully tied with tape, and, seating herself in the rocking chair, began to unwind the string, while tears gathered in her eyes. Her hand trembled as she removed the lid, and, taking out some broken toys and a little shoe, worn and soiled, began to kiss them and talk to them as though they were vital things. Thus has many another mother done before her. Human nature is ever the same, no matter how different may be the texture and color of the skin.

While the mother sat fondling and talking lovingly to these relics of an early lost darling, her heart becoming softer and softer, she thought she heard a moan just below her window. Hastily gathering up her treasures, and concealing them in the box, she stole noiselessly to the window and looked out; then asked, "Who's there?" Waiting for a moment or so, and receiving no reply, she concluded that she had been mistaken. It was a trifling circumstance, and she soon forgot it. Grief is selfish, and monopolizes too much to allow even a thought to stray off in search of other matters. Rachel had pondered too long and absorbingly upon the conversation of the morning to be disturbed by what she decided to be a mere trick of fancy.

"Ah," she thought, "harboring fugitive slaves seems to be a dreadful crime. Andrew thought hardly of it; he is a determined character; I must heed his will in this affair. If my cabin becomes a place of suspicion, I shall find but little rest; perhaps *he* may not be able to protect me from the fury of the mob. Well, I shall be particular in future; these poor runaways must find shelter somewhere else; I will never take another one in."

With this resolution, Rachel satisfied herself, or imagined that she did, and so, with a lightened heart, set about her every-day's work.

But, toward twilight, as she sat at the door, watching the dusky shadows as they crept over the still landscape, she heard again that piteous moan. "What can it be?" she asked; "is this place haunted?" She looked around, went to the corner of the cabin, and peered among the tall weeds and grass, but could not see any person or thing to frighten her. "Why, this is too curious," she murmured; "I never heard these sounds before, and yet I've lived here a long while." A superstitious fear began to come over her, her blood flushed and chilled alternately, her limbs trembled, and she would have been glad, in her fright and loneliness, to have welcomed any human face. That fearful dread of the nearness of the dead, that apprehension of a spiritual visitation, which freezes the blood and unstrings the nerves of the boldest, was too much for this delicate and sensitive woman. Her position was becoming painful in the extreme.

"I cannot stay at the cabin to-night," she thought; but she had no place to go to, and, reentering the cabin, she lighted her little tin lamp, took her thimble from the work-basket, and began to sew, although she trembled violently. However, hearing no further repetitions of the mysterious sounds, she began gradually to resume her accustomed calmness.

As she sat rocking, singing and stitching, a wild, weird, black face looked in at the open window upon her, and a pair of shriveled, claw-like hands were stretched out in supplication toward her. The face and attitude looked terrific in that uncertain glimmer of lamp light. There was no cry, no murmur or moan—only that dreadfully agonized face, and the supplicating motion of the hands.

As if by some subtle magnetic charm, Rachel turned her head toward the window, and, as she met the gaze of those bleared eyes, she screamed aloud and fell forward on the floor.

"My God!" she cried, "is it the devil come to torment me—come to take me off, body and soul, before my time?"

The strange figure did not move or change its supplicating position. At length, Rachel recovered by degrees, and, pressing her hand over her eyes, rose—never daring to turn even her body toward the fatal window. But we know that terror fascinates as irresistibly as beauty, and the eyes of the affrighted woman could not long remain covered or avoid a glance toward the window. Half reluctantly, half willingly, she moved her body slowly, gradually round, until she faced the terrible apparition; and looking at it now, with the conviction that she was to see something frightful, was enabled to control herself. As she gazed toward it, with distended nostril and flashing eye, never daring to trust her tongue with words, the thing made an attempt to speak.

"Bread—water—a crumb—a drop—please"—were the broken syllables that issued from those dry, withered lips.

"What is *it?*" inquired Rachel.

Still the thing, with one long finger upon the parted lips, seemed to beg for food or drink. In a little while, Rachel divined this, and, seizing a cup of water, she ventured to draw near the goblin. The wretch clutched at the cup, swallowed down the water, then moaned out—

"A bit of bread, for God's sake."

This, too, was furnished. By this time Rachel had divined the truth. A poor runaway negro woman, starved and famished, was asking for relief. She forgot the resolution of the morning, and said to the wretched beggar at her window,

"Come in, I will give you what I can; come at least and rest awhile."

The poor woman, half walking, half crawling, groped round to the doorway and entered the cabin, with the assistance of Rachel's hand. And how tenderly Rachel waited upon her! how she laved those flesh-wounds, bound camphor to the aching temples, and, by kind restoratives and soothing words, recalled the poor wandering vagrant to consciousness and human life.

"Tell me," said Rachel, "what brings you to my cabin? I know, of course, that you are running away from your master, but why did you come to me?"

"Oh," replied the poor wretch, who now began to revive under this kindly treatment, "I didn't mean to run off, but my old mistress, a widow woman, was gwine to move off to the Sonsie country, an' I didn't want to be separated from my old man, an' ole miss wouldn't sell me nor hire me out where I could see him, but sed to me, 'come 'long an' git 'nother husband.' Now, I never ken do that—'cause I jist believe de Lord married me to my old man, an' I kan't consent to leave him, no how an' no way. I talk to ole miss 'bout it, but she would think this here way. Then I spoke to Peter, an' asked him if he wouldn't look round 'mong some of 'em rich gentlemen that he chops wood fur of winter nights, an' ax 'em if they wouldn't like to buy me; fur I thought if they'd offer a good big price, old miss would consent, fur she do love money. Well, Peter he went round an' tried, an' Lawyer Thompson wanted a house gal. I'm good hand at house-work, an' Pete told him so. He come out to see ole miss, an' offered her eight hundred dollars, cash down, fur me. Well, at fust 'peared like she was gwine to take him up, but she 'gin to think on it, an' she said she fotched me up an' wished allers to keep me in the family, so's me and my chillen might 'long to her an' her'n allers. Now, when I hearn this, and found I got to leave Peter, why I jist kinder all sink down an' go 'way to nothin' like. So, when Peter come, last Saturday night, I jist told him I couldn't stand it, no way an' no how, an' meant to run off. He sorter 'suaded me not to; but when my mind's once made up, it's hard to git me to change. So, on last Monday, I made up my bundle, an', at twelve o'clock at night, stole out of the house. I allers slept in the little room at the end of the long porch, close to ole miss's room. They wouldn't miss me till daylight, so I 'spect to git a good start; but I lost my way in the woods, an' went wandering 'bout, feelin' my way, hidin' 'hind bushes every time I hearn a squirrel or bird move; an' when day come, I had to hide away, an' by night I was so tired, hungry an' dry, I couldn't walk much; all I'd had to eat was two or three green berries, that I pulled as I laid hid under brushwood. I daresn't hardly move, so I didn't git fur that night; I was so faint an' weak like that many times I wish I was back 'long wid ole mistress, an' so it was most all of time since I lef."

"Do you want to go to your old mistress? What's her name?"

"Why, laws, honey! Now I'se started, sick and weak as I be, I 'gins to feel like a free 'ooman, an' 'pears to me as I'd rather die jist here at yer feet, an' in dis fix, than to go back and be slave to my old miss, widow Vitertor; tho' I kant say as how she is good enuff to me; I had, shure, enuff work to do, but I generally made out to git through with it. Thar was five in family; I had to wash an' cook, clean house, an' work in garden of summers; 'tend to cows, keep the poultry yard, an' make butter fur market. I only had little time of Sat'day nights to talk 'long my old man; but I didn't mind that much, fur the comfort of seeing my old man was joy enuff; but now I kant no ways go off outer him."

"But if you run off—"

The woman laughed a strange sort of laugh, and, shaking her head, replied:

"He has legs 'an can come arter me."

"Are you not getting sleepy?" asked Rachel.

"It 'pears so kurus to be under kiver agin; but if I gits laid down, an' my mind sorter easy like, may be I will sleep."

Rachel put her away on a pallet in the little room, and, taking down her Bible, read a chapter of the New Testament, and, kneeling down, begged of God to give her patience and charity to bear with and feel for her suffering fellow-creatures.

She thought, It is not much that I do for this poor wretch, to feed and shelter her for one night. I will do as I would be done by, and leave the result to God.

This would indeed be a Christian age, if we all—great and little ones—judges, jurors, and private citizens—followed the course of this simple-hearted mulatto woman, who, living away from the world and proscribed by civilized and polite races, with a mind not overlaid by false reasoning and state policies, could listen to the voice of God as it whispered to her soul.

VI

The village of L——, usually so quiet, dull and drowsy, was quite alive and active now, for it was "Court day"—always an important day in inland towns. Swarms of people crowded round the Court-house; and along the fences, and in front of the taverns, store-houses and public buildings generally, horses were tied up, by every variety and style of bridle, from the gay red list and stout leather to the broken and knotted rope.

At the corners of the streets, under awnings, negro women sold apples, melons and ginger cakes to hungry boys.

Everything and everybody were astir. Groups of farmers, in white hats and country jean coats, stood-about the pavements, discussing politics, or settling, according to their own notions, some old and long-pending law suits; while tobacco juice and oaths flowed in plentiful streams.

Two men, in rough blue jean coats and dirty straw hats, and carrying large riding switches in their hands, passed down the main street, and, pausing in front of the clerk's office (which adjoins the Court-house), began to read the advertisements and notices that were posted upon the fences. Let us quote two of the these:

$500 REWARD!—Ran away from me, on last Monday night, two negroes—a man and a woman. The man is about thirty-five years of age, a dark mulatto, six feet high, with a scar under his left eye, stout shoulders, able body, and a good-natured face. Had on when he left blue cotton pantaloons and a roundabout. The woman is about thirty, looks older, very black, with a heavy face, and slightly lame; wore a striped calico frock, white apron and neck handkerchief. The above reward will be promptly paid, if apprehended in this State, or lodged in some county jail and sent to me.

A. D. VERTNER.

$50 REWARD if taken in the State, $75 if caught out of the State, or within five hundred miles of—County——.

Ran off from the subscriber, on last Friday, a likely negro woman, about twenty-five years of age, very black, appears to be upwards of thirty, hard set face; about five feet two inches in height. Wore away a check domestic frock, walks a little lame, and is quite glib of speech. The above reward will be paid if found, or information sent to the subscriber.

A. D. VITETOR, per JANE M. VITETOR.

There were a number of similar notices, all of which were carefully read by the two comrades in jean.

"'Pears to me, Mac," said the older one, "thar's bin a stampede 'mong the niggers. Any o' your'n bin 'mong 'em?"

"No, d—d if mine gits a chance. I doesn't pity a man whose niggers runs off; it's a sure sign he's bin 'lowin' 'em liberties—lettin' 'em visit an' keep company. Thar's nothin' so bad for niggers as a visitin'. I never allow strange niggers in my kitchen or cabins. I made that rule, and I don't 'low it to be broken. Why, bless you, if visitin' was 'lowed 'mong 'em, I'd never be able to keep an egg or a spring chicken on the place; they'd all be stolen. It's as nat'ral fur a nigger to steal as 'tis fur a white man to eat when he's hungry."

"I don't know so well 'bout that, Capt. Mac; I haven't got, to be sure, a great drove, like you. I only keeps three—two farm hands an' one woman to cook an' wash. I don't own 'em even. I hire, but then I have bin a hirin' these steady on fur the last ten years, so they kinder 'pears like my own. I ain't had occasion even to strike one of 'em a lick. They's all of one family—a man an' his wife an' brother; and, Capt. Mac, I do find 'em as faithful as though they was my own family."

"Do they belong to the Church?" inquired Mac, with a quizzical look and tone.

"Yes, they all belongs to the Baptist Church, an' I 'lows 'em to take turn 'bout in going to the meetin' in the school-house. I belong to the same meetin'; indeed, Jerry an' me jined church at the same time an' was baptized together."

"I hope he wasn't dipped with you, Sam Bosby?"

"No, Capt. Mac, Brother Downes allers baptizes the whites first, an' the niggers afterwards; an' that's right, you know."

"I ain't so sure of that, Sam Bosby; if you baptizes a nigger at all, I think he should be dipped 'longer the rest of you. If you give him the right hand of fellowship, do it in the clean way."

"Yes, but the Church doesn't mean to equalize whites an' niggers."

"Then the Church tells a d—d lie, for it says all is on an equal footin'. Come, now, Sam Bosby, 'tain't no use talkin' yer religion to me, 'cause I don't think it's worth a snap of my finger."

"Oh, Capt. Mac, you are a very irreligious man. I ask yer pardon, but r'ally I can't hear you talk so without feelin' it my bounden duty to tell yer of it, fur the sake of yer immortal soul."

"Oh, hang it! quit yer fudge. Who told you my soul was immortal? I tell you ag'in an' ag'in, Sam Bosby, I don't believe in yer churches; I don't believe in any of yer good talk; I don't care blazes for the soul, because I only believe in what I've seen an' felt."

"Haven't you felt that you had a soul? Haven't you had immortal longings?"

"I never had longings fur anything but money, an' some how or other, by hook or crook, I've managed to git a pretty round sum of that. Niggers ain't no more to me 'an horses or cows. If I believed in God, heaven, hell and the soul, why, I'd believe at once that it was wrong to hold niggers in bondage."

"Oh, no, Capt. Mac, the Scripter justifies slavery. Many times my own heart has bin agin' it, but then I'd turn to the Scripter an' find it justified thar, an' so I've eased myself of any scruples an' smitings I had afore."

"Yes, that Bible! every body proves his or her ism by it. My 'pinion is that's it's good enuff book for wimmin an' chillen; but men—'tain't fit fur men. It does to skeer the wimmin. They likes to read 'bout the New Jerusalem an' sich towns, because that sort of trumpery of gold streets an' shiny gates pleases 'em; but it's trash to men. Now, I likes well enuff fur my wife to belong to the church; I kind of encouraged her to jine, for its a sort of excitement, this goin' to meetin' of Sundays; rain or shine, I have to gear up the old carry-all an' drive my wife over to the school-house. 'Pon my word, I kan't see no immediate good in it, an' yit it 'pears kind o' necessary fur the wimmin folks."

"Oh, yes, Capt. Mac, yer wife is one of the sure ones; her salvation is sartin. I've watched her in meetin' an it 'pears likes her face is bright with divine promise."

At this the facetious MacFarland gave a contemptuous sneer; and the two moved away in the direction of the Court-house. Encountering Col. Vertner, they bowed very politely and halted, MacFarland remarking—

"Well, Colonel, I see, from a notice stuck up, that you has bin losin' two niggers."

"Yes," replied the Colonel, "but as Tom Hynes has undertaken the job, I've no doubt they will soon be returned to me."

"Yes, Tom an' his hounds is sure on a scent; them niggers is safe. But, Colonel, I niver has any of these disturbances on my place. I keep my slaves tight."

"So I have heard, Capt. MacFarland," replied the Colonel, "but I do not believe in severe treatment. Negroes are human creatures, and I have established the mild rule on my place. I have repeatedly turned off overseers because of cruelty, and now appointed one of the slaves to over-look, give out and attend to the work, and I find that we get along with less whipping, less complaints.

"And on account of this mild rule, as yer call it, two niggers runs off together one night. Ah, ha! ha! Colonel, the laugh is agin' yer."

"So it may be, Capt. MacFarland, but for all that I shan't allow cruelty; mild measures are wise measures; so, good morning, Captain—good morning, Mr. Bosby."

"The Colonel is a gentlemanly man," observed Bosby.

"Yes, but he can't keep a hotel," replied MacFarland, as he gave his companion a familiar nudge.

Bosby seemed to enjoy the wit of the remark, if we might judge from the laugh he gave.

"Yes, sir," continued MacFarland, "these readin' men ain't much fur actual life. They judges too much from the books. My man Tom allers laughs, and says to me, 'Master, Col. Vertner's niggers says that their master wants 'em to farm 'cordin' to the newspapers, but some how 'twon't hang.' Yer see, in that case, the niggers knows better 'an thar master; fur it won't do to introduce yer machines upon farms. Niggers don't understand 'em. The only machine I believe in is the big greasy arms of niggers, kept in good order by a smart whip."

"That's the one yer uses too."

"Well, it is; an' nowhere 'bout in these parts can you match my niggers."

In such conversation as this the two men continued, as they walked up the street.

They passed a quiet, neatly-dressed gentleman, who was walking leisurely down the street.

"Ah, who is he?" inquired Bosby.

"That's the new schoolmaster, who's come here from some of them Yankee States. He is tryin' to git up a school here."

"He is nice lookin'."

"Yes, fur a schoolmaster or a storekeeper, but I am sure he knows nothin' 'bout business."

"Them guessing Yankees, clock-makers, &c., ginerally has a turn fur luck."

"Oh, they are shrewd enuff, an' can lie as fast as you or me can count, an' that's a way to git along."

Meanwhile, the stranger, whom our friends recognized as the "Yankee schoolmaster," pursued the even tenor of his way, all unconscious of the novel criticism which his gentleman-like appearance provoked. He was indeed a remarkable looking person, and, seen among these rude villagers and country people, seemed like a swan among a swarm of crows. The whole manner of the man was that of utter self poise, self-trust, as though he realized his manhood and determined that others should respect it. The figure was that of a conscious, satisfied man; the face was cold, and slightly severe in expression, with a clear, pale complexion and prominent brow. Thought, culture and fine speculations looked out from those calm blue eyes, while the brown hair (of which there was a plentiful crop) was cut short and brushed close to the head, giving to the face a somewhat curt and shrewd expression, which was not natural to it. The neat suit of black broadcloth, black kid gloves and shining hat bespoke a well-to-do sort of condition, and strongly contrasted with the coarse home-spun of the surrounding farmers.

On and on he continued his walk, until he got far beyond the town limits, into the outskirts of the woods, admiring, at every step, some new charms of the magnificent forest. True, though he missed the faithful cultivation, the patient toil and tasteful elaboration which have made his own native New England's rocky soil to blossom and bloom like a very garden of roses, here, at least, he found nature in all her wild and rollicking luxuriance, bursting into full-hearted beauty, running over with glee and laughter, like a maiden of seventeen. It was as if he had stumbled upon enchanted ground. He looked round expecting to meet fairies, wood nymphs and sylvan goddesses, and lo! one did come almost at his call; for, as he turned round, Madge Vertner came galloping by on her sleek little pony, her face looking as bright and blooming as Aurora's, beneath the shadow of her riding-hat, with its waving black plumes.

Observing the nonplussed air of the stranger, with all a Southerner's genial readiness, Madge remarked:

"Have you lost your path, sir? Turn to the right, and, by crossing that little thicket, you will strike the main road, which conducts to the village."

As she gave these directions, she indicated the way by a graceful motion of her riding-whip. Without waiting for a reply, she rode swiftly on.

"Surely, that is the original Die Vernon," thought the stranger; "or I am in the heart of enchanted land. Everything is glorious here."

With these pleasant fancies working in his heart, he turned away from the wood and followed exactly the direction which Madge had given.

Along the public way he frequently encountered, as he returned, negroes half-clothed, ragged, dirty and deplorable looking; so he began to question his first suggestions of fairy land.

VII

We will ask the reader to accompany us to a beautiful house
on the outskirts of the village of L——. We will walk into the parlor,
examine the room, and listen to the two colloquists seated on the sofa;
for we recognize in one of them our young friend Madge. But, first, let
us observe the taste displayed in the elegant fitting up of the apartment.
There are gorgeous pictures—perhaps a little too modern; fine statues,
buhl tables of curious workmanship, curtains of gold-colored silk,
festooned with laces, flowers blooming in rare antique vases, chairs
of unique style—everything, in short, that bespeaks the presence of
recently-acquired wealth. You miss the dear old-fashioned tables, the old
family portraits, the odd, stiff uncomfortable old straight back chairs
that belong to families with whom wealth and social position have been
a birthright. There is a questionable sort of elegance about the house
that makes one suspect the owners to be people of yesterday. Madge
Vertner, in her full riding costume, is seated in a large arm chair, with
her tiny foot resting upon a blue velvet footstool, and the heavy folds
of her black habit sweep the carpet. Her companion is a lady of about
twenty-three. The face is a pleasing one—pleasing, perhaps, from a
certain subdued expression which, if not that of thought itself, is that of
its semblance, quiet. This expression is, no doubt, increased by the dress
of deep mourning which she wears. The lady's face occasionally breaks

forth into a sweet smile, which lights up the features and gives them beautiful animation. Madge is rattling on in a very enthusiastic manner:

"Now, you see, Helen, I shot a bird on the wing yesterday."

"You have done that before, haven't you?"

"Oh, no, indeed; this is my very first exploit of the kind. Papa says he was never able to do such a thing."

"He doesn't give his whole mind to it, as you do," replied the other, with one of her peculiar smiles.

"No, indeed, for it seems to me he reads all the books that are published. I have known him to sit in the library poring over a book from seven o'clock in the morning until seven in the evening, scarcely taking time for his meals. I don't see how he *can* do it. His legs must feel very uncomfortable, and need the exertion of a good run. 'Tis enough to put one's eyes out, so constantly to follow those printed pages."

Again the lady smiled.

"Why, Madge, dear, half the pleasure of my life is in books. Since my father's death" (the lady sighed), "I've found them an immense consolation. I never feel lonely if I have an interesting book."

"Dear me! how queer it seems! Now, when I feel lonely, which is seldom indeed, I call for my pony and go galloping through the woods; and as soon as my blood begins to flow, all is right again with me."

"Madgy! Madgy! you are a happy child. All things bright and joyous seem to flow to you and from you."

"I can't understand, Helen, why people are ever otherwise than happy, unless indeed" (and Madge's voice grew softer) "they have lost near friends, as you have, Helen."

"Yes, Madge, but are there not other troubles in life almost as heavy as the loss of friends?"

"I can imagine none other; can you?"

"Yes."

"What are they?"

"Their name is legion."

"Can't you answer me more directly, Helen? You know, dear, how much I dislike this kind of round-about talk. Say *the thing*—never mind the dress. Now, give me a true idea of these troubles you nickname legion."

"Perhaps 'tis as well, Madge, to leave you awhile longer in your happy dream. The knowledge of evil, of pain and human suffering, will come soon enough."

"You half frighten me, Helen. Why are you always so serious? Mamma says when you were a very little girl you had this same curious, odd way."

"Does your mamma say so, dear?"

There was a questioning sort of earnestness in Madge's eyes as she regarded her friend. She looked as though she were trying to read her through, and pluck out, if possible, the heart of the mystery; then, playing with her riding-whip, cutting at the skirt of her flowing train and tapping the toe of her little boot with an anxious impatience, she burst out into a happy-hearted laugh, saying:

"'Tis no use for me to puzzle my head over what can't get into it. I know I am happy, and I believe everybody else is. Why should they be otherwise? Look out at that west window, Helen; see the ample stretch of green wood; gaze up at yon blue arching sky; see the sun shining splendidly; feel the earth warm and glowing beneath your steps; fill your heart with this fresh air, and then say how it is people can be unhappy! We live here happily and securely with our friends, and feel that a good God holds us under his wing. This we realize most truly in the green old woods, or on the sunny meadow side. I have observed that unhappy people are those who read a great deal. I am afraid there is poison hidden somewhere between the pages of those books. You needn't laugh so, Helen, for I believe what I am saying."

The lady rose and wound her arms round Madge's waist, pressed her chilly lips on that sweet young brow, and murmured—

"God bless you."

Madge looked up, surprised to see tears glistening in Helen's eyes.

"Why, bless me! Helen, what *is* the matter?"

"Nothing, dear—positively nothing"; but as she tried to utter these words calmly, her lips quivered, and, yielding to the pressure of the moment, she laid her head upon Madge's shoulder and wept. Our little heroine did not understand a word of it; did not know how to offer consolation, or what soothing words to speak; but, with that ready sense which belongs only to fine, intuitive natures, remained quiet and allowed Helen's emotion its natural and healthy vent.

How many of us have felt the cruelty of that common, vulgar inquiry, "What's the matter with you?" Better a thousand-fold leave the sufferer to nature's care—silence and reflection. A fine grief, that lies hid away in the heart, must never be insulted by such a question. Who, thus interrogated, does not hug all the closer his or her peculiar sorrow, and feel that it is all his own? Our sorrows are peculiar, and oftentimes personal; we do not wish strangers to take stock in them. The story of the poor old hunted, insulted cripple contains a solemn truth. Children had worried him all day, as he sat on the wayside rock, eating his crust—wearied him with incessant questioning—when, at length, teased beyond the limits of his patience, he broke forth—

"Children, be gone, let me have at least my trouble to myself."

We are all willing to share our pity, but, for charity's sake, leave us alone with our troubles.

After a few moments' silence, Madge, speaking cheerfully, as though nothing had happened, said:

"Helen! mamma, papa and I are going to the Mammoth Cave next week; will you not join us? Take the vacant seat in our carriage. We shall be so glad of your company."

Helen smiled, evidently quite pleased at the prospect of such a trip.

"I should, indeed, love to go with you, but I don't know what mamma will say to it."

"Oh, she'll give consent, I am sure; let me propose it to her; come, let us go to her room."

The two girls passed through the broad hall, up a curved flight of stairs, and entered Mrs. Mason's private sitting room. Here also everything was arranged with the same eye to gorgeous effect. Brilliant colors and elegant design without simplicity of taste manifested themselves in a striking manner.

Mrs. Mason, a cadaverous-looking invalid, enveloped in laces and wrapped in a morning dress of plaid silk, sat in an arm-chair, beside a small table, which contained a silver tea service, and she was sipping the delightful beverage from a Sevres cup.

"Good morning, Madge; I am taking my lunch."

Madge stepped forward, and, warmly kissing the lady's brow, replied:

"Yes, I am glad to see you so well."

Seating herself on an ottoman near Mrs. Mason, she began some pleasant, cheerful conversation upon out-door life, which charmed the fashionable invalid into a moment's forgetfulness of her pains and ills. Sweet child of untaught life, who carried in her heart truth and love, and wore them pictured like sunshine on her fair face! She made all who came in contact with her happy, for she had no theories, no art, no questioning of mysteries, no searching into the future. Life was not a problem to her, or if it was, she found its solution in a quiet, happy conduct, and lived her own sweet life in her own sweet way; and like those same wild-wood flowers amid which she played, she made the atmosphere in which she lived pure and fragrant by the perfume and beauty of her character.

Before she left, she had obtained Mrs. Mason's hearty consent to Helen's joining the party for the Cave; and with a few more pleasant words, she bade them good-bye, and galloped off, leaving Helen Mason in wonder how any one could be so happy and free from care.

VIII

"Now, I tell you, Peter, them ar niggers is gwine to be found out, kotched an' brung back."

Aunt Polly said this, as she entered the cabin where Uncle Peter sat smoking away at his old pipe.

"Who tole you so, Polly?"

"Why, Peter, Lord love you, I hear masser a-talkin' to 'em about it, an' he says he's done gone an' got Tom Hynes an' his men sot on thar track, and then they's kotched as clar as guns."

"Humph!" muttered the old man, and smoked away at his pipe. His wife knew that it was not worth while to ply him with further talk, so she set about furbishing up her pans and arranging the scanty furniture of her cabin. It was Saturday afternoon, and she said that she must "fix up for Sunday." What a blessed and beneficent institution in the slave's life is the Sabbath! The pleasant sunshiny afternoon was drawing to a close, and the quarter looked unusually cheerful. Each little grass-plat in front of the cabins had been carefully swept. Two or three of the negroes were dancing, while an old man played upon a fiddle. Over by a broken fence, and upon an old topple-down keg, which had been used for an ash-bucket, was seated the negro girl Ruth, engaged in an apparently interesting *tete-á-tete* with Daniel, the dining-room servant. She practised, in an humble and grotesque way, all those blandishments of manner that render the city belle so attractive. Negro women, old and middle-aged, sat out in front of their respective cabins, darning socks or patching old clothes for Sunday wear, while a group of half-dressed boys played marbles, and our little Pomp, in the rear of one of the cabins, but within hearing of the music (if music it was which came from feeble, untaught hands and broken bow), had a private dance all to himself. His motions were quite remarkable, and would no doubt have greatly startled a French dancing-master. Though not such graceful pirouettes or such dexterous vaulting as we have witnessed upon the stage, still, his leapings and twirls were admirable, if it were only for their accurate regard of time. His body seemed a musical instrument in perfect tune. As he danced, he accompanied himself with a unique song, the chorus of which we give for its very oddity:

> "Jump up, Ginny, with your booties on,
> Three or four yards of calico."

The boy seemed to be in the very rapture of enjoyment. His eyes sparkled, and his shining brown face literally ran over with mirth and frolicsomeness.

Scenes of animal life and enjoyment such as these—little gleams of sunshine and pleasure in a world of blight—form the basis upon which certain wiseacres build up a wondrous superstructure of argument in favor of slavery!

When the fun was at its highest, Madge Vertner, like a visiting angel, passed through the "quarter." She was dressed in white, with a few blue ribbons fluttering about her arms, neck and waist, while her straw hat sat jauntily upon her head, and the brown curls, thrown back from her face, swept over her neck and shoulders. Of course she was followed closely by her companion, Rover.

The dancers did not stop—the frolic did not halt for a moment. "Miss Madge" was no stranger to them, no stiff, exacting visitor, only a higher inspiration to increased pleasures. As they skipped, shuffled and danced along, their black, shiny faces looked happier for the coming of young mistress. As she passed gayly through, she had a word for each— some patronizing comment upon the dance, some joke to give vent to. When she came to an old or a sick slave, she made a kind inquiry after his health, or proposed some nice little remedy which he could get by sending to the house; or, she drew from her pocket a little roll of tea, sugar, or some such luxury, which she gave to him; and so her visits were always welcome. Pomp spied her, and, forgetting both his song and jig, rushed up to her, extending his hand, and cried out—

"Please, Miss Madge."

"What, sir?" and she knocked off his hand with a small stick. "What is it you want?"

"Please, ma'am, some of that 'ar."

"What?" and she held out her two empty hands.

"Some dat 'ar you's givin' Uncle Ned."

"Uncle Ned is sick, and I brought him a little parcel of tea and sugar."

"Please, ma'm, give me some sugar."

"Why, you are not sick."

The boy paused a moment; then, assuming a serious expression, said:

"Yes, miss, I'se sick—I'se had headache in my back fur long time."

"The headache in your back!—how is that?"

"Why, you see, Miss Madge, Uncle Ned say de headache is de worst of misery, an' I knows I'se got de worst of dem 'ar in my back." Suiting the action to the words, he put his hand upon his back, and began to distort his face.

"Come, now, Pomp, no 'possuming," said an old negro.

"No, I feels de pain, I does; I 'clar' I does."

Madge laughed heartily, saying, "Well, Pomp, you are such a good actor that I suppose I must give you a cake"; and she threw him a ginger-bun, and continued her walk. For a moment she paused to look at Daniel and Ruth, smiling half pleasantly, half contemptuously, as she looked. Pomp, the cunning rascal, who, like Rover, loved to follow his Miss Madge, remarked:

"Them's sparking over dar, Miss Madge"; and with this he ran his tongue out, rolled up his eyes, snapped his fingers, and ran off.

Ruth was the first to see Madge, and, with an affectation of timidity, she began to hang her head and turn away from Daniel. Seeing this, Madge, who at times was the very incarnation of Frolic, bethought herself of a little plan for teazing the lovers.

"Now, Ruth," she cried, "what are you doing there—idling your time? Don't you know mamma wants you? And as for you, Dan, I think you had better be about your work in the dining-room. It must be near tea time; get away to your work."

Without specially heeding her assumed tone of command, Daniel began to vindicate himself, with an air of true manliness.

"Yer see, Miss Madge, 'tisn't near tea time as yet; my dinin'-room work is all done up; it's Saturday evening time, when we all takes rest and play. I doesn't see as how Ruthy an' me is a-doin' any harm when we has a little quiet talk 'long of ourselves; an' I'se sure, Miss Madge, as how you'd be the last one as would want to be a-interferin' wid us."

"But, Daniel," said Madge, trying very hard to look stern, "how do I know that you and Ruth are not forming some plan to run off? You see you all need to be watched, and we have a right to be suspicious of two persons who are standing off talking in a low voice to themselves."

"What does yer suspect of us, Miss Madge?" The youthful lover looked curious. Ruth began to twist her body about, pull at her fingers, and look as awkward as possible.

"Laws, now, Miss Madge, an' didn't you hear noffin of what Danel has bin a sayin' to me? I does declar', 'tis orful foolish like, an' I wan't no ways listenin' to it."

"Well, what did he say, Ruth?" inquired Madge.

"'Taint no kind o' use, Miss Madge, to be a-tellin' of yer all his foolish talk, but you see as how Danel, he—well, Miss Madge, Danel, he—Danel, he—"

Ruth broke down for want of feminine courage. Madge, with a predeterminate wish for fun, continued:

"Well, Ruth, Danel, he—what?"

"Laws, Miss Madge"—the girl began to interlock her fingers, bend her head still lower, work her toe into the ground, and writhe her body like a serpent. "Danel, he—pshaw! Danel, he—axed—Danel—pshaw! Danel, you say it yerself." And she darted off to hide herself in one of the cabins.

"Come, Daniel," said Madge, in a jocose tone, "can't you tell me about it?"

"Well, yer see, Miss Madge, yer see as how I'd like to do what you wishes me to, but I kinder feels as how I'd rather not, specially as I ain't spoke to Ruthy on de subject."

"Oh, then, I don't care to know," replied Madge; and, whistling to her dog, she walked off in the direction of Uncle Peter's cabin. On arriving there, she received a hearty welcome from the humble occupants.

"Laws, now, Miss Madge, an' ain't us glad to see you?" said Aunt Polly, as she stopped rubbing her tin pan and set forth the best chair for Miss Madge. "Now, take a seat, an' rest yer pretty self in this ar' dirty ole cabin. I 'clars I'm shamed o' myself to be all in suds so late of Saturday even'. Things ar'n't fit fur de like of you, Miss Madge."

"Don't make any more apologies, Aunt Polly; everything is as clean as possible, you know."

The old negro woman broke out into a hearty laugh, for she was well aware that the cabin was clean. She had been too hard at work upon it not to know the fact, but it is etiquette with slaves to depreciate everything they do, or that is their own.

Madge took the old split-bottom chair which Aunt Polly had wiped off with the dust-mop and set out for her, and, seating herself near Uncle Peter, began to talk with him. After lightly touching upon several subjects, such as the old man's rheumatism, the crops, &c., she ventured to ask if anything had been heard of the fugitives. Uncle Peter shook his head.

"I doesn't know, young missy, but I s'poses as how, if dey reached de river an' crost, dat dar ain't much hope of trailin' 'em. Dey does say a show 'tis mighty diffikilt to ketch 'em on t'oder side. Yer see, over dar in Indiany, dem 'lishionists hopes 'em heap—dat is what dey say."

"Who are them 'lishionists?" asked Madge.

"Ah, honey," exclaimed Aunt Polly, "dem's de mean ole dirty white folks dat hopes to steal niggers from dar rightful masters, an' den sells 'em down de river, an' puts de money right into dar own pockets. I wishes now dat de dogs would git arter dem 'ar—dat's what I wish, I does; an' I tell Peter so t'oder night." To enforce this assertion, she struck her hand violently against the bottom of a tin pan which she had been polishing, and gave a defiant shake of the head, as much as to say, Who can gainsay that threatening wish?

"Oh, Polly, you go 'long; what does you know 'bout dis here? You jist talks crazy like; nigger wimmin is got no bisness a-talkin' 'bout sich things. Yer jist look arter yerself, an' see dat you doesn't be a-doin' no sich tricks, an' leave de rest to de Lord. He knows well enuff how to punish 'em dat offends him, an' He don't want none of yer help."

"But, Uncle Peter, what do you mean by helping the Lord. Oughtn't we to help do His work by living up to what He tells us is right? Don't we all help Him in this way?" Madge's theology always cropped out when she talked with Uncle Peter.

"Ah, now," said Uncle Peter, as he knocked a few ashes off his clay pipe and rolled up his old blear eyes with an expression of comical reverence, "'pears to me, young missy, as if none on us would hope Him any how; when we does good, we ain't a-sarvin' of Him, but our own selves. Ain't we a-strivin' for dat 'ar home of de New Jerusalem? ain't we a-doin' of de right way to git a home up dar? De Lord, he doesn't want us—what is we to He? Dar He done set on dat great golden throne from de beginnin' of time, an' dar He am a-gwine to set 'out'er any hope from us. We sarves Him bekase He is a good Master, an' we wants to find a good home longer Him, or else be sole down dar (pointing downwards), to de ole bad fellow."

Madge recognized, though in a different dress, the usual and accepted style of religious reasoning. What if it did not altogether agree with her fresh and original views? What if she thought there was a question of the beauty and faith of that service which is only rendered with a hope of reward? What if it appeared to carry with it too strongly the odor of the world-spirit, and to lack the disinterested heart-glow which her simple nature accorded to religion? She did not speak—durst scarcely entertain views which so clashed with the sermons that were poured down each Sunday from a purple velvet-cushioned pulpit, by a reverend man in a black gown. Madge was not wont to confuse her mind with thought or speculation; she had been too active and happy for that; but one cannot live long among that lowly but suggestive negro race without finding, at least, his imagination wonderfully accelerated. The immortality of the soul forms one of the chief subjects of conversation in the slave cabins. To that beautiful and untried Hereafter they direct all their thoughts, aspirations and fancies. Their conversion to religion is always signalized by some wonderful trance, in which special revelations are made to them. An old negro man, whose all-embracing love was sufficiently strong to "cast out fear," once declared that he had been to heaven, and there beheld Satan, pardoned of his ancient offences, and, with crown upon his brow, seated upon the right hand of God; "for, dear," added the simple old man, "de Lord he ain't gwine to stay mad with nobody forever."

Madge Vertner went too frequently to the quarter, sat too often in the cabins, and listened too long to the spiritual experiences of the old negroes, not to be impressed thereby; and now, as she walked back to the house, she debated with herself that profound question of "free agency." "How queer that I should be expected to work and help God, if all things are foreordained! Plainly I see with Uncle Peter that I can do nothing; God is all-powerful; and yet I *must* do right. How is this?" She looked puzzled. "Oh, well, I'll ask Dr. Doremus—he can tell me." And so, in her old way, she put the question out of her mind.

IX

When Madge returned to the house, she paused upon the
verandah to catch the last glimpse of the setting sun, which was painting
the western sky with purple, crimson and gold, glinting the tops of the
old elm trees, flecking the lawn with varied tints, and bathing the whole
landscape in a warm, soft and loving light. Instinctively she removed her
hat, and, leaning against the flower-twined pillar, turned her sweet face
full toward the west and drank in the charm glowing from that scene of
beauty. Rover came bounding along, and, crouching at her feet, turned
his queer, intelligent eyes also toward the sunset. His mistress, however,
did not heed him. One of her old dreaming fits was upon her. She was
silent and happy, but could give no reason for it. God's actors are never
theorists. They live what other people think and write. How natural
and rightful does it seem for this young girl, this bud of seventeen,
to be in close communion with nature—to love the forest—find her
companions among the birds—listen to "sermons in stones"—read
"books in the running brooks"—find poetry in the flowers, and admire
the pictures painted by the gorgeous sunset.

Yet we suppose that most of her friends complained of her as a
hoiden, and marvelled why the elegant Mrs. Vertner did not break her
child of such vulgar habits, refine and make a lady of her. But Madge's
life was as unconscious as that of the flowers. She was blameless and

guileless; yet she was by no means "a model," or a record of human virtues bound in flesh and blood. She was bold and wilful, with a flash of temper which sometime kindled up her whole frame and lit her face as lightning lights up and brightens the summer sky. Col. Vertner had never allowed her will to be curbed, so that she oftentimes appeared imperious though never harsh. "*I must*" and "*I shall*" were never, even in her childhood, idle threats, but intimations of a settled purpose, from which nothing could swerve her. Her father, who took great pride in her determined character, used to say, in his jocose way, that "she was a d—l one minute and an angel the next." Though her life was, to all appearance, so very objective and external, so full of dashing animation and boisterous frolic, those who knew her best—the negroes, and especially the old nurse—declared that she was watched over and guided by angels—that spirits whispered round her cradle; and though this was generally set down as idle negro talk, yet we have seen her at times when her face bore a strange expression, the eyes being wild, her lips parted, and the thin, fine nostril distended as if snuffing air purer than that breathed by common nostrils. So it was now. As she leaned against the pillar, gazing at the sunset, a soft, dreamy langour seemed to encircle her, and to make her eyes dewy and her limbs heavy.

"Madge, Madge," called her father's voice from the parlor; "Madge, darling, come here."

"Yes, papa, I am coming." Still she did not move, or change the earnest fixedness of her gaze.

Pomp, who had been following her at a distance, now stole up and laid himself down on the door sill, fixing his eyes inquiringly upon his young mistress.

"What's it, Miss Madge, up dar?" and he pointed his finger toward the sunset. "Is it God's house—door open—an' is all dat splendid red an' yaller his carpet?"

"Who told you so, Pomp?" she inquired.

"Nobody, miss—nobody at all; only I hearn 'em say dat God lives up dar in de sky, an' so I jist s'posed dat yonder mout be his front door, what somebody's lef' open, so dat us can see clar in."

Madge, not displeased with the unique idea, was disposed to pursue the conversation a little further, and said:

"Well, Pomp supposing that to be an open door of heaven, tell me what you see beyond."

"Laws, Miss Madge, I doesn't see no furder 'an de front passage an' de big winders. Yer see dem big red curtains, jist like de ones missus hangs up in de drawin'-room in de winter, comes down so long an' broad like, dat I can't see fur inter de house; but I knows it is splendist like, an' I should love to have a peep in dar—I would, now, best in de world."

"Well, Pomp," said Madge with a sudden energy, "if you are a good boy and a faithful servant, and do all that you are told, and don't steal or tell stories, you will go there when you die."

The boy's eyes were stretched widely open; he rose and looked at his young mistress with an expression of delighted wonder.

"What, Miss Madge, me gwine to heaven when I die?"

"Yes, if you are a good boy."

He hesitated a moment, as if weighing in his mind the chances and possibilities of such a destiny. For a moment his black face grew bright, as if he half accepted the promise. 'Twas but a gleam, for, quickly resuming the old expression, he shook his head, saying—

"But, laws! Miss Madge, de kitchen an' de quarter won't be nice, an' I'll hab to go in dar 'long wid de oder niggers."

"No, if you are good when you die, you will go to heaven, where there will be no kitchen, but all the saved souls will live together."

"Den dey ain't gwine to hab a kitchen up dar? And de white folks will go 'long de niggers? Oh, no, Miss Madge, God ain't gwine to hab no sich house as dat."*

Madge felt herself a little puzzled about the matter, and, her idea of social order being somewhat disturbed, she laughingly remarked—

"Well, Pomp, be a good boy and leave all to God."

As she turned to enter the parlor, a rough, shabbily-dressed and dust-bespattered man rode up to the verandah and, hastily dismounting, called out to Pomp—

"Here, boy, here! is your master at home?"

---

* Author's note: This is a literal transcript from the conversation of a slave.

"Yes, sar, he's in de drawin'-room," and Pomp made a bow, touching his hand to his fore-lock, in imitation of taking off a cap. "Walk in, sar, please—walk right in to de house."

Madge did not halt or speak to the man, but, remembering that her father had called her some moments before, she entered the drawing-room, where she found him busy with his newspaper.

"Well, darling, I've been thinking over our trip to the Cave, and trying to arrange in my mind the day we shall start."

"Oh, papa, that's very pleasant news: when—"

Here the conversation was broken off by the sudden entrance of Pomp, followed by the rough-looking stranger.

"Master, here's a gemman wants to see you." There was a very obvious emphasis upon the word gentleman, and a queer, cunning expression in Pomp's face, as if he doubted the stranger's right to that much-used and more abused title. After glancing shrewdly towards his Miss Madge, he darted off, declaring that he meant to hold the stranger's horse and see if he wouldn't give him a dime or sixpence.

Col. Vertner rose from his seat, and, with a cold word of recognition, welcomed Tom Hynes to his mansion.

"Well, Colonel, I'se got 'em fast an' shure, lodged in the town jail."

The Colonel was about to reply, but remembering his daughter's presence, he said:

"Madge, I have business to attend to."

The girl retreated from the room, but not out of hearing. She ensconced herself behind an open shutter upon the verandah, where, unperceived, she could hear every word of the conversation.

"Where did you catch them?" asked Col. Vertner, with a little more cordiality in his tone, as he pointed to a chair.

"Well, thanky, Colonel, I feels sorter tired, but this here cheer is altogether too fine fur one o' my trim to sot on. Why, I'll squash this green velvet right into a holler with my weight an' dirt. I did mean to smart up a little afore comin' here, but I was in sich a hurry to let you know the good news."

"Be seated, say nothing of your dress, but tell me how, where and when you caught the negroes."

"Well, now, Colonel, you see them dogs of mine is as sure an' sartain as ken be; they ken scent a nigger true an' fur. I jist whistled 'em out an' followed along the course pretty direct from your place to the river. I have scented an' treed so many niggers that it 'pears to me now as though I could do it most without the dogs. I has my hand in, an' seems to have a faculty that way; an' though I don't mean any vanity or self-praise like, you know, I does say it, who oughten ter, that I has picked up more runaways than any other fellah of my size an' age in these parts."

Col. Vertner was growing tired of this kind of talk, and, waving his hand, called Tom back to the original question, by asking—

"And where were they arrested?"

"Oh, I ax yer pardon! but I forgits sometimes; true, as you was sayin', whar was they caught? We walked along the fust day, an' I seed from the way the dogs smelt and snuffed along that we was on the right track. All along through them flat thickets and right into the swamps we marched fur two days, when, nigh about the close of the third day, as we drawed close on to Squire Martin's farm, I seed the dogs begin to snuff and fume away at the ground, and Cuff—he's the best of the whole pack—jist tore round an' snuffed up as though he'd have a fit. Then I knowed he smelt nigger flesh, an' sure enuff he did. I began to beat about a little myself, an' thar, hid away behind a pile of old fence rails, I found 'em both, Jack an' Milly. At fust the boy showed a little resistance, swore he wouldn't be took back alive, an' that he never meant to be a slave again. Wall, now, you see, I never 'lows any o' that kind of talk 'bout me; so I fetched him a blow across the head with my powder-horn, which I think done the business, an' give him a pretty bad headache; then the woman fell to a-cryin' an' beggin' an' sayin' they would go back peaceably. Well, I had no more trouble, you may say, after that. With the assistance of Bill Bunce, I tied 'em both, an' they walked along with us as peaceable as could be, except the woman, who kept up a good deal of sobbing an' sniffling; but Jack was as still as though he had bin dumb. Milly took on a good deal when she found that they was goin' to jail an' not comin' home; but they's fast now, an' you can do what yer likes best with 'em."

"And now you wait for your pay."

"Yes, Colonel, I should like to git the money now if it suits your convenience; but don't hurry yourself you'se as good as the bank, an' any man can 'ford to wait your time."

"It suits me to pay you now"; and Col. Vertner withdrew to another room, while Tom Hynes was left sole occupant of the parlor. How admiringly the vulgar man's eye wandered about, and occasionally lingered for a moment or two upon some rich article of furniture. How he envied the owner of so much splendor and luxury, and perhaps he dreamed of the time when he too should be master of such an establishment. But if he did, such pictures and visions were soon dissipated by the return of the owner of the mansion, who counted out to him, dollar by dollar, every cent of the reward.

"Thanky, Colonel, I'm much obleeged," said the obsequious Hynes, as he carefully rolled up the bank notes and deposited them safely in his old, worn leather wallet. "I s'pose, Colonel, you'll be comin' in to town to-morrow or next day to see to them runaways, or would you like me to fetch 'em out to you?"

"No, I shall go in myself to-morrow; I never wish to have them again on the place, and shall dispose of them as soon as possible."

"Now, if you'd be fur sendin' 'em down the river, I ken tell you of a trader who would give you as good a bargain as any man. He is buyin' up now, an' I know that he gives good prices. If you would like, I ken bring him to you, here, if you say so, or in town."

Col. Vertner hesitated a moment, and then said:

"Bring him to me to-morrow in town. We can take him to the jail and let him look at the negroes."

"Sartinly, Colonel, it's jist the same to me; we'll be on hand, near about the tavern. I have only one other job on hand at present; that's to look up that gal of the widder Vitetor; I guess it won't be more 'an a snap of my finger to git her. Them wimmin ain't smart in the legs like the boys. Now, I believe, if it hadn't bin fur his wife, your Jack would have bin clean off t'other day, but the wimmin is slow and hinder us. This gal of the widder Vitetor's went off, I understand, without any sign of a cause. I was talkin' 'long Andy Vitetor, the other day, an' he says his mother is goin' to move out to Missoury, an' the gal didn't want to leave her husband, an' had bin beggin' a good deal to be hired out or sold here, but his mother wan't willin', an' so she started off. They have had her husband up, tryin' to make him tell whar she is, but they kan't git nothin' from him. He is John Green's man Peter. They say they give him an orful whippin', but to the last he held out that he didn't know nothin' of his wife."

To none of this talk did Col. Vertner lend a willing or attentive ear; indeed, he felt a sense of degradation in remaining so long in the presence of such a vagabond as Hynes. But the wealthy gentleman must needs remember that he was in his own house. Moreover, the slave-catcher—degraded though he be socially—has certain responsible political possessions; he is a voter—one of the Democratic sovereigns—and his existence cannot be quietly wiped out or overlooked, as though he were a woman. Even the nabob, at certain times, condescends to salute him. So Col. Vertner bore, with a show of patience, a monologue which was utterly distasteful to him. But, after awhile, Hynes took his leave. When he remounted his horse, there stood the expectant Pomp, bowing very politely to him, and insisting upon giving him his stirrup. He followed him down the avenue, opened the gate, and saw the rough rider depart without bestowing upon him a cent. With a disappointed expression of face, the boy looked after the horse and rider, and, turning away, whistled "Nary red."

....

The glowing twilight had faded into the dark shadows of evening. Everything looked chill and gray. The lamps were unlighted in the parlor; Col. Vertner sat alone. Madge stole from her hiding-place; and, still as the moon gliding from behind a cloud, she crept up to her father's side and laid her hand upon his shoulder.

"What is it, daughter?" and the fond father's hand was upon her head, with his fingers twining her long curls. She gazed full upon him; in that equivocal light, her great eyes shone out like stars.

"Papa, Milly and Jack have been found."

"Yes, my dear." He tried to smile.

"When are they coming home?"

"I am not going to let them come home at all."

"Yes, you will, papa."

"No, my dear; now don't think you can persuade me to do such an unreasonable thing. You are a very young girl, Madge, and can't understand business affairs. I'll buy you as many ponies, dogs, dresses or pianos as you want; but I will positively not listen to you when you urge such a foolish request."

"Papa, it isn't right to sell them away from home; they want to stay with us."

"Then why did they run off?"

Madge was a little dashed.

"But, papa, we should forgive them and not make them unhappy. I know it was wrong of them to run off, but I am sure that they will not do so again. You will try them this time, won't you, dear papa, for my sake?" And she wound her arms round his neck, and pressed her cheek close to his.

"Come, now, that's a dear good papa; he will do it for me, I know."

"But, Madgy, darling, what of our promised trip to the Mammoth Cave? Have you seen your friends, and does Helen consent to accompany us?"

"Yes, papa, she is anxious to go with us, and her mamma has given consent; all that matter is pleasantly arranged; so we need talk no further about it. Let us have it settled, *between ourselves,* that Jack and Milly are not to be sold, but brought back home, and kindly forgiven. Come, papa, you are not used to refuse *me* favors."

"No, child, not when you ask things within reason, but now you are going far beyond your privilege."

"*My privilege!* Why, papa, what that is in your power should limit *my* privilege?" She half drew away from his embrace and eyed him with a look almost of defiance.

"Well, little lady, you needn't be so very haughty about it, but I shall have to teach you that my business affairs *must not* be interfered with, even by my precious, pouting, saucy little Madge Wildfire."

"But, papa, I mean to beg and tease and worry you until you say yes. Ah, but there comes mamma; I mustn't speak of it while she is by."

Mrs. Vertner came sweeping in through the open folding-door, as stately and chill as an ice queen.

"What, Mr. Vertner, are you and Madge alone in this gloomy room? Why didn't you ring for lights?"

"Gloomy is it, my dear? I am sure I thought it a fine pleasant sort of light. Daniel came in with the lamps, but I would not allow them to be lighted. 'Tis so much pleasanter to sit thus through the twilight."

"How very odd you are; I am sure it is very gloomy. I *must* have a lamp."

She rang the bell, and Daniel soon appeared with the lights. Madge screened her eyes with her hand from the bright blaze, and Col. Vertner sank back in the pillowy depths of his arm chair, to dream dreams, perhaps, of what "might have been." Mrs. Vertner drowsed over her embroidery—that unceasing occupation of vacant minds—while Madge sat lost in a brown study, locking her fingers together, knitting and unknitting them, as scheme after scheme dawned upon her rapidly-awakening mind. All three were silent or preoccupied with themselves. The tray of tea and sandwiches, which Daniel brought in, was sent out again, its contents untasted. Thus the hours wore on, until the hand upon the dial-plate of the alabaster clock, which stood on the mantel, pointed to the hour of nine, when Madge rose and wished her parents good-night. As her lips lingered, for a moment, upon her father's brow, in the good-night kiss, she whispered—

"Dear, papa, you will grant my request, will you not?"

He shook his head decidedly, and said, in a clear tone—

"Go to bed, Madge; say your prayers, darling, and try to learn obedience."

When she entered the weird little room where she slept, she did not light the lamp, but seated herself at the open window and looked out upon the still, star-lighted summer night. Hour after hour glided by, and Madge still sat by the window, dreaming dreams and forming plans of which we shall have more hereafter. The thoughts which come to us in the stillness of the night are generally serious and earnest, and the convictions of duty which we have then are mostly true and good. No man could live a wrong life who accustomed himself every night to quietly think over the actions of the day—to analyze his motives, criticize his behavior, and "post" the books of conscience.

X

The next morning Madge met her father at the breakfast-table, with her usual cheerful and affectionate manner. Her mother, who was a careless observer, noticed no change; but Col. Vertner, to whom that young face was a familiarly studied book, fancied there was a shade of determination unusual to it. He sought to divert the conversation into the most pleasant channel.

"And so, my dear, Helen Mason consents to join our party for the Cave."

"Yes, sir." Madge played with the spoon of her coffee cup.

"I can't say," said Mrs. Vertner, "that I am glad to have that girl with us. She is so gloomy and disagreeable."

"Not disagreeable, mamma. I know that she is gloomy, but then she can be very agreeable, and I don't think her gloominess is so very unpleasant. She always seems so good and sensible."

"What do you mean by good and sensible, Madge?" asked her father.

"Why, what Helen Mason is."

"And what is my little Madge?"

"I suppose, papa, you would call me independent and wilful."

"Or wild and boyish," added her mother. "I tell you, Madge, we must take you to New Orleans next winter, and see if a few months of town life will not polish you a little."

"I shall die if you take me to town, mamma; 'tis no use for you to expect to make a fine lady of me. I can't be that; the very attempt at anything so false would take the life out of *me*."

"Madge, why are you so determined and wilful? You know nothing of the pleasures of the city, and yet persist in saying you will not go? How do you know but you may be charmed?"

"At any rate, mamma, don't let us talk of it now. Wait till winter comes—time enough then to arrange. *Now* I feel as if I should like to have a swift gallop through the woods." And pulling the bell, she ordered her pony, and then went to her room to get ready for the ride.

"Only see," said Col. Vertner, pointing to Madge's plate, "the child has eaten nothing; her breakfast is left positively untouched."

"I can do nothing with her, she is so wild and freakish. I am sure, Col. Vertner, I don't know where the girl got *such* a disposition."

"I am sure neither can I say, my love. She is an independent little elf, as uncivilized as a bird or a squirrel; yet, for the life of me, I can't say that I would have her otherwise. She is so natural."

"What nonsense, Col. Vertner, for you to talk! Why, if you wished to keep her in an entirely natural state, did you send her to school at all, or have her taught anything?"

"Well, my dear, so far as school goes, I think she has had very little of it. All the teachers we have ever employed have given out that she had very little faculty for the acquisition of knowledge; and yet they loved her dearly, and admitted the singular readiness of her mind for the reception of thoughts, though unmindful of mere technicalities. One insensibly acknowledges a power in the child; though what it is I am puzzled to say. Hers is a character which, perhaps, takes precedence of especial talent. Sometimes I think she has not been properly taught. I mean that her attention has not been rightly directed to studies. You know when Miss Pauline took her out botanizing in the woods, she learned the analysis of plants and flowers with wonderful facility, and seemed fond of the science. So it was when Mrs. Poe took her out of evenings and pointed out the stars, planets and constellations; she became greatly interested; but a lesson learned from a book and recited from memory seems to disgust her."

"I am sure she could never be taught to play a tune on the piano."

"And yet I heard her, the other day, singing a wild air in the woods, which charmed me more than any music I ever heard at the opera. It was as clear, twittering and melodious as that of any bird."

"Yet, if you seat her at the piano, and ask her for the simplest tune, her fingers blunder over the keys, and she makes a fearful discord."

"I admit that; but she is, I repeat, a child of nature, and requires the woods-life setting to be seen to advantage."

"Something must be done for her. I can't consent to have her brought up in this half-heathenish manner."

While the father and mother discussed the child's faults and virtues over their toast and coffee, Madge, habited in her riding-suit, was walking through the quarter, with her long train caught up and thrown over her arm.

In some way the negroes had heard of the capture of the fugitives. Perhaps Daniel had reported the news to them. Gliding about the dining-room and through the house, he had, no doubt, heard of it from the family talks. Madge observed the negroes, grouped about in little squads, talking—such of them, viz., as, from age or household occupation, were not engaged upon the out-door work. She stood at a little distance from them, and earnestly contemplated the group. She was very quiet, and her eyes were earnest and thoughtful, more so than usual. She stood but for a moment, then, without speaking to any one, turned and left the quarter. She entered the house, passed through the front hall, and out at the front door, where she found Pomp holding her pony by the rein.

Patting Silk on the neck, with a caressing word, she was soon in the saddle, and, with a "Good-bye, Pomp," she fled along the wood-path swiftly as the wind. Silk seemed possessed of his mistress's spirit.

"Now, jist look dar at Miss Madge, Rove; you kan't keep up 'long her an' Silk. They jist shoots 'long like flyin' birds." But no sooner was Rover loosened from the kennel than he rushed after and soon overtook Madge.

In about an hour afterwards, Col. Vertner came out, and, mounting his horse, rode toward the town.

And now let us look into the jail, upon our humble friends, Jack and Milly. They are in a low, dirty room, with iron-grated windows, the narrow bars of which are half-curtained by dust and cobweb. The floor is strewn with dust, dirt and rubbish, while rats and mice are scampering to and fro. In the darkest corner, as if shrinking away from the partial gleam of daylight which stole through the begrimed and grated window, are Jack and Milly. It is a deplorable sight—the fallen aspect and hopeless, dejected manner of that poor black man. His heavy-featured face looks heavier than usual, for the little animation which naturally belongs to it has gone out with the loss of hope; and there he sits, in that dirty jail corner, still and silent, hugging to his heart his despair and anguish, seemingly unconscious and heedless of his wife's reproaches.

"Now, you jist see, Jack, I tole you so. I tole you we would be cotched an' brung back, an' den sold down de river. I wish you had done as I said, an' not brung all dis trouble 'pon us. Master will never forgive us—he'll jist sell us right 'way on the spot, I know he will. O Lord, O Lord, 'pears as if trouble will never end. I wishes I had never listened to you. I wishes I hadn't gone. We had a good enuff home, an' now de Lord only knows whar we'll be sole to. We'll go down the river, I am sure, an' be sole apart, too. O Lord, Jack, I does wish I had never seen you. You hain't done nothin' but bring trouble onto me since I knowed yer."

In this manner Milly rattled on, reproaching and quarrelling with Jack. Not that she blamed him especially for their present luckless situation, or that she felt unkindly toward him, but because, in the brokenness of her grief, words, and words of severe blame to another, afforded a sort of bitter relief. But Jack sat still and motionless; no word or groan escaped him, and his face appeared rigidly unconscious of what was going on. Only once did he betray sign or symptom of emotion, and that was when Milly, in the highest transport of her furious grief, cried out,

"Why don't you speak to me, Jack? What makes yer set dar like yer was wood, an' won't be a comfortin' me, when I'm takin' on so? Yer knows 'twas you dat brought dis on me, an' now you sulks dar as if yer warn't to blame! Do pray talk 'long me, or I'll go smack crazy."

Then, making an effort, he turned toward her; the rough
purple lips seemed to move, but no sound followed. The hard, black
hands began to fumble and feel about the floor upon the space which
separated him from her; but the motion was feeble, the bleak, staring
cold eyes looked toward her, while a film of mist overspread them. There
was a moment's pause—he gave a faint cry, and fell forward on his face
upon the floor.

"My God! my God!" screamed out Milly, as she reached forward
and lifted him in her arms, as though he had been a babe; "oh, good
Lord, Jack, what's the matter? Yer ain't gwine to die right here, afore my
eyes! O Lord, forgive me for all dem ugly, mean things I said."

Just then the heavy grated door swung back on its rusty hinges,
and the coarse jailer, with more than his wonted politeness, ushered in
Madge Vertner.

Milly was bending over her husband, too much absorbed in his
condition to notice the entrance of the visitor; and Madge walked up
close to her, and even spoke, before the poor creature became conscious
of her presence.

"Why, Milly, what's the matter?"

With a bewildered and affrighted expression, the woman glanced
up to her young mistress, stared at her for a few seconds, then hid her
face in her hands. But Jack seemed roused, as if by magic. In common
with all Col. Vertner's slaves, he had shared in the general love for Miss
Madge. Her walks through the quarter and occasional kind words to
him had always been gleams of sunshine in his life of bondage; and
now her cheering presence and clear voice half brought back the life
to his heart. He looked up with a reässured countenance, for he hoped
she was the bearer of good news. Madge Vertner marked the change in
the negro's face and read its meaning. Her heart almost failed her at the
instant, as she remembered her father's determined words and tone; but,
never having been thwarted in her life, she could not easily despond. So,
with a gay and half railing tone, she said,

"So, Jack, you and Milly have been running off?"

The slaves did not reply, but hung their heads in apparent shame.
Madge turned to the jailer and asked,

"Can I have a chair?"

"Certainly, marm."

Quickly the jailer withdrew, and soon returned with a chair, cushioned and covered with calico (no doubt the best one his house afforded).

"I am sorry, miss, to have a lady like you sit in such a lookin' place as this. Hold up your ridin' dress, if you please—it's all in the dirt; an' them rats and mice keep runnin' round; I'm 'fraid they'll git on yer feet."

Madge took the chair without any further notice of the man than a smile and a nod.

When he had withdrawn, she again began conversation with the negroes.

"What made you run off?"

Jack did not answer, but Milly began in a beseeching tone:

"Oh, laws, Miss Madge, we's sorry enuff fur it. De devil got inter my poor Jack's head, an' 'suaded him to run off; but he's sorry enuff 'bout it now. If master'll only let us off now, we'll be better sarvants 'an we's ever bin; an' 'pears to me as I've got enuff freedom—'tain't what it's tole us."

Madge was silent, but sat tapping her foot with her riding-whip. Milly went on—

"Now, Miss Madge, if you'd only jist be good enuff to beg for us with master, an' ask him not to sell us down the river! Oh, Miss Madge, I'd never forgit you if you'd do it."

Jack had resumed his stolid expression—no word escaped him.

"But, Milly," said Madge, "how can you think papa will forgive you? It was very ungrateful in you and Jack to do so. You had a good home. Papa is very angry with you, and you know he has good cause for it. How many masters do you suppose would forgive servants such offences?"

"I know," said Milly, in a self-depreciating tone, "that we have bin very bad an' don't desarve anything from master; but I thought, Miss Madge, if you'd only speak a word fur us."

"But he is determined not to let you come back to the place."

"Then may be he'd hire us out to some of the neighbors, whar we would be close by home, and if not together, at least nigh enuff to see one another some, Saturday evenin's."

"No, Milly, I don't think he will consent to do that."

"Oh!"—the woman's words broke hoarsely from her throat—"oh, Miss Madge, is he 'termined to sell us?"

"Yes, Milly."

"An' down river?"

"To a trader."

"O Lord! O Lord!" She locked her fingers over her knees and rocked her body back and forth in the very sickness of grief.

Madge's eyes were moist, but she did not wipe them, nor permit the tears to fall, but sat quietly tapping her foot with her whip.

At length, with a strong effort, Jack ventured to speak.

"As for me, Miss Madge, 'tain't no difference what 'comes of me; but Milly 'pears to take on so dat, if you pleases, I'd like you to ask master to take her back; an' den, if he's a mind to, he may sell me to de trader. I'se willin' to go any whar, down de river as well as not; all places is all de same to a slave, only I jist hopes I'll be sole to a hard, tight place next time."

"Why, do you want to go to a hard place out of repentance for having run off?"

The negro shook his head, and smiled broad enough to display a solid, unbroken row of firm white teeth, as he replied:

"You see, Miss Madge, if a nigger has a good home an' some holiday, he naterally begins to think; an' sure as he thinks, 'tis allers of his freedom; an' dat don't 'pear to be right fur a slave. You see, in dem long winter nights, when I made baskets by fire-light, I began to think to myself that 'twas no how right fur me to be workin' all de time fur somebody else; an' as I set thar workin' an' thinkin' side o' the fire, a light broke out over my mind, jist as clar as day light, that I had no right to be givin' all de strength thar was in my marrow-bones to any man—even if he was white. It seem to me as how God made me to own myself; an', Miss Madge, when dis yer took holt on my mind, it jist fastened itself thar as fast as a snake. I couldn't git rid of it; it stuck by me day an' night. Then I didn't kere to eat or to sleep; I jist thought on it. Well, then I had to tell Milly 'bout it, an' she didn't seem to feel it so much; but she was willin' to go 'long with me, though, to be sure, when we laid out o' nights in the woods, wet with rain and nothin' to eat, poor critter, she would wish herself back to the place an' say I had brought her off fur no good. I never thought to be took an' brought back alive, but some how things didn't work right, an' here I is in the jail."

"Don't you see, Jack, that God wouldn't help you off?"

"Oh, no, young miss. Who put dem thoughts in my head 'bout freedom but de Lord? No, it wasn't, I s'pose, de right time, but I does know an' feel dat de Lord loves freedom."

"Hush now, Jack, don't be a-talkin' that ar' way any more, but jist ask pardon fur what you's done," said Milly.

Again Jack's white teeth shone out in a furtive smile, and he shook his head, muttering words which were not audible.

"But, Miss Madge," he continued, "if I might ask a favor, 'tis dat you'll git Milly back home. 'Twas no fault of hern—let me answer fur it—'twas me who 'suaded her off."

"No, no, Jack. I ain't gwine home widout you; 'twould be worse 'an down de river. Oh! de sight of our cabin widout you would kill me." And Milly crept a little closer to his side, and laid her hard, rough, withered, black hand upon his arm, with something of the dog's show of fidelity.

Madge, though silent, was not unimpressed by the scene. Large, bead-like tears hung on her eye lashes, and the quick beating of her heart was almost as audible as the whip-tap upon her boot toe.

The silence was at length broken by the jailer's opening the door and admitting Col. Vertner, Tom Hynes, and a flashily-dressed man, whom we suppose to be a wholesale dealer in human flesh and black skins.

XI

The jailer had told Col. Vertner that his daughter was with the slave prisoners; so he was not, as we had expected, startled by her presence. But Madge's keen eye detected the frown on her father's brow, which he so vainly tried to conceal from her. Nodding to him, she said,

"I am before you, papa, in my visit."

"Yes, dear; why didn't you wait for me, or let me know that you were coming?"

Madge did not understand so well as we do the courtly politeness which locked down a falsehood, and, deceived by his manner, she believed that he was not displeased with her for going to the jail. But she gave a curious, inquiring glance toward Hynes and the trader, both of whom took off their hats and bowed to her—an act of politeness to which she made no return.

Milly shrunk farther into the dark corner, but Jack looked full into his master's face.

"And so, my boy," observed Col. Vertner, "you have been running away, and have had bad luck!"

There was no reply. Jack twisted his fingers in and out, and wove them together in every possible contortion of pain, while his face was unmoved.

"Since you are tired of living with me, and seem to have a fancy for travelling, I am going to give you a chance to try your luck in another part of the country." Col. Vertner smiled as he said this, and continued: "Here is your new master, and I hope you will do better and fare better with him than you have with me." As he uttered the last part of the sentence, he pointed to the trader, who, with a sycophantic smile, advanced a step or two nearer the slaves, whom his eyes had been all the while closely examining with the practiced air of one who was accustomed to such merchandise.

"Stand up, boy," said he, in a swaggering tone, as he replaced his slick hat on one side of his head.

Jack stood up.

"Turn round."

Jack obeyed.

"Put out your hands. Eh, pretty good fingers! long and slim! Open your mouth; teeth fair. How old are you?"

Jack looked toward Col. Vertner, as much as to ask, "What must I say?"

His master, with a laugh, said,

"Jack, ain't you smart enough to know your age, or isn't that as easy as running off?"

"I thought, sir, I was about turned forty."

"The advertisement said thirty five," remarked the trader, as he gave Col. Vertner a quizzical glance.

"I think Jack has over-calculated by five years. It appears to me that he is not over thirty-five at the farthest; but be that as it may, he is not past his prime, and a good worker; a good boy, I should say, too, if it had not been for this runaway freak."

Jack's gaze was fixed intently upon his master's face, and, as he listened to the latter part of the sentence, his eyes began to blink and quiver a little, as though he felt tears gathering there—tears that must be kept back.

All this time Madge had remained sitting quietly in the chair, still tapping her boot with the riding-whip, but listening attentively to every word that was uttered. When her father spoke of Jack, she leaned a little forward, to catch the expression of the negro's face, and the plume of her cap brushed against her father's arm.

"Well," continued Col. Vertner, "how much will you offer for the boy?"

A terrible agony went over the slave's face; the muscles worked, actually seemed to writhe; the mouth quivered; the eyes closed with a spasm, then opened as suddenly; but no relieving tears gushed out. The moment of physical trial passed, and the victim stood calm and subdued before his torturers. But that look of anguish—that black figure, stony in its fixedness of grief—went to Madge Vertner's soul, and seemed to create her anew. She now no longer pitied the slave; she sympathized with him; his trouble became hers. Her whole heart was open, and, as if by a sublime apocalypse, she saw at once the wrong, the sin in which her father was playing a part. She had risen from her chair, and was about to lay her hand upon her father's arm, when she was arrested by the trader's saying,

"Well, I think he's worth about nine hundred; but afore we comes to terms 'bout the boy, let's see the woman. I'd like to lump 'em—take both at a fair price." Then, turning to Milly: "Git up, gal; stand up here, 'long your husband I s'pose; let's take a look at you."

Milly, by an effort, crept out of the corner, and, holding on to Jack, actually climbed up, and then stood by the side of and still clinging to her husband. The sight of that face, so stricken with terror, was enough to rouse the pity of any human creature; but a slave-catcher and a slave-driver are not human, but a sort of hybrid creation between man and beast.

"Open your mouth, put out your hands and feet," was the trader's order to Milly; when Madge, placing her hand firmly on her father's arm, and fixing her keen eye upon the trader, called out—

"Stop! these negroes are not for sale."

She felt her father's arm tremble (with surprise) beneath her firm grasp, and the trader and Hynes glanced first at her, then at Col. Vertner, with an inquiring look; but Milly, upon whose ear those words had fallen like a new life, sank down at Madge's feet and clasped her round the knees, while tears fell like rain. And Jack's countenance! Ah, Madge never forgot that look!—it went through and through her heart, and thrilled her as she had never been thrilled before. It was a glance of such piercing warmth, such entire gratitude, that it would have thawed the most frozen soul. Col. Vertner felt himself shaken by it, though he only caught the last gleam of it; for he first turned his face to Madge, and it was her wonder-working eye that first drew his attention to the slave. Had he seen that indescribable look, we believe his heart would have melted, for he was a man of kind and good instincts, over whom education, pride and family training exercised a controlling influence. As it was, he commanded himself in a moment, and said:

"My daughter, this dirty jail is no place for you. I cannot let you remain a moment longer."

"Papa, you are here."

"I have business, my dear, and *must*—since you will not willingly obey—*order* you to leave instantly."

He had never before spoken to her in such an authoritative tone and manner. She was surprised, almost frightened at it; but, with a spirit of determination akin to his own, she replied,

"I will go, if you will promise me you won't sell Jack and Milly."

"Madge!"—and his voice was very stern—"I cannot have you interfering in my business affairs. You must not forget your proper place. Now, go at once, my dear"; and his voice softened a little.

"Papa, these negroes belong to me, or will, for I am your only heir. Now, it is not right for you to sell my property; besides, it is a pet plan of my own to retain these two servants. Now, papa, dear, oblige me in this."

It had been a sterner parent than Col. Vertner who could have denied the soft persuasion of those upturned eyes, and the beseeching beauty of those ripe, red lips.

"Well, daughter; if I don't sell them, I must punish them, at least, for running off, by hiring them out for a year."

Madge remembered that Milly had proposed this herself, and, thinking anything better than having them sold, she replied,

"Ah, well, you may do that; and now, papa, I'll obey you. Good-bye, Jack and Milly; in a year you shall return; and I am sure you will be better servants after this." Then, shaking hands with each of them, she left the jail, remounted her pony, and galloped off in the homeward direction.

After she had gone, Col. Vertner, Tom Hynes and the trader, all three, experienced a sense of infinite relief; each one, no doubt, thinking "Now we can come to business." But the poor trusting negroes believed, with the innocent Madge, that Col. Vertner's word was pledged, and that they were not to be sold. Meanwhile, the three—Col. Vertner, the trader and Hynes—held a little private conference, in which there seemed to be a good deal of discussion.

"Well, Colonel, call it an even eighteen hundred."

After a little hesitation, Col. Vertner agreed to this, and, taking out of his pocketbook two half-dollar pieces, he gave them to Hynes, saying, "Give them this when I leave; I don't want to see them when they learn that the bargain is closed."

Lordly owner of broad acres and troops of slaves, he yet trembled before one of his humblest. He meanly shrunk away, not daring to meet the trusting glance of the poor creatures whom he had deceived.

"Well, Colonel, jist step with me to my office an' we'll close the bargains, draw up the papers, and I'll fork over the cash; an', Hynes, you jist 'tend to them 'ar niggers, an' see to fetchin' 'em right away to the pen."

Accompanied by Col. Vertner, the trader left the jail. On the steps they encountered the jailer.

"Well, Colonel, has you an' Mister Harrison come to terms yit?"

"Oh, yes; and now I will settle with you for the jail fees."

"Oh, any time'll suit me, Colonel; I'm in no hurry; your time is my time; jist suit yourself."

But Col. Vertner, who was used to this accommodating style of conversation from the villagers, was shrewd enough to interpret it as meaning, "I can wait, but I'd prefer the money *now*"; so he at once settled his account with the jailer, and then set off with the trader to receive the blood-stained gold.

Tom Hynes, when left quite alone with the slaves, assumed his most important and swaggering air. Approaching Jack, he said, as he punched him with his hickory cane,

"You didn't spect to see me so soon agin, I reckon, ole hoss, did yer?"

As Jack vouchsafed no answer, he went on:

"Now, you's goin' with me to a different sort of home; yer to go to Mister Harrison's pen, an' next week, I reckon, if Providence don't spile the fun, you'll be floatin' down de river on de Ohio; and if you behaves yourself, you'll git a pretty good home on some of 'em cotton or rice plantations."

Milly glanced from Hynes to Jack, and from Jack to Hynes, in the most rapid manner. She could not understand what she heard. Did her ears deceive her? Hadn't Miss Madge got master to pardon them and promise that they should not be sold? And yet Tom Hynes said they were to go down the river next week. What did it all mean? Jack was turned, as if by a magician's stroke, to stone. Madge's gentle voice and his master's promise had brought back the warm glow to his over-tried frame; but now he was chilled and frozen again. Poor Milly's eyes wandered over his face, hoping to read something like comfort there, but the rigid, ice-locked features terrified her.

"Oh, Massa Hynes, what does you say?" she broke out; "we ain't sold, is we? What was it master promised to Miss Madge? Didn't he say we was only to be hired out, an' not sole?"

"Well, you is a cussed black fool, if yer didn't know that the Colonel was only a-talkin' so as to git his darter out of the way."

At this announcement, Milly sank down upon her knees, clasped her hands together, and cried out, "Good Lord! have mercy on us."

"Here is a half-dollar a-piece that your master left fur you, with good-bye; here, take it, an' then git up, an' come 'long with me, fur I ain't got no time to stand here listening to you fussin' 'bout what you know you desarves; so make haste an' come on; I won't be hard with you, unless you hinders me too long, an' then, if you does, I shouldn't mind smashing this stick across your pates in the snap of a finger; here, take your money." He threw a half-dollar on the floor at Milly's side. She picked it up, with a "thanky, sir," which came mechanically from her lips; but when he offered the coin to Jack, the negro refused, saying, between his shut teeth,

"I doesn't want it, sir; he wanted to save his darter's feelin's, an, so he tole a lie, but didn't kere fur our feelin's."

"Look here, boy, what's you a-talkin' 'bout here? I'll try my stick over your head, if you don't mind yer words," said Hynes.

"Poor Miss Madge," wailed out Milly; "poor little angel, she didn't know nothin' 'bout this; an' if she had uv had her way, 'twouldn't a bin so."

This thought appeared to comfort her—the thought of sympathy—and she said, with more firmness than usual,

"Come on, Jack, we'll do the best we kin, an' may be we'll be sole to the same place. I hope so, indeed." And, wiping her eyes with the old rag of an apron which she wore, she rose and laid her hand tenderly upon her husband's shoulder, adding, "Come on, ole man; let's go an' trust in de Lord dat we'll be kept together. Come 'long, Jack; don't stand here so stiff an' cold like. Come, Master Hynes is in a hurry, he wants us to set off wid him."

"Yes, come 'long," put in Hynes; "I ain't got another minnit to wait 'long with you."

Milly took Jack's hand and led him out of the dirty, dark room, and down the dusty stairs, out into the open entry, where they met the jailer and his wife.

"Well, nigs, you is goin', is you?" asked the jailer, in a most unfeeling tone.

"Yes, massa, an' we thank you for what you has done fur us while we has bin here."

"Wal, you ar' welcome fur what little you got from me," replied the man, somewhat touched by the woman's humility.

Jack was stony and unmoved, and suffered himself to be led along by Milly and watched by Hynes. Thus they passed out of the jail yard, down a quiet street and across a green common, until they reached a small, low, brick building, enclosed by a high plank fence; and soon they were securely locked in the "slave pen," with about a dozen other marketable men and women, with black and yellow complexions.

XII

Several weeks after the events recorded in the last chapter, Col.
Vertner's travelling carriage, heavily laden and tightly packed on the
outside with trunks and valises, was slowly winding through a public
highway, lined on either side by a thick, deep forest. It was the middle
of a warm afternoon in September. The sunlight flickered across the
road, and played on the tree-tops, spotting the green leaves with golden
specks. It was a lazy, drowsy time; the coachman was half asleep on his
box, and the carriage moved but slowly. Mrs. Vertner, with her head
on her husband's shoulder, was quietly enjoying her siesta, while the
Colonel nodded over a book. On the front seat Helen Mason was also
sleeping, with a gauze veil thrown over her pale face, and an open book
on her lap. By her side was Madge Vertner, wide awake, gazing out of
the carriage window upon the quiet woods, with an admiring eye. She
looked very bright and happy. Glancing around at the sleepers, she
said, half aloud, "what stupid people, to be sleeping at such a delightful
time! I can't stand being cooped up here any longer"; and, opening the
carriage door, she sprang lightly out, and bounded rapidly along the
road for some distance, before the occupants of the carriage became
aware of her absence. It was the third day of their journey, and they were
now drawing near the Mammoth Cave; their route had lain through
the middle counties of Kentucky, the scenery of which was very varied,

occasionally wild and uncultivated, and then again rich and blooming with cultivated farms, or smiling with white-spired villages. Col. Vertner enjoyed the face of the country, and admired the farms; while Madge never tired of gazing at the old primeval trees of wonderful size. But Helen Mason remained unconscious of all around her, totally absorbed in her book, while Mrs. Vertner quarrelled with the slowness of the horses, complained of the ruggedness of the roads, and was totally out of patience with Madge, who had occasionally insisted upon mounting the box and driving the horses. And now, starting up from her nap, and missing her daughter, she exclaimed, "Where upon earth is that madcap child? I should not be surprised if she were again on the driver's box. Wake up, Col. Vertner, and see where Madge is."

Helen Mason started up, dropping her book from her lap, and exclaimed—"Why! Madge? she was here a moment ago."

Just then our heroine came running up to the carriage, with her arms full of flowers and leaves.

"Oh, papa," she cried out, "only see these beautiful things!" and, dashing the leaves and flowers into the carriage, she broke out into a long, loud peal of laughter, that seemed to wake the echoes of the woodlands.

"While you, old sleepy heads, were drowsing the time away in stupid sleep, I was scampering along the side of the woods, gathering those pretty things. Helen, you had better come out here than be cooped up in the carriage; come, let us take a walk. I met a man who told me we were only a few miles from the Cave, and I should like to walk the rest of the way, papa."

"Madge, Madge, are you crazy," said Mrs. Vertner, in a quick reproving tone; "come, get into the carriage immediately. A pretty sight it would be for you to be seen walking up to the hotel."

With reluctance Madge obeyed her mother, and entered the carriage with a sigh.

"How my little Madge hates a cage!" said her father, smiling. "I am glad she has not a pair of wings, or she would be flying away from us."

"Indeed she would," answered Madge, with a degree of fervor that surprised her father, and caused Helen Mason to start and exclaim—

"Why, Madge, would the possession of a pair of wings make you fly from your friends?"

"Sometime I would come back; but, Helen, don't you think it would be a delightful way to travel—sailing through the air, buoyed up by your own white, feathery wings, rather than creeping along at this pace?"

"It would be more practical, Madge—and perhaps more natural; for we rather seem defrauded of what would be a useful human appendage."

"What crazy talk!" exclaimed Mrs. Vertner. "I am astonished at you, Helen, for I thought you had more religious perception. Such talk sounds positively irreverent."

Helen was mortified, but Madge, who was used to her mother's reproofs, only laughed as she replied,

"Why, mamma, I should think that you would be very covetous of a pair of wings, since you seem to dislike walking and all other kinds of active exercise."

"I never care to criticize the workings of Divine Providence, my dear." There was an immense depth of self-satisfaction in Mrs. Vertner's tone, which effectually silenced Madge, and caused a most provoking smile on the part of the Colonel, as he glanced toward his child.

When within a few miles of the Mammoth Cave, they turned off from the main road and entered a quiet wooded road, more like a foot-path than the public entrance to a place of great resort. All travellers will remember the singular beauty and attractiveness, the quiet and repose, the coolness and stillness of the path. Madge was in ecstacies, and constantly swinging herself from the carriage window, calling out to the driver to halt or to drive more slowly—insisting, to her mother's terror, upon getting out and walking.

"Oh, I *shall* suffocate in this close, warm carriage; I *must* get out."

"No, Madgy dear, be patient a little longer; we shall soon be there, and then you may run and romp to your heart's content," said her father.

With a frown gathering upon her brow, and a vexed expression, Madge sank back into the carriage, and, covering her eyes with her hands, said:

"Since I can't be allowed to enjoy the cool shade and beautiful trees, I'll not look at them, but make a complete prisoner of myself."

When the driver pulled up in front of the hotel and opened the carriage door, Madge sprang out, exclaiming,

"Well, I *am* glad to be free again."

The hotel, which had been put up for the accommodation of summer visitors, was a long, low, wooden building, painted white, with a trellised verandah, overgrown with grape vines, extending its entire length. Groups of persons were standing about the yard, on the verandah, and in the door-ways, while a party of two or three ladies and gentlemen, in fantastic Turkish costume, with tin lamps in their hands, were returning from an exploration of the Cave. Madge laughed outright, as she looked upon them.

"How funny they look, papa! Helen, only see!" and she pointed toward the group.

"Fie, fie, Madge," whispered Mrs. Vertner, "how very rude to point and remark upon strangers! You will give mortal offence; pray be more particular."

It was near tea time. Mrs. Vertner and Helen complained of fatigue; and Madge and her father wishing for an immediate visit to the Cave, were met by Mr. H., the proprietor, who told them that, for the sake of affording the guides rest, no admission to the Cave was allowed after six p.m.

"Let us venture without guides," urged the enthusiastic Madge, but, being overruled by her father and friends, she consented to wait until the morning.

Refusing all solicitations to visit the ball-room, or take part in the dance, she soon retired to her chamber. About an hour afterwards, Helen Mason came into the room, saying—

"Oh, Madge, I have just seen the celebrated guide, Stephen, and he is a splendid-looking creature."

"Is he not a negro?"

"No, you would scarcely take him for a mulatto or quadroon; he looks to me more like a handsome Spaniard, a Hidalgo, or a proud Mexican, with fine, straight hair, and deep electric eyes. I declare he is magnificent."

"But he is a slave," said Madge.

"He ought not to be."

"Why?"

"Because he looks like a gentleman."

Madge was silent for a moment, and then said, in a quick tone,

"Helen, when I was in the jail, where poor Jack and Milly were locked up, I felt as if *no* one should be a slave; I can never forget the impression those poor helpless fugitives made upon me. Helen, it did seem so strange to me to see a stout man like Jack so prostrated. He was not handsome, Helen; he did not look like your proud Mexicans or Spaniards; he was a poor, ignorant black fellow, who could not speak decent English, but he uttered some words that went direct to my heart, and some of his thoughts, though roughly expressed, seemed to cleave my adverse judgment like swords of justice, and change my whole way of thinking. Helen, he said that God loved freedom, that He had put the thought of freedom into his head, and that he felt that he had a right to all the strength of his own sinews and bones. His words come to my mind, Helen, with the force of solemn truths. I do not read books, or know anything about the sciences; but my heart tells me when a thing is true. I think what is good for me is good for another, and I see that every living creature, from man to the brute, loves liberty. Why, my dog Rover is restive in his kennel, and the birds I have tried to cage always touched my heart so much by their vain attempts to break through the wires that I have liberated them."

Madge had spoken rapidly, and with a flash of the eye. As she paused and drew a long breath, Helen bent down and kissed her brow, saying,

"Madge, you are a darling child; and though I do not entirely agree with your sentiments, there is a magnetism in them that I cannot resist; but now I must not keep you up longer, for to-morrow will be a busy day with us"; and, wishing her good night, she retired to her own room.

Madge was not inclined to sleep, but, extinguishing the lamp, she drew her chair to the open window. It was a clear starlit September night, warm and breezeless. The sky seemed literally alive with stars; and the constellations were pouring down their silver light, and planets were twinkling like living human eyes. Away to the north-west, red Arcturus was shining out like a lamp, and steady and sure in the northern heavens twinkled that old, changeless pole-star, the light and guide of many a poor, wandering fugitive, and upon this star Madge fixed her gaze. Music from the ball-room, softened by the distance, stole gently upon her ear.

She did not at first observe two figures, that were seated upon a bench just below her window, conversing in a subdued tone. They were so much in the shadow, it was impossible to distinguish whether they were men or women, until one of them spoke out in a clear, manly tone:

"Yes, Matt, he is a true gentleman; I was in the Cave with him for six hours, and had much talk with him. He is as good a geologist as Professor N.; there was not a rock or pebble that he could not classify; and when we got to Cleveland's cabinet, he sat down there and fairly clapped his hands with delight. He gathered up whole handfuls of that sulphate of soda, seized upon those encrusted roses and lilies, and laughed over them and talked over them as if they had been as much gold and diamonds. I tell you I have been in that Cave with all sorts of wise men and professors, but I never heard one talk to my mind like this one."

Madge thought she had never heard so sweet and thrilling a voice as the one in which these words had been spoken. She was sorry when he ceased speaking, not that the words had any special interest for her, but the tone was more soothing and melodious than the music that came to her from the far-off ball-room.

"Yes," said another and coarser voice, "that man is a gentleman. I liked his looks, Stephen, from the first time I saw him, and hoped he would choose me for his guide; but I might have known he would select you, for you are so much more learned than I, all them great gentlemen want you to go with them. I wonder, Stephen, if I will ever be liked as much as you?"

"Oh, yes, Matt, by the time you have been here as long. You see I have almost grown up with this Cave. I think you have picked up a good deal, considering the time you have been here. Exploring the Cave with those professors is an education for any one. I have learned much from them. It was Professor N. who first put it into my head to learn to read. He never told me the alphabet more than three times before I knew it. I shall never forget him for it. He woke up a great power in me, which, once set going, like steam, won't stop until it puffs me into *something.*"

There was a strong emphasis on the last word; and as Madge looked from the window, she could see that the speaker had risen from his seat.

"Do you see yonder star, Matt, in the north? Do you know what it points to?"

"To Canada."

"*To Liberty!*" The voice, though hushed, had something of a clarion sound, and made Madge suspend her breath.

"I love that star," continued the same voice, now resuming its sweetest tones; "and if I could be an idolator, I would build altars to it, I would pray to it, for it has been Liberty's lamp, and pointed the safe way to many a weary fugitive. God bless that star! As long as its light remains undimmed, my faith in the Eternal shall endure."

It is impossible to give any adequate idea of the pathos of tone in which these words were uttered, and the few moments of silence which followed seemed fitting and appropriate.

"How much longer have you to serve, Stephen?" asked the one whom we have heard called Matt.

"In two more years I shall make my last payment, and then I will be a freeman, and will soon set sail for Liberia."

"Then you are going to leave this country."

"Yes, indeed; why should I stay here, to be scoffed at by those whom I despise as my inferiors; why, Matt, the man who owns me knows less than I do. The other day, he jeered at me and said he would not be willing for me to know so much, if I were not a guide in the Cave. *Niggers,* he said, when they knew a good deal, were apt to be saucy; but as my knowledge brought him higher wages for me, he would not object; and, said he, twitching me by the arm, 'I ought to ask you a few hundred dollars more for yourself.' I tell you, Matt, this riled me up dreadfully; I bit my lips until the blood came, to keep from speaking; I went then and took some liquor to drown my feelings."

"Yes, Stephen, that is what they say is undoing of you."

"I know it, Matt; I know it does me no good, and may be much harm; but what am I to do, pulled about by so much trouble? Every year my old master raises a hundred dollars on me. At first he was to let me buy myself for a thousand dollars. I have paid him every cent of nine hundred, to say nothing of little sums of five and ten dollars at different times, which he came to me to borrow and has never credited me with. Now he says I still owe him four hundred; it is not fair, no way you fix it, but what can I do? I am his slave, glad enough to get away on any terms, no matter how unjust."

A few more indistinct words were spoken, and the two colloquists arose and left their seat. As they moved more into the light, Madge could distinctly discern the figures of two tall, well-formed men. Her eyes followed them anxiously, until they turned an angle of the building, and were lost to her view.

The next morning, after an early breakfast, Mrs. Vertner, Helen and Madge began to prepare for a visit to the Cave. Mrs. Vertner demurred at wearing the Bloomer costume, which, however, the proprietor assured her was necessary to her comfort in the subterranean world she was about to visit. Helen Mason was also reluctant to adopt so unique a dress, but Madge was delighted—declared she never before had such free use of her limbs.

"Oh, papa," she cried, "I should like to wear this dress all the time; it seems so much more natural than the other."

And in fact she did look very pretty in that short red skirt and trousers, with a crimson and black scarf wound around her head, like a Turkish turban. The party proceeded down a path which crossed the lawn at the back of the main building, and walked about one hundred yards from the house, when they reached the entrance of the Cave. Here they were met by the guide, a colored man of rather pleasing appearance, dressed in linen pantaloons and shirt, a straw hat upon his head, and a bundle of unlighted torches in his hand.

"I am sorry," said Col. Vertner, to Helen, "that I could not procure the celebrated guide, Stephen, for he had been previously engaged by another party. This one is Matt, very good they say, but not such a curiosity as Stephen, who, I have heard, is a very cultivated man and a good practical geologist."

While Col. Vertner was saying this, the guide had been busy lighting the lamps; and now presenting one to each member of the party, and taking up a well-filled basket of provisions which sat upon a rock near by, he said:

"This is to be your dinner; and now, ladies, if you are ready, we will begin our journey. Take one last look at this world above ground, and follow me."

Helen Mason shuddered at the yawning mouth of the Cave, and feared to enter.

"Come on," cried our adventurous Madge, as she plunged in directly after the guide; "come, Helen, the frowning mouth is passed."

"Ah," cried Helen, as she clung to Col. Vertner's arm, "I feel as if I were entering Hades."

After passing the Narrows, they were soon beyond all signs of daylight, and realized that peculiar sense of mystery which one experiences in a midnight world. Here they were, one hundred feet below the upper earth, shut out from the activities of every-day human life, darkness and wonder all around, breathing an atmosphere purer than that of Italy, and a strange sense of pleasure thrilling their nerves. The blue gleam of their Bengal lights, reflected against the massive sides of the grand Dome, produced almost the effect of enchantment. Stalactites and stalagmites, in every variety of beautiful style and cluster, hung around. It was like a fairy palace. The whole party stood in mute admiration.

Pretty soon the exhilarating effect of the pure air acted upon Madge's frame with a resistless power. She shouted aloud, flourished her lamp right and left, and scampered about like a kitten.

"We can't stop long here," said the guide; "there are plenty more wonderful places than this to be seen, so we must take up our lamps and be getting on."

It would be impossible to give a full and faithful account of all the beautiful and wondrous spots which they paused to admire, but we must not fail to notice the "Old Arm Chair," which is a large rock, formed like a great chair, and which affords a comfortable seat.

"Jenny Lind sat there, and sang us a song," observed Matt. "Stephen, too, sometimes stops there and sings the 'Old Arm Chair.' He's got a clear, fine voice."

"And can't you sing it for us?" asked Madge.

"Oh, no, young miss. I can't sing like Stephen. I am sorry you didn't get him for your guide. He's been here longer than I have, and, besides, he is smarter and knows more than I can ever hope to. The professors, who used to come here examining and testing the quality of the rock, took a great fancy to Stephen, and so he learned a good deal from them."

It was a wonderful sight when they reached the celebrated "Gorin's Dome," and looked down into the frightful "Bottomless Pit." Above rose the majestic dome, and far below, at a distance of three hundred feet, sank the pit, a dark and yawning chasm. Matt threw down a lighted paper, dipped in oil; the illumination was beautiful, betraying, as it did, crevices and fissures in the vast shaft. A sense of solemn awe, such as they had never before known, took possession of each member of the party. The cold and moveless Mrs. Vertner was even excited; a tremor seized Helen Mason, and our wild, elfish little Madge was melted to tears.

Bill, Col. Vertner's coachman, who had been allowed to come with them, looked down into the frightful abyss, and exclaimed, in his sincere, naïve way,

"'Twould be all day to any one as got down dar."

Crossing the pit by a frail little bridge which tottered beneath their steps, they made the descent of the first ladder, which brought them to the river "Styx," one of the smallest of the three cavernous streams, which is supposed to flow into Green river. At "Echo River" they took the boat. It is a small, transparent stream, about a quarter of a mile in width and ten feet in depth. Matt rowed them gently along. They were surprised to discover that the lightest sound, almost a whisper, was echoed. The merest tap of the oar upon the side of the boat was repeated a thousand times, receding at each successive echo, until the sound faded away in the most distant chambers above, assuming the liquid, melting tones of the finest Eolian harp. Our party was delighted; their ears were never tired of the delicious sounds. They tried every variety of noise, which always brought back a recurrence of harmonious sound; the spirits of the Cave, wild with glee, seemed to answer their lightest or merriest call. Madge and Helen sang an old familiar song, which was replied to by the most bewitching melody from the airy chambers and musical apartments above. The guide proposed discharging a pistol, which was readily assented to by the party. The effect was startlingly grand; loud thunder burst upon their ears, almost deafening in its effect, growing fainter and fainter as it receded, until it died off in the airiest melody. Truly did our friends deem this fairy land.

"Yes," said Matt, "Stephen says this Cave has been a world of comfort and pleasure to him. He lives most of his time in here; for when he isn't guiding visitors, he is hunting about through these rooms and halls, to see what new things he can find. I want very much to see if I can't discover another opening in this Cave. A gentleman who sometimes comes here has offered me two thousand dollars if I'll find it, and let him know."

"I hope you will find it," said Mrs. Vertner.

Madge had been surprised to observe how freely and unrestrainedly her mother talked to or listened to Matt. And a fact it is that the most aristocratic ladies and gentlemen who visit the Cave seem to forget for a time those unnatural distinctions of race and caste, and associate with the colored guides in the most familiar manner. Perhaps it is the pure air of the Cave, acting upon their minds as well as bodies.

"Yes," said Matt, "in a sociable way, to Mrs. Vertner, "when I get that money, I won't be a slave long. I'll buy myself at once."

"Why, Matt, are you a slave? You ought to be free," said Mrs. Vertner.

These words seemed to surprise the coachman. He looked earnestly at his mistress. Alas! the generous wish did not extend to him. Afterwards, in speaking to Helen, Mrs. Vertner said, "Oh, I only said that because I was afraid of the negro. I didn't know what he might do with us 'way off in that strange, dark world."

After they had crossed the river, in one of the winding paths leading to "The Cabinet," our party became conscious of the approach of persons. Suddenly they were met by Stephen and a gentleman whom he was guiding. The effect of the meeting was picturesque in the extreme. Stephen's swarth, olive face, dark, flashing black eyes and rough dress, were set off in bold contrast to his companion, who was a tall, spare man, with fair complexion and light-blue eyes, and a countenance expressive of the highest thought and culture. A few stray locks of iron gray hair escaped from his crimson velvet smoking-cap, and his blue slashed raglan heightened the dramatic effect of his costume.

Now, as they paused in front of the new party, each holding their lamps so as to reflect fully upon the others, they formed a picture fit for the pencil of a Rembrandt.

Madge gazed at the stranger with undisguised admiration, while he gave back her glances with equal pleasure.

What a meeting!

Seven miles from the mouth of the Cave, seven miles away from the glorious light of the sun, seven miles off from the upper world of life! Miniature rivers, valleys, mountains and rocks, that had never in all previous and primal time drank in or reflected back the joyous light of heaven, lay around them on either hand. Here in an interior, subterraneous world, "rock-ribbed and ancient," giving back no answer to man's idle questioning of its past—here in a solitary world of darkness and splendor,—these two met for the first time!

Madge could not tell why it was that this stranger's glance still haunted her as they continued their long windings and threadings of the Cave! Sometimes his face, seen for but a moment, and then by the blue flicker of their lamps, seemed to connect itself with everything that she saw afterwards, and gave to the cavern a new and deeper interest. When, on their return from the "Rocky Mountains," which was the terminus of their first day's trip, they paused at "Cleveland's Cabinet," our heroine was in higher spirits than usual. This Cabinet, named from a Mr. Cleveland, who is said to have first discovered it, is one of the most interesting apartments of the Cave.

The reader must conceive a vast room, arched over by a roof twenty feet in height, the sides and arcade of which are encrusted by a thick coating of pure white frost, through which protrude in every direction buds, vines, tendrils, rosettes, sunflowers, cactus leaves, lilies and every variety and design of fanciful formation, from the simple flower to the exquisite finish and elegance of a Corinthian capital—all wrought from a material the most frail and delicate, and of a soft, pearly whiteness—and he will then have some faint conception of this beautiful and unique Cabinet. At some points the over-arching roof is thickly studded with small snow-balls, which have apparently been frozen there, and present innumerable mirrors wherein the light is reflected with a glow and glitter as if from ten thousand diamonds.

Imagine such a fairy scene, a mile in extent, every turn of your foot revealing some new vegetable form?

After remaining for an hour or more here, wondering and admiring, Matt proposed that the party should adjourn to "Table Rock" and partake of their collation. All had good appetites, and ate with a zest, and for the first time in all her life Madge beheld her mother drink from a cup and hand it to a negro.

Truly, the Mammoth Cave should be the temple of abolitionism.

Soon after this, as Mrs. Vertner and Helen were quite fatigued, they took up a hasty march for the "mouth," reserving "Serena's Bower" for another visit.

How strange the upper air and world looked to them, as once more they emerged from the cavernous darkness! The sun hung low in the west—red, gold and purple clouds were floating about the horizon, and Helen cried out,

"This sunlighted world is the loveliest, after all."

XIII

In the evening, to Mrs. Vertner's surprise, Madge proposed to visit the ball-room.

"Why, what a curious, almost contrary child you are, to be sure," put in her mother. "Before this you have resolutely declined to go to balls and parties; last night, when Helen and I were quite well and willing to go, you refused to even look in upon the dancers; now, when we are jaded and tired out with a long jaunt, climbing over rocks and descending slippery ladders, you suddenly propose to visit the ball-room! It must be only a freak of perversity."

"No, mamma; I just felt as if it would be a pleasant sight; and if you and Helen are too much fatigued to go, why, I am sure papa will attend me. Ah, here he comes."

"What is it, my child?" he asked, as, with a weary air, he tossed himself down into a chair.

"I wish to go into the ball-room to-night. Mamma and Helen are very tired: won't you escort me?"

"Certainly, my dear; and though I am very much fatigued by the day's long walk, yet am I so glad to see you in the mood for something like civilized gayety that I shall be delighted to wait upon you, and even offer to dance the first quadrille with you."

"No, no, papa, I don't care for dancing, and am afraid I should make a sorry sight upon the floor. I shall only look on quietly for awhile"; and with this she left the room, to seek her own apartment and make ready for the evening.

"This *is* an unexpected crotchet of Madge's," observed Col. Vertner to his wife; "she is constantly betraying some new feature of her strange disposition. I declare the girl is a puzzle to me. After this day's hard exercise, climbing, jumping, leaping and walking, to be willing to sit up late and enjoy a dancing party!"

"Yes, and the very thing she has always despised and laughed so much at," said Helen Mason, who was reclining in a large arm chair, near the bed upon which Mrs. Vertner lay.

"I really have no pleasure in the girl. Each day she appears to grow more eccentric. It is such a pity that my only child should so disappoint me."

"Ah, my dear," put in Col. Vertner, "you must not speak so discouragingly of Madge. She will outgrow this wildness and peculiarity, which seem to annoy you."

"I have been hoping so for the last three or four years, but now I begin to despair. I see that time only confirms her peculiarities."

"No, my dear," added the Colonel, with a smile, "I argue a good deal from this evening's freak. You see she wants to go into gay company—has determined upon it for this one occasion at least. By and by, she will acquire a taste for society, and then she will be all that you wish her."

Mrs. Vertner shook her head distrustfully, but Helen felt like putting in a disclaimer. Madge was her very ideal of ripe, fresh girlhood, and to hear her so unjustly criticized half provoked Helen.

In the meantime, Madge was in her own room, overhauling her trunk, taking out dress after dress, shaking the wrinkles out, examining and laying them aside, unfolding laces, collars, sleeves, laying out ribbons, bows, &c., without number. Never before had our little heroine been so occupied with toilet flummery. "Let me see," said she, half aloud, as she sat beside a large, open travelling trunk, with silk dresses, crape shawls, laces and ribbons all around her in heaps and piles—"let me see. Helen once said that pink was most becoming to me; but, then, papa likes me best in blue"; and she leaned her pretty head thoughtfully upon her little hand, her mind being occupied fully and wholly with that usual and all important subject of "maiden meditation"—*dress*. "But," she continued, after a moment's pause, "I like white the best, and feel the most natural in it. But, then, a ball-room is *such* a gay and fashionable place, where, mamma thinks, no one should be natural, and so I expect I had better wear this pink flounced grenadine"; and, shaking out the slightly crushed fabric, she rose from the trunk and began to make her toilet for the evening. She worked very slowly, as all unaccustomed hands will. Her curls seemed stiff and unpliant to her; she positively quarrelled with the paleness of her complexion, and for the first time took a long, anxious look at her reflection in the mirror. "Well, I am ugly," she murmured in a dissatisfied tone; and, after arraying herself in the pink grenadine, entwining flowers in her hair and winding a strand of fairy-like pearls round her throat, seizing an ivory fan and a pair of white gloves, she again seated herself, with a dissatisfied expression of countenance. "Well," she muttered, in vexation, as she pulled on her glove, "I may spend hours in dressing, and it's no use. After all, I can't make anything out of myself but plain, ugly Madge Vertner. It is just as mamma says, and I don't in the least blame her for being so unhappy about me." A little knock at the door here interrupted her complaint.

"Come in."

It was the colored chambermaid, who came to bring fresh towels.

"Good even', young miss"; and, with her eyes fixed in very evident admiration upon Madge, she exclaimed, "Laws, but ain't you putty; you's jist the puttiest young lady as has bin here dis season."

Madge's face brightened. Though she was used to such flattery from slaves, at this moment it came so opportunely, so like consolation, that she accepted it with gratitude, and, with one more glance toward the mirror, started off for her mother's room.

And we may well wonder what had so suddenly changed Madge. We have seen how indifferent she has hitherto been to all matters of personal beauty, or of feminine vanity, but there always comes a time to woman, sooner or later, when she wishes herself more beautiful, when she sighs for the powers of fascination—when, without even looking into her heart, she is half conscious of a new guest there, whom she strives and strives to please and trembles before!

"Why, Madgy," cried Mrs. Vertner, "you have indeed dressed yourself with great taste and care. Doesn't she look well, Helen?"

"Oh, yes, Madge, I never saw you look half so pretty; your dress is beautiful. And how could you arrange your hair so well? did you have the girl do it?"

"No, I was my own maid; and I expected you would say that everything was awry."

This was the occasion of great pride and joy to Mrs. Vertner; she actually took hope from it, and began to think perhaps Col. Vertner was not altogether wrong in his favorable conjectures and prophecies of their wild and unfashionable daughter. And the Colonel himself regarded Madge with even more than his customary fondness.

"Why, little darling," he exclaimed, "you look fresh and beautiful as a blossom. No one would suppose, to see you now, that you had been all day leaping rocks, climbing ladders and crossing rivers in the cave. But, come on; let us now make our way for the ball-room."

Taking her father's proffered arm, with a free step Madge entered the ball-room, where everything was ablaze with light, beauty, grace and fashion. The place and the scene were alike new to her. However, with that unconscious freedom of a thoroughly self-poised nature, she remained free from embarrassment or constraint. Glancing quickly round the large and brilliant room, her eager and detective eyes singled out from the crowd one marked figure, and, with a nervous clutch at her father's arm, she cried out,

"There *he* is?"

"*Who?*" inquired Col. Vertner, in surprise.

"Oh"—and suddenly recollecting herself, she added, "no one— pshaw! only the stranger—that peculiar, foreign-looking man whom we so suddenly encountered to-day in the Cave."

"I had almost forgotten that we met any one; and if we really did, I am sure I cannot now identify him."

"Yonder he stands, papa, over in that corner—a tall, graceful, sad-looking man, dressed in gray."

"He—why, he looks like an Englishman, and seems to be far past his prime. I see nothing peculiar or distinguished in his appearance. I am sure I might meet him a dozen times without thinking of bestowing upon him any especial observation."

"Why, papa?"

Just then the band struck up a lively polka, and a dozen or more couples went whirling, twirling and eddying round in that most beautiful and bewildering dance.

"How pretty it is," said Col. Vertner. Madge, however, was all the while watching, in a furtive sort of way, the stranger in gray, who quietly occupied his corner without any apparent interest in the dancers.

Our heroine did not long remain unobserved. The freshness of her beauty, the artless grace of her manners, soon attracted attention, and introductions and solicitations to dance came pouring rapidly upon her. Declining to take part in the merry-making upon the ground that "she never danced," she was soon seated in the recess of a window, talking with a gentleman chiefly distinguished for his moustache and immense quantity of beard; but every moment or so her eye wandered off in search of the stranger, who, meanwhile, had not been altogether unmindful of her. From the safe retreat of his corner, he had seen her graceful entrance, and had anxiously watched her unaffected manners; by and bye he found it convenient to emerge from the corner and mingle a little more with the crowd. After a few passing remarks to some of the most prominent and best-dressed belles, we find him getting round into Madge's neighborhood. And now, as he stands within a few inches of her chair, notwithstanding the loudness of the trombone and violin, he hears every word of her simple and child-like conversation. Let us likewise join him and eaves-drop a little.

"I suppose, Miss Vertner, you read all the new novels—Reade, Bulwer, Bronté, Dickens and Thackeray?"

"No; I don't read novels; I never could get through with but one, and that, I believe, is by Charles Reade, and called 'Never Too Late to Mend.' It made a deep impression upon me."

"Why, it's rather queer—you don't dance, don't play, nor even read novels. I never saw such a young lady."

"Perhaps not."

"Do you read history—Prescott and Irving?"

"No, I have literally read nothing, and you will not find me at home on any of your favorite subjects."

She turned half away, with a tired and irritated manner, when her eyes suddenly and fully encountered the clear, approving glance of the stranger who was standing quite near her chair. She blushed, smiled and half bowed; then, turning abruptly away to hide her confusion, asked her companion if he would call her father.

In a few moments Col. Vertner came up, and, to his daughter's surprise, smiled and bowed when he perceived the stranger, saying,

"Mr. Butler, allow me to present you to my daughter."

Madge's glance met those cold, clear gray eyes; and instinctively, as if by a resistless impulse, she put out her hand, which Mr. Butler cordially grasped, saying,

"This is the very favor, Miss Vertner, I was about to solicit of your father."

"Why, papa," replied Madge, "I did not know that you were acquainted with Mr. Butler."

"I have had that pleasure, my dear, only for a few moments since I left you. Mr. Butler is from England, and is now making the tour of our country. He has but lately come to Kentucky. I hope he will remain some time with us and learn something more of our people than English tourists generally do."

Mr. Butler smiled and returned thanks for their gracious remarks. Madge said nothing, but looked a great deal.

"I think, Miss Vertner," said Mr. Butler, bending over her chair, "that we met to-day in the Cave."

"Oh, yes," replied Madge, "I remember it quite well, and recognized you at once when I came in this evening."

The gentleman bowed very low, and a close observer might have seen a slight pink tint spread over his face. There was something so natural and artless, so truthful and simple about Madge that it struck him pleasantly.

"How far did you explore?" he asked.

"We went to the Rocky Mountains, and chiefly through the main cave. To-morrow we are going to 'Serena's Bower.'"

"Ah! that is the most beautiful spot in the entire cavern; at least, I enjoyed it most," observed Mr. Butler, with that clear, cultivated English accent which Madge thought perfectly delightful.

"I was also more fortunate than you, Miss Vertner, in the choice of a guide. Matt, though very good and shrewd, is not the character and person that Stephen is, whom I consider as great a curiosity as the cave itself."

"We were sorry not to have him, but I believe you were in advance of papa and had secured his services."

"Yes, and I have also engaged him for to-morrow, but I should be delighted to have your father's party join me. I am sure you will enjoy it more with Stephen for a guide."

"Oh, thank you; I shall mention your offer to papa, who, I am sure, will gladly accept, for he was quite disappointed in not getting Stephen," said Madge.

"I should like," continued Mr. Butler, "to be with you when you first see 'Serena's Bower.' It is a fairy place, and seems the chief apartment, the presence chamber of the unseen queen of that palace cavern."

Thus, in talking upon subjects of mutual acquaintance and interest, they came to know each other directly, and chatted away with great freedom and ease.

There was a charm and grace about Madge's conversation when she once became excited. She said *things* rather than words. One was astonished at the closeness of her observation. She understood nature practically, as a woodsman does; and though Emerson and his books were unknown to her, yet we believe that even that subtle philosopher would have been pleased with the astuteness of this simple girl's remarks. She could tell every variety of forest tree, the peculiarity of its growth; and all the family of tiny wild woods flowers, hiding and blooming away under clefts of rock or at the roots of trees, had names and language for her. So now, when, in the progress of their conversation, they glided away from the Cave to the woods and waters, the birds and flowers of Kentucky, Mr. Butler thought Madge a charming and spirited talker. He found her possessed of a clear, true mind and strong native understanding, uncolored or clouded by theory, dreams or speculation. She saw life and nature as they were, not as other people represented them. Insensibly the hours wore on; Col. Vertner was suprised to observe his wild and flitting butterfly sort of child so interested, apparently absorbed, in a long and continuous conversation. It was late when she declared herself ready to leave the ball-room. Mr. Butler and Col. Vertner satisfactorily arranged, before separating for the evening, that they were to form one party for the Cave the next day, under Stephen's guidance.

"Well, daughter," said the Colonel, as he parted from her at her chamber door, "you seemed to be fascinated by, as well as fascinate, the Englishman."

"Why, papa!" was the only reply. And that night, before retiring, she sought Helen's chamber.

"Oh, Helen," she cried, as she seated herself on the side of the bed and took her friend's hand within her own—"oh, Helen, I've seen that stranger whom we met in the cave, and I like him so much."

"Who, that old-looking man we met with Stephen?"

"Yes."

"It isn't possible, Madge Vertner, that you are so charmed by him? He looked older than your papa."

"I am sure I neither care whether he is older or younger. I only know that he is a splendid-looking person, and I dare say is as full of character as he is of fascination and genial urbanity."

"This is very funny, Madge."

"What is?"

Helen Mason half rose from the pillow and, resting her head on her arm, looked earnestly into Madge's face.

"Madge," she said, at length, "please put out the lamp, and then come and sit on the bed beside me; I have so much to say to you."

Madge did as she was desired, curious indeed to know what her friend could have to say. She drew very near to Helen and laid her arm about her neck, while a wistful, anxious gleam stole out from her pretty eyes, but said nothing, and waited for Helen to commence.

"Madge, dear," Helen began in a whisper, "you are half in love with this Englishman, and you only went to the ball in the hope of meeting him. No; now you needn't start so, and try to pull away from me; I'll hold you fast. I knew from the first that you were very much pleased. I observed the peculiar look you gave him in the Cave. You almost started toward him; and he looked more intently at you than at any of our party. I revolved it all in my own mind, saying I shouldn't wonder if something grew out of this romantic chance meeting."

She paused, but Madge did not reply. She still sat quietly with one arm around her friend's shoulder and the other hand pressed closely to her own face. Helen went on.

"'Tis no harm, Madge; you needn't hide your face; besides, the lamp is out; we have only the pale starlight, coming through that window; so you must not shrink from me."

She coaxed the hand away from Madge's face, and by one or two lively sallies reässured the half-frightened girl.

Madge was too truthful and honest to deny the gentle charges brought against her, and yet a sort of feminine delicacy forbade her frankly acknowledging.

"Now," said Helen, with a quick breath and in rapid, partially indistinct tones, "I am going to tell you something of myself. I, too, love a stranger; one whom, I suppose, my good mother will pronounce inferior to me, though, Madge, I am no more worthy of him than I am of the first angel in heaven. I'll spare you any enthusiastic description; but when we return, I shall insist upon your seeing him, and I am sure you will admire him. Oh, Madge, he is so good and noble; he is too lofty a character to love me, I am sure; and yet there have been moments when I almost felt that he did."

Helen did not cower and shrink as Madge would have done. There was so much of pride in her love that it infused into her very nature a finer consciousness and made her glow and beam. So now she raised herself fully and sat upright in the bed, with her long hair streaming over her arms and neck.

"Who is he?" asked Madge, in a whisper.

"A Mr. Norton—John Norton—a teacher lately arrived in our village from one of the New England States."

"I didn't know, Helen, that you were acquainted with such a person. How does it happen that I have never met him at your house and you have never spoken of him to me?"

"You have not been to our house very often, dear, within the last few weeks; neither does Mr. Norton call frequently; I have met him oftener at friends' houses, when we have talked a great deal. He has, in this very short time, got quite a large school, and the children are all very fond of him. But do you know that they whisper he is an *Abolitionist?*"

Helen looked frightened, but Madge did not start or betray the least sign of surprise or disgust. Helen waited for her to speak. At length she said,

"And what of that, Helen? I see no reason why he shouldn't be, if he thinks that way; nothing is more natural than to declare his convictions."

"But an Abolitionist! isn't it a horrible word?"

"No word is horrible to me, Helen, that means something."

"I am glad, dear Madge, to hear you speak so; for I feared this would alienate us. Do you know that when I listen to Mr. Norton, he half persuades me to be an Abolitionist. There is no possibility of resisting such words and tones as his. And now, dear, I feel better that I have confided in you; 'tis such a relief to talk of what is weighing upon one's heart; and, dear Madge, now that you love also, we can sympathize with each other."

Madge did not speak, but, with tears glistening in her eyes, laid her head upon Helen's shoulder, and together they wept tears of pensive pleasure. It was a pure and touching sight—one worthy only of the eyes of guardian angels—and so we drop the curtain over it.

The next morning Helen and Mrs. Vertner both declared they were too much fatigued to pursue their explorations of the Cave, but Madge and her father determined to continue. However, it may be well to state that the latter would gladly have foregone further explorations for another day or so; but seeing his daughter so resolved, he could not refuse to join her.

At the mouth of the Cave they were met by Mr. Butler and Stephen, each prepared with torches, the guide also carrying, slashed across his shoulder, a can of oil, with which to supply the lamps.

"Good morning, Miss Vertner," said Mr. Butler; "I trust you slept well and feel strong enough for to-day's difficult rambling."

"Oh, yes," answered Madge, "I am quite in the humor to-day for scaling rocks, walking topple-down ladders—in short, of braving all the difficult passes of this lower world. Good-bye, daylight," and she plunged quickly into the Cave, following the guide.

"The entrance," observed Mr. Butler to Col. Vertner, "is one of the most frightful features of the Cave, I think. Some how, man as I am, and fond of adventure, I always feel an involuntary shudder as I pass under this frowning arch."

"It sharpens my ardor," exclaimed Madge. "I have a natural love of the daring and frightful."

Mr. Butler smiled at this, saying,

"I suppose Stephen is glad to hear that you are not easily frightened; one of his greatest troubles here is the guardianship of timid ladies. Didn't you say so, Stephen?"

Thus addressed, the guide turned toward the party, and now, for the first time, Madge had a full view of his remarkable face. It was a face that should have been seen under a tropic sky, for one in looking at it insensibly connected it with feathery palms, bright and gorgeous lilies, and the glancing of strange and bright-winged birds. The clear olive of the complexion, with a slight red glow of the cheek, were in admirable harmony with the soft velvety blackness of the large oblong eyes, fringed by heavy, curling lashes. The features were small and delicate, and as finely shapen as if finished by the touches of an elaborate sculptor; but then these minute physical details, perfect as they were, formed but a minor portion of the beauty of that wonderful face. They were to the soul-light and brave, though melancholy, countenance what the mere mechanism of a piano is to the wild melody which its mystic keys can produce when touched by the hand of a master.

Madge could scarcely suppress a burst of admiration as those splendid tropic eyes were bent upon her in a clear, penetrating glitter.

"Yes," he said, in reply to Mr. Butler's question—and his voice was rich and liquid—"yes, I have had some curious and even trying scenes in this Cave with timid ladies. I have had to carry some of them in my arms along the narrowest defiles, bordering the edge of rocks where the least misstep would have tumbled us down a chasm hundreds of feet in depth. Even this I shouldn't have cared for if they had only known how to keep still, but they frightened me by the sudden nervous clutches they would give my arm, and evident attempts to stop me at places where it was difficult to maintain my foothold."

"Well, I shall give you no such trouble," said Madge.

"Ah, no, indeed," cried Col. Vertner to Mr. Butler, "I believe my daughter is a very chamois for lightness in bounding over rocks. She surprised me yesterday; and as to fear, it is a foreign element in her character."

Thus, in pleasant chit-chat, they continued to perambulate this dark and wondrous cavern, pausing at every two or three steps to admire some new beauty or wonder of the strange place. At length they arrived at "Star Chamber," one of the most beautiful and unique compartments of the Cave. It is a large oval room, the roof of which is covered with stalactite formation, in exact copy of the starry heavens. It is as perfect and natural as though nature here, in some artistic freak, reproduced a copy of her own first grand work.

Stephen, after desiring them to seat themselves upon a bench, which had been provided, deprived them of their lamps, and, wishing them good-bye, started off for another part of the cavern, leaving them for an instant or so in that fearful, rayless, subterranean darkness. The first sudden effect upon the eyes was painful and trying. Madge, who was seated between her father and Mr. Butler, began to tremble, and, in a dismal sort of whisper, asked,

"Where has the guide gone? will he leave us long?"

"No," replied Mr. Butler, who understood the trick, "he will be back soon enough. But now only lift your eyes to the star-lit heaven."

And there above them shone out, as one at first thinks, the same splendid "starscape," that each night greets the gaze from the beautiful upper world. There were the sister planets, the fast old stars and the clustering constellations, and conspicuous among them all was the majestic sweep of a comet, while a solemn *blue darkness* gathered round and seemed to enfold our party.

Mr. Butler traced out with great ease some of the most noted constellations, and Madge saw her own favorite "Corona" glittering up in the vaulted roof, a semi-circle of twinkling gems.

"How exquisite," "how wonderful," they simultaneously exclaimed.

"Why, my daughter, is it," asked Col. Vertner, "that you always, in looking at the stars, first see that small and to me scarcely distinguishable constellation of 'Corona'?"

"I don't know, papa."

"Because," gallantly put in Mr. Butler, "a queen will naturally see a crown; and I am sure Miss Vertner is worthy of a starry one."

It was well for Madge that they were in the midst of unrelieved darkness, else might her deep blushes have betrayed her. It was the first compliment that had been paid her to which she had ever listened. And now it went like a stroke of lightning through her frame, heating up her blood, thrilling her nerves, and creating for her a new and delicious sensation.

By and bye the guide came back, and restored to them their lamps, saying,

"Now, if you have rested enough, we'll take up our line of march, direct for the 'Rocky Mountains' and 'Serena's Bower.'"

They toiled on for hours, seeing wonders and contending with difficulties, walking gossamer bridges, such as were only fit for the foot-fall of Titania and her fairy train, until at last they reached that long, stupendous ridge of piled up rock, known to pilgrims in the Cave as the "Rocky Mountains." Most truly and appropriately is it named. "Grand, gloomy and peculiar," it frowns upon the foot-weary passenger who stands below contemplating the daring venture of scaling its formidable heights. Stephen lit the Bengal lights, which sent a blue glow over the awful scene. Our party paused and were silent with awe.

"Great are thy works, oh Lord," murmured the Englishman, as he lifted his cap from his head.

Madge proposed that they should take their lunch here.

"Had we not better wait until we reach the 'Bower'; and then, young queen, you may dine amid fairy beauty?" said Mr. Butler.

"No," replied Madge, "I prefer dining upon this rugged mountain-side. It will be something strange and new."

Accordingly they opened their baskets, and there, with gloom and grandeur all around, they ate with as keen a relish as if they had been seated at a banquet-table amid worldly comfort and ease.

Taking up the order of march, and scrambling over rocky ledges and mountain heights, still further on, and thirteen tedious miles from the entrance, they came to the famous "Serena's Bower," the gem, and supposed to be the terminus, of the monster Cave.

This beautiful and fairy-like spot is entered by a very narrow and difficult aperture. However, our party crawled and worked themselves through, and were well repaid for any difficulty of access.

The interior of the Bower is one of the most beautiful places human imagination can conceive of. It is a small but deep base, with an umbrella-shaped roof, studded with stalactites of the most beautiful design. From the ceiling the stalactites join and run down on the sides, floating out like the long, depending locks of a woman's hair; and from this fancied resemblance the grotto takes its name. There were fan-like pillars dividing the bower into smaller and various sized compartments. In one corner of the grotto, and about three feet from the floor, is a basin of the purest and most limpid water. Stalactite formation of pillars stand round the edge, as if to guard and protect the sacred waters. The guide hung a lighted lamp inside the columns and immediately above the waters. The illumination was brilliant, and made the scene glow like magic. Madge was in ecstacies. Mr. Butler drew from his pocket a small leather travelling cup, which he unfolded and, filling it with water, offered it to Madge, saying,

"Will you not honor my cup by sipping of the waters of Castaly from it?"

She drained the cup, and, turning to him, said, with great animation,

"Now, I shall be inspired."

Ah, the "Mammoth Cave" did truly open new worlds to her. She is not now the lively, careless Madge Vertner that she was when we first met her. A new purpose is working in her life, and the illumination of a new and glorious sentiment is firing up and shedding radiance upon that inner and deeper world of the heart and the affections.

XIV

Thus several days passed very pleasantly; Madge and Mr. Butler becoming better acquainted, and, consequently, better pleased, with each other. They now went into the Cave together, wandered about through the woods, or promenaded the long verandah on moonlight evenings.

Of course, in their numerous matters of conversation, the important and much discussed subject of slavery came up for due consideration; and Mr. Butler was charmed with the naturalness and originality of her views. She had a straightforwardness and downrightness of manner which was perfectly captivating to the slower judgment of the cool and clear-headed Englishman.

One afternoon, as they sauntered along through a fine park-like wood that adjoined the Cave-ground, Mr. Butler said to her,

"Miss Vertner, you seem so naturally opposed to all systems of human cruelty—all organizations for the abuse of human rights and Christian principles—that I am surprised you have not turned your attention to slavery as an institution rather than as a system of cruelty."

Madge paused for a moment; then, looking up brightly, her eyes gleaming from under her hat, she said:

"Because I understand the subject rather from my heart than my head."

Mr. Butler smiled; he was not wont to look at great social questions through the light of human feeling alone. He was an abstract thinker, and reduced everything—human life itself—to a question of science. He would have ridden rough-shod over a poor way-side beggar, condemning him as one of the accidencies of life, to establish and engraft upon society some great idea which he had toiled over in his keen brain. Slavery was, to him, a wrong, one that belonged to a false condition of society, which he looked calmly upon, believing it would be exterminated when his social theory got a practical recognition from the world. He was a great and good man, whose heart was held in abeyance by his intellect—one of the world's *best thinkers*. When he talked to her, Madge felt an instinctive respect; yet his ideas were not always clear to her understanding.

"Now, Mr. Butler," she was often heard to cry out, "I can't follow you through that tortuous, winding path or ratiocination; tell me the *thing itself*; never mind about *the how* and *the why*."

She was a pleasing puzzle to him; though not a companion for his highest thoughts, yet an impetus to them. He was often astonished at certain wise sayings of hers, and would abruptly ask,

"Where did you get that?"

"I don't know. I thought it," was always the artless reply.

Taking up the line of her remark, he now replied:

"But is it not a safer way of arriving at the truth to judge social problems and social errors according to the head?"

"I don't judge at all," answered Madge; "I *feel*. Now, I am sure, Mr. Butler, that cruelty would be terrible to me. Why shouldn't it be so to another?"

"That is, assuredly, a Christian way of viewing the subject; but let us now examine it philosophically. Slavery *is* unquestionably a wrong, a very great one; but we must work for its extermination in a cautious manner. We must, as it were, *feel* our way. Now, the plan that occurs to *me*, as the most feasible, is to depreciate slave labor; make a direct appeal to the pocket of the slaveholder, and you catch him in his only vulnerable point. Machinery is a more active and efficient Abolitionist than twenty William Lloyd Garrisons. Supersede by machines the negro hands employed in the culture of cotton and sugar, and you will have half stricken off the bondman's fetters. Let the Northern brain work instead of the Northern tongue revile its Southern neighbor, and a brave work will be done. If the great idea of association could be promulgated and practically introduced at the North, then would you see the slave begin to lift his head. We must not only preach, but pave the way for the introduction of a beautiful and unflinching morality; show by our own lives that we properly esteem labor; make it honorable before the world; and then will a true reform be inaugurated."

"I don't know or care about the means, Mr. Butler; I only wish some way could be found to check cruelty. I suppose slavery *is* right; at least I've been brought up to believe so; but my heart refuses to acknowledge the necessity for cruelty, or even harshness."

Mr. Butler smiled, as he answered,

"You are wrong in your premises, my young friend; for if slavery is right as an institution, then it legitimately follows that severity is right, should the slave rebel against his condition. We ought to quarrel with the system upon higher grounds than that of its severity and rigor. The worst feature of it is its outrages upon mankind; its coarse insults to the human race; for surely there is no darker disgrace to humanity than the reduction of a brother man to a chattel."

"If the slaves had good and pleasant homes, Mr. Butler, shouldn't you call the system a correct one?"

"No; I should still despise it. The strict or the lenient rule has no bearing upon the primal question; they only determine the individual character of special owners."

Madge was bewildered; it was an entirely new presentation of the subject; yet gleams of its truth flashed across her awakening intellect.

In the course of their walk, and at a turn of the woodland path, they came upon Stephen, sitting alone upon a rock, smoking his pipe.

"What a handsome creature he is!" said Mr. Butler.

"Yes, indeed," answered Madge.

"Shall we stop and talk to him?"

"Certainly."

"You are not engaged with parties for the Cave to-day, Stephen?"

"No, sir. I have rest for the first day since the busy season set in. Matt, I believe, has gone in with two gentlemen."

"Does the upper world look dreary to you?" asked Mr. Butler.

"Oh, no, sir; though I love the Cave so much, and seem to have *lived* the most there, yet I find a day up here all the more pleasant for my long banishment from the sunlight. I find, however," he added, as he rose and threw aside his pipe, "that the effect upon my eyes is very bad. I can't now, as I used to, stand the full glare of sunlight."

Madge thought it a pity that such splendid eyes should be injured, and there was a depth of tender anxiety in the glance which she gave him.

"I have been telling Miss Vertner," said Mr. Butler, "that you expect to purchase yourself in about two years, when you shall have made your last and final payment."

"Yes, I calculate that two years will set me free, unless my old master raises a hundred or so on me."

"Is he likely to do that?"

Stephen smiled. "Ah, sir, money is a thing that my Boss loves better than his meeting-house; and some how he thinks that my blood and bones ought to be a California to him."

"How much have you already paid him?" inquired Madge.

"Something over nine hundred dollars," answered the mulatto, with a tone of pride; "every dollar of which I made mysel except little presents that have been given me by gentlemen whom I have guided through the Cave, but my boss seems to think he ought to have more for me, and this puts off my freedom."

"What is your master's name," asked Mr. Butler, "and who is he?"

"Old Mr. Sam Hemingway is the man who owns me; he is a farmer of this county, and lives about six miles from here. He is moderately well-off, and a very tight, close master. However, he has never struck me a lick."

"He doesn't whip his slaves?" asked Mr. Butler.

Stephen gave the interrogator a searching look, as if to satisfy himself that he was sincere in his question; then, turning away his head, with a scornful laugh, said:

"You better go over to those corn fields and look at those negroes' backs before you ask me that question."

"Tell us something of your past history, Stephen. I am sure Miss Vertner will be pleased to hear it."

"Indeed, I shall," said Madge, as she seated herself upon the rock from which Stephen had just risen.

The guide smiled, saying, "My life hasn't much in it to interest a young lady and a cultivated gentleman; yet, if it affords you any pleasure or amusement, Mr. Butler, I shall be glad to give you my experiences, such as they are."

Mr. Butler threw himself upon the grass at Madge's feet, and Stephen seated himself also on the grass, quite near his two auditors, and, after a moment's silence, in which he appeared to be regaining and re-collecting all his wandering thoughts, began:

"I remember my mother but indistinctly, but I have not forgotten that she was a beautiful mulatto woman, full of kindness and love to me. She was sold" (there was a tremor in the man's voice), "I believe for debt. I have heard that she was sorely troubled because she could not take me with her. What became of her I never heard; no doubt she died upon some of those hard rice or cotton plantations. Perhaps it is well for me that I never learned her fate. Slaves had better be in ignorance of what becomes of their friends who are sent down the river. What we do hear from there is terrible. My disposition is a little fierce." He stopped for a moment, dashed his hand across his brow and brushed away the moist mass of black hair that rested there. "Well," he continued, "I went on growing just as the weeds do on old Mr. Hemingway's place, working in the corn fields, doing odd jobs about the farm and going to mill every two weeks. I was a quick, and, they said, a bright and saucy boy, so going to mill was a great thing to me; there I met white boys who went to school and could read, write and cipher. They were farmers' sons, no wise proud, so they'd stop sometimes to play marbles with me, and tell me about their school. I was pleased with all that they told me about their books. *To read* became the one object of my ambition, so I traded with a boy for a primer, giving him in payment my bag of marbles. This primer was the key I coveted most. I hid it away behind a log of the corn crib, and at odd times, at nights and on Sundays, I used to study. It was up-hill work; I didn't know what to call the first letter; and once, when I was sitting behind the corn crib, poring over my letters, not knowing what to make of them, one of old master's sons, Jim Hemingway, came by and snatched the book from me and tore it up. This put an end to my trying to learn to read; but I never forgave Jim. It seemed one of the chief aims of his life to torment me; and when I heard of his being killed in a street fight in New Orleans, I am afraid I didn't care much, but rather felt that he had met his desert. I jogged on in a pokish sort of way until I was eighteen, when I fell in love with a bright mulatto girl, belonging to a man who owns the next farm to my master's. We were engaged, and about to be married, when a trader came along and offered Kitty's master a fair price for her; he couldn't refuse the money; she was sold and shipped off for the South before I could get time to see her. I went, as usual, on Saturday night to see her, and old Nancy, Mr. Johnson's cook, met me with the news that Kitty was sold down the river and had started off that day with a trader, who was camped about four miles off. This came upon me like a rock of ice. I got cold and hard all in a minute. I couldn't speak to Nancy, but stood, she said, looking at her and yet not seeming to see her. She told me that Kitty's whole trouble was that she couldn't see me to say good-bye. And, 'Stephen,' said Nancy, 'she left her best handkerchief for you, and said you must not grieve about her, and yet she didn't want you to forget her.' Well, sir, I swallowed down something hard and heavy like in my throat, and, with something of a man's walk, went round to the front of the house, and there I met Mr. Johnson. I walked up to him and looked him full in the face 'Mr. Johnson,' said I, 'is Kitty sold down the river?' Well, sir, he began to cough. I do believe, slave as I was, that there was something in the way I spoke that made that man know it was no use to fool with me; and, sir"—Stephen poised himself upon his elbow, and his fierce eyes seemed to dart black lightning, as he continued—"I do believe that for a minute Johnson was cowed; but pretty quickly he got over it, and said, 'Yes, Stephen, I had to sell the gal; I'm sorry fur you, but I couldn't help it; I was in debt, and a good price was offered me for Kitty, so I had to let her go.' 'And you didn't give her time to tell me good-bye?' 'No; but wasn't that the best? You see, Stephen, it would only have been more trouble to you both.' When I was about to speak to him, may be to strike him, for *something* was strong in me, one of Mr. Johnson's daughters—Sara Jane, I think, they called her—rushed out of the house, crying. 'Is that you, Stephen?' she said. 'Well, I'm glad you are talking to father; he had no business selling Kitty. I begged him not to. She was a good girl, and I loved her as if she had been my own kin. He needn't have sold her; I had rather the farm had gone than Kitty. I never shall forgive father.' She went on crying and saying many more things of her father. I blessed her from my heart; I have never forgotten her; and if she wanted a friend now, or one of her children—for she is now the mother of several girls and boys—needed anything, I'd serve them gladly. The negro never forgets or outgrows his gratitude. She told me, moreover, that she wished I would go to see Kitty, 'for, Stephen,' she added, 'all the girl's trouble was not seeing you.' I didn't thank her; I couldn't; but I turned away from that place; instinct or God guided me to the negro camp; I reached it at ten o'clock. It is a good many years ago, but I can still see that camp, those linen tents, that guard and patrol, as they looked then, under the still, white moon. The trader called out 'Who comes there?' I answered that I was Mr. Hemingway's Stephen; that I'd like to speak a minute with Mr. Warder (that was the trader's name). 'Well, what do you want with me?' I told him I'd like to see Kitty and say good-bye. He was pretty gruff about it; said that he didn't want any fussing, but, if I'd agree to keep quiet, I might see her. I went into a little tent where Kitty was lying, with one or two other negro girls, *handcuffed*. At first I thought I would choke; then I remembered my word had been given, and I thought it would be best for Kitty if I didn't show much feeling. I can't forget her poor, sick, dumb look. The creature had fretted and cried so much that all the spirit had gone out of her, and I do believe she didn't know me. But when, after two or three words, I rose to leave her, I took off my black cravat—the one I wore on Sundays or when I went to see her—and tied it round her neck; she seemed to come to herself, and, with one great howl, she fell forward and caught at my leg; then I heard her chains rattle, and something or somebody hurried me off. How I got home that night, I don't know, for I didn't seem to remember anything until toward daylight, when I found myself near home. I got through that day with my usual work, and at night I started off again to the camp. Of course I knew that the negroes were not there, for the gang had moved off at daylight, toward the South; but I wanted to go to the place where she had been; I knew it by the holes in the ground where the tent spokes had been driven. It was all still and dead as my own heart. I laid down on the ground; I rolled over the grass; I looked up at the great strange moon, and wondered if there was a God in heaven or pity any where. As I rolled and tossed about, my hands caught at something soft

in the grass; it was the cravat I had given to Kitty; it was stiff, no doubt
with her tears, poor thing! I knew she would grieve for it; I had hoped
that it would be a kind of comfort to her and a reminder of me; but
may be it was best that she should forget. I suffered a good deal after
this. I had no friends: mother and sweetheart had been stolen from me;
I couldn't read, so all my odd money was given to a grocer in exchange
for whiskey. Drink gave me relief. A good while passed off, and then a
large hotel was opened at the Cave. I was hired first for a waiter, but
pretty soon I acquired such knowledge of the Cave that I was appointed
guide. Then my true life began. In there I found so much to interest and
excite me that I never tired of hunting about through its wonders. Many
learned gentlemen came to visit here; for days they would be in the
Cave alone with me, and of course they talked freely; I gained a good
deal, particularly from Professor N———, who has spent several seasons
here; he is the geologist of the State of Indiana, and first taught me the
alphabet and aroused my desire for knowledge. I had no difficulty then
in learning to read: it seemed that I naturally took to it; I spent all my
leisure hours in poring over books; gentlemen used to give them to me,
and I've blessed the day that brought me to the Cave; it has been heaven
to me." He ceased speaking, sprang up from the grass, and stood with
his face full toward the sunset. "Such sights as those, sir, keep us from
going mad," he said, as he pointed toward the west: "it makes us think
and dream of what lies beyond that gorgeous gateway."

As Madge looked at him, she cried out, "It is a shame for you to
be a slave. Old Hemingway ought to give you your freedom."

A bright, red flush passed over the mulatto's handsome face as he
turned toward her, and, making a graceful bow, said,

"Your kind words, Miss Vertner, will never be forgotten."

He did not wait for a reply, but turned off into a cross path and
was soon lost in the thicket.

That evening, as Madge and Mr. Butler sat talking upon the
verandah, she said,

"I believe that I begin to look upon slavery itself as a wrong.
Stephen's story has made a great impression upon me. We shouldn't take
liberty from any one. I am going to speak to papa on the subject, and
urge him to free our slaves at once."

"And will he do it?"

"Of course he will, when he once understands it to be wrong; but I have never mentioned the matter to him. He very readily forgave two of our servants who had run off and given him a good deal of trouble. He was on the eve of selling them to a trader; upon my intercession, however, he at once forgave them."

Madge then related the story of Jack and Milly; she had never learned the truth of that affair, and believed that her father had scrupulously observed his promise, and only hired out the slaves. When the truth does come to her, she will learn how light a thing is a slaveholder's conscience. He who can, in a country like ours, willingly defraud a fellow-creature of his "inalienable right" to liberty will, of course, make no honest scruple at violating his word or promise.

While Madge was speaking, her father's coachman passed, with Matt. They were talking low and earnestly, but Madge's ears caught these words from the coachman:

"I wish I could dar' to look forward to de time when I might be my own master; but, Matt, I 'spects to die a slave; 'tis a mighty hard thing for a slave to save up money enough to buy himself; owners axes so much fur us."

"Did you hear that?" asked Madge. "Poor fellow, he ought to be free, and he *shall.*"

With these words she concluded the evening's conversation. Alas! she has yet to learn how difficult a thing it is to fight against self-interest and hereditary power. When we think of the tenacity with which (apparently) civilized people cling to the vile system of American slavery, we can only account for it by a belief in the old doctrine of utter Human Depravity.

XV

We must leave the Vertners for a while in their enjoyment of
the Mammoth Cave and turn our attention to our humbler friends
at Rachel's cottage. We have not looked in upon them since that
memorable night when the worn-out and tried fugitive found shelter.
No event, however, of special importance has occurred. The fugitive
found homely comfort and kind care from Rachel, but was unable
to continue her flight, as she knew that the whole neighborhood and
county were on the alert for her capture. Rachel's fears were all forgotten
when she found her sympathy and shelter so touchingly appealed to.
Putting behind her the threats of Col. Vertner, she opened her heart and
her home to the friendless runaway. She went now oftener to the village
and moved about more familiarly with the people, trying to learn what
they were going to do with her poor charge. On one occasion, when
she went in to sell eggs, she gathered from chance talks that a scouting
company had gone over to Indiana in search, and that Peter had been
questioned about his wife's fight, and, when protesting that he knew not
of her whereabouts, had been severely whipped. Moreover, she learned,
with fear, that some idea was entertained that the fugitive had been
secreted in the neighborhood, and a thorough scouring of the country
was proposed. Of course, she knew that her house would be suspected
and probably the first place examined. This filled her with fright, not so

much for her own complicity in the affair as her apprehension for the
safety of her *protégé*. Rachel had a kind, womanly heart, added to heroic
courage and self-endurance. Slavery to her was odious; and for her own
choice, she would have preferred death itself, by means of the overseer's
whip, rather than live even in petted or pampered slavery. Her body was
able to endure any amount of pain and ill-usage, encouraged, as it was,
by such a high and indomitable spirit.

But now, when this village gossip, magnified, as it always is,
by many repetitions, came to her in such a threatening form, she
bethought herself of the best and safest means of protecting Maria.

One day, as they sat in the little inner room of the cabin, talking
in a half-whisper, for they were obliged to be very cautious, fearing that
scouts and spies might be lurking about the place, Rachel asked:

"Maria, if they were to take you, what would you do?"

The woman, who had been crouching down in the corner, close
to Rachel's side, looked up, with terror written all over her face, and
said:

"If dey takes me! Is dar any idea dat dey will?"

"You know, of course, that you are always in danger of being
taken."

"Yes; but, Rachel, has yer hearn anything dat makes you say dis
here to me?"

"Don't be frightened. Keep your wits about you. You have, poor
creature, need of all the senses God gave you. I did hear that the white
people suspected that you were hidden somewhere in the neighborhood
and meant to search. Of course, my cabin will be one of the first places
to which they will come."

Maria, with wide-starting eyes, crept yet closer to Rachel's side,
and laid her black hand firmly on Rachel's wrist, and, pausing for a
moment, as if to refresh her courage, said,

"Rachel, dig a big hole in yer yard, dis night, and bury me alive in
it, rader den sen' me back to be a slave."

The woman who uttered this sentiment had a black, weather-
beaten, ill-favored, ill-featured face; was rough and rude of speech;
but, at that moment, her spirit was as proud and great as that of many
a white woman whose name has been enshrined and preserved as the
boast of a nation; yet such is the blind and insane prejudice against

color and race that what constitutes heroism in the white woman, in the negro is called heresy.

Rachel caught hold of Maria's shoulder, exclaiming,

"They shall *not* take you; my life first."

There was something splendid in the aspect of the two women as they sat gazing full into each other's eyes. That proud, untamable something—that wild, electric, lightning-like spark, which we call spirit—shone from the flashing depths of Rachel's eyes, and was answered by the determined glance of the aroused creature at her feet. Poor Maria was not all a brute, nor yet a slave, as some might suppose. *Now* she realized herself, almost for the first time. She had scarcely tasted of liberty; but the one drop that had come to her lips so excited her thirst that she longed for a deeper draught, as the wounded hind for the brook-side.

Animated by such noble feelings, the two women grew into a warmer sympathy; and Rachel, in a simple, friendly way, tried to instil some of her own pride into the mind and heart of the ignorant creature at her side.

"Does you tink," asked Maria, "dat my ole man could cum to see me here?"

"Mercy, no; are you crazy, Maria?" asked Rachel. "Do you think that the white folks are fools? No, indeed; I expect people are watching round here now. You must not sleep, but live every moment as if you were treading a broken bridge that spanned the Ohio."

"I wishes, in my heart, that I was on t'other side of de Ohio ribber. Dey does say as how dat dar is a set of folks over dar dat will help de black people. If I could git to dem once, den I'd see my way clar to Canaday; but gittin' ober de ribber is de worst t'ing. 'Pears like it's mighty hard to run off, Rachel, now Col. Vertner's Jack an' Milly was cotched. Dat Tom Hynes and his pack of hounds can tree a nigger jist like a rabbit or fox."

"Yes, and he is after you, and I am afraid will soon be on the right track."

"Laws, I hopes not; for he is one of dem venomous kin', and never misses de scent of a nigger. If he is arter me, I is as good as cotched."

The woman began to tremble and shake as though suddenly stricken by the ague.

"The Lord is stronger than Tom Hynes; trust in Him, Maria."

"Yes; but does 'pear sometimes as if he was so far off, way up dar in de sky, dat he don't kere much 'bout what happens to niggers."

"He isn't far off; he is close to us, this moment. He is here in this very cabin."

"Now, Rachel, if I believed dat, I wouldn't be de least bit afeared of Tom Hynes or his dogs; but den I doesn't tink dat he is right here on de spot, else he wouldn't let so many wicked t'ings go on."

"He lets a great many strange things come to pass. We can't understand how it is, but by and bye it will all work right."

"How does you know it, Rachel?"

"I *feel it,* Maria."

"Well, but don't it 'pear as if de wicked was de most favored of Providence. Why, dat ar cussin' and swarin' Tom Hynes, he jist thrives like wild oats. I hearn my ole man say dat he see Tom Hynes at de camp-meetin' wid his pockets cram full o' money, an' jist a cussin' like a dead-drunk sailor. Now, what you make ob dat? De Lord lets him thrive, while my ole man, who is as good and prayin' a creater as can be, is kept in de hardest kind of slavery."

"The Lord don't work as we *think* He ought, but upon a higher plan. Moreover, Maria, the end has not yet come. We can't tell whether Tom Hynes thrives or not; wait till the end."

"Yes, de preacher said dat de Lord made dem dat he love suffer, but I kant see dat way; 'pears to me as dem dat does to please Him should be taken kere of an' seen arter; dat is de way good masters does."

"But the reward is to come after death. We will enjoy heaven more if we have had a hard time here. Did you never hear any of those pretty Scripture stories read?"

"Oh, yes; ole Miss used to hab me come in to prayers when de preacher staid all night wid us, and read de Bible and prayed night an' mornin'. Some of dem stories was most beautiful. Dat one about Joe or Joseph, whose brothers sold him, an' den he come to be a king. I jist tole my ole man dat was de kind of slavery I'd like. Dey may sell me to dat kind of a master any time."

"Let me read to you from the good book." And Rachel took her little Bible down from the shelf and read from the book of Job, in a slow, hesitating voice, as if pausing to taste of the very words so full of Christian promise.

"You see how Job suffered, Maria, and what constant faith he kept in the Lord. We must depend upon the Lord; never give up our trust or forget to pray to Him. He is our only trust and hope."

"I wishes de Lord Jesus was here, for dat ar book say he made Peter walk on de water by means of His grace. Now, if I jist could get dat faith dat would make me strong enough to walk over de Ohio, I could be a long way ahead of Tom Hynes before de mornin', but dem ar things ain't done in dese times, Rachel, is dey?"

"Maria," said Rachel, as she replaced her Bible on the shelf, "I don't think it is quite safe for you to sleep in this room. The cabin is liable to be attacked at any moment. Here, just step in this closet; do you see that the bottom of the floor lifts up? and when you hear any signs of noise, raise that up and go down. Let me show you."

Rachel lifted up the floor as lightly as if it had been a door; revealing, at the same time, a hollow in the earth, to the depth of three or four feet, sufficiently large to furnish a bed for a human body.

"In that you can snugly hide yourself; then let this planking drop thus, and it fastens by a hinge, and he must be a smart man, indeed, who can detect the trick. I have concealed many a poor runaway slave in there. You see, now, it passes for a wardrobe, with my dresses hanging around."

"I s'pects you is right, Rachel; I had better sleep in dar; jist gib me a blanket or quilt to fling over me, an' I'll sleep dar as well as I ken when my mind is so 'sturbed."

Rachel did not sleep much during the night. An impression of danger seemed to haunt her, and the two or three minutes of sleep which she did catch were tormented by frightful dreams. But the poor fugitive slept soundly. Rachel got up in the night, opened one of the little windows, which let in a flood of moonlight, and sat gazing at Maria, who was sleeping so unconsciously on the closet floor.

"Poor wretch," she thought; "you can sleep soundly whilst storms threaten around. It is a blessed thing. I'll not waken you."

The next morning she rose early and went out to milk the cow. She was not surprised, though a little troubled, when, on returning to the cabin with a pail of fresh, rich milk, she met a suspicious-looking man, quite near her gate. Upon being asked if he wanted anything, he carelessly replied,

"No; I was only lookin' at yer little place; it's very nice. I am a little tired, and shouldn't care if you'd let me rest awhile inside and give me a drink of yer fresh milk: thar's nothin' I like so much as a tumbler of good milk."

Rachel did not fancy having such a looking character tarry long at her cottage, and yet she had too much policy to refuse him a few moments' rest and shelter.

"Come in, then, and take a seat," she replied, in an indifferent sort of tone, taking, at the same time, from the cupboard shelf a tumbler, which she filled with the foaming, creamy milk and offered to him.

"Ah, I'm obleeged to yer. This is very rich milk. I hain't drunk sich this many a year. Has yer got one 'em Durham breed cows?"

"No; I haven't one of those full-blooded ones; my little red cow is one of the common kind, but just as good a cow to give milk as your Durhams. I ain't one of the sort as believes one breed is better than another in cows, horses or human creatures; all are alike, and good enough, too, if you let 'em be."

Rachel said this in a peevish tone, and the man looked up with a surprised expression; then, breaking out into a hearty laugh, said:

"You is one of 'em free rights an' equality sort, ain't you?"

"I am for letting what God made alone, and not troubling myself which is best and which is worst. God made people and things just as they are, and you might let 'em be."

"Well, them's good enough sentiments; and now that I've been to your cabin once, Rachel, and made myself acquainted like, I shan't mind to come agin, if you is willin'."

"Well, I ain't willing to have you or any of the like of you prowling round my cabin; I live here peaceably, and don't interfere with anybody, and don't want any one to come troubling me. I don't wish visiting from any white men."

"Oh, hush now, Rachel; don't you reckon I knows about Col. Vertner's comin'.'."

The woman turned pale, and quivered in every limb. She moved toward the man with a partially uplifted hand and a dangerous flash of the eye.

"If," she said, and her voice was thick with passion—"if you don't quit this cabin at once, I'll knock you to the earth; I'll—I'll—"

Here she fairly broke down with passion.

"An' what'll I be a-doin', you imperdent yaller wench, when you are knockin' me down? Do you s'pose I'll stand and take it? I'm a white man an' belittling myself to talk with the like o' you."

Rachel had taken a chair, and sat pale and panting as the man finished his tirade.

"Then, if you are a *white* man and so proud, I want you at once to take yourself off from my cabin."

"I'll go when it suits me; but look here, gal, 'tain't no sort of use for you an' me to be a-quarrellin'; we had as well make it up, an' settle things the right sort o' way; I ain't goin' to bear malice agin' you because you spoke just now when you was mad; words don't mend the matter at all, so we won't say nothin' further. You are devilish putty, fur all you has yaller skin. Come, give me a kiss, an' we'll be good friends."

As he approached her and was about to execute his request, she drew back her hand and, with all the vindictive power of an insulted woman, struck him, full across the face, a blow which made even the strong man reel, coming, as it did, so unexpectedly. He staggered a few steps; the blood gushed from his mouth and nose; and, springing toward Rachel, he caught her light form in his grasp and shook her violently, aiming, at the same time, blows at her head and face.

"There—there, you yaller wench, take that; an' this shan't be the last you hears of me; I meant you well, but, after this, I'll mean you ill. My name is John Sharpe, an' you may look out for me agin. I'll have vengeance, an' you'll know of it mighty soon."

With these threats, and muttering oaths, he took his leave. Poor Rachel was bewildered, frightened and stunned from the blows and the shaking she had received; she had not heard distinctly all that he said, but had caught enough to know that further ill and outrage were threatened her. After regaining something like composure, she went in to see Maria, who was fastened in the closet.

"Oh, laws, Rachel! what *has* happened? I heard sich a fuss, and was skeered most to death. Do tell me 'bout it."

Rachel recounted the whole interview as faithfully as her scattered wits would permit, concluding with these ominous words:

"I'll look now for heavy trouble."

"Oh, yes, indeed, I knows dat John Sharpe; I'se hearn my Master Andy talk 'bout him; dey say he is drefful spiteful an' full o' bad 'tentions."

"I wonder," murmured Rachel to herself, as she glided about preparing breakfast, "when the Vertners will return? If Andrew was here, he *might* protect me."

XVI

Tom Hynes was loafing on the stoop of the tavern in L——,
chewing tobacco, betting on the probable result of some State or
county election, and talking with his friends, the tavern-keeper, the
hog-drover and the racerider; while in front of the house a lazy black
ostler was holding a horse by the bridle, waiting anxiously, no doubt,
for the sixpence which the rider was expected to throw to him. The little
dirty-faced white boys were playing marbles in the sand, and a mulatto
girl, ten years old, with a tin pail of water balanced upon her head, was
walking past, singing, at the top of her voice and in a clear, musical
tone,

"Oh, Susanah, don't you cry for me."

"That gal has got a voice, I tells you, as might make a forten,"
said Tom Hynes. "She ken jest run up an' down them scales equal to
any bird. She can Do, re, mi as good as any singin'-school master. I'm a
mind to make her stop a bit an' give us a tune. Here, Grace, stop a bit."
The girl ceased her song suddenly, and answered, in a rough tone,
"I kan't, Mister Hynes; I'se got to take this pail of water to
mammy fur to cook white folks' dinner wid."
"D—n it, I say, stop this minnit, an' I'll give you sixpence."

The dinner was instintly forgotten, and the pail of water deposited on the ground, and Grace immediately began to sing, in a pathetic voice, "Way down on Swanee River."

There was something peculiarly fascinating and picturesque in the child's rendering of the song. To a fine, clear, natural voice she added an accurate ear for music and a dramatic power of expression which were perfectly unique and charming. She seemed literally to feel and act the song. When she had finished and stooped to pick up the money that had been thrown to her, Hynes called out,

"Give us 'Juba,' an' I'll let you have another sixpence." At this Grace began to sing in a low, muttering, humdrum, but entirely musical tone,

"Juba here an' Juba dar,
An' Juba everywhar,"

accompanying her voice, at the same time, by a slow, stately sort of foot-measure, more like a grand march than a lively dance, patting her breast and sides all the while; then, as the tune changed, she moved off into a lively quick step, out of which, with accordant music, she bounded off into a smart, rapid country-dance, flinging herself into the wildest, most grotesque, but by no means ungraceful attitudes, winding up with a rapid shuffle, then gyrating, curvetting, wheeling round on alternate feet, in the most singular, agile and vivacious pirouettes imaginable, improvising, as she went along, a narrative song commemorating the exploits of "My old master," sung in an appropriate tune. For rapidity of motion, litheness and facility of limb, time and tune, and comicality of attitude, this negro dance excelled any *pas-de-seul* we ever witnessed upon the stage. Lola Montez's somewhat celebrated "Spider dance" was nothing to it. When fairly out of breath and borne down by the exertion, she stopped suddenly, and, looking at Hynes, said, in the most familiar tone,

"You oughter gib me a quarter-dollar fur dat, 'kase I'se done tired myself, an' mammy'll beat me fur not comin' long wid de water."

"You thinks you ought to have a quarter? Well, now, you'se 'bout as sassy one as I'd wish to look at. I'm a stont mind to give you nothin'; but here's yer sixpence"; and he tossed it toward her. But Grace was nothing daunted; she picked up the coin, and, walking forward, with a bold expression, said,

"May be some of 'em oder gemmen what's settin' dar an' bin a seein' me will gib somet'ing more."

"Well, I don't mind to give her a sixpence," said one, "fur I hain't seen anything equal to that; so here's fur yer."

Accordingly each one of the company gave her a sixpenny piece. She felt quite rich, and, making a curtsying sort of acknowledgment and thanking them for their kindness, she took up her pail of water and marched off with a quick step, towards home, when she was suddenly encountered by a stout-looking negro woman, with a leather strap in her hand.

"What's you bin a singin' at de tavern fur, dancin' an' cuttin' round fur a parcel of men, an' I waitin' in de kitchen fur dat ar pail o' water, afore I could put in de backen an' cabbage to bile fur de white folks' dinners. Oh, yes, yer wants to sing an' dance in front o' public houses does yer, yer black imp, an' be a-talkin' long o' white men, who had best be a tendin' dar own bisness? But I'll take de very hide off yer bones. No chile o' mine shall do dat ar way, if I ken fetch 'em up different." And here she brought her leather strap down on Grace's shoulders with the most unsparing severity, observing, however, the wise precaution to first take possession of the bucket of water. "Now, git yerself along brisk like or I'll tell mistress on yer, an' she'll make de old red cowhide walk on yer back. Best believe I ain't gwine to be a-foolin' 'long wid you dis sort o' way."

"Now, mammy, jist please don't beat me so, afore I tells you all 'bout it. Yer see, Mister Hynes say he would pay me if I'd sing him a song an' pat 'Juba,' an' so I done got de money an' bring it here to yer."

"Whar is de money? Gib it ter me. 'Tain't right, Grace, dat yer should be takin' money from Tom Hynes; I ain't gwine to hab you a-doin' so; jist gib it here to me." And, taking the money from Grace, she began to count it slowly over in her hands. "Yes, dis here'll buy me a drap o' tea an' a little sugar fur Sunday mornin'. Grace, don't yer let me hear ob yer speakin' any more to Tom Hynes an' 'em men in front of de public-house; if yer does so again, I'll take de hide off yer. Now, 'member dat, an' don't take no more money from Tom Hynes."

"Well, that ar nigger is worth a pretty good sum o' money," said Hynes to his friends; "she's as smart an' slick a hand as I ever saw. Seems to me as it would be a good bargain fur Harrison. I'll tell him of her when he comes round buyin' up fur the next lot."

"How is niggers sellin' now?" inquired one of the men.

"Oh, putty far, indeed; they run 'em up in Orleans last year to from sixteen hundred to two thousand a head fur a smart man. It's a mighty lucky bisness; all other sorts of trades seem to fluctuate, but thar's very small difference in nigger-tradin'. Now, thar's Harrison: he begun the bisness a poor man. Why, ten years ago, when I fust knew him, he wasn't worth shucks, an' now he's got between sixty an' a hundred thousand dollars worth o' stock in different banks; he has tole me that he jist clars money like sand on niggers. He has a sharp eye at trade an' knows a sound nigger better 'an any o' yer doctors. You kan't begin to deceive him about 'em; he jist knows 'em same as a storekeeper knows a bit o' wash calico. 'Tain't no use a-talkin', it's the right sort o' bisness, an' I'm goin' into it as soon as I ken git enough scraped together to make a start. Harrison has hinted a little 'bout takin' me into partnership; an' if he makes me an offer, I'll take him up at the snap o' my finger."

As this conversation was going on, the negro ostler, who had been relieved of his duty of holding the traveller's horse, came up and seated himself upon the step of the stoop, not far from Tom Hynes and his group, and appeared to pay very evident attention to the conversation. Every now and then he would wipe the perspiration from his brow with his shirt sleeve. Though it was not a warm day, and he was not actively exercised, still large beads of perspiration were constantly gathering on his brow and sometimes rolling down his black face in sluices. There he sat, with his woolly head bent a little forward, and his ears drinking in every word of the conversation.

"Talkin' 'bout niggers," said the landlord, "puts me in mind o' what I hearn some one say t'other day—I doesn't know as I can jist now call to mind who it was tole me—that the new schoolmaster had bin a-sayin' as how he didn't believe in keepin' niggers in slavery, an' that thar seemed to be a kind o' dissatisfaction growin' up towards him in the town. I don't know as it is jist so; but, from the fust, I did not believe in that man; he was too smooth—always 'peared to me like,

when I see him round, as a cat was mousing 'bout, huntin' for no good.
At fust I thought we might have had him fur a boarder; he come here
an' looked at a room an' sorter engaged it. He slept here two nights,
but couldn't stay any longer because the young men drunk so hard; but
I doesn't believe as that was the reason. He seemed pleased enough at
fust. I tuck him a dollar cheaper than customary, fur he said he'd likely
be permanent; but a mornin' after he come, one of the nigger wenches
give some imperdence to my wife, an' I jist thrashed her pretty roundly
an' sorter bruised and blackened her eye a little. Well, that mornin', at
breakfast, my Yankee turned jist as sick and white as a two year old baby
at sight o' that wench's eye. Seein' him sorter squeamish, I asked him
what's the matter; he looked toward the gal, then made one run from
the table. I follered an' found him in the yard a-spewing and heavin'
like a baby. I wanted to laugh, fur I never had seen a man behave so
much like a gal afore; but I kept my face straight an' said: 'I'm sorry, Mr.
Norton, that the wench has turned yer stomach; if I'd a-known you was
so weakly, I'd not a let her come in to the table.' I offered him a drop o'
brandy, thinkin' it would settle his sickness, but he shuck his head an'
said it wasn't the sight so much as the idea what had been done to the
woman; an' then he went on with some o' his meetin'-house talk; so I
jist stopped it up by sayin' 'nobody was a comin' to my house, either as
visitor or boarder, an' try to advise me 'bout my family arrangements;
I controlled them things my own way'; and so I walked away an' left
him to be sick over it. The next day he made some complaint 'bout two
young men drinkin' the night afore, keepin' him awake an' sich stuff—
said he had concluded to git more private board, paid his bill an' went
away. I wasn't sorry either, I ken tell you."

"If he's one of 'em Abolitionists, I'd like to see him," said Tom
Hynes. "I ken take the stiff out o' thar back bone, I ken tell yer. One
of 'em kum up to me when I was in Indianny, and I shut him up at
once. They's the meanest, sneakenist sort of folks, an' jist as 'fraid as a
nigger—glib on the tongue, but skeery an' shimble-shamble as an old
blind horse."

"But, then, he mustn't be allowed to go 'bout tamperin' with
niggers, or he'll put notions in thar heads as'll give trouble."

"I don't care," said Hynes, as he stretched out his legs and threw his arms above his head, "how many niggers he persuades off; 'twill be all the better for my bisness; I ken ketch all he starts."

"By the way," asked the landlord, "have you got any news from Andy Vitetor's woman?"

"Not yit; but I'll let 'at one lie in the grass awhile. I'm a-workin' my plans; an' afore anybody knows it, I'll pounce down upon her."

"Do you think Peter knew where she was?" asked the drover.

"No, I doesn't think that gal tole anybody whar she was a-goin'; an' its putty well settled in my mind that she hasn't yit got across the river. Thar's them on t'other side that works 'long with me in this bisness, an' the traps is all laid. She couldn't git by. I'll beat about little more in the woods 'bout here, an' I'll come out with her; she's hid somewhar, I'm sure."

The negro ostler here turned his face full upon Hynes, regarding him with that peculiar, wondering, anxious expression which, in the lower order of negroes, has struck us with such pity. There was no spirit in the glance, but a dead, cold eye that hoped nor asked for nothing, gazing out upon vacancy with a bleak glance, just the same asking look which we have noticed in the innocent submission of a lamb.

"Bill, kan't you find some work to attend to, an' not be idlin' round here, as if 'twas Sunday? Git yourself off to the stable or somewhar to work."

Thus addressed by the landlord, Bill, who knew no other law than that of obedience, betook himself to the kitchen, where he seated himself upon a stool and was soon engaged in a lively chat with the cook. The landlord did not care particularly for Bill's idleness; he only wished to get him out of the way of their conversation, which it was not altogether the most prudent to carry on in a slave's hearing.

Soon after Bill's withdrawal, the party received an addition in the person of Mr. John Sharpe, who looked very angry, swore very hard, and finally got Tom Hynes into a more private place and a private talk, in which they both grew very much excited, and Sharpe was noticed to make very threatening gestures.

XVII

The next day after John Sharpe's visit to the cabin, Rachel felt so uneasy and excited that she could not remain at home.

"Maria," she said, "I feel as if I most go over to the Vertner place and find out when the family is expected home."

"What fur, Rachel? Does you know 'em quality folks? Why, laws, I'se never bin thar in my life. Col. Vertner's black folks thinks tharselves better 'an any of de rest of de niggers 'bout here, 'cept it is some of 'em town darkies, like the widow Mason's. But I does tell you, dat ar' Miss Madge, she's one uv 'em rale quality. I'se saw her many times ridin' on her pony, an' she allers stopt an' spoke to me in a rale quality sort of voice. I hearn my white folks say she wa'n't proud like her master; dat she didn't try to cut a splurge, an' didn't kere fur nothin' but shootin' an' ridin' on horseback. Dey say dat a good many white gals 'bout here tried to do like her, but 'tain't no use. Dey wasn't Col. Vartner's darters. Dat Miss Minervy McFarland got her a hoss an' tried to race 'bout de country, but den she didn't have Miss Madge's putty face an' lady ways. I 'members, one Sunday, when I was comin' from town, right long de big road, I met Miss Madge, ridin' on her little black pony, wid dat 'ar dog o' hearn runnin' arter her. She dropped her little white handle whip: I picked it up fur her, an' she said thanky in sich a nice voice, an' look so good an' putty, 'at I'd heap rather had it 'an a quarter-dollar."

"I never saw Madge Vertner but once, and then it was only a glimpse; but I dare say she is a good girl." Rachel said this in a serious tone. Maria looked up in very evident surprise.

"Why, Rachel, how ken you talk dat ar way 'bout sich grand quality folks?"

Rachel frowned, and was about to speak, perhaps in an angry tone, when suddenly recollecting herself, she walked off, as if to hide a rising emotion. Soon after, she hid Maria away in the closet, closed down the windows, locked up the house and set out on foot for the Vertner place. Her course lay along a dusty public highway. With her sun-bonnet pulled down over her face, she walked briskly along, occasionally passing persons, single horsemen or foot-passengers, some of whom gave her a nod; others passed on, scarcely seeing her. For herself, she did not see or hear anything. All her senses were introverted; only memory was busy at work. In about an hour she reached the Vertner place. Pausing at the gate of the avenue, she looked long and wistfully up the elm-shadowed walk, almost fearing to enter. A few birds were glancing through the trees, and flies were buzzing in the warm September sun; it was a tranquilizing sort of day, dreamy and drowsy, and Rachel felt its mellow and subduing influence.

At the "quarter," Uncle Pete was sitting out in the sunshine, enjoying his pipe, while Pomp was frolicking with Rover, and squads of half dressed negro children were playing round about the grounds, turning summer sets, tossing balls and hallooing in the most vociferous manner.

"Won't yer be quiet thar, chillen?" cried Uncle Pete; "yer never gives a body time nor peace to drop asleep; here, I'se almost off in a nap, and yer hollered out so dat you'se done skered all sleep away fur to-day. Be done dar wid dat dog, Pomp; an' tell 'em chillen to go in de cabin an' keep still while I sleep a bit."

"Yes, sar," answered Pomp, "me'll make 'em hush"; and, turning off, with an impish laugh, he stuck his finger to his nose, kicked out his foot in the direction of Uncle Pete, and made a determined rush upon the group of children, commanding silence in the most authoritative tone, at the same time twitching one of the boys in the side, causing him to scream out in a frightful yell.

"Laws, Dick, isn't you 'shamed o' yerself to be makin' sich a noise when Uncle Pete wants to sleep! Laws, now, Uncle Pete, I bin tryin' to keep dem ar' chillens still, but dey's jist de noisiest critters I eber see—heap sight worse 'an Rover. Here, Rover, here, here"—and, whistling to the dog, he bounded off in the direction of the mansion, when unexpectedly he met Rachel. Stopping directly in front of her, he opened his eyes and mouth and stood still in surprise.

"Which is the way to the quarter?" inquired Rachel.

"Laws a marcy!" be exclaimed, never heeding her question—"laws a marcy, but I hain't seed de like o' you afore in dis place. Whar's you come from, an' what does yer want here? All de white folks is gone off."

"When is your master coming back?"

"Oh, I doesn't know; but afore long I 'spects, bekase Dan is bin a airin' de house, an' Ruthy's all de time workin' round fixin' t'ings; so I 'spects de white folks is comin'. I'll be glad, an' so'll Rove, bekase we wants to see Miss Madge."

"Can't you show me the way to the cabins, or let me know where I can see some one of the house servants who can tell me when the family is expected back?"

"Oh, yes; jist come 'long wid me, an' I'll take you to Aunt Polly, an' she ken ax Dan; he knows 'bout it; but what does yer want longer master an' missus? or may be yer wants to see Miss Madge?"

Rachel did not directly answer this question, but began talking to the boy on what she rightly supposed would be a favorite theme with him.

"Is that your dog?"

"Which, dis here one?" (placing his hand on Rover). "No, indeed, dis is Miss Madge's dog, an' she thinks sight o' him an' her pony, Silk, I ken tell yer, an' Rove loves Miss Madge. De fust day an' night arter she went 'way, Rove just howled round de house as if somebody was dead, an' he wouldn't eat his bones, but kept huntin' 'bout, as dough he was a-sarchin' fur Miss Madge. Dat dog jist knows her name"—and turning to Rover he asked, "Rove, does you want Miss Madge?" Whereupon the dog looked up, with a kind of intelligence gleaming from his eye, and whisked and frisked around in very evident pleasure.

"Dar, dar, didn't I tell you him knowed? he's jist as smart as anybody; Miss Madge talks to him same as she does to me."

By this time they had crossed the yard and were in the quarter, where they found the children in a most riotous play, Uncle Pete standing in the midst, brandishing his hickory cane right and left, to the perfect unconcern of the group.

"I jist wishes," cried the old man, "dat Alic would cum in from de fields, an' he'd settle yer quick enuff, you young scamps. Yer jist keeps a noise here all de time, an' dis is de way yer's bin a-carryin on ever sense de white folks went away."

"Never mind, Peter," said Aunt Polly, as she joined the group, "don't be a-frettin' yerself 'bout dem ar' chillen; dey ain't worth yer notice; jist go in de cabin, an rest yerself an' smoke yer pipe a bit."

"Who's dat?" asked the old man as he faced Rachel.

"Dat dar? why, I knows Rachel; dis here is de seamster dat I met, at town once"; and she dropped a low curtsy, and, wiping her hand with her apron, offered it to Rachel in a very cordial manner.

"Well, now, Rachel, I'se right glad to see you; it's 'mazin' kind o' yer to 'member old nigger like me; but yer knows I tole you den if you jist would come to see me, I'd be powerful glad to see you, an' so I is. I never shall forgit how good 'twas o'yer to gib me sich a lift dat time. Yer see, Peter, dis is de werry 'un what sarved me sich a good turn when I was in town. You member, Peter, doesn't yer, what I'se tole yer 'bout de 'oman, when I was so tired, an' she gin me a good ride on her own hoss, an' walkt herself 'long de big road until we got to whar she say de path turned off to her cabin? Well, dis is de one; she tole me her name was Rachel, an' dat she was free. Well, you see, I hain't forgot you, honey, fur 'twas a monsterus lift you gin me dat time; 'kase I was sufferin' a little longer rheumatiz. But come in, Rachel, come to my cabin; sit down an' rest yerself."

Rachel followed Aunt Polly and Uncle Peter to the cabin, and was glad enough to avail herself of the rest which they offered, as she was a little tired from her long walk.

"Come in, Rachel; take dis here cheer; sit down an' rest yerself. I'm 'shamed o' dis ole cabin—it's so dirty an' all tossed up; don't look round you, please, Rachel, bekase I'se 'shamed to death of everyt'ing, an' jist has to shut my eyes right tight to keep frum seein' de dirt; but I'se sich little time to do anyt'ing 'bout here; I'se not bin quite so bissy sense our people went off, fur most o' my work is washin' fur de white family.

Missus is so 'tickler wid her little fineries, dem lace collars, sleeves an' caps—all dem little fine jobs is mine; but I'se had a rale good play time sense our people went off."

"When are they coming back?" asked Rachel.

"Laws, honey, I kan't say; not soon, I hope, fur I'd like a bit longer o' play time, an' yit I does want to see Miss Madge; 'pears like de birds all went off wid ker, an' dars her dog Rove—poor dumb brute jist hunts round arter her as sorrowful like as any human critter. I likes to have her 'bout—she's so lively like—allers runnin' an' laughin' an' playin', wid a good word fur us all. Now, take kere dare, Rachel, don't be a-lookin' at dat ole cupboard; it's jist as dusty as if I hadn't wiped it off dis blessed mornin'." And Aunt Polly waddled up to a little wooden press, which was entirely guiltless of the slightest spot of dust, and began to rub it furiously with her apron.

"Come 'long, Polly, an' quit yer fussin' 'bout nuffin'; yer knows dar ain't no dirt an' dust 'bout here, 'kase you clean all de time; didn't I see you a-scrubbin' at dat same cupboard dis mornin', an' now you is a-wipin' it off as dough it was all kivered wid dust!"

Aunt Polly began to laugh heartily, and, turning her head to one side with a sort of grand-folks air, replied,

"Psha! Peter, dat's de way you allers sarves me when my company draps in. Men folks is so quare; dey never t'inks us wimmin has anyt'ing on our minds. Now, Peter, he is allers complainin' dat I cleans too much, an' anybody ken see what dis cab'n is. Laws, ef 'twasn't fur Peter, I'd hab t'ings 'pear rale nice an' sot in order; but he fusses so; an' when a 'ooman has got an ole man, Rachel, she kan't no more do her own way. Now, I does love to clean an' scrub; I ken use a brush wid any 'ooman o' my age, but den I done clar got out de way of it sense Peter an' me got married. 'Tain't no use a-tryin' to git yer own way, 'kase men folks is so 'termined to git de best of dar wimmins. I'se picked up many a resolution, but jist had to put it down dar under Peter's feet, 'kase he'd worry so I'd be 'bleeged to do as he says."

This mournful criticism upon the sorrows of matrimony was pronounced in a short staccato tone, which gave to the words a kind of terse force from which their was no appeal. Uncle Peter sat eyeing his old woman with a glum sort of smile upon his face, whiffing away every now and then at his cob pipe. Rachel was highly amused. From the moment of her entrance, she had observed the scrupulous cleanliness of the cabin, but she well understood the negro etiquette, which delighted in abusing everything belonging to oneself, and was not surprised to hear Aunt Polly decry against the dirt of this well-swept and well-dusted cabin. She endeavored, in the most adroit manner, to draw off Aunt Polly's attention from surrounding affairs. The truth is, she had almost forgotten ever having met the old woman, and had come to the Vertner place to boldly inquire for the return of the family; but now she gladly accepted the pretext which Aunt Polly's mistake afforded, and let her errand pass for a social visit.

"Dis is de fust time you'se bin here, Rachel, ain't it?" asked Peter.

"Yes."

"Wal, den, Polly, take her roun' an' show her de place; go down to de house an' let her see everything; 'twill be a sight fur her, sich, I s'pose, as she never seed afore."

"Is yer rested enuff to go roun'?"

"Oh, yes; I shall be very glad to see the place."

"Well, den, let's go fust to de house. Ruthy is down dar; she's bin a-cleanin' an' airin' up afore our folks gits back. Missus is powerful 'tickler an' kan't bar to see de least t'ing out o' order."

They passed through the garden, which was still looking beautiful and fresh, notwithstanding the lateness of the season. A colored gardener was weeding out the flower-beds and clearing the awarded walks and paths.

"You see, over dar is Missus's green-house; she has a power o' flowers all de winter, an' some o' 'em is heap puttier 'an dese what grows in de summer."

Rachel looked at everything, every spot, almost at each particular flower, plant and shrub, with an intensely interested eye. Polly observed this and was pleased, and experienced a kind of pride as she exhibited the beauties of the place. Slaves feel a peculiar sort of personal interest in their master's property, and believe that they themselves catch some portion of the glory reflected from their master's wealth. It was this pride which now induced Polly to resume her usual depreciatory style of conversation, which, let us here remark, always proved that she was at the very height of satisfaction with all around; and if any one had chanced to agree with her, she would have soon let them know that things were entirely above criticism.

"Dis here garden," she continued, after being satisfied of Rachel's entire admiration—"dis here garden looks poor now; 'pon my word, I neber did see it look so shabby; yer see, Ben, he is de garden man an' don't take a bit o' pains sense Missus lef'. I jest knows what missus'll say when she comes back; she'll jest fret an' carry on 'bout it till master'll hub to see dat Ben is lookt arter; yer see, Ben jist needs a-combin' up once ebery season; he kind o' drinks, chile, an' den he don't 'tend to his work. Las' year, missus say she wouldn't keep him on de place no how, an' master cum mighty nigh sellin' him. In fac', I t'ought once he was clean gone, an' I couldn't help feelin' sorry fur him, fur all he had bin a-drinkin' an' a-swarin' at an orful rate, an' I jist b'lieved mas'er tole de truth when he say de place wa'n't safe wid sich a boy on it; but den de fellar did seem so much 'stressed 'bout bein' sole; why, bress yer, honey, arter he done hearn he war gwine to be sole, he neber slep' a wink for smack four nights; he jist roamed 'bout de place same as one o' 'em dumb brutes, an' he lookt 'orful, I tells yer."

"But he was not sold, it seems."

"No, honey, but he would o' bin ef it hadn't bin fur Miss Madge. She jist went an' tole mas'er she didn't want Ben fur to be sole, an' den 'twas all right. Mas'er tole Ben as how he'd let him off if he'd make a promise to Miss Madge dat he wouldn't never touch anoder drap; an' Ben made dat promise, an' he's kep' it ever sense, widout he's bin takin' a bit lately, sense dey all went away, an' sure dis here garden looks as if he mout a bin."

"Your Miss Madge appears to be a great favorite with you all," said Rachel.

"Laws, yes, indeed she is; I jist wishes you could sot yer eyes on her—you'd t'ink yer had come 'cross an angel; she is jist de puttiest chile you ever saw; she looks fit to eat. I s'pects you'se hearn of her ridin' 'bout de country; she's allers out on her pony. But, psha! 'tain't no kine o' use fur de poor people roun' here to be a-talkin 'bout Miss Madge; she is got plenty o' fine close, an' could dress an' dance 'long wid any o' 'em, ef she was a mind to; but she jist don't want to, an' she is rich enuff, an' putty enuff, an' has plenty o' black folks to wait on her; so she ken jist foller her own mind. Dat's what Peter said to me t'other day, an' it's true—bress your heart, it is—ebery word of it. Now, here we is at de house; it don't look no ways as it does when our folks is home."

They passed through a side door and entered the linen-room, where Ruth was seated in the centre of the apartment, with a quantity of white muslin curtains lying around her on the uncarpeted floor; she was busy mending some of them, and running strings into others, talking quite animatedly to Daniel, who stood over in the corner, with a large tin basin, busily engaged in washing and wiping some rich Bohemian glassware. The sunshine came in from a large open window, and filled the room with a warm, pleasant radiance as it glinted over the painted floor and shone on the gay-colored glassware.

Ruth looked surprised as Aunt Polly and Rachel entered, but began to smile quite complacently when Aunt Polly said,

"Dis here is my frien' Rachel, Ruth; she has come to make me a call, an' I has brung her down to see de house, as I knowed you was a airin' an' puttin' 'tings to rights, an' wouldn't mind showing me roun' a bit."

"Oh, no! I'se glad to see yer frien', Aunt Polly, an' will show her all de rooms in de house if she'll only 'scuse de order dey is in at present." Looking over to Daniel, she added, in what she meant to be a very stylish sort of manner, "Dat young gemman is Mr. Dan'el Vartner." Daniel acknowledged the introduction by a very polite bow, and immediately laid aside his towel, forgot his work and drew a chair up near the group.

"Oh, don't stop your work on my account," said Rachel; "we can talk just as well if you go on with your business."

"'Tain't no sort of consequence; I'se plenty o' time, an' had jist as lieve rest a bit as not; but you look tired; let me give you a glass o' wine—thar is some very good close by."

Rachel, who well knew that Daniel had no right to make this offer, and knew that he was only purloining it from his master's cellar for the purpose of making a show, declined taking any, saying she never drank wine; but Ruth and Daniel both insisted, and even Aunt Polly ventured to suggest that Rachel might as well indulge after her long walk, adding that she believed "the wine was quite handy."

"Git some, Dan'el; I'm sure Miss Rachel'll drink a drop when you brings it up; an' I'll git some cake, so as she can hab some lunch," said Ruth.

Aunt Polly knew all this was contrary to the slave's duty, but she had, in common with all other politicians, public and domestic, a sort of private casuistry by which she reconciled these little peccadilloes with her otherwise strict ideas of honesty; she believed, and sometimes went so far as to express it, "dat niggers had a right to all dey could eat an' drink dat belonged to dar masters; an' if it wasn't give to 'em, dey had a right to take it fur 'emselves." To speak the truth, we are somewhat of her way of thinking, and quite justify the slave in this kind of larceny. Since his master goes into the larger system of stealing the time, life and body of the slave, why should not the other, in a smaller way, imitate the example furnished by his master?

Daniel soon returned from the cellar with two bottles of the famous "Sparkling Catawba," and Ruth brought out a plate of fruit cake, some cheese and crackers, with a little of her mistress's most delicate currant jelly, which she ventered to say would do "for a relish."

A small table was drawn out in the centre of the room, plates of white and gold china (belonging to Mrs. Vertner's most elegant tea set) were furnished, and wine served in the Bohemian glasses. It was really a comically pleasant sight to see those three negroes—who had been used to take their meat and bread as best they might, sometimes on plates, but oftener in their hands, in the roughest and quickest manner—now partaking of an exquisite collation, using the best table-furniture, and drinking the best wine their master's cellar could afford.

"Doesn't yer like de flavor of dis wine, Miss Rachel?" inquired Daniel, as he drained off his glass and replaced it upon the table with a slight sort of jingle, as he had often seen his master do. "I likes it much better than that sour hock; an' as fur claret, it ain't got enuff sperit in it fur me."

"No," said Ruth, lolling back in the chair and poising an amber-colored wine glass upon her finger, "I doesn't at all like dat sour wine; it kind o' riles me all up an' makes me as sick as dough de gall-bag had broke in my stomach. Now, I likes dis de best; it makes me feel light like. We had some of dat bitter t'other day, an' it didn't 'gree wid me." As if to enforce her words, she gave her head a gentle toss, and, by some unlucky chance, she let the glass slip from her finger; it fell to the floor and was shivered to fragments. "Laws, Dan'el, you made me do dat 'ar—yer know you did," she exclaimed in terror; but, alas for the truth of her accusation, Daniel had been standing some distance from her at the time of the luckless accident.

"I'se bin a watchin' yer, Ruthy, and I jist knowed dat was gwine to happen; 'peared as dough I seed it fall afore it did," said Aunt Polly.

"Den, may be you sot a spell on it. I'se hearn o' sich tricks bein' done afore now."

"Wal, we hadn't no right to be a usin' of white folks' t'ings, an' dat is de reason it happen'd; fur my part, I done 'gin to 'pent o' my part and shar' in dis bisiness, an' wishes I could throw up off o' my stomach all dat I'se swallowed, for it wa'n't right to be a-robbin' of our master."

Daniel, who valued the privilege of showing himself a munificent host far more than he feared punishment, put on quite a lordly air and endeavored to treat the whole matter as the most trifling affair. With something of the grand gentleman's manner, he said:

"What does yer mean, Aunt Polly? 'Tain't no kine o' conserquence; it's only one wine glass dat is broke. Who keres fur dat? Missus ain't gwine to notice it. I doesn't even b'lieve it's worth talkin' 'bout; let it pass frum yer minds; don't speak of it; it's no sort o' conserquence. Here's another—a red one. Let me fill up yer glasses agin, ladies, an' we'll drink to de health of Col. Vartner."

"I 'grees to dat," said Ruth, who had recovered from her fright; and as Daniel gave her another glass, he said, *sotto voce:*

"Be pertickler wid dat glass; don't git in any more o' yer ways an' smash it." Then, filling the glasses of the others, Col. Vertner and Madge were separately pledged.

Rachel was growing tired of the frolic, and began to fear that the definite object of her visit would not be attained if this style of entertainment continued; so she ventured to remind Aunt Polly that her time was limited, and the day wearing on.

"Laws, yes, honey; an' I promised yer dat Ruth would show you de house. Here, Ruthy, kan't yer take Rachel an' me through de rooms?"

"Of course I ken, an' am happy to do it too. Whar's my keys, Dan?"

"Now yer see, Miss Rachel, what kine o' housekeeper we has here; if 'twasn't fur me, Ruthy would lose her keys." So saying, Daniel drew from his pocket a huge bunch of keys. Ruth snatched them from him, with a half peevish, half playful speech, then, requesting Rachel and Polly to follow her, led the way through the mansion. She conducted them with pride through the wide, airy hall into the elegant parlors, the sitting room, the library and breakfast apartment.

"Yer see the house don't look so nice as common; the curtains is all down, an' the picters kivered, an' a good many little ornaments put away till missus comes back. I'm jist tryin' to git things inter order afore they gits here."

"And when are they coming?" asked Rachel.

"Oh, Mrs. Mason's man was here yisterday to say his missus had a letter from Miss Helen, sayin' they was comin' the fust of next week, and dat my missus sent me word a gentleman was a-comin' 'long with 'em, an' I must have de spar room ready; so I'se jist as busy as ken be. But, Rachel, wouldn't you like to see Miss Madge's room? Jist foller me up stairs."

Everything in that strange little chamber struck Rachel with surprise; she looked around upon the guns, the stuffed animals, the queer pictures and the oddly-painted floor, and her amazement was very strongly expressed in her face.

"Ain't it a quare room?" said Ruth. "Miss Madge is more like a boy 'an a gal; she gives her ma a heap o' trouble 'bout her bein' sich a Tom-boy. Missus thinks it orful, an' she scolds enuff 'bout it; but master, he jist laughs an' says Miss Madge must have her own way. Peter says dat Miss Madge is a fair angel. Don't yer know 'at she went into town to see Jack an' Milly when dey was in jail, an' dat she jist stood up to her pa an' dat trader an' spoke her mind right out. She made master promise not to sell 'em, an' she don't know yit but what dey is hired out. When she git's word dey is down de river, she'll make an orful fuss, fur she's got a mighty strong way o' her own, she has." Aunt Polly shook her head as she finished this sentence.

"I tell you what," said Daniel, "I'd jist give my life to sarve Miss Madge. I don't b'lieve none of the talk I hears at meetin'; I didn't begin to know what they mean by religion till I heard Miss Madge talk 'long wid missus one evenin'. She knowed all 'bout Milly and Jack's runnin' off, for she heard 'em, the very night they went off, a-talkin' under her winder, an' she never told on 'em. I heard her tell missus she heard it. An' that's what I calls religion."

"Well it was, but I never knowed dat she knowed 'bout 'em gwine off, Dan," said Aunt Polly; "but, den, she is jist one of de best gals dat ever was born, an' dar ain't a nigger on dis place, from de biggest to de littlest, but loves her like dar life."

"Yes, but I allers wonders dat she don't love to dress finer, an' go, like oder young white ladies, to balls. I wish she'd go to town an' let me go 'long to wait on her. She ain't got none of 'em lady ways; she don't like to ride in de carriage, but gits on her pony an' goes 'bout de country by herself. Dat ain't right, miss knows."

"You hush, Ruth," put in Daniel; "don't yer say nothin' 'bout Miss Madge."

This conversation surprised and pleased Rachel; she was delighted to hear such glowing accounts of Col. Vertner's child from those who knew her so well; she saw at once that the master and mistress were both forgotten in the deep reverence with which the slaves regarded their young mistress.

"I am glad to hear that Miss Madge Vertner is such a kind and good-hearted person," she said with great earnestness; and, giving another long look at the room, as if to daguerreotype it upon her mind, she declared that as the day was wearing away so rapidly, she must be setting out for home. In taking leave of Col. Vertner's servants, she thanked them cordially for their kindness; and though they invited her to come to see them again, it was noticed that she did not reciprocate the politeness by asking them to her cabin.

When Rachel was gone, Ruth called her "an impudent free nigger, stuck up an' proud because she was light-colored and free"; but Aunt Polly smoothed it over by saying that "Rachel forgot to ax 'em, she knowed."

A thousand strange thoughts and old memories were aroused in Rachel's mind, as she retraced her homeward steps. The rich man's house, the account of his wild and spirited child, the devotion of the negroes to her, mingled up in the mulatto's mind with other thoughts, and she went plunging through her own past, digging up recollections that she had well-nigh forgotten. Though the orbit of her life had been

comparatively small and insignificant, we do not know what worlds
of beauty and stars of promise may have shone along the horizon of
her spirit. And now, when weary with the exercise and excitement
of the day, she paused to rest by the wayside, and, throwing off her
sun-bonnet, wiped the damp from her brow and pushed the masses of
heavy black hair from her forehead; her eyes shone out with a strange
and beautiful lustre; she looked like a sybil. A gentleman who was
passing by seemed suddenly struck by her appearance, and expressed
his admiration in a very decided look, which brought the red blood in
flashes and ripples to her brow and cheeks; but there was that in the
mien and glance of the man which told her he was a gentleman and
that she had no reason to fear insult from him. This stranger (who was
no other than the Yankee schoolmaster of whom we have heard) really
wished to stop and talk with her, but was deterred by a fear that it
might imply insult to her color, and so be passed with only that kind,
admiring look which first startled her. When she reached the cabin, she
found everything quiet and still; but poor Maria, who was fast shut in
the closet, told her that she had heard men's voices round the cabin, and
that some one had tried to open the door and had knocked two or three
times at the window. This alarmed Rachel, and made her long the more
intensely for Col. Vertner's return.

XVIII

Toward the close of a pleasant afternoon, just about the red, gloaming twilight time, the Vertner carriage drew up in front of the Vertner mansion; and before the coachman could dismount from his box, or swift little Pomp reach the side of the coach, Madge had flung open the door and leaped from the vehicle.

"Oh, I'm so glad to be at home!" she cried out, as, shaking hands with Pomp, she seized hold of Rover's ear, gave it a smart pinch, then threw her arms round his neck, and laid her own soft cheek upon the dog's shaggy head, saying all the while, in a low, affectionate tone, "Poor fellow—poor fellow—did he think I was never coming back to him? did he miss me? did Pomp neglect him? Never mind, old fellow, I've come back now, and we'll have famous romps together."

Rover received this salutation in the most beautiful and commendable manner, rubbing his head against his mistress's cheek, licking her hand, pressing close to her side, wagging his tail, all the while regarding her with a tender and intelligent eye.

Just behind the family carriage came a chaise, driven by Col. Vertner. By his side was seated Mr. Butler, whom he had persuaded to make him a visit.

"Only see my wild child," exclaimed the Colonel; "she has found her dog and really seems delighted to meet him; she is now lost to everything else."

"Madge, Madge, for shame," whispered Mrs. Vertner, as she rushed up to her daughter; "don't behave so; remember you are a young lady. Come away from that dog, and enter the house in a proper manner. Mr. Butler is looking at you."

"And what if he is?" asked Madge, as she turned her bright face up to her mother's. "Why, mamma, poor Rover is *so* glad to see me; he would feel hurt if I did not give him some sort of welcome." And, rising from the ground, she smiled and blushed as she glanced toward Mr. Butler, and asked, in a frank voice, "Are you disgusted with me for being so familiar with my dog?"

"Not at all; I was only admiring the reciprocal affection."

By this time Daniel had come to the door; smiling and bowing to his master and mistress, he said,

"Yer is welcome home."

"Well, Daniel, my boy, has everything gone on right?"

"Oh, yes, master, ever'thing has went on like clock-work. How's you and mistress bin?"

Colonel and Mrs. Vertner nodded to the servant, but Madge and Helen shook hands with him. Mr. Butler observed this difference. Daniel, assisted by one of the coachmen, began to detach the trunks from the carriage-boot, and Mrs. Vertner, followed by Helen Mason, Col. Vertner and Mr. Butler, entered the mansion, while Madge, eager to see the servants, ran off with Pomp and Rover to the quarter, where she was warmly welcomed. On entering the parlor, Mrs. Vertner's eye ran searchingly round the room, as if to detect some evidence of neglect or ill-usage, but, discovering nothing out of order, her features resettled into their calm, rigid expression.

Col. Vertner invited Mr. Butler into the dining-room, where, upon a marble sideboard, they found wine; and after refreshing themselves, the Colonel remarked,

"Now comes the favorite task of a Southerner. I must make a visit to the quarter and say how d'ye to the slaves. Would you like to take a turn among my people?"

Upon Mr. Butler signifying his pleased acquiescence, the two set out for the quarter.

As the negroes were expecting their master's visit, everything was in more than usual order. The children were dressed in their best clothes; the men and women, with pleasant, smiling faces, were sitting in front of their cabins, laughing and talking in a more than usually moderate tone; Alec, the overseer, dressed in his best Sunday gear, stood in a quite conspicuous place, prepared to give his master welcome and to render an account of his stewardship. Madge was seated at the door of Uncle Peter's cabin (with Pomp and Rover on either side), conversing with the old couple, telling them of all that she had seen, when a cry ran round the quarter, "Master's comin', master's comin'. Hurrah! welcome home," which was followed by a tossing-up of hats, waving of handkerchiefs and vociferous clapping of hands. When this noisy demonstration had ceased, and Col. Vertner had bowed to them, Alec stepped forward, almost immediately in front of his master, and, bowing very low and holding a somewhat worn straw hat in his hand, began his carefully-prepared speech:

"Mas'er, you'se welcome home; we is glad to see you back agin, lookin' so hale an' portly; we is pleased to know 'at you'se bin enjoyin' yerself in a nice little visit; an' we is allers glad to have yer come back to us in health an' life, an' de grace ov de Lord. I has done my best to keep things straight an' in order; I is pertickler pleased to tell yer dat all our people has 'haved 'emselves well an' wid 'priety; dar was no drinkin', card-playin', swearin' nor partyin' on de place whiles yer was absent. Here is de keys (holding up a huge bunch of heavy keys), an' I 'vites yer to visit every part of de place, de stables, cow-house, barn, an' all 'em buildins as comes under my jisdiction, an' see for yerself. An' now, wid wishin' yer agin, in de name of all yer sarvants, a welcome home, I'se no more to say"; and, bowing very low, amid the clapping of hands (in which Col. Vertner and Mr. Butler joined heartily) he retired. Col. Vertner then waved his hand very blandly, and, stepping a little in front, said:

"I am glad to hear such good accounts of your behavior in my absence, and thank you for the fidelity with which Alec says you have each and all of you discharged your work. Good servants will always work as well in their master's absence as when he is present. I believe my people have a feeling of honor; you all know that I trust you—that I leave you, to go on journeys, with a full faith that you will do your duty. I have always tried to be a good master to you, and I believe the relation which subsists between us is one of mutual affection; you are each and all bound to me as members of my family, and so I believe we shall always remain. None of you here present have ever given me trouble; and when, as in one certain case, I found that two of my slaves were discontented, it gave me a sore pang at heart. You all remember that case: pass it by" (he waved his hand as if anxious to sweep away the recollection of anything so unpleasant). "I think, at least, all of *you* are attached to me, as I certainly am to you, and I thank you again for your devotion. If any one of the number has any particular thing to say to me, he is privileged to come forward and do so. Take this, my people, and make merry over your master's return"; and he tossed a handful of coin into the group. Great scampering followed among the younger slaves, while several of the older ones, availing themselves of their master's permission, gathered round him to make personal inquiries after his health or to speak of some of their own little affairs. One woman, bearing a sick baby in her arms, came to have master look at her weakly one. With a kind inquiry and a good word, the master slipped a quarter of a dollar into the child's scrawny hands, and turned off to speak to Mr. Butler, when Pomp, running up, said,

"Master, Alec didn't tell yer, in his speech, dat de blue sow has a litter full o' little pigs, an' de brindle cow is got a calf, an' de ole brown mar' has a colt. Mas'er, ken I break dat colt when he's ready to be broke?"

Laughing heartily, Col. Vertner replied,

"Quite an accession to the family stock," and was moving off, when Pomp, springing in front, said,

"An', mas'er?"

"Well, what else, you young rascal?"

"I didn't git any of dat change you flung at us; de boys scrouged me out."

"I can't help that; you ought to have been faster; besides, I don't think, Pomp, you are likely to be behind the others when money is in the matter; but here, take this."

"Oh, thankee, sar—thankee"; and pocketing the shilling, he rejoined the group, boasting that he had got more than any of the others, for he had, by being fast, picked up the most, and also master liked him best and gave him a shilling because he had told him about the old sow and pigs.

The master's speech, which had been attentively listened to by the slaves, was followed by a great deal of coughing, a profuse fluttering of old, faded cotton handkerchiefs, blowing of noses, &c., by way of testifying to the roused emotion, sensibility and tenderness of the negroes.

"Did yer ever hear anything equal to dat 'ar speech o' mas'er?" said one of the black men; "it 'most broke my heart; he does kere heap fur us; 'pears like we's ongrateful to him."

Aunt Polly was particularly demonstrative in the expression of her emotion; she had made a great noise blowing her nose, and groaning out "bless Lord," "bless mas'er," and such expressions.

"I ken tell yer," said Uncle Peter, "dat Alec's speechifies well; he most come up to mas'er; dat 'ar Alec has got a spirit in him, an' talks like 'em folks as reads in de books; I didn't know de nigger could talk so well."

"Ah, Peter, how are you and Polly getting along?" called out the cheery voice of the master as he walked up to the cabin, with Mr. Butler.

"Putty well, I thanky, mas'er; how's it wid yerself?" answered the old man, rising from his chair.

"And Polly, how is it with your cabin? Any cleaner than usual?" As he said this, Col. Vertner pushed the door farther open with his cane, and peered curiously in.

"Oh, Laws, now, mas'er, to be sure, ever'thing is dirty and torn up as ken be; 'tain't bit fit fur yer eyes to look on; but Peter, he takes on so. Don't look in now, mas'er, fur marcy sake, an' let dat strange gemman see my cabin, all turned inside out"; and Polly pretended to hide her face with her apron, when, in truth, she was secretly chuckling over the fact that the cabin looked, to use her own phraseology, "nice as a bandbox."

"Things do look a little upset, Mr. Butler." Col. Vertner gave his friend a mischievous nudge, whispering at the same time, "The old woman is full of deception on these matters"; then speaking loudly, and turning to Polly, he added, "'Tis a pity, old woman, that you can't keep your cabin in better condition. If you don't mind Peter's comfort more, I shall have to make a change here, and send you off—hire you out, perhaps."

"Oh, Laws, mas'er, now, to be sure, you must be jokin', like, for dis here cab'n's done been rid up dis mornin', an' I scrubs it twice ever' week, an' dar ain't no chillen 'bout to unrange t'ings arter I fixes 'em, an' Miss Madge say she b'lieves it is de cleanest cab'n on de place; but den I'll be smarter arter dis, be up sooner in de mornin' an' knockin' roun' airlier."

"I'se right glad mas'er's done said what he has, Polly; now I hopes you'll quit dis here way o' lyin' dat you is allers in; you knows, an' you knows you knows, an' oder folks knows you knows, dat 'tis a lie when you says t'ings ain't clean 'bout dis cab'n, an' now I'se glad mas'er's done shot you up like a box."

"Well, to mend matters, Polly, here is money to buy you a new head-handkerchief and some tobacco for Peter's pipe," and, amid thanks, bows and curtseys, the master and his guest moved on round the quarter, pausing occasionally to speak to some old slave or throw a half-shilling to some crawling child.

Except for Mr. Butler's astuteness in perceiving a claw through a velvet glove, he might, like many another hospitably entertained stranger in Southern society, have been delighted with the seeming beauty, unity and happiness of the "patriarchal institution." As it was, he looked a little deeper; and that evening, when they sat round the elegant tea-table, his eye followed Daniel, who moved about, to all outward appearance a mere waiting-machine, a puppet, pulled whither and as his owners desired; but to one skilled in the analysis of that curious and illy-read book, the human face, this waiting-man's countenance had an expression which was not too full of content. Mr. Butler knew that though he appeared wholly occupied with his business, he was listening to every word of the conversation.

"Our good people, my dear," said Col. Vertner to his wife, "were, as I expected, delighted to have us come back, and were full of inquiries after your health. It really makes a master happy and proud to see so many poor dependent beings around him looking up to him as their benefactor and the dispenser of all their comforts and happiness. It makes my heart swell with gratitude to God, Mr. Butler, when I think of the great privilege I have of shedding peace and pleasure around. A sense of my own dependence upon the Good Being comes over me, and I bethink me of my duties and the responsible station to which I have been called; and thus, sir," continued Col. Vertner, as he replaced his empty cup in the saucer with a ringing sound—"thus, sir, I am confirmed in my original belief that slavery is a divinely ordained institution, acting for the mutual benefit of the white and black race. In this seemingly, to you, hard relation of master and slave, the best feelings and instincts—that of guardianship on the one hand and trusting dependence on the other—are kept alive. This ownership of slaves tends to awaken on the part of the owner all his best and highest social feelings. I've often travelled through our Northern States, and have been kindly entertained in Northern homes, but I always missed that genial, warm and ruddy glow of confidence and feeling which belongs only to Southern households, and is born of this very system of slavery which the insane Abolitionists would so cruelly crush out."

"Papa," said Madge, "if the slave system alone produces this genial glow of sentiment which you say is entirely peculiar to Southern homes, why don't we find it influencing Mr. McFarland's family, or General Dade's, or Capt. Wilson's, and many other families, where you and I know the greatest cruelty is practised and the greatest unhappiness endured?"

"My daughter, the persons you have named are mere brutes; they are not masters, and such men as you speak of are liable at any time to a presentation to the grand jury, and to be severely punished for their cruelty."

"Can any one present them, papa?"

"Yes, my dear."

"Then, why don't you do it? for I've heard you often say that such cruelties were intolerable."

"Madge," said Mrs. Vertner, in an under tone, as she pressed her foot rather heavily on her daughter's toe, "you must not join in gentlemen's conversation; 'tis not polite."

"Oh, mamma," cried out the girl, "you hurt my toe when you bear on it so."

"Madge!" exclaimed the terrified mother; but Col. Vertner indulged in a hearty roar of laughter, exclaiming,

"Ah, Madgy, darling, you are your own honest, single little self, and can't be otherwise. Mamma must excuse you. You see, Mr. Butler, my daughter, being an only child, has been allowed to grow up in a free and natural way."

Mr. Butler did not make any reply in words, but his eyes spoke volumes. Madge blushed deeply; perhaps she was beginning to read and interpret such glances. Pretty soon after, and to Mrs. Vertner's great relief, the gentlemen adjourned to the library to discuss politics, slavery, and perhaps *religion (?)*, over their wine and cigars. Madge went off for a stroll to the stable to see after Silk, and Helen Mason sat down to run over the keys of the piano and play some snatches of tunes as an accompaniment to her thoughts.

XIX

Days glided pleasantly on at the Vertner mansion. Helen Mason had gone home. Mr. Butler enjoyed himself in a quiet sort of manner, walking through the beautiful autumnal woods, roving about the "place," talking occasionally with the negroes or watching them at their work, all the while drawing his own inferences and deductions from the working of the slave system, of which he had heard and thought so much. Sometimes Madge walked or rode with him; not often, however, for, since her return home, she very naturally fell into her old habits, and he did not ask to be much with her, for he wished to study her character, and so gave her full liberty. Sometimes, it is true, he did wish she would not so steadfastly persist in her habit of retiring at nine o'clock in the evening; for when she left the drawing-room, he felt as if the brightest lamp had been put out, and the conversation always grew dull and heavy. Not that she ever talked much, but her very presence seemed to give an increased flow to his own ideas. She warmed and brightened him like sunshine, all the while herself unconscious.

One morning, as they sat round the breakfast-table, Col. Vertner, whose face looked a little disturbed and anxious, said,

"Madge, I shall leave Mr. Butler in your charge this morning; I am going out for a little ride, and may not return until after dinner."

Without noticing the first part of the sentence, she replied,

"Going out for a ride? Why can't I go with you?"

"Because I am going on business; and pleasant as your company is, I must decline it this morning."

"Where are you going?"

"Madge, why do you ask so many questions? hasn't your father told you he was going on business?" said Mrs. Vertner.

"Yes; but why can't he tell *me* what his business is? I want to go with him, and shan't disturb him in the least."

"No, my darling, I cannot let you go with me; stay here and entertain our friend Mr. Butler; you and he can take a ride or drive. To-morrow I shall be glad to have your company."

"That's the way I'm always put off with to-morrow; I never have anything my way."

"It seems to me, dear," replied her father, with a good-humored smile, "you have everything your own way, and that is why you are so petulant when the least opposition is offered to your wishes."

Madge was silent for a few moments, but there was a ruffled expression upon her face as she sat playing with her napkin-ring.

"Papa," she exclaimed, as the momentary cloud faded from her face, and a bright, happy expression succeeded, "do tell me where you have hired Milly and Jack. If it is near enough, I'll ride over and see them for awhile this morning; it will so please them."

Col. Vertner's face wore anything but a pleased expression as he answered,

"'Tis too far off, my child—quite a journey."

"But they are to come home next year, and it would be nice to make them a visit; I am sure they will be pleased to see me, for I was a favorite with them. Ain't you glad, papa, that you did not sell them? it would have been mean and cruel, and I shouldn't have loved you."

Col. Vertner rose from the table; his face was pale; Madge sprang to his side and wound her arms around him.

"Are you going now? *Must* you go? Well, give me a kiss; good-bye."

She followed him to the hall door, and stood looking affectionately after him as he rode hastily away. Mr. Butler lingered at the table, talking with Mrs. Vertner. Madge's eyes were yet gazing down the avenue in the direction her father had gone.

"I don't feel like talking to Mr. Butler this morning," she murmured; "I can't bear the house, and mamma is always scolding. What if I ride over to see Helen? No. But I shan't stay here; I'll have a gallop at any rate. Here, Pomp (she had spied the little elf peering round the gable), have Silk saddled and brought round; I am going out."

"Does yer want Rove let out de kennel? Is him gwine 'long too?"

"Oh, yes, let him come; he would whine if I left him behind." And Madge, after excusing herself to her mother and Mr. Butler, went off to get ready for the ride.

"A singular child," said Mrs. Vertner, as her daughter left the room.

"A very lovely one, I think," replied Mr. Butler; "her naïvete is perfectly irresistible."

"It gives me great pain to have her grow up so rude and uncultivated, but all I say to her falls on empty soil; indeed, I sometimes think the girl doesn't hear me when I am speaking to her, she is so indifferent; but her father, who has some most absurd notions, professes to consider it all right, and is insane enough to say he wouldn't have her changed. Though she is my own and only child, I must say that she is very far from being what I wish her."

The conversation was interesting to Mr. Butler simply because it was of Madge. Mrs. Vertner's perpetual note of complaint, her rigid formality, her want of literary culture, and undisguised assumption of high-breeding and fashion, disgusted him; but as Madge's mother and his lady host, he treated her with the utmost respect, although her conversation made him stifle many a good yawn.

....

If we look in at Rachel's cottage two hours later, we shall find it cleanly swept and everything set to rights, while she, in a fresh white apron and handkerchief, is seated on a low stool, close to Col. Vertner's side; her head rests on her thin hand, while the elbow is firmly planted upon the arm of the chair in which Col. Vertner is sitting. Her large eyes are fixed full upon his face; they are moist and anxious. He looks puzzled, moves about nervously in the chair, taps his foot with his riding-whip, puts his hat on and takes it off, puts it on again and again removes it, as one who is nervous and agitated. All the time, her eye has

been riveted upon him; never has it moved or quivered, only when she
brushed away a few tears that were gathering on the lashes.

"What is it, Andrew?" she at length asked. "Can nothing be done?
Am I to be tormented by such men, with no hope of protection?"

"I don't see, Rachel" (he placed his hand upon her head), "what
can be done; you are a mulatto and free; therefore it is hard to say it,
but, nevertheless, it is true, no one can assume your affair; if you were
a slave, it might be otherwise; you would be under the protection of
your—"

"*Master,*" she added, with a curling lip. "Andrew Vertner, do you
think this is right—is it Christian—is it human?"

"Certainly not, Rachel; I feel it as much, almost more than
you do; but how can I avoid it? It is one of the evils that grow out of
condition. If I could make it better for you, I would; but I have no
power in these affairs."

She drew back from him for a moment, ran her eye down the
whole length of his person, as if taking in at a glance the dimensions of
the man, then said, in a slow, sarcastic tone, as if counting her words,

"If you could make it better for me, you would! Are there no
others for whom you would make it better?" and, putting her lips close
to his ears, she hissed out two words that made him turn pale as death.

"Good God, Rachel!"—he seized hold of her arm; drops of
foam flecked his lips, and his eyes were blazing—"what do you mean,
woman? Do you try to drive the knife where my heart is sorest?" and,
releasing his hold upon her arm, he sank back into the chair and
covered his face with his hands; great hot tears broke through the parted
fingers, and the strong, rich man sobbed aloud.

Rachel was frightened; she had never seen Col. Vertner so moved,
and she now became fully conscious what a powerful spring in his
nature this one was which she had pressed. She sat still, watching him
as the cat watches the mouse it is charming through fear. All her nerves
were strung to the highest; her pulse was bounding like a mad cataract;
one moment she was about to leap upon her victim, with the bitter
word and the terrible threat, when suddenly the woman returned to
her. She was softened, and creeping closer to him, gently drew his hand
from his face, and, looking up into his eyes, while tears stood in hers,
she said,

"You need fear nothing from me, Andrew; I am true; from my love you can expect hereafter, as in the past, everything."

He put his arms round her; he drew her to his bosom; he kissed her brow, cheek, lips, neck and hands.

"Rachel, Rachel, tell me that you will never make this matter known; tell me that you will be true; I am a miserable man; God knows, if I have sinned, I have suffered severely. Rachel, have I been unjust or unkind to you? Tell me what I can do to make atonement, and I will, freely; only be true in this one matter; will you, Rachel?"

His face was full of pain and his voice earnest and beseeching.

She looked around startled. Laying her hand on his shoulder, she said,

"Speak low."

"Is any one concealed here?" he asked, rising hastily.

She threw wide open the door that led into the inner room.

"See for yourself," she exclaimed.

Satisfying himself that there was no one there, he asked,

"Why, then, were you afraid of our being overheard?"

"People might be loitering round my cabin, you know" (with bitterness); "there is nothing or no one to protect a free woman of color."

"Rachel, you know well enough that, so far as I can, I will protect you; you know, or you ought to know, that the blow which falls on you strikes also upon my heart—that your interest is near and dear to me."

Her head had fallen upon her breast; her long arms swung gracefully down; the attitude was full of significance, and seemed to strike Col. Vertner. He caught her by the arm; he stroked her hair, and spoke words of kindly soothing: she was cheered. We are all children, and never outgrow our love of bon-bons, no matter whether they are manufactured of sugar or that still more dangerous material, *fond words*.

After a few more instructions and cautions to Rachel, he signified that to remain longer now would be dangerous. "The danger," however, did not impress him until after he had decidedly obtained the object of his visit; *it never does*. When he had found out all he wanted to learn, then the *danger* increased and culminated. Springing quickly into the saddle, he paused for a moment, to hear a few farewell words, which poor Rachel, in her foolish fondness, needs must address to him. The bridle-rein hung loosely over the neck of his horse; Rachel was close at his side, with her hand resting on the saddle, and, as she spoke low and tenderly, she forgot where and with whom she was; not so with her companion; no personal or affectionate feeling so utterly occupied his mind as to blind him to the probable dangers of his position.

"What noise was that? Some one is coming up the wood-path; I am sure I heard horses' feet," he said, breaking in upon some loving phrase of hers.

"No," she replied, with a smile, "'tis only the cows, that have not been turned out to-day. How easily you are alarmed now-a-days."

"There again," he exclaimed, "some one *is* coming."

Scarcely had the words died on his lips than Madge Vertner rode up to the gate.

"Why, papa!"

"Madge!" It was not the usually tender expression of his voice.

"Papa, whose cabin is this? and what a pretty ride through the thicket. I was surprised on the main road to find what appeared to be a pretty and romantic path leading through the woods, and determined to explore it; it led me here; but I didn't expect to meet you. Who is that woman?" pointing her whip toward Rachel, who had, during the first part of the sentence, retreated to the cabin-door.

"Don't forget to have the sewing done in time," cried Col. Vertner to Rachel.

She nodded assent. Madge's eyes were fixed upon her.

"Who is *she,* papa?"

"A sempstress, my dear, who is doing some work for me; but come on, now, we'll have a ride; I am through with my business"; and, giving Silk a cut of his whip, and drawing his own rein a little tighter, both horses started down the path at a quick rate.

"But, papa, that was a very beautiful mulatto woman. I liked her face so much. How lady-like she appeared; are you quite certain she *is* a *sempstress?*"

Madge's eyes were fixed inquiringly upon her father; he quailed a little before the keen glance, but, with an effort at his customary self-possession, replied,

"Yes, she *is* a sempstress. I wished some sewing done for some of the servants, and have employed her."

"I should like to come here some time with you and see about the work; this woman strikes my fancy."

"Perhaps so."

"Is she free?"

"Yes."

"It would be a pity for such an interesting and lady-like woman to be in slavery. What's her name, papa?"

Madge bent forward and peered into her father's face in a manner which was not at all agreeable to his self-complacency. He gave her hasty answers, and seemed anxious to change the subject of conversation, but Madge was wilful and asked fifty questions.

"I tell you," exclaimed her father, in an irritated voice, "that I know nothing of the woman except that she is a good sempstress."

"Well, I *must* know more of her; and as I have nothing particular to engage my time, I'll attend to this sewing you are having done, and can ride over to the cabin every morning."

"Madge Vertner, don't you *dare* to go again to the cabin of this free negro. If you do, I shall not soon forgive you. Madge, I have never been seriously offended with you; but if you violate my wishes in this respect, I shall be deadly grieved."

"Why, papa, how very odd this is. What possible objection can you have to my going to this woman's cabin?"

His voice and manner were a little softened and rather more careless as he now answered,

"Is it odd, my dear, that I should feel some little pride in you? that I should prefer that my only daughter should be choice and select in her associations, and, above all things, guarded and particular about the places she frequents? It might not appear well for you to be dropping in, making social calls at the cabin of a free negro woman; you don't know to what rudeness or insolence you might be subjected."

"I should go to see her only as a sempstress, and am not afraid of being rudely or insolently treated. However, it is of no great consequence; and if you don't wish me to go, I shan't; that ends the matter"; and whipping up their horses, they were soon cantering off in the direction of the village.

Very little more was said between the father and daughter; they now rode rapidly on until reaching town, when Madge signified her intention of visiting Helen Mason, and, bidding her father a cheerful good morning, turned down a private street. She found Helen in the parlor, with a gentleman whom she introduced as Mr. Norton, and whom we recognize as the Yankee schoolmaster, supposed by the villagers to be tainted with the odor of abolitionism. After the formality of the introduction had passed off, Mr. Norton remarked,

"I think I've seen you before, Miss Vertner."

"Ah?"

He then referred to the time when he met her in the woods, and she had so kindly directed him the way to the village.

"Perhaps so," said Madge, "but I have certainly forgotten it."

Mr. Norton was too earnest a man and close a thinker to talk twaddle or nonsense, so he soon directed the conversation to *subjects*. But when he spoke of books, Madge acknowledged, with unaffected frankness, that she never read; he then spoke to her of her out-door life, her love of animals, her horsemanship, her sports with the gun, &c.

"I never liked fishing," she said; "perhaps because I am not contemplative, and am too rapid of movement. To sit on the river side, with a hot sun pouring down upon you, waiting for a fish to nibble, would be as dull to me as reading a book or a newspaper."

"Don't you read the morning papers?" inquired Helen.

"No, indeed; I learn the news just as the negroes do, by hearing it talked about."

This allusion to the negroes was the suggestion to Helen of directing the wheels of conversation into another groove.

"Do you know, Madge," she added, "that I have told Mr. Norton how near you are to being an Abolitionist?"

"Well, how near am I?"

"*Madge!*"

"Why, Helen, I don't know fully what the word Abolitionist means; papa and mamma make it stand for something very dreadful, irreverent and wicked; but Mr. Butler has a very nice and humane definition. Now, I have always thought, of course, that slavery was right. Our servants seemed contented and happy, and were looked upon as part of our family; but then, if they are dissatisfied and wish to quit, I surely think they ought to go, and that no one should prevent them."

"That would be voluntary servitude," put in Mr. Norton; "but don't you think they should be paid fairly for their labor, Miss Vertner?"

"Are they not fed and clothed?"

"Yes, and, without inquiry about the style, quality and quantity, I'll go on to say, that I object to a system which so nullifies the energies of a whole class. When a man works for his money, and then, when it is acquired, exercises his own faculties in the disbursing or investing of it, he is strengthening his power, developing himself and growing; but there is another and higher view still to take of the subject: Can man have property in man?"

Here followed the clear statement of ideas which are old to our readers as a hundred-times-told tale, but were entirely new and startling to Madge and Helen. They gathered close to his side and listened with earnestness. Madge threw off her hat, brushed back her curls and fastened her eyes eagerly upon Mr. Norton's face; she marvelled at his quietude; once, in her excitement and in her own intense manner, she seized him by the arm, exclaiming,

"But, sir, the remedy? What would you do to stop all this?"

"Ah," he said, in a slow, calculating tone, "there comes the difficulty; it is a monster work, a huge, horrid Iniquity which we cannot strike down at once; we must go cautiously and gradually to work, use method and means, arrest its growth, confine, limit it, cut it off limb by limb, crib and cabin it, keep it out of the territories, restrict, imprison it, until, for want of room, it turns and bites itself. A bold blow now, directed to the evil itself, would be fatal."

Madge hesitated, was silent; there was a doubtful expression upon her face; she played with the strings of her riding-hat, which lay upon her lap; she bit her lip; light and shadow flitted alternately across her face; when at length, looking up, with a clear, open countenance, she said,

"No, Mr. Norton, I don't see your way; if the thing is wrong, it ought to be abolished at once; if it is a sin to hold slaves, let them be freed to-day; don't tamper with wrong; overthrow it at once; strike it a good open-hand blow—that's my doctrine."

"Yes, you are a good-hearted child, and speak from your own generous inexperience. The cure of evil will be the work of years, and a slow work too, I regret to say."

"Well, it needn't be slow," said Madge, "if people are earnest in what they say. I don't see why you urge no tampering with slavery as it now exists. If it is wrong, fight it; you wouldn't tell me to gradually abandon the practice of lying and stealing; you would say, quit it at once. The temperance preacher tells the drunkard to give up drinking at once, not even to handle the bottle, touch not and taste not. Let the anti-slavery preacher teach the same. When you once convince the slaveholders of the wrong of keeping slaves, they will give them up."

Mr. Norton smiled incredulously, and Madge continued,

"Of course they will. People wouldn't do wrong if they knew it; they are deceived."

Madge became so deeply interested in the conversation that she remained several hours. Helen was delighted to find her friend and lover chime in so well. On bidding Mr. Norton good-bye, Madge insisted that he should come out to the "Vertner place" and that they should talk the matter over in her father's and Mr. Butler's presence.

XX

The thought of Rachel, and the desire to see and know more of her, did not long trouble Madge. She soon put it out of her mind; but Mr. Norton's conversation constantly recurred to her. Pondering upon it, she did not quite understand his arguments, for hers was one of those open, straightforward, spontaneous minds that take in the sum-total of an idea in a single glance, and do not gradually approach or grow up to it. If received at all, it was taken *at once and wholly*. So now she began to think "if slavery *is wrong, it is wrong,* so there's the end of it. We should not compromise with or excuse it." She did not like Mr. Norton's talk about caution, waiting, working by inches, slowly strangling slavery, at the same time pampering it. This was not in accordance with her simple ideas—for she was no politician. Wrong was wrong. But then, with all her wilful determination, there was a slight distrust of her own powers which sometimes made her slow to act. She now thought long and earnestly upon the subject, and watched the servants with greater interest. Their very faces became a close study; she questioned them a great deal, and they answered her with frankness. Col. Vertner observed the thoughtful expression of his daughter's face, and marvelled at the cause. She now rode and walked oftener with Mr. Butler; but his calm, practical, prudently-expressed views upon the subject of slavery did not suit her impetuous enthusiasm. The difference between her and him was that he *thought,* while she *felt;* her dislike of slavery was a passion, born in the very heat, intensity and redness of her heart; while his was a calm thought conceived of the brain, matured and grown by long, timely and philosophical reflection; it had all the coolness, calmness and prudence of the head unfevered by the heart. Madge used sometimes, in her own rapid way, to break off the conversation by saying,

"Oh, nonsense, Mr. Butler, the thing is either right or wrong; if it is wrong, why, it's wrong, and let us do away with it, not in two or three years, but right off. I don't care about the 'advisability,' the 'practicability,' and those sort of things; let us have freedom at once."

"But, my dear young lady," pursued the sober Englishman, "let us look at its political aspects; let us consider—"

"No, I shan't consider its political aspects, because I can't understand them; let us look rather at its moral deformities."

In this way she often fretted him out of his coolness, and puzzled him as only a pretty and wilful girl can puzzle a sober and serious man. But she had determined to have a talk with her father, and, contrary to her usual manner, she deferred the interview from day to day. Two or three times she went to his library door, put her hand upon the knob, intending to enter for the purpose of having a serious conversation with him, but her heart failed her, and she whispered to her conscience, "Be still till to-morrow; then I'll speak fully, clearly to him"; but when the morrow came, she always found that her timidity had increased, and she was still another day off from the purposed interview. Yet the thought worked anxiously in her heart. At last, nerving herself, she ventured to ask him if he would not join her in a woodland walk. Readily consenting, they set out, one bright October morning.

"Well, daughter," said Col. Vertner, as they sauntered along through the gloriously-colored woods, "you have been looking rather more serious than usual; what is the cause of it?"

This direct question relieved her of a great deal of embarrassment, and she began at once:

"Yes, papa, dear, for the first time in my life I have been thinking deeply. Now, is it right for white people to keep negroes in slavery?"

The question was simply, but earnestly, asked; there was something in the tone that made it impressive. Her father started, but quickly, in a moment's time, recollecting himself, said,

"Why, yes, Madge, I think it is entirely right for a noble, powerful, rich and dominant race to subjugate and hold to drudge-service a weak, ignorant and servile one."

"How do you make it out, papa?" She drew a little closer to him and took his hand within hers, while they slowly continued their walk.

"Ah, well, my little girl, it is a difficult question to answer; I should have to go into a great deal of dull, dry, and perhaps unprofitable, talk before I could make you understand it. Suffice it, my dear, that your father, mother, minister and friends believe it to be true, and don't vex your young brain with such useless cogitations; think of something else. Tell me, however, dear, who has been worrying you with this cant about the injustice, the right or wrong of slavery? Has Mr. Butler dared to forget the duty of a guest, and so abuse my hospitality as to tamper with the peace of my child's mind?"

"I have talked freely with Mr. Butler on this subject; but, then, *I* always introduced it. So far as etiquette is concerned, papa, he has violated no rule; yet he has not refused to answer my questions on the ground that *I could not understand him.*"

"Don't be piqued, dear; I did not mean to insult your judgment. Yet slavery is a subject that I don't wish to bother your young brain. Think of other and more pleasant matters. Women who talk and rave about the moral wrong of slavery are, for the most part, poor, unhappy, unsexed sort of creatures, odious to society and cut by all respectable people. I don't wish my child to be of them."

"Yet, papa, I don't believe slavery is right, and with *respectable people's* opinions I have nothing to do. My own conscience is arbiter alone in this matter."

"Again, Madge, I must warn you not to speak of this to me or to any one; *think* what you please, but be careful what you *say.*"

"Rest assured, papa, I shall always say what I think; I am no slave, to meanly hide my opinions. Who and why should I fear?"

"Don't you fear your father's displeasure?"

"Yes, if I feel I deserve it; but when I know I am doing right, I can even defy my father's displeasure. A great principle, papa, does not, should not, consider relationships of any kind. 'Forsake father and mother for Christ Jesus' sake,' is one of the favorite maxims of our good old minister, and I think I am prepared to act upon it."

Col. Vertner had never heard his daughter speak with such earnestness, and was not a little surprised.

"Ah, dear," he suddenly cried, as he flung his arm around her, "see that squirrel leaping from the limb of yon beech tree; if you had your gun, he would tax your sight."

"Oh, I am sure I could shoot him; I've fired at more uncertain marks than he. How I wish that I had my gun! See, see, papa, he is still now; how prettily he sits on that bough, cracking his nuts; only look at him; pretty Bun. Now he is gone; how swift! almost equal to a bird. It would have been a pity to shoot him."

Her father had struck upon the right subject for the diversion of her thoughts, and now an animated conversation upon shooting, horseback riding, field sports, &c., ensued, in which full confidence and affection were restored between the father and child. Madge's spirits were soon as high as ever; she bounded back to her old accustomed mood quick as a bough from which a bird of ill omen has flown away, or like a spring the moment pressure is withdrawn. Col. Vertner's eyes flashed with pride as he watched her scampering along, hallooing, singing, whistling, calling to the squirrel, throwing sticks at the birds, paddling her "wee sma' feet" through the fresh fallen leaves of October, while her long curls were blown about by the fresh autumnal wind, her eyes sparkling and her cheeks flushing with the excitement.

"How she loves nature!" he exclaimed; "what an untamed and untameable child she is! God grant that no shadow ever may fall upon her! Be careful there, Madge; don't run against that tree; you might put your eye out; see, the limb swoops down quite low; do be careful."

"Why, papa, don't you think I can take care of myself? I have almost lived in the woods, and it is funny for you, now, to fear the bough of a tree or a hazel bush."

The echoes of her merry laughter resounded through the forest, pleasant as the chimes of May-day bells.

When they returned to the house, Madge was surprised to find Helen Mason and Mr. Norton. She gave them a cordial welcome, and insisted upon their remaining until after dinner.

"Oh, Mr. Norton," she cried, as she grasped his hand in the most friendly manner, "I'm so glad to see you; we shall have a real good, true talk; I have been thinking of what you said ever since we parted, and I long to have the conversation repeated."

Her artless and enthusiastic manner greatly pleased Mr. Norton, though he had rather she would not advert to their former topic of conversation; but Madge determined her father should have the full benefit of such arguments. Her mind was beginning to take fire on the subject, and she could neither think nor speak of anything else.

"Come, Madge, let me go to your room," Helen asked, "to take off my bonnet and shawl."

When once fairly domiciled in Madge's unique apartment, Helen caught her friend by the hand, exclaiming,

"Oh, Madge, I've something to tell you, which I am afraid will make you very angry."

"What is it?"

"Promise me that you'll not be *very* angry."

"I can't promise until I know what it is you have to tell."

"Well, well, Madge—oh, I hate to tell you."

"But you must," answered Madge, in a firm tone.

"Well—oh, I can't—"

"You *must* speak." Madge took hold of both of Helen's hands and held them tightly. "Tell me at once, in the fewest possible words, Helen Mason."

"Your father told you—did he not?—that he had only hired Jack and Milly."

"Yes."

"Well, it is false; he sold them both to that horrid trader whom you met in the L—— jail."

"*It is a lie!*" was Madge's prompt and emphatic reply.

"*Madge!*"

"*Helen!!*"

Our young heroine was very pale, and her eyes flashed scornfully, as she still held Helen's hands tightly clasped within her own, and her lips trembled, while a bluish-gray tinge began to settle about her mouth.

"I have not repeated to you, Madge, an idle, floating village rumor. I inquired and found out that it was true. Your father has deceived you."

For a moment Madge stood very still, with an erect head; then, suddenly loosing her hold upon Helen's hands, she said, in a low, scarcely audible tone,

"If he has deceived me, cruelly, wickedly trifled with my sympathies, I shall hate him."

"Madge Vertner!"

Helen was frightened; she had never heard Madge speak thus of her father. "Madge Vertner," she called out a second time, but Madge stood quiet and firm, with her eyes bent upon the floor. "Yes, yes," she muttered to herself, "and this is why he would not tell me where he had hired them. He said it was a long journey, and now, as I recollect, he *was* a little confused. Oh, yes, I begin to understand—he has deceived me—treated me as though I were a foolish, fretful child; he has *lied* to me, and I'll confront him with his lie." She moved toward the door. Helen stepped in front.

"What, Madge, you will not go to him now? He will blame me for telling you. Please don't go to him yet; wait awhile, please."

"It is no matter, Helen, what he thinks; you and I know that he has lied; he knows it; that jailer and trader know it; worse than all, *God knows it.*"

"But, for my sake, Madge, dear, don't speak to him just yet. Remember there is company in the house."

"Helen, I can't think of anything else but the lie my father has told me, and the poor trusting negroes believed so entirely that I could and would save them. Why did I leave that jail? Because I had faith in my father's word; and he has lied to me! Helen, as you urge it so strongly, I'll wait until after dinner before I speak to him; but be sure I shall not spare him."

"Now, Madge, try to be calm; look and act like yourself; don't let any one suspect how you are feeling."

"Oh, yes, Helen, you wish me to look a lie, as my father has uttered one."

Madge was very bitter; her confidence in her father had been so entire, so perfect, that this revelation came to her as a crushing blow. However, governing herself as best she could, she and Helen soon descended to the parlor, where they were joined by the rest of the company. Madge's eyes were often, and for several minutes at a time, fastened upon her father. Helen thought she saw the eye flash, the lip quiver and the nostril dilate with scorn.

<h1 style="text-align:center">XXI</h1>

John Sharpe and Tom Hynes were in close conversation in a corner near the stoop of the L—— tavern. Evidently they had some important affair to consult upon, for their heads were very close to each other, and they talked in a low tone, looking round cautiously every two or three moments, as if fearing listeners.

"I tell yer, Tom," said Sharpe, in a grave voice, "I jest believes some runaway is hid in that free nigger's cab'n. I was prowlin' 'bout thar, t'other night, an' I hearn talk till a late hour. I crawled up putty close to the side of the winder, but I couldn't ketch any words, but the buzzin' of voices was plain to me as that nose in yer face. Well, I watched thar' smack till daylight, an' nobody come out of that cab'n. 'Twasn't none o' the neighborin' niggers a-visitin' Rachel. I'd give the very pick o' my pigs to ketch that gal in some kind o' mischief. Consarn her imperdence, she once riled up agin' a little fun I offered her, jest the same as if she war white. Them merlattoes is orful proud, an' the free ones mightily sot up. But do yer know, Tom, that folks in these parts is beginnin' to talk about Col. Vartner; he's bin seen a heap o' times stealin' away from that cab'n. Now, I sorter 'luded to this to that yaller wench, an' she jist flew at me equal to any tabby cat, and clawed an' scratched my face. Well, I swore then I'd be trouble to her, and I means to keep my oath."

"I've no objections to yer bringin' the yaller hussy inter trouble; but what do you want to draw me inter yer work fur? I've nothin' agin' the gal; besides, I don't want to make Col. Vertner mad; he is a rich man an' a gentleman, an' spends his money freely. I doesn't want no fuss with him."

"Not if you can git a job o' work as'll fetch you a fat fee?"

"Now, you're comin' to sense. I ken listen with consideration to you when you talks 'bout fees. That view of the subject alters the case very materially. Now to bisness. What is it you mistrusts?"

"I ken change yer way o' thinkin' an' reasonin' mighty quick, Hynes, when I talks 'bout money; I tells you I jist b'lieves if you war' dead an' a person was to lay a sixpence under yer nose, you'd come back to life."

"Consarn yer triflin'; go on with bisness. What rat have you bin a-smellin' round that free nigger's cabin?"

"I tell you I does know an' feel that thar' is a nigger hid thar'—a runaway *too;* how does you know but it may be the widder Vitetor's Maria? I'd be glad to have that gal kotched; she b'longed to a widder woman, an' I ain't fur them sort a-bein' cheated out of their rights; an' then, too, I'd like to have that gal, Rachel, well punished fur her tarnation imperdence to me. Now, I'm goin' to keep up a close watch round that cab'n, but I ain't nothin' in trackin' runaways to what you are. S'pose you jist gives that cab'n an eye?"

"Well, I will look after it now, since you seem so sure that somebody is hid thar'. I'd like to ketch that Vitetor gal: she was rale ungrateful to her old mistress, who, they say, raised her jist as kind as though she'd bin her own child; but them's the kind as allers gives the slip when they gits a chance. But darn my buttons if I don't b'lieve, after all, that a nigger an' a hoss both has a right to tharselves if thar legs can carry 'em off."

His companion looked at Hynes distrustfully; he was puzzled, and, for want of a proper expression of surprise, laughed. Some brutes are not all brutes; occasionally we see a faint, very faint, flash of something better, something that gives us a partial promise of *what might be,* under different and better training.

"Well, I'll see 'bout this job, John; I'll be lookin' round that cab'n; an' if I find a runaway thar', he may look out fur sure ketchin'. Good mornin'; I must be off now"; and, whittling at a stick, Hynes moved away in the direction of a group of idlers seated upon the front steps of the building.

"Good mornin', 'Squire; good mornin', Capt. McFarland; good mornin', Mr. Bosby"; and touching his hat slightly, Tom Hynes was soon at home with the *precious* crowd; while John Sharpe, not altogether pleased with his chum's treatment, skulked quietly off to indulge his revenge in secret. Rachel's insult had never been forgotten, not even for a single moment, but was nursed in his heart, and he looked forward with anxious hope to the day and the hour when he might bring ruin to her. His dull brain, which had never known the higher enjoyment of thought, was now never weary of plodding and devising plans and schemes by which best to carry out his wicked design against a helpless woman. As he walked down one of the streets of L——, with his head slightly bent, a sickly sort of light broke over his countenance; the usually sullen eye began to twinkle most viciously and his lips to wreathe or writhe themselves into a sardonic smile.

"Yes," he muttered, "I'll hunt up that nigger man Isaac and set him on this bisness, and I'll be bound matters'll soon come to a head."

Pursuing his walk for some yards until he reached the outskirt of the village, he stopped in front of a blacksmith's shop, and stood, with his arms resting upon the sill, gazing into the open shop window.

A large, heavily-built black man (slightly lame), in a leathern apron, stood over the red, glowing fire, looking down into the blazing coals, singing fast as the sparks flew from his heated forge. Sharpe's figure darkened the window and the smithy looked up suddenly, while a broad smile spread over his face.

"Good mornin', Mas'er Sharpe; good mornin'"; and brushing the heat from his forehead with the sleeve of his tow shirt, he left the furnace, and, coming close to the window, seemed to know that he was wanted for a special purpose.

"What is it, Mas'er Sharpe?"

"Oh, nothin'; I only thought I'd look in on you a bit; hard work that, ain't it?"

"Putty hard, Mas'er, but still heap better than no work."

"So yer wouldn't like to live easy an' be without work?"

The negro laughed aloud as he replied,

"No, mas'er, I'd not like to live all the time widout work to do; work is jest as wholsesome fur me as meat; but den I likes fur Sunday to come; I couldn't live widout it. Sunday sorter hopes one up fur Monday, and I kan't say I'se sorry to see Monday come round agin."

"Wal, Isaac, you're one of 'em rare niggers that loves work; 'tain't common fur a nigger to work 'cept he is afraid of the cowskin."

"Ha, ha, ha!" Isaac's loud laughter rung out in a peal at this. "Dat ain't me, Mas'er Sharpe; dat ain't me, no how; I don't work bekase I'se afeared. No, sir-ee. I works bekase these hands won't be still. I had a bilious fever once, an' my ole miss declared dat my fingers wouldn't hold still; I jist fumbled an' worked 'mong de bed-close until it tired 'em all to look at me. Ya, ya! I hain't got none of 'em lazy bones in dis ole carcass of mine."

"Well, now, I have got a job o' work fur you that'll pay well if yer 'tends to it right.

"What is it, Mas'er Sharpe?" The black man's face began to fairly *shine* at the prospect of making money. "What is it, Mas'er Sharpe?" He limped a little closer, until his woolly head touched Sharpe's hat; and here an earnest little conference ensued. Isaac looked troubled; he shook his head—occasionally bowed; his countenance all the while wearing a serious, puzzled expression. "But, Mas'er Sharpe," he said, raising his voice from the whispering tone in which the colloquy had hitherto been conducted, "dis here may bring us into trouble; you can soon git out of it; but what's a nigger like me gwine to do? I'se not very skeery, but den I'd rader not hab anyt'ing to do long o' dis here; it's gwine to bring trouble; I seems to see dat much."

"D—n it, how ken it bring trouble to your black skin? I tell you again, I'll take kere of you; an' if you sarves me in this job, you'll not have cause to be sorry; but if you doesn't do what I asks, you'll have occasion fur trouble in real earnest. You remembers that ten dollars I lent to you?"

"Yes, Mas'er Sharpe, I 'members it well, an' hopes soon to pay it back."

"Wal, I sarved you then; you sarve me now."

"I'll do what you wants, Mas'er Sharpe." The negro's tone was hopeless, but Sharpe spoke in a lively manner,

"Cheer up, Isaac; the day is gittin' brighter fur you; you will yit be a free man, it's plain to me; I'm willin' to help you."

"Ah, mas'er, it 'pears to me that day goes furder an' furder off. When I was a young man, 'bout eighteen, I hoped dat twenty-five would not find me a slave, Oh" (he heaved a deep sigh), "dat day looks mighty fur back in de old times now; here I is forty-five an' no nearer my freedom now than I was den." The head went down lower and lower on the breast until the face was entirely concealed. Sharpe stood curiously watching his victim and his tool; large drops fell down upon the negro's dirty tow shirt, but they were not tears (those old hard-worked eyes could not weep), but bitterer drops than tears: they broke from the skin in a sweat of chill agony, and burst out thickly over the brow, throat, cheeks, and, in fact, from every pore of that black body. It was the gathered rain shed from clouds of grief old almost as the slave's life. But they did not tell upon the sympathy of his curious beholder. Sharpe gazed at that drooping figure with as careless an eye as he would have looked upon a horse.

"Come, don't be down-hearted; cheer up; all will be well with you after a bit; only sarve me, an' yer wont be forgotten."

The interview was here cut short by a man calling out, "Come, Isaac, I wants you to shoe this horse."

<h1 style="text-align:center">XXII</h1>

When Isaac went that night to see his wife (who was owned by one of the villagers), she was surprised to find him so silent. At first, Hetty appeared not to notice him, but flourished round the kitchen, manifesting the usual amount of feminine and conjugal contempt; but seeing that Isaac did not observe her, but sat absorbed in himself, she could stand it no longer, and broke out,

"Well, now, *Isic,* what does you call dat 'ar? Come here to see me and jist sets dar like an ole hen on her nest, fur all de world. Yer doesn't see me more 'an two nights out of de week, an' yet yer jist sets dar an' don't speak a word. I'd like to know what company you considers yerself fur me. Ain't I bin all dis day a-hurryin' thro' my work, so as to git a bit o' chance to talk long wi' you when you come? I kan't see no use in yer comin' here at all, if dat is de best you ken do. Now, jist look at yerself, will you? You is old enough, an' big enough, an' ugly an' black enough, to know how to behave yerself when you comes to see yer wife. You never brings me anything, not so much as an apple or a cake. What 'comes of yer money now? I knows you makes some. You needn't deny it to me, but you takes mighty good kere to keep it all to yerself; do you hear dat, Isaac?"

While saying this, she had been, all the time, busy in preparing the supper, pausing every two or three moments to use her arms and hands in gesticulation. Receiving no answer from Isaac, she burst out in a louder tone,

"No, you is not de man to take kere of yer own. I gits no money 'cept what Grace makes, and she, agin' my will, sings an' dances in front of dat tavern, an' white men flings her money, an' I takes it from her."

This roused Isaac.

"What! does my gal sing an' dance before dat tavern? I never hearn dis afore. Let me ketch her at dat an' I'll take de very hide off her. She had better be after her work. Look a here, Hetty, I doesn't want to hear no more of dis. Dat gal is a smart gal. I knows she is black; I knows she is a slave; but den she is *my chile,* fur all dat, an' I ain't gwine to have her a-singin' songs an' dancin' in front o' public houses."

Isaac had risen and stood facing his wife.

"An' what is yer gwine to do to help it, if I says she may?" Hetty's eyes were glaring upon her spouse in the most *unconjugal* manner.

"Why, why"—Isaac drew closer and closer to her, and, laying his hand heavily upon her shoulder, said, "why, I'd knock her an' you both in de head."

"We don't b'long to you; we b'longs to master; we ain't yer niggers; we b'longs to them folks in de house."

"Psha! Hetty, you pesters me when I'm in trouble; you ain't no wife to help yer ole man, to feel sorry fur him when he is in misery; you jist quarrels wid me an' makes me more miserable."

The supper, which the white people were waiting for in the house, was forgotten; dishes were set down, temper was quenched, and Hetty came close to the side of her husband, with a different expression of countenance, and said, in an altogether softened and faltering tone of voice.

"Isaac, I didn't mean a word o' all dis here I has bin a sayin'; I was only riled up. Forgit it, Isaac, an' tell me if anything troubles yer. What's de matter? Has yer white folks bin hard on yer? Don't you git 'long well at de blacksmithing? I hearn 'em say you was doin' well."

"So I is doin' well."

"Den you won't be 'stressed 'bout me. Now, Isaac, you oughtn't to mind me when I'm mad; you knows I ain't myself. But den I wants to try to aggravate you, bekase I doesn't like to have you seem as of you didn't kere 'bout talkin' 'long wi' me. Grace has been a givin' me a sight o' trouble; dat chile is rale smart, an' she shows herself too much in front o' dat tavern. Now, I switched her well an' tuck de money frum her; but she's bin at it agin; I kan't send her to de pump fur water but she stops dar; an' if one o' 'em traders gits his eyes sot on her, she is clean gone, an' dat would kill me. I has seen too many o' my chillen sole down de river. I kan't bar to see dis last one go. Somethin' is gwine on in de house; strange men comes here an' walks round an' looks at things. S'pose we is all to be sole, an' I sent away frum you, bekase we'd go straight down de river ef we was."

"Hetty, you is too easy skeered, an' allers thinks de worst is gwine to happen, but I'se got a good friend, an' he said to-day, if I'd sarve him, I shouldn't suffer."

"Who is he?"

"Mas'er Sharpe."

"What, Isaac, John Sharpe? Whew! whew! I doesn't b'lieve in him no more 'an I do in a spider. He is jist a-spinnin' his web round you, an' he'll ketch you jist as de spider ketches a fly; I wouldn't trus' him, Isaac; now you mind my words."

At this juncture of the conversation Grace came in.

"Laws, mammy, ain't de supper ready? White folks waitin' fur it, an' ole miss is in orful hurry. How d'ye, pappy?"

"Come here, Grace," said Isaac; "tell me where you got dem red beads dat's roun' yer neck?"

"A man gib 'em to me fur singin'."

He caught hold of the strand with a quick jerk; the thread snapped and the beads went spinning and whirling over the brick floor.

"Now, dat's what I'll do wid all sich trumpery you gits. Let me hear o' yer singin' at de tavern agin, an' I'll take de skin off yer back an' de blood out o' yer body. Stop, don't be a-pickin' up dem beads; let 'em lay dar an' be stamped to pieces."

The child began to cry, but the angry mother here put in her threat.

"Yes, Grace, I has bin a-telling yer pappy how you does, an' he ain't no ways pleased wid yer; he wants you to keep away from dat tavern, jist as I has bin a-tellin' yer, but yer won't mind me; yer thinks yer knows best. Never mind now 'bout cryin' over them beads; if yer don't mind, you'll cry wusser 'an dat when white folks sells yer."

"Who's gwine to sell me?" inquired Grace, as she stopped gathering the beads and looked up inquiringly into her mammy's face.

"Hush, Hetty, stop yer tantalizin' dat gal; send yer supper in to de white folks, an' let Grace 'lone; you ken keep her frum gwine to taverns widout all de time tormentin' of her wid what you doesn't know *is* gwine to happen. Come here, Grace, an' give yer ole pappy a bus."

Thus addressed, the child sprang upon her father's knee, threw her arms round his neck and kissed him.

"Now, git down, puss," said the father, "an' go to yer work; take de white folks' supper in de house; don't be hurt bekase pappy broke yer beads; when I gits some money, I'll buy you a puttier string of 'em den dat was. Go, now, 'bout yer work."

She slid down from his knee and, with a pleasant smile, took the dishes from her mother and went into the house.

When the supper had been fairly dished up, and they were quite alone, Hetty drew her stool close to her "old man's" side.

"Now, Isaac, what is dis plan between you an' dat John Sharpe?"

"I'se mos' 'fraid to tell yer, Hetty, bekase I fears you is sort o' loose-tongued."

"I ain't, not a bit, an', moreover, I'se not gwine to tell anything as'll bring you into trouble. Come, now, you mout as well tell me."

"Ken I trus' yer, Hetty?" He fixed his eyes fast upon her. He turned her face so that the blaze of the wood fire in the wide chimney shone full upon it. He seemed to search every feature, almost to penetrate the flesh and reach down to the heart.

"Yes," he added emphatically; "yes, I'll trus' you dis time anyhow."

"*You ken.*"

"Wal, den, John Sharpe b'lieves dat dar is a runaway hid in Rachel's cab'n, an' wants me to look him out an' tell him."

Hetty's hand was on Isaac's arm.

"What! not Rachel de seamster?"

"Yes, dat one."

"An' you ain't gwine to do it fur no John Sharpe."

"I has promised him."

"Well, you shan't; bekase I am 'termined no harm shall come to Rachel, if I ken help it. Why, Isaac, has yer done forgot how she nursed me when I had cholery? Ain't I hearn de doctor say many times, if it hadn't bin fur her, I'd died, bekase all my white people had done run off to de country, an' none o' de niggers 'bout would kum to me; an' didn't she send me things, lint an' ile, when my poor boy got burnt? and didn't she cry 'long wi' me when my chillen was sole down de river? No, now, I tell yer, Isaac, I ain't gwine to set idle by an' see trouble come to dat 'ooman; she is good enough lookin' and knows enough to be white, an' I has hearn dat dar is dem dat keres fur her as is de fust here; an' if you goes to troublin' her, I hope dem dat is rich an' strong an' likes her will be arter yer."

"Does yer wish it agin' me?"

"You has no bisness puttin' yerself in sich ugly work. Kan't you 'tend to yer own matters, an' let de 'ooman alone? She's done nothin' to you."

"But if I sarves John Sharpe, he'll help me along to gittin' my freedom; he said he would."

"No bad work o' dat kind is gwine to help yer to yer freedom, I ken tell yer. De devil is in dat 'ar, an' he never helps you to freedom. I'd rader be a slave all my days 'an bring harm to a poor 'ooman, an' one dat had sarved me an' my chillen too."

Issac did not reply, but sat with his head drooping on his breast. Hetty sighed heavily, and clasped her hands over her knees, while her eyes scanned the fire. The little low-roofed, brick-floor kitchen was dusky and still; only the flickering blaze of the firelight, every now and then darting into a blaze, then fading out, shed light upon them.

....

Rachel had closed the cabin door and windows, lighted her little wick lamp, and was giving Maria her supper, while everything looked cosey and comfortable in the cabin.

"Here, child" (this is a kindly mode of expression peculiar to the negroes, and is generally applied without regard to age), "take something to eat; drink this tea; it will give you strength. I want to have a little talk with you."

"Has anything happened, Rachel?"

The poor fugitive was trembling with apprehension.

"Nothing new."

"You looks so serious."

"Do I?"

"Yes, an' you skeers me. Do tell me right out, an' at once, what it is dat's on yer mind. Is dey arter me? has dey foun' out whar' I am?"

The poor, wretched creature crawled closer to Rachel; her eyes were staring fearfully; each feature wore an anxious expression, and every limb of her body trembled; creeping up nearer and nearer to Rachel's side, she seized hold of her garments, clutched at them, with mute entreaty in each gesture and motion of her body.

"Oh, Rachel, hide me; don't give me up if dey come fur me. Take kere of me, bury me, kill me, do anything, but don't give me up. If ole miss gits me agin, dey'll persuade her to send me down de river, an' I couldn't stand dat. Oh, Rachel, don't give me up. Save me, an' God'll bless you; I know he will."

Rachel's eyes were full of tears, but she turned aside to hide them from Maria.

"Let go me, Maria; don't be so frightened; you know I will do the best I can for you; but if the worst comes, I shall be ruined with you."

"You, Rachel! why, what could dey do to you? You is free."

"But I am *yellow*-skinned; negro blood is in my veins. I have no citizenship; I am a mulatto woman, on a par with slaves and cattle" (there was inconceivable anguish and bitterness in the tone).

"Isn't free people safe?"

"Safe from what? Surely not from the white man's insults, malice and oppression. No, Maria, I have no power to assist you when your place of concealment is once discovered; then I shall lose all that I have, perhaps my own freedom."

The poor fugitive did not perfectly understand this, but she caught at the latter part of the sentence, and, recoiling a few paces from Rachel, she wrung her hands violently, drew a long, determined breath, then said, in a composed tone,

"No, Rachel, I isn't gwine to stay here any longer; I'll go out dis very night an' try to make my 'scape by myself if I ken; if not, I hope Tom Hynes's dogs'll kill me, tar' me all to pieces afore dey takes me back to bondage; but I ain't gwine to stay here an' bring trouble on you, who has befriended me. No, I kan't do dat no how. What! take yer freedom from you? No, indeed, dat trouble mustn't come to you by me. I knows, from dis little drop I has had, how sweet freedom is, an' I ain't gwine to be de means o' yer losin' it. I'm gwine now, Rachel."

"What do you mean, foolish woman? You cannot think of venturing out into the woods to-night; you do not know a single path, and it's a dark night."

"God is in de woods, Rachel, same as He is here. I'll call to Him. May be He'll hear a runaway's prayers."

"And He'll not return a fugitive." Rachel said this in a low tone and with uplifted eyes. Taking Maria's hand within her own, she added,

"You shall stay with me awhile longer. To-morrow I'll see your husband. We must have him interested in our secret. Perhaps he can assist in getting you to the river; he may know the names of some of the friends on the other side who will assist you. I can't think it is right for you to stay here another week; I have had bad dreams, and all the time I seem to see trouble before us. To-morrow I'll try to arrange. Go now to your closet."

Maria caught Rachel's hand and held it for a moment within both of hers, showering it with her fast-falling tears. When she had been fairly stored away for the night, Rachel trimmed the lamp, drew out the little table, and began to sew; she was too anxious to think of sleep. Belonging, as she did, to that wild, poetic negro race, she also inherited their susceptible temperament, and was subject to strong mental impressions, which almost amounted to foresight or clairvoyance. She was accustomed to say *I feel* such and such things, or *I see it so,* and no reasoning or statement of fact could change her impression, which, when examined, always proved a revelation. Now she *felt,* almost realized, that trouble was at hand. Her fingers moved nervously along the seams of her work; her eyes, too, were restless and anxious, searching round, every moment or so, as if expecting to see something or some one. As the hours wore on, her fears began to subside, and quiet was gradually returning, when she heard sounds of footsteps under the window. She listened nervously, stole to the window, put her ear against the closed shutter, but could distinguish nothing. Concluding that the fancy had deceived her, she began to prepare for bed, and was soon sleeping soundly as if there was no such thing as care in the world.

Next morning, she was surprised by a visit from Hetty. After the first salutations had passed, the woman, without any formality, explained at once the object of her visit.

"I know, Rachel, you'se s'prised to see me here, but I jest got off from my folks by sayin' I wanted to go have a frock cut out. I hain't much time, bekase I mus' be back in time to git de dinner. Rachel" (the woman was a little embarrassed and began to play with the corner of her apron), "you's bin kind to me. You helped me at a time when everybody else forgot me. I'se not de one to overlook or misremember dat, so I come to you now to warn you dat you is in danger, an' to say dar is dem about dat means to bring you harm. Now, don't ax me no questions, bekase I kan't answer none; all I ken I'se tole. I'se got no more to say. Only, Rachel, I begs you, if you has got rich white friends what'll save you, to go to 'em at once an' let 'em help you."

"Can't you tell me what kind of danger I am threatened with? I shan't ask you for names or persons; only let me know what I am suspected of or how endangered?"

Hetty hesitated a moment or so; then, brightening up, added, in a brisk tone,

"Yes, I'll not forgit what you'se done for me, an' I'll tell you dis much. Folks, some folks, b'lieves you has a runaway hid here. Oh, Laws!" (she pressed her hand to her lips and looked round terrified) "oh, Laws! is anybody in dar (pointing to the chamber) to hear me? I'se most feared of de sound of my own voice."

Rachel thanked her heartily for the kind interest she had manifested, but did not say that there was a necessity for the warning.

"Now, Rachel, I must be gwine, but do, chile, be lookin' arter yerself. I kan't bar to think any trouble is gwine to happen to yer. Good-bye, an' take kere of yerself."

Shaking hands, they soon parted. Poor Rachel! A great stone seemed rolled tightly against her heart; she was in an agony of doubt and vexation, and, like all generous persons, feared most for Maria, and determined at once to hunt up aid in some friendly quarter. Of course the first one whom she thought of was Maria's husband.

XXIII

"PAPA," exclaimed Madge Vertner as she entered the library, where her father sat reading—"papa, where did you hire Milly and Jack?"

Col. Vertner turned his head toward his daughter, laughed, held out his hand, but did not answer her question. She stood a few paces from him, with her hand resting on the door-knob and her eyes fixed firmly upon his face.

"Come here, my child." His hand was still extended toward her; refusing to take it, she answered,

"No, papa, I shall not go to you nor take your offered hand until you tell me what you have done with those negroes. You promised me not to sell them; you surely have not lied to me?"

"*Madge!*"

"Yes, papa, I ask again if you have lied to me?"

"I don't understand this language. You are not used to speak so to me. I have spoiled you, as your mother says, by over-indulgence."

"Papa, where are Jack and Milly?"

"I do not recognize your right to interrogate me. You are my own petted child, the dearest thing on earth to my heart; but if necessary—as I now begin to see it is—I can restrain you and urge my authority

191

against your wilfulness and insolence. Is it fit that I should be cross-examined by my own child about my own business affairs?"

"Papa, I do not cross-examine you, but propose one simple, direct and earnest question; I only ask if you have violated a promise made to me, and I hold that there is nothing unfilial in this. You ought to answer me *directly*."

"Do you think, dear, I would deceive you, save for your own good?"

"Papa, you have sold those negroes; you sold them to that trader whom I saw in the jail. You have broken your solemn promise to me. I trusted you as I would have trusted Heaven. When I first heard of this lie (papa, you need not start nor get so pale; I know the word I use; it is the word that fits your action), I could not believe it, and did not until evidence was given. I wish I had never heard it; for, papa, though I still love you, my *respect* is gone forever. You are not the father of whom *I* can be proud. After this, I shall require something more than your assertion to prove a thing to my reason."

"Madge, go out of this room."

"No, papa, I am cooler now than you, and here I shall stay until I tell you all that I feel. I have been thinking much of this matter. Oh, papa!—"

He had risen from his chair and was pacing the room with a nervous and rapid step; a deadly whiteness overspread his face, and he ground his teeth in silent rage, all the while locking and knitting his fingers together. Stopping quickly in front of his daughter, he seized hold of her arm, saying, in a slow, husky tone,

"Girl, do you suppose I'll be bearded by you in this way? Get to your room quickly, or you will urge me to do something I may regret."

Never once, not even for a single moment, had she allowed her eye to leave his; it was fastened, locked upon him—that eye of such wondrous power, strong enough to be the tamer of the fiercest passions! He seemed to realize the charm, and, passing his hand over his own eyes, he said, in a kind voice,

"Don't look at me that way; don't; you will kill me. Madge, Madge, your father is unhappy—is miserable; pity him"; and, sinking down into a chair, he covered his face and wept as a child.

Without seeming to regard him, she still stood with her eyes drooping, as if anxiously studying out the figures upon the carpet.

Col. Vertner soon re-collected himself, and, resuming his wonted air, asked,

"Madge what or who has set you upon this catechizing of your father? Yes, I did sell the two slaves for whose pardon you begged with all the pretty grace of a pretty girl. I sold them because they had betrayed their master's trust and confidence; they were petted slaves—had a comfortable and happy home, which they could not appreciate, and I have provided another for them, where they will learn the value of the one from which they tried to fly."

Her eyes were fixed upon him; he marked their varying light and the alternate flushing and paling of her cheek; but still she did not speak. He smiled kindly; her features, however, did not relax; they were moveless and rigid as marble. He again held out his hand; she seemed not to notice it.

"Madge, my girl, what does this mean? You are not angry with your papa? Come, my bird, come, sit upon my knee. What! you won't come? Well, get your hat and let us have a ramble; the keen air will give you a better mood."

"I don't wish to."

Her head was now partially turned from him. He walked up to her and passed his arm lightly round her waist, but she gently slid from him.

"What! won't let your father come near you? How is this, Madge?"

"You have *betrayed my trust and confidence;* when slaves do this to their masters, they are sold; but when parents betray their children's confidence and trust, what, then, is the forfeit?"

Her eyes were glittering like a serpent's when she fastened them upon him. Determined not to be again daunted by her, he extended both hands, and, with a smile of admiration, said,

"It seems that my only child is going to do worse than sell her father—she is going to desert him, take her love from him, and so let his heart starve. Now, when I sent Jack and Milly from this home, I provided another for them; but where can you find me another child?"

"It is no jesting matter, papa; moreover, you did not find Jack and Milly another home; you sold them to a negro-trader, who bought them as if they were cattle, fully resolved to sell them for the highest market value, either together or separated, as circumstances might determine. All this, papa, you knew, and had promised me differently. You have *meanly* deceived me."

"And can't you forgive me? I am sure they have good homes. I'll see Harrison (the trader) and ask him how and where he sold them; and if they haven't good homes, I'll try to get them back. Now, are you satisfied?"

"*How can I believe you? I had your word before.* I trusted it fully, but you deceived me. This time I require something stronger."

He bit his lip, frowned slightly, turned away from her, and, after a moment's silence, began to hum an old air, perhaps by way of showing indifference, but we know that these bitter taunts and home-thrusts stung him to the quick. Madge, without fully comprehending her power, yet understood that she could move him. She remained silently observing him. He felt that her eyes were searching his face like a basilisk's, and tried, by every possible little artifice, to avoid their sharp glancing; by walking about the room and playing with the books upon the table and in the cases. It is a terrible thing when a father is humbled and confused with conscious guilt in the presence of his own child.

"Come, Madge," he at length said, "sit down on this sofa beside me, and let us talk the matter over. I am sorry, dear child—"

She came forward and took the seat designated by him. He attempted to take her hand; this time she did not resist, but passively submitted.

"Darling," he began, in a slow, low tone, "you are the closest and dearest thing to my heart; if you turn away or grow cold, I shall have but a small hold upon life. You are the one sweet, precious link between myself and a happier period of existence. Madge, I watched and waited anxiously through all your wayward, uncertain infancy (you were at first a feeble child); and when you began to wax in strength and grow in beauty, I felt as if life were not all a blank, for you were the charm. You have been very dear to me—a solace and comfort. How tenderly I have watched the unfolding of your true character, feeling every day that you grew dearer and dearer! Your out-door life, your woods-sports, your quickness and boldness, though displeasing to your mother, were delightful to me, for I recognized in them the freedom and honesty of a brave nature. Day by day you have grown more into my heart, until now I feel that you are its very light and life. I am getting old; and as the sands shift and the colors get dim in my glass, I cling the closer, sweet, child, to you, and in your blithesomeness realize and renew the flowers and sunshine of my lost May."

His voice grew faint and tremulous, and a moisture was on his eyelids. These signs of emotion were observed by Madge. She slid a little closer to him, pressed his hand, turned her face full upon his, and, observing the tears in his eyes, her head sank upon his shoulder, and she broke out in an impulsive voice,

"Dear, dear father, do you love me so *much?* Am I all this to you? Are you unhappy? I thought you kind and affectionate, but I believed that you lived more in your books and thoughts than in your child."

He held her long and close to his breast; she distinctly heard the quick and rapid beating of his heart, and her tears (she scarcely knew why) fell thick and fast. They were tears wept from April clouds, and were quickly succeeded by a flash of sunshine.

"Come, papa," she added, in a lively tone, as she lifted her head from his shoulder, "come, let us have either a walk or a ride."

"Certainly, my child. Shall I order the horses?"

"Yes."

As she was crossing the hall, on the way to her room to prepare for the ride, she was met by little Pomp, who gave her a note.

"Here, Miss Madge, dis was lef' here by Miss Mason's man, an' he said I mus' give it to you right away."

Madge took the note, read it over several times carefully, and then asked,

"Where is the man? Did he not wait for a word or message?"

"No, ma'am, he was in a hurry."

"No, matter; order my pony; I must ride over to Mrs. Mason's, papa," she added as Col. Vertner approached from the library; "Helen Mason has sent an urgent note for me to go to her instantly. We can't have a long ride. Will you go with me there?"

"Yes; I have business in the village, and will accompany you as far as Mrs. Mason's, where I shall leave you for an hour or so to talk over matters with Helen, then call and bring you home."

XXIV

Madge found Helen Mason, looking very pale and worn, lying on a sofa in the pretty little oaken breakfast-room.

"What is it, Helen? Not sick, I hope? Your note was so urgent that I came right away, although papa and I were preparing for a nice long jaunt together. What is the matter, Helen? Sick, dear?" And Madge knelt down beside the sofa and wound her arms around Helen's neck in the prettiest and most coaxing manner.

"Yes, Madge, I'm sick again; that troublesome little hacking, throat-tickling, sleep breaking, good-for-nothing cough has returned; it bothers me all the while. Yesterday I raised a little blood, which seems to have done me good. The doctor was here again this morning, orders me to be quiet and not to take exercise, keep within doors for a week, and live on low diet. He says, however, I shall be the better for the escape of that hot blood. There, Madge dear, reach me that phial, and, if your hand is steady, count out a dozen drops; thank you, I shall feel able to talk presently; this cough mixture is truly a composing and comforting draught."

She looked at her little French watch, and smilingly added,

"I must have twelve drops more in half an hour. This being sick is something you can't understand, Madge."

"I was never sick in my life. Mamma says I am not elegant enough for an invalid; can't afford a pet cough; too unrefined for a head-ache or heart-ache. Mamma, you know, is often sick."

We don't know that Madge meant to be malicious or wicked, but there was certainly a very queer sort of expression out her face. Helen Mason smiled, and only reached out her hand to clasp Madge's with a loving pressure.

"But, Helen, how and why did you take this ugly cold?"

"Mamma has not been well for several days—unusually wakeful and restless of nights. I watched a great deal with her, and perhaps was not careful of myself, though I tried to be."

"Why did you sit up with her?"

Helen turned her head wearily off.

"Never mind, Madge; but then I will speak. You know poor mamma has been a weary invalid. She is querulous, hard to please, and full of sick people's crotchets, and poor Lydia was almost broken down with constant waiting, and mamma—she is not *naturally* fretful, she is sweet-tempered—was harsh to the girl. Mind you, Madge, she did not *mean* to be unkind. So I dismissed Lydia and took the post myself."

Madge had been earnestly gazing at her friend's face, while her own countenance changed with almost every word.

"Helen," she asked, "isn't it strange mothers never love their children so well as fathers?"

"Why, Madge" (Helen smiled), "they are generally thought to be the most fond and devoted. A mother's love is a synonym for faithfulness and tenderness."

"Your story-books say so, but I never relish reading them; they are untruthful. Helen, I can count on my fingers the tender words my mother has spoken to me, and I never felt a particle of warmth in her kisses; but my father, his very heart dissolves in love for me. I have come to realize the depth and fervor of his affection. Is there any love like a father's, Helen?"

"Madge, your pulse quickens as you ask that question; hasn't Mr. Butler taught you that there is another? What makes you start so? Stay, don't pull away from me. I must hold this wrist a little longer till it tells me all your secrets."

"Nonsense, Helen; don't be so foolish. Let me go; talk of something pleasant; only see what a fit of coughing you have brought on by this little wrestle; you have quite spent your strength. Helen! Helen, what is that upon your handkerchief? Gracious! it is blood, and how pale you are, dear Helen!"

"Madge" (in a half whisper), "reach me the salt-cellar from the side-board, and a goblet of water; there, now, I'm better; the blood does not come; it was only a small vessel of the throat which that jerking, nervous little cough broke; don't be frightened, Madge; it's of no possible consequence; I feel much better now. Let us go on with our conversation. Where did we stop?"

"No, Helen, no," Madge broke forth, "you are not well; don't strive to hide it from me. You feel weak; you are pale and wasted since I last saw you; and there is an anxious look on your face. What is it, Helen, that so troubles you? Come, tell your own Madge."

There was a large, shining, bead-like tear in the sick girl's eye when she reached forth her hand to take hold of Madge's.

"No, darling, no, I am happy to-day; anxious I may be, for life is uncertain to all and short to me; but do you know, dear Madge, that I sent for you to tell you that I am soon to be married?"

"Indeed! Helen."

"Yes, dear."

"*To be married soon?*"

"Yes," with a bright smile and a gentle pressure of the hand.

"Helen, what shall I do when you are married?"

"*Go and do likewise.*"

"Nonsense! ridiculous! silly! Helen, you don't mean really *soon?* You mean in two or three years?"

"No, in two weeks."

"*You shan't!* I'll oppose the bans."

"Where is Mr. Butler?"

"Gone to New Orleans."

"When does he return?"

"I don't know; some time next spring. Papa had a letter from him last week."

"And when did Madge have hers?"

"What a question, Helen!"

"You are not so free and frank as you used to be, dear; there was a time—it does not seem long gone—when I was the first one to know all your affairs. Now you keep your secrets. But never mind, Madge, if you had rather not tell me *all* now, I can afford to wait; for certain I am that the time will come when you will tell me everything."

Madge tried to speak, but her lips only worked nervously; the tongue was silent. Words would not come forth; tears were in her eyes, which Helen perceived, and, kindly taking her hand, said,

"No, Madge, no, I'd rather not hear it now. Wait awhile. Nurse your secret longer; it is not old and strong enough to bear the air; hide it longer; don't be confused and shy; don't turn away from me. I will tell you now of my plans. Mr. Norton and I did not at first intend to be married so soon. We expected to wait for two or three years; but mamma's health is so frail, and I am not strong; we need a gentleman in the house; it has been so forlorn since poor papa's death that we have all, in council assembled, concluded it is better to hasten matters a little, and, indeed, Madge, I am not sorry. I feel constantly the necessity of near intellectual companionship and the presence of a watchful friend. *He* will make things look brighter in the house. You will come to see us often, Madge?"

"Yes—but, Helen, tell me how Mr. Norton talks; he is in raptures, I suppose."

Helen smiled as she replied,

"*He is a lover, Madge,* and, of course, for the while, has lost somewhat of his cold, quiet dignity. Yet I have a half fear at times that he will grow tired of me, his life is so intensely intellectual. I have said this to him, but he is so good, so condescending that he says I will always be a spring of delight to him. Yet it does seem as if one of the sons of light had become enamored of a daughter of earth. How can he decline to my level? It makes me tremble, and I shade my eyes from the dazzling glare of the future."

Helen's cheeks were suffused in crimson and a beautiful enthusiasm lighted up her usually pensive eye. Madge marked these signs.

"Helen," she asked, "what will he do with your negroes?"

"Set them free, of course, dear; I am perfectly willing; and mamma, though not an Abolitionist, will not now object. Mr. Norton has gained such complete power over her that she will not dispute his authority in anything; and who *could*, who would fight against his keen sense of right?"

"Will he do this, Helen?"

"Certainly, dear, for he abhors slaveholding; it seems the strongest article in his creed, and so powerful and earnest have been his arguments that I am quite won over to his way of thinking. Slavery is an institution as old and near to me as any home relation or domestic tie I have on earth; I had, from custom, come to think it right; but his mind, like a great lamp swung up in the darkness of my life, has revealed to me the horrors amidst which I dwell. I am determined not to be any longer unjust and cruel. Our slaves, at least, *shall* be free. I sometimes fear that I will be too weak to bear, in every word and act of my future, an unflinching protest against the system. I so much dislike making a crusade against the community in which I live, but then *he* will be by to encourage and strengthen me, and I'll not falter. This question has taken very great hold upon my thoughts. Though I am not like you, Madge, active and demonstrative, I *feel* keenly, and hope to do my little part as well as I can. If I remember aright, Mr. Butler has a strong feeling against slavery."

"Not a *feeling*, but a principle. Everything with Mr. Butler comes from his head. He *thinks* about Right and Wrong, and reads and writes about it. I only *see* these things. They are before me like sunshine, starlight; I know them, but cannot define their laws. Papa says Mr. Butler is a safe man, and has no temerity. Helen, papa explains my idea of right-doing by the name of temerity. He says if a man attempt to preach anti-slavery in a slave community, he is a rash man. I should call him a good man. Papa said, the other day, when I pressed him hard, that *perhaps* slavery was wrong in the abstract (he talks so much about the abstract—I'm sure I don't know exactly what he means), and that it would probably die out with the advance of a more perfect civilization. This kind of talk is very puzzling to me; it bothers my head and puts me all wrong. I can't follow papa and Mr. Butler when they spin out their thoughts, fine as a spider's web."

Just then a mulatto girl, with a bright eye and a clear, golden complexion, came into the room. She was tidily dressed, and had such a fresh, smart manner that even in a drawing-room she would have been a noticeable person.

"How d'ye do, Lyd?" exclaimed Madge, in her free, careless way.

"Good mornin', Miss Madge; how is it with herself?"

"Well as usual, Lyd; but what makes you let your Miss Helen get sick so often?"

"Laws, Miss Madge, Miss Helen is one of 'em sickly sort. It 'pears to me she's too delicate fur anything but to look at, just like 'em white lilies. I always thinks of Miss Helen when I looks at 'em lilies; but you, Miss Madge—laws, now, you's jest for all this world like that big, red monthly rose—always fresh and gay. It does us good to have you come here. You fills up this room and makes it sweet and cheerful, like the roses and the sunshine. I do wish you'd stay more 'long Miss Helen, for you always helps her up mightly; she is better for two or three days after you comes. But she'll soon have somebody else to keep her company an' cheer her up; then she'll git well." This allusion was followed by a hearty burst of good-natured laughter, in which Madge joined while Helen smiled.

"Poor, faithful girl," she exclaimed as the mulatto left the room, "she well deserves to be free. How lovingly she has served us. Her good humor is almost without a parallel. I never knew her spirits give way under the most trying circumstances, when, indeed, I have seen her in situations where almost any nature would give way; and, Madge, her natural sense and shrewdness are very remarkable. When I am sick or '*dawncy*,' as she expresses it, she comes to my bedside with some pleasant news or ready jest, which quite enlivens me. I don't think I could get along without her. At the time of my father's death, she was my greatest consolation. She felt that affliction deeply, yet all the time sought to conceal it from me, lest she might deepen my own grief."

"Yes," said Madge, slowly, "these poor negroes, coarse, rough-appearing as they are, often show the most delicate and refined sensibility. They are constantly surprising us in such fine little ways. I always loved them, even before I began to see the unjust position in which they are now placed, for I found, in all my little childish troubles, that they sympathized more truly with me than any others. You know, Helen, I had an old negro woman for my wet-nurse, and they say she was unusually kind, tender and affectionate. Poor mamma was so sick after my birth that I was sent off with old mammy Luce, and was never seen by my own mother until I was two years old, and then only at rare and distant intervals. They say that mothers who do not nurse their children seldom love them much, and my old colored mammy seemed to fear that my mother did not love me enough."

"Where is she—your old mammy Luce, I mean?"

"Oh, papa liberated her. I have often heard him say that he couldn't bear to hold in slavery the woman at whose breast I had nursed. He also gave her a handsome amount, which keeps her from want. I wish I could see her; but I suppose she is happy in some of those populous free States. I often think most tenderly of her, for, as I remember, she was kind to me. Ah, how often I wish that my own mother were half so fond; but it's idle to make such wishes. Helen, when I used to—as a child—go up and fling my arms round mamma's neck, she always seemed afraid that I would crush or injure her fine lace collars, and I learned to know that my place was not closest to my mother's heart; her lace and jewels were nearer."

"Madge, you may do injustice to your mother. She is different from you, and has these fine, fashionable tastes; but I don't question her affection for you. Why, just think, you are her only child; she *must* love you, though she is undemonstrative. But tell me, did your father acknowledge that he sold Jack and Milly?"

"Yes; and, Helen, I said frightful things to him. They seemed almost to crush him; it was in that terrible interview I first learned how dear I was to his heart. My words cut him like a knife. Poor papa, he will never break another promise to me, or sell another slave, I am sure."

The servant here announced Mr. Norton, and also told Madge that her father was waiting for her. She rose to go, and, flinging her arms round Helen's neck, exclaimed,

"Dear Helen! God bless you. I am rejoiced to find you happy, so happy in this new relation you are about to form; but—but—but" (with sobs) "don't forget your poor Madge"; and, without waiting for an answer, she ran out of the house and rejoined her father at the gate.

XXV

Madge was very thoughtful as she rode home. Her father had rarely seen her so quiet and silent. He could not arouse her. Even when they sped along, in a swift gallop, he missed her wonted exhilaration of spirits. The various efforts which he made to rally her failed of their object.

"What had Helen to tell you, dear?" he inquired, as resting from a mile's swift gallop, with loosened rein they walked their horses slowly through a quiet part of the road.

"She is going to be married, papa, very soon."

"To Mr. Norton, I suppose?"

"Of course."

"When?"

"In a few weeks."

"I hope she may be happy, and yet I question it. If my judgment is not wrong, Mr. Norton is not the man to make a suitable husband for a pure and delicate-minded Southern girl."

"Why, papa, he is one of the most agreeable gentlemen I ever knew; highly cultivated, of gentle and kind manners, and, Helen says, full of affection."

"This outward seeming is very fair, but I distrust it. Let us know him better first. The villagers have none too much respect for him."

"Oh, they would suspect him because he does not believe in slavery. I love to hear him talk. He has made Helen an Abolitionist."

"Pity he couldn't make something better out of such good material!"

"*Papa!*"

"Well, darling, we shall see what her slaves will make of *him!*"

"I can tell you what *he* and Helen mean to make of them."

"What?"

"*Human beings;* free men and women."

Col. Vertner broke out in a prolonged burst of laughter, the wild peals and echoes of which floated off and back from the ridges of leafless forest trees and died mockingly in the distance.

"Helen told me so to-day."

"Did she, dear child? Well, I dare say she thinks so, simple girl that she is; but she will learn, so will my little Madge, that a man don't lightly throw away forty thousand dollars."

"Who said anything about a man's throwing away forty thousand dollars?"

"Well, forty-five or fifty negroes certainly represent that much money, particularly in the present high and prosperous state of the slave market."

"Papa, you make me sick with such shallow and disgusting talk. Why, you are not any better than that negro-trader whom I saw in the town jail. You are every bit as vulgar in your ideas."

"Upon my word, you are complimentary. But, I want very much to know, Madge, where you learned this sort of reasoning."

"Human reason, you mean. Well, papa, I am a human being, not a pig, and so I claim to have reason, sentiment, emotion, if you will, which I believe distinguishes men and women from brutes."

"You make a strong statement, my dear," he smilingly answered.

"Is it not true?"

"As a generalization, certainly it is; but I see how you mean to apply it and then I take issue against you; however, we will not discuss these ugly matters now. Let us have a pleasant ride home and a pleasant talk."

"I'd rather speak of this. It is a subject that lies nearest my heart."

"I wish it troubled you less."

"Papa," she answered, without observing his remark, "suppose that pretty seamstress, at whose door I once found you, and whose fine face comes over my thoughts often now, was a slave, would she not bring a high, a very high price in the market? Doesn't the slave buyer pay a premium in such cases for beauty, mind and character? Can you tell me in what our morality is better than that wretched code of Turkey, or Circassia?"

Madge had not looked toward her father while saying this, or she would have been startled by the exceedingly painful and harrowing expression as well as the ghastly paleness that overspread his face. Col. Vertner was a strong man, a bold and brave one, full of vigorous passions, and not wont to give up to fright or agitation; yet Madge, in her unsuspecting innocence, had touched upon a sensitive chord of his heart, which now went moaning and wailing through all the secret places of his nature, even as the Æolian harp vibrates when swept by the fingers of the straying wind. Col. Vertner was not a bad man, nor yet a good one; had he been brought up under the finest and best social influences, it is quite likely he would have been a remarkable character, for there were flashes of feeling, touches of sentiment and nature which gave indication of the susceptibility of his disposition and mind; but, growing up beneath the fostering influence of a society which recognized a wholesale wrong and encouraged and supported the worst of evils, how could a pliant and yielding nature become other than ruined for life? The very diamond owes much of its beauty and brilliancy of the skill and taste of the cutter. So also society is the lapidary which fashions and shapes character according to the prevailing mode, sometimes so skilfully carving a gem that each little cone and facet are made to sparkle and refract; or again so clumsily hewing and rounding as to obscure half the jewel's glory.

Without observing her father, Madge continued:

"And that poor guide at the Mammoth Cave, what a terrible injustice it was to retain such a person in slavery. Why, papa, he was almost a scholar. Mr. Butler said he was one of the best practical geologists he ever knew, and that he himself learned a great deal from him."

"Yes, dear, Stephen was one of those exceptional characters we sometimes meet. But such geniuses are rare as diamonds. Occasionally we find a remarkable intellect flashing out from the gloom and ignorance of the negro race, shining all the brighter for the darkness by which it is surrounded. We, however, estimate a race in the aggregate, not by chance and rare specimens."

"But, papa, may we not argue a great deal from one or two specimens? A whole gold mine is sometimes discovered by chance particles found in the dust."

Thus they whiled away their half-hour's slow ride homeward, in pleasant and quiet conversation.

Soon after reaching "the place," Madge, who seldom found her mother an agreeable companion, returned to her own room. She was more thoughtful and silent than usual. But not liking and scarcely understanding the mood, she needs must—like all active persons—occupy herself with some sort of manual work; and taking down her rifle and pistols, she began cleaning them nicely, all the while humming a low air to herself, and gradually growing more and more cheerful.

"Come in," she called out, in answer to a low knock at the door.

"Well, Daniel, what is it?" she inquired, almost without looking at him.

"Please, miss"—he stood fumbling at the door knob, with his eyes cast down—"please, miss, I'll clean them for you."

"No, thank you; I can do it best myself; I am really in want of something to do."

"You'll git your nice hands all siled with that 'ar."

"Why, Dan, you know I always clean my guns myself. What makes you *so* polite?"

"Nothin', miss; I only wanted to do dat 'ar fur you."

He lingered a moment, eyeing his young mistress wistfully; then, with apparent reluctance, withdrew.

At first, Madge did not heed this, but after awhile it occurred to her mind that Daniel's manner was strange.

"What," she said to herself, "if he had something particular to say to me? He had a strange expression of countenance. I'll send for him."

As she was about to ring the bell, Daniel opened her door.

"Oh, you have come—by instinct," she added, in a lower tone; then, speaking louder, "Well, Daniel, this is prosy work. You may clean that gun," pointing to one.

"Thankee, Miss Madge; I thought may be you might git tired, so I come back to see."

Crouching down upon the floor, he began to rub away quite industriously at the plated mounting of the gun, but his interest in his work soon began to flag, notwithstanding his young mistress plied him with questions about the affairs of "the place"—even ventured to joke him about his courtship with Ruth, and asked when the wedding was to come off.

"Laws, Miss Madge, I don't know as it will ever be. 'Pears to me I kinder think a slave had best never marry."

"And why?" she asked, looking him steadily in the face. The negro halted, stammered, then, gathering up all his courage, said, with a quick and rapid breath, "Slavery is mighty hard to bar, young miss, by your own self, but worse when you has a family."

Madge walked up and down the room two or three times, evidently in great agitation; then, going close to the negro, said, in a quick, *staccato* tone, "Dan, why don't you run off?"

"Oh, Miss Madge, Miss Madge, if I dars to tell you, dat is what has bin a-runnin' in my head for a long time, ever sense I overhearn you a talkin' longer miss 'bout Milly and Jack, and said you didn't blame 'em. *If I should be caught,* thar's the bother. Then, I've no money, an' they tells me you had better not start widout some change in yer pocket."

Madge was silent a moment or so; she stood with her finger pressed upon her half-parted lips, her eyes wide open, as if searching through space for a solution to the questions which an anxious heart and an excited brain were proposing.

Daniel, who did not fully understand his young mistress, feared that he had gone too far and began to repent his precipitate confidence.

"If I has said anything wrong, Miss Madge, I hope you'll excuse it."

"Hush, hush," she whispered, as she waved her hand toward him, but did not turn her head or move her fixed eye.

A moment or two of bitter suspense went over the slave's soul. Madge turned toward him, took out her purse, and counted ten dollars in small coin, saying.

"There, Daniel, there is all the money I have; take it; and if it buys you a safe passage to freedom, I shall think it worth more than hundreds to my heart. Take that pistol also; load it well; and here, hide this little sword in your bosom. Defend yourself bravely against those who attack or seek to recapture you. Now start for Canada when you please. Follow the North Star, and my blessing go with you. Don't say anything more to me about the matter, for I am now plotting against my father. Your secret is safe with me."

"*Oh, Miss Madge!!*"

"Hush, no thanks; I have done all I can for you. Go now and say no more to me about it. I do not even wish to know when you intend to start."

Waving her hand to him, she turned away, walked to the window and looked out.

He obeyed her, and left the room without saying another word. When he had, however, closed the door and was no longer in the presence of his mistress, his deliverer and his friend, his courage failed him; he broke down; his heart poured out blessings and tears. He paused a moment upon the threshold; then, slowly, noiselessly opening it, he crept up to Madge, knelt down and fervently kissed her foot, then stole away without word or sob. But Madge, who was fully conscious of his gratitude, felt a dampness upon her thin satin slipper and knew that the slave had wept his thanks.

"Dear papa," she murmured, "I wonder if I really do *him* a wrong? God knows how I love him; yet there is a little voice deep down in my heart which pleads so strongly for the slaves. I *can't feel* that I do wrong in thus conniving at and aiding them in their escape."

She was not wont to grieve or ponder long. She only thought in action, never planned or arranged beforehand; and now that she had acted, the matter was put entirely from her mind, and she set to work with a lighter and a happier heart. A good deed performed in behalf of another is the best medicine for sadness or low spirits.

A great impetus was given to poor Daniel's life; and he moved about that day as though his body had been set on springs. His mistress, who was wont to complain of him, even unbent her quiet dignity sufficiently to praise him. Ah! little did she know whither his thoughts were travelling, or what proud, sweet hope was now animating and blessing him. Could she have looked upon him late that night, when, making up a small bundle, and stealing softly out of the cabin, he stood for one moment in the still starlight, and gazed around him, for the last time, at "the old Kentucky home," where, after all, he had passed some pleasant hours, and, with his hand on his heart, and his breath stilled, he fled away from it forever, to seek "life, liberty and the pursuit of happiness"—on British soil. If she could have looked at him then, we say, she would have found him there a *man;* hitherto she had only known him as a chattel.

We will state here—for we shall not again see him—that Daniel reached the Canadian shore in safety, and, as we learn, lived long and happily, without one regret for this ill-advised leap.

....

Daniel's departure created a very slight surprise at the place. Col. Vertner swore one of his "*neat*"(?) little oaths. Mrs. Vertner expressed a desire that all the negroes might follow; for, she declared, "they were nothing but a ceaseless trouble and a dead expense upon her husband's hands"; whereupon, Madge suggested that if such was her mother's belief and wish, she thought deeds of manumission had better be drawn up at once. This, of course, was called impertinence. The slaves gossiped about it; and many a timid one shook his head, saying,

"Oh, Daniel will be sorry for dis afore long; dem hounds is sure to git him."

Madge sought her father at the first convenient moment, and extracted from him a promise not to advertise Daniel.

"Papa, may I trust you?" she asked, with earnestness, as she stood beside his chair in the library, where they had but a short while ago had such a fierce and exciting interview. But though once so egregiously deceived, she was too young and confiding not to quickly renew her faith in one whom she loved.

"What ardently we wish we long believe,"

is particularly true of the young.

....

Preparations for Helen Mason's wedding were now in active progress. Madge spent most of her time in town, and at Mrs. Mason's house. She and Helen were constantly with milliners, dressmakers, &c. Madge grew tired enough of satin and lace.

"Oh, Helen," she warmly exclaimed, "getting married costs you a great deal of useless trouble. I can't see any possible use in all this preparation and spending such frightful sums of money. It is just one of those nonsensical fashions which quite puts me out. Why are you obliged to have a trousseau? I'd just as lief be married in my old riding-habit as that lace and satin dress you have there. It's too absurd."

"Miss Vertner will not think so when she comes to be married," interposed the sapient dressmaker.

"Yes, I will, if ever I am married."

"Ah, Madgy," exclaimed Helen, smiling, "don't you recollect one certain evening, at the Mammoth Cave, how a certain independent and careless young lady suddenly became very fastidious about her dress? After making quite a superb toilet, this same indifferent young lady complained that her sleeve was awry, or that the set of the waist was imperfect, quarrelled with a stiff and unyielding whalebone, made war upon a set of graceful ringlets, declaring them to be limpsey, and"—

"Fie, Helen, you are crazy; do hush; don't worry me so. I know what and who you mean." And Madge hid her blushing face upon her friend's shoulder.

Though Helen looked so entirely recovered from her recent attack—though she moved about with such a buoyant and elastic step—though her eye was so lustrous and her cheek and lip so rosy and full, the physician, who still called, looked at her with a questioning, doubtful eye: he was very precise to count over and over again her pulse, and warned her, in the strongest terms, to be very cautious about much exertion; not to sit or stand where there were any particles of floating dust; to watch and guard the temperature of her chamber; sleep with a high pillow, &c., &c. All this Madge anxiously heard and understood.

One day she followed the Doctor out of the room down to the front door; large tear drops hung on her eye-lashes, when she inquired, with a nervous voice,

"Doctor, is she very ill?"

"Not ill, Madge, but"—he looked round to assure himself that no one was within hearing—"but she is failing very fast; one lung is entirely gone and but a shred of the other remains. Her life can only be held by the greatest care. Do caution her against over-exertion."

Madge's heart trembled as though a great and unexpected blow had fallen upon her. She went into the little breakfast-room, sat down upon the sofa and wept bitterly.

"So much trouble seems crowding upon my life," she murmured; "what *will* come next? Am I the gay and happy Madge Vertner of six months ago? I can scarcely believe it. How quiet and tame I am. Silk and Rover seem to feel that *I* have changed; and so I have. Experience is a harsh teacher; she is making me old and unhappy; my life of wild woods frolic was happier. I'll return to it—give up social friends—go back to sports; Silk and Rover shall be glad again."

She dried her tears before Helen found her; and when they again sat together playing with their work, laughing and chatting amid gauze, lace and satin, no one could have guessed that, an hour before Madge had been weeping violently. The troubles of petted youth are but April showers, and the sunshine of a genial humor paints a rainbow on the canvas of each retreating cloud!

XXVI

Helen Mason's wedding passed off, in due course of time, as all weddings do, with the usual amount of show and pomp; a retinue of brides-maids, parties, trousseau and corbeille, after which she settled down to commonsense and domestic happiness.

Madge returned to her former life with a feeling of *seemingly* renewed and increased interest. She now rode out oftener, played the more with Rover and chatted with Pomp and the "old folks" of the quarter; but still she found it difficult to get up the same amount of *real* animus. Insensibly, to herself, she watched the coming of the tri-weekly mail from the South, and, what was quite unusual with her, she was the first to seize the bag from Tom and hastily examine the budget of letters. Her father observed how eagerly she read the news from Mr. Butler, and how irritable and impatient she grew when his expected letters failed. On such occasions she generally complained of headaches, when Col. Vertner would quizzingly ask, and "how is it with the heart?" But, then, she was one with whom you could not take liberties, for what she did not resist by force of native dignity, her father was wont to declare she could annihilate with a few austere frowns and pouts.

Things were gliding along in their usually quiet and apparently indifferent way at "the place," Madge declaring that "times were as dull as blue Mondays," when, one morning, the sober current was suddenly broken up.

As Madge came in to breakfast, she observed that her father was unusually interested in the morning paper. The expression of his face was painful and his manner nervous and absent. Mrs. Vertner addressed a question to him two or three times without eliciting a reply.

"Why, papa!" exclaimed Madge; but, suddenly checking herself, she cunningly observed the page and column of the paper upon which his eyes seemed so tightly glued.

The breakfast was summarily and silently despatched. Col. Vertner gulped down his coffee at one draught, not withstanding Mrs. Vertner and Madge simultaneously cried out, "it is boiling hot, you will scald your throat."

It might have been an iced lemonade, for all the discernment he then possessed. Seizing his overcoat, hat, riding-gloves and whip, he rushed out to the stable, and, almost before the hostler could saddle his horse, mounted and was off.

"Your father seems annoyed," said Mrs. Vertner; "I have observed that for the last two or three days he has been uneasy and fretful. What can be the reason?"

"I am sure I cannot say," replied Madge, "but suppose he is not entirely well. People can't afford, mamma, to give a reason for every whim of conduct, particularly spontaneous persons, like papa. We must not watch so eagerly."

"How curious you are," was the laconic reply.

Madge secured the paper and stole away to her room. She soon found the column and there read what had so stunned her father. It was as follows:

"The examination of the Court yesterday resulted in a conviction of the free mulatto woman, Rachel, a slave man, Peter, and two other negroes, for aiding and secreting the slave woman, Maria, the property of Mrs. Vitetor, late of this State and County, now residing in Missouri. The punishment affixed by the statute to such offences is nine-and-thirty lashes, to be administered at the public whipping-post. Thursday next is the day appointed by the Court for the execution of the sentence. We hope it may prove a useful and salutary lesson to the other slaves."

Then followed a long tirade, by the editor, against free negroes and the dangers resulting from their residence anywhere in the neighborhood of slaves. *The example* was pronounced a bad one.

"And so it is," acquiesced Madge, "a bad, very bad example. Freedom is always dangerous to slavery; but poor Rachel, I pity her. She is the beautiful seamstress at whose cabin door I once met papa. Poor woman, how I pity her the mortification of this public whipping. I am sure she is sensitive and delicate; her countenance and manner expressed it. I wonder if something can't be done for her. I shall speak to papa about it. I am sure, if he can, he will aid her."

And she did speak to him, but he assured her that it was impossible to do anything.

"The decree of the Court, my dear," he replied, "is unalterable, and any interference now, on my part, would only ruin me and do that unfortunate woman no good."

"Well, where is she, papa?"

"In jail, my dear." His voice faltered a little.

"In that old, horrid, dirty jail, where poor Jack and Milly were kept?" she eagerly asked.

"Yes, dear."

"Oh, papa, how cruel and wicked."

"It can't be helped, Madge; I feel bitterly for the poor woman, and wish that I *could* save her."

After a moment's anxious silence, she said,

"Well, papa, at least *I* can do one thing."

"What is that?"

"Go to see her, comfort and sympathize with her, as she lies in that horrid jail. I can and *will* do that."

"No, no, my child, you must not."

"Yes, I *must*."

"Madge, it is not *proper*."

"Papa, I can't bear your *proper* talk. I don't care whether it is proper or not, so it comforts that poor woman; so I'm going at once."

"No, dearest, no; it will not comfort the woman, and will injure me greatly. If you could save the woman, I would allow you to go, without a thought of myself; but, believe me, you can do her no possible good and me much harm."

Sadly she answered,

"Well, since I want to comfort her, and do not want to injure you, I shall have to give up this little plan."

She said no more about the matter; but while she remarked her father's gloomy face, he, too, observed the paleness and sadness of hers.

XXVII

Hetty's warning to Rachel, though instantly heeded, came too late to save Maria or her protector. Closely watched by anxious scouts, the hiding-place was easily ferreted out. Rachel had gone, the day after her interview with Hetty, to see Maria's husband, and interested him in the secret. Though the poor negro's very life seemed bound up in the result, he had no power to stay the cloud of trouble which was hanging over his wife. He planned and directed a hundred ways for immediate flight, but each one seemed so utterly impracticable that they were bound to be abandoned. All through the dark hours of the two nights preceding the discovery he and Rachel sat together in the cabin, scheming, making and altering plans. Poor Peter was timid and could not give in to the bold ideas of Rachel.

"Why not start at once?" she inquired, "this very night?"

"We kan't git over de ferry; dar is no boat. You see, Rachel, if we waits a little bit longer, till I look round a bit, an' find two or three friends to help me on, and git a boat an' sich like things, why, I b'lieves we can git away very easy and widout much trouble to anybody."

"What do you mean, poor fool," exclaimed the energetic woman, "by waiting a bit? Haven't I told you that there are those who suspect us, who watch round this cabin, and stick like bloodhounds upon my very tracks? By tarrying longer here, you not only expose me to danger, but peril your wife's liberty. Go at once if you would save all. To stay here is to perish."

She spoke quickly and glanced round as if afraid that her very words had raised up spectres of armed men.

Maria crawled out from her closet close to Peter's side, and, laying her hand upon his arm, said,

"Come, Pete, let us go now, dis very minnit. If I am to be kotched, I doesn't want it to be in dis here cab'n, whar I'se bin so kindly took kere of. I doesn't want to pay back Rachel's kindness in dat sort of way, no how. Come, let's go at once. De sooner we is out from here, de better it'll be fur all sides."

Rachel was pleased at this show of determination on the part of Maria, and she said, in a cheerful and encouraging voice,

"That's right, Maria; be brave; keep up your heart and spirits, and you will come out right; trust in God and your own prudence. I hope it will end well."

Though she spoke hopefully and tried to *feel* so, her blood was chilly, and the shadow of a great danger seemed to loom up before her at every step. Dashing her hand across her eyes, as if to disperse a mist, she rose and began to make up a bundle.

"I will only give you a little provision, Maria; it will not be well for you to take clothing; you must do the best you can with what you wear away; and I am sorry I cannot give you food enough to last for several days; but I fear that even this small bundle will be a disadvantage; try to get along the best you can, and look to God for help."

Saying this, she placed the little bundle in the fugitive's hands, and was about to call down a blessing upon the prepared flight, when they were all startled by a quick knock at the door.

"Oh, my God!" cried Maria, "who is dat?"

Shrinking back into her closet, Rachel as hastily concealed her as possible, and called out, in an intrepid tone,

"Who knocks?"

"Let us in, at once," answered a gruff voice.

Between fear and surprise, she thought she recognized the tone of Sharpe.

"My God, what *can* it mean!" She trembled violently, but dared not open the door.

"Will you let me in at once?"

"I cannot open the door to strangers at this hour of the night."

"If you do not open it, we will break it down."

"There are more than one. They have come for no good purpose. Don't hide, Peter," she added in a whisper; "it will excite suspicion; stand your ground boldly. I had better open the door, I suppose, for they have power to force it."

"Stop that d——d whispering, and let us in without another minnit's parley."

Pressing her hand close to her heart, and collecting all the forces of her soul for such a trying moment, she approached the door with a steady step, turned the key and drew back the bolt. There stood Sharpe, Hynes and Isaac (the colored blacksmith).

"You are devilish long openin' of yer door, you yallow wench," said Sharpe, as he swaggered into the room.

"What ar' you doin' here, boy?" and Hynes laid his hand on Peter's arm. "Who do you belong to, and what brings you to this cabin at sich an hour of the night?"

The timid, trembling slave, whose very life and spirit had been ground out of him by long usage and slave service, tried to explain that he had come to make a visit to Rachel and had overstaid his time, &c.

"All that is putty plain to see, and you needn't be a tellin' us of it; but out with yer bisness; what brought yer here?"

Peter began to tremble more violently.

"Oh, Mas'er Sharpe, Mas'er Hynes, please"—

Hereupon Rachel interfered.

"What is it to you, Mr. Hynes or Mr. Sharpe? The negro doesn't belong to either of you; and the cause of his visit to me is my business and not yours; so tell me what *you* come for, and leave pretty soon, or I'll turn the whole of you out."

"You will, ha—will you?" and Sharpe seated himself in a chair just in front of her, drew out a couple of cigars, offered one to Hynes, lighted the other and began smoking in the most indifferent manner, all the while regarding her with an impudent expression. The woman, though dreadfully frightened, did not quiver or quail, but answered his impudent glance with a look of the sternest defiance.

"Well, let's have a bit o' talk 'bout it, Rachel, afore we settles it. Now, we doesn't mean to stay long on yer premises; but afore we goes, we counts to take more 'an we brought with us; we'll have the pleasure of yer company, if you pleases, to ride into town with us and to take a look and stop awhile at the jail. How would you like to spend some time thar?"

Removing the cigar from his mouth, while a cloud of offensive tobacco smoke filled the room, he eyed her with the malignity of a devil; still, Rachel's fortitude and self-possession did not forsake her. Crushing down her wounded pride and sensibility, she determined to meet the wretch with a manner that should be equal to his own audacity.

"I guess you will not take me to your jail, or five steps from my own cabin," she answered, with a seemingly *nonchalant* tone.

"That's got to be seen yit. I s'pose by the time I git through with this smoker" (alluding to his cigar), "you'll be ready to start?"

With a laugh and a wink, he turned to his friend Hynes, saying,

"Wal, now, Tom, I s'pects it's time for you to begin the sarch."

At this, Rachel forgot herself, and gave a little nervous start, which was quickly observed by Sharpe.

"Oh, ho! Rachel, you is comin' to yerself, I see, and begins to git skittish like; don't shy too soon, colt, for we hain't fairly begun yit; you'll want yer blinders soon enuff."

All of this provincial gibberish fell unheeded upon the woman. She felt herself growing stony. With that one phrase, "search the house," she read her warrant. Now she fully understood Hetty's warning. All was discovered, *all* was lost! She put her hands out piteously and pitiably, as if clutching at some immediate means of help or safety.

"What is it, Rachel, that skeers you so?" asked Sharpe; but her eyes only closed as if to exclude some horrid sight.

"Well, Peter," put in Hynes, as he knocked the ashes from his half-consumed cigar, "tell me where is that other member of yer company, that woman that has bin a stayin' here for some time? I'd like to see her, too."

"Dar isn't no other 'ooman here, Mas'er Hynes—no other 'ceptin' Rachel."

"Thar isn't, ha!"

"No, mas'er."

"Well, now, Pete, you ginerally lies putty well; but this time you has done *too* well. We'd like to have you fetch out that gal you'se got hid here. I want to see how much she looks like the widder Vitetor's Maria."

The suddenness of this speech took the poor negro quite by surprise and threw him utterly off his guard. Thinking only of his wife's danger, forgetting prudence and everything else, he fell upon his knees at Hynes's feet, exclaiming,

"Oh, pray, Mas'er Hynes pray don't—pray—please"—

"Fool! fool!" cried out Rachel, as she dashed Peter aside, and, walking up to Hynes, said,

"What is it you want with me? I am the only woman in this house, and you know it; look at me and see who I resemble; be quick about your look, too, for I want you gone from this cabin; it is late at night, and neither right nor agreeable for you to stay any longer."

"Yes, but before I go, I tell yer, you merlatter wench, that I am goin' to examine this cabin. I'm goin' to look in every hole and corner till I git that nigger, that run away nigger you has got hid here. I am goin' to take her back to her rightful owners. 'Tain't no sort o' use in you opposin' me, fur I ginerally has my own way with the like of you; so it behooves you at once to give up to me. Look here, gal, when Tom Hynes says a thing, he means it, and the like o' you is no more in my way 'an a cow, an' not so much as one o' them good Durham stock. I looks upon niggers as a cross between a baboon and the devil."

Insults such as these and from *such* a source had no gall for Rachel. She heeded them no more than the ravings of a madman, but her heart forboded evil, trouble. She knew that these two men were determined, if possible, to find the wretched fugitive who had begged shelter from her. And this it was that so wrung her soul and wrote her face over with grief. Seizing a lamp from the table, Hynes called out to Sharpe to follow him into the inner room and begin the search. The confused noise of voices had reached poor Maria in her closet. She crouched down under the planks, closer and closer, scarcely daring to breathe, lest she should be heard. When Sharpe flung the closet door open and held the lamp in, looking behind every little box, removing every bundle to see if she was there, some rays of light penetrated the crevices of her hiding-place, and she almost screamed aloud in terror.

"Wal, Hynes, she ain't thar, as I can see."

"Give me the lamp," cried out the burly negro-catcher; "I'll find her if she's anywhar about. My dander is up now, and she is obleeged to be found, if any whar about."

He carefully reconnoitered both rooms, not overlooking a single spot or failing to remove each and every article of furniture. Determined not to be baffled, he swung open the closet door, saying, with a coarse oath,

"I'll rip up this floor, like all thunder, till I find her. Whar is she? D—n it, Isaac, didn't you tell me she was hid somewhar here?"

"Yes, mas'er, to'ther night, when I was prowlin' round, I seed or thought I seed a woman settin' here, talkin' 'long with Rachel, and, from de way dey seemed to hide round, I tuck her to be a runaway, and de bit of a sight I got of her face, when I stole up to de winder, looked mightily like de widder Vitetor's Maria, as I 'members her."

The negro hung his head as he finished the sentence; he dared not meet the full, penetrating glance which Rachel fastened upon him.

"Let's rip up the floor," suggested Sharpe.

"Begin with the closet," cried Hynes.

Poor Rachel! her last hope fled affrighted. Clasping her hands tightly over her breast, she turned her eyes to heaven, resolving to meet the worst with composure.

In a few moments the slight board floor was torn off, and there, crouching closely down to the ground, shivering, trembling, half dead with fear, cowered the poor hunted fugitive.

"Well, this is a putty sight!" shrieked Hynes.

"Jist as I said—jist as I told you," cried Sharpe, rubbing his hands with delight; and, turning to Rachel, he added.

"You'll smart for this, I can tell you."

She did not speak, but stood with her glassy eye fixed on Maria.

The poor fugitive turned her eye from one to the other, with an eager, dazzled sort of look, scarcely seeming to comprehend the scene. The very lamp light was too strong and bright for her eyes, which had been so long accustomed to the darkness. Once only she extended her long black arms to her husband, as if begging from him that protection which she ought naturally to expect; but he was powerless, and turned from her to conceal, if possible, his own anguish.

"Rachel! Rachel!" she called out, in a heart-broken tone, "will they kill me? I wish they would."

It was a great blow. A blasting bolt come at the very moment when Hope seemed fairest! Liberty was lost, and she had no further wish, but, with a sullen sort of indifference, resolved to go and endure. So she soon commanded herself with such a show of resignation that Hynes afterwards declared he believed she was willing to go back to slavery. This assertion is often made by slave catchers, and we doubt not with as little truth.

"Come, every one of you," said Hynes; "come, right away, and git in my wagon. I'm goin' to take you to jail; and as for you, Rachel, I guesses it won't go well along with you. Thar has bin already a good deal of talk 'bout free niggers in the neighborhood, and a putty strong feelin' is got up agin' 'em, an' I guess you has put the finish to it. But, come, git on your bonnet an' bustle into the wagon."

She did not stop to look round her cabin, but only secured the key of her bureau, and, folding a shawl about her form, signified her readiness to follow. Maria's wrists were tied with a slight cord, and she was assisted into the wagon and seated near her husband.

They drove along rapidly in the still starlight, never speaking a word to each other, and scarcely heeding the coarse jokes and ribaldry of the men, who were smoking furiously all the while.

A dismal sense of loneliness and destitution came over Rachel when the grated door of the jail closed upon them, and the rusty lock clicked as if in mockery of her grief and shame.

XXVIII

Rachel, Maria and Peter, with one or two other innocent *accomplices* (who were arrested, tried and proved guilty on the merest suspicion), were hurried through a sham trial and sentenced by the bogus Court to receive nine-and-thirty lashes upon the bare back, at the public whipping-post. All through the trial, Rachel bore the most stolid and indifferent appearance. She knew, from the first, what would be the decision of *such* a court, and she possessed her soul in true bravery, little caring what might come; but Maria constantly wept and wrung her hands, all the while exclaiming, with groans and sighs, "I brung it upon you all; oh! that I had died first"; while Peter sat with sullen, silent face, not seeming to see or hear what was going on around.

It was a squire's court, and the case was soon disposed of. Only once, after Rachel had heard the Court's decision, and when they were taking her back to the jail, did her eye run round the house, as if in search of some one. She looked disappointed, and a half sigh escaped her, but, with that strong courage which heroic women realize in the moment of trial, she gathered up the forces of her soul (grief, shame, mortification were frozen upon her heart), and moved with as proud a step from that courtroom to the jail as though she had been going to a throne.

Once returned to the jail, with a generous self-forgetfulness she sought to minister, by manifold acts of kindness, to the comfort of Maria and Peter.

"Come," she said, with a pleasant, almost lively tone, "we mustn't be sad; let us not forget that pain only lasts for a short while. We do not feel that we have done wrong; our consciences are right; let us be bold and fear nothing else. What are thirty-nine whip lashes? they only cut the body, and cannot mortify the soul. The sting and smart are nothing. Come, cheer up, don't care for it."

"Yes; but, Rachel," said Maria, "I has lost freedom; I thought it was almost mine; 'pears to me now as if I had done lost everything. Ef they'd only kill me an' be done wid it, I'd thank 'em; but I kan't go back an' sarve agin as I has done. Dis little drap o' freedom has done got up my thirst, so dat I'll parch an' go mad if I has to be a slave agin; an' den, too, dey'll either take me to Missouri or sell me down de river, 'part from Peter, an' I shan't have no bit o' comfort."

Rachel felt all this; the slave woman's grief entered her heart; yet she forbore any words of encouragement to a grief so dreadful.

"Well, what of that?" she replied. "This life only lasts for a little while. You may soon die; and if your faith is good, you surely believe that it will be better hereafter. Come, cheer up; this world, with all its cruelty and oppression, will soon pass away, and the next one shall surely be better for you and me."

"Oh, Rachel, I is a poor sinner; and while dis great trouble is upon me, I kan't think 'bout de next world: I only *feels* dis here. I knows it all does very well for 'em as has got things nice an' fa'r to be a-talkin' 'bout de next world; but poor slaves, like Peter an' me, kan't afford to look away from dis here. Trouble sticks you down to dis. Why, Rachel when a chile is burnin' in fire, it don't do it no good to know dat dar is an ice-house quarter a mile nigh; de chile don't care for nothin' den; it only feels de burn; so you kan't git me off dis here. Den, too, I knows dat I has bin de cause of bringin' sufferin to you an' Peter; 'pears like I *could* bar it all to myself, but I doesn't like it to come to de rest o' you."

"Never mind 'bout me, Maria," added Peter between his sobs; "never mind 'bout me, ole 'ooman; only take kere o' yourself; 'tis 'bout you I keep all time studyin'. 'Tain't no use now kering 'bout anything, bekase we is jist got to walk up to dat whippin'-post, as we has walked up to a good many other trials; we has jist got to look it in de face, an' think 'bout dat 'ar cross dat dey hung de good Lord on; an' I tells you, it'll make us forgit de pain. I does," he continued, as he dashed his hand across his eyes, "feel sorry for Rachel; she is a lady person, an' it will go hard with her to stand up dar afore so many people an' be whipt like a dog; it's a great shame."

Rachel's face turned a shade paler, and her thin lip quivered, while the dilating nostril and flashing eye told how hard a struggle was going on between her pride and submission to circumstances.

"Why is it thus with me?" was the one bitter question that constantly flashed through her brain; yet, putting it aside, crushing down all useless repining, she took the rough hand of Maria within hers, and, in an altered voice, said,

"If I have been able to do you a kindness—if the cup of cold water and the crust of bread which I gave you, in the name of Christ and Humanity, have been of grateful service to you—I will now ask in return that you show your regard for me by trying to bear this present trouble; don't repine; you have need of all your strength; don't think of me. I can and *shall* endure my punishment with indifference, for I have a peace within my heart which no whip can lash out. All that I want of you and Maria is to try to be brave; and in order to do so, you must not again speak of the matter; by thinking and speaking of it, you lose your power of resistance. Talk about some more cheerful subject, and your spirits will be better.

"My sperrit is done knocked clean down; it's lying flat in de mud; an' I don't never 'spect to see it rise agin. I ain't one of 'em dat is of a willin' mind; I kan't be, like you an' Peter, reconcile. May be I hain't seen de Heavenly Dove. Dey say 'em dat sees dat is allers safe. Oh! Lord, I is so wicked dat I'm even 'fraid of '*a sign.*'"

In her generous effort to comfort these two poor, trembling slaves, Rachel was so completely drawn away from herself that she, too, received consolation. But let no one suppose that she was as indifferent to the impending punishment as her words seemed to imply and she believed. There were moments when the rush of grief and shame seemed almost ready to overwhelm her—when she stood faint and weary, ready, in her agony, to curse her fate. Let it be borne in mind that she had been comparatively delicately reared—that she was *free*—and though

oppressed for the few drops of dark blood that stained her veins, yet she
had never been a slave; and now to be humiliated by a public whipping
was bitter and galling.

....

Madge did not speak further with her father about Rachel,
but she was observed to be often alone, unusually silent. The negroes
remarked the change; poor Rover *realized* that something was wrong
with his mistress; he missed her usual playful fondling; he stole up to
her side, licked her hands, practised all his prettiest pranks and antics,
as if to win her back to sport and pleasure. Pomp often stole to her side,
and, with more than his wonted tenderness, asked, "Is yer sick, Miss
Madge?" But still she could not be beguiled.

"What is it, Madge?" asked Mrs. Vertner.

"Oh, nothing, mamma, only the world is so wicked."

"I don't think so, my dear. It has been, I am sure, a very good
world to you. I only wish, Madge, that you could see some of the poor
suffering people who live in the city alleys, who beg their bread from
door to door, who have scarcely clothes to protect them from the cold.
They have a *right* to complain, but you have every blessing, every luxury,
and yet sigh because the world is unkind."

"I think, mamma, you have made out my case for me, and
furnished me with the best arguments. I would that my condition
were less luxurious, since I am surrounded by so much suffering.
Now, if there are so many poor creatures starving, suffering for the
barest comforts, I do not believe we are entitled to so much ease and
luxury. We have no business owning all this land, keeping up such an
establishment, least of all holding so many servants."

"Why, Madge is an agrarian," exclaimed Mrs. Vertner to Helen,
who was sitting near.

"A what?" inquired Madge.

"Agrarian, my dear; that is, you think people should hold
property in common."

"I don't know what you call it; I only *feel* that it is wrong in
the sight of God for my father or any one to hold such an amount of
property, to live in such style, while hundreds are suffering for ordinary

comforts, and the only wonder is that God does not send us some signal punishment."

After Madge had left the room, Mrs. Vertner said to Helen,

"That girl grows stranger and more peculiar each day; I don't pretend to understand her; indeed, I am sometimes afraid that I do not feel rightly toward her; I often accuse myself of a want of maternal affection, but she is so singular, so perverse, so rude and almost rowdyish. You know she was sent away from me for the first years of her life to be nursed by old Susy, and I have often fancied that the old negro set some spell upon her; I have heard of such things, and am half tempted to believe them."

Helen laughingly answered,

"Well, the spell has only been one of great fascination. Madge charms everybody. My husband thinks her the most enchanting person he ever met; and as for the charm she exercises over me, I find that it increases with every year and month of my existence. One of the strongest ties my frail life bears to this world is Madge's love; and, dear Mrs. Vertner, I can't bear to have you speak and feel thus toward her. Madge observes it and is pained." Helen's voice faltered; tears were in her sweet eyes; but that little cough, which the least excitement produced, now came to the relief of her emotion.

"Now, Helen, dear, why will you excite yourself?" cried Madge, who opened the door just as that paroxysm of coughing began; "what have you been talking about—what has so agitated you?" and Madge wound her arms round Helen's neck, stroked her cheek, and said the most affectionate and soothing things to her.

Mrs. Vertner's face was very pale. Helen's words she felt to be a truth. She had often suspected that her child, her wild and truant, but loving and earnest, Madge, felt the want of genuine sympathy—pined for a mother's heart and a true mother's love; but when these doubts occurred to her mind, as they often did, she put them aside with the deluding assurance, "The child is so wild and boisterous that love would only be one of the many refinements which she puts scornfully under her feet"; and so the mother turned again to her jewels, laces and satins, and found ample pleasure there.

"Helen," whispered Madge, as she bent over her friend, "I want to go home with you this evening and stay to-night and to-morrow with you."

"I shall be delighted, Madge."

"Tell mamma—nay, Helen, ask her—perhaps she will be pleased by it."

Helen observed that Madge's eyes were wet with tears, and she felt touched by this pretty and affectionate little compliment which she wished to pay her mother, for it was a well-known fact that Madge went where and did what she pleased, asking no one's permission. Such had been the plan adopted by Col. Vertner. He, who stripped negroes of every shred of personal liberty, allowed the largest amount to his wife and child.

"Helen," said Madge, as they drove slowly into the village, "do you know why I proposed to spend to-night with you?"

"No, dear; it is, I suppose, only one of your fascinating whims, which, like all the rest, brings pleasure to me." She warmly pressed Madge's hand.

"Thank you, Helen; but, then, I have a particular reason for wishing to be in town to-morrow."

"Why, Madge?" Helen again pressed the little hand which still rested within her own. "And yet I half suspect your reason."

"And, Helen, you do not object, and will not attempt to thwart me?" She fixed her large, anxious eyes full upon her friend.

"I cannot oppose you, Madge, in anything, yet I wish you would consider this matter well. You surely do not mean to go to the—?"

"You cannot even say the word, Helen, your nerves are so weak; but I know what you mean. Yes, I shall go to the whipping-post. I shall see it, and then, afterward, determine what to do."

"Oh, Madge, why uselessly torture yourself by such a terrible sight?"

"If the *sight* will be terrible to me, what will the feeling be to the poor victims? My eyes are not more delicate than their backs. I shall be present at the whipping. Will you lend me your carriage?"

"Certainly; but can't I dissuade you?"

"No, don't attempt it; my mind is fully made up."

Helen's only answer was a silent pressure of the hand.

When they reached Mrs. Mason's house, they found Mr. Norton standing at the door, anxiously watching for them.

"Dear Helen," he exclaimed, as he gently assisted his wife from the carriage, "I hope this day has not been too much for your strength."

"Oh, no, indeed," she replied, as she leaned heavily upon that strong, protecting arm, "Madge always inspires me with a sense of her own infinite life. Do you know I seem to borrow strength from her?"

"Yes, my dear, and venture, perhaps, to build too largely upon that borrowed power, and so exhaust the loan before you are aware of it."

"Dear Helen," cried Madge, "I wish indeed that I could largely endow you with my surplus strength; but then it would not be well to have you too strong; who asks or expects, or even wishes, that the rose shall be strong? its very frailty and delicacy are portions of its wondrous beauty." Drawing a little nearer to Helen, she whispered, "Don't tell your husband where I am going to-morrow; don't tell any one."

Helen answered by one long, confiding, earnest, affectionate glance, which seemed to say, "Thy will shall be my law."

XXIX

Madge resolutely kept her intention. Helen dared not say a word further to dissuade her; too well she knew the determined temper of the girl she was dealing with. All through the evening Madge was as bright and animated as usual; no one but Helen could detect a cloud upon that brow or observe anything peculiar in the tone of her laughter. Once only—when Helen stole close to her friend's side, and, unobserved by the others, whispered, "Oh, Madge, what a fiery-tempered blade you are, to be sure"—did she start or tone down her exuberant spirits.

"Don't speak to me, Helen," she answered, in a whisper; "my heart is all on fire; and if I didn't laugh, I should be forced to cry. Can't you see that it is unnatural, forced, and—and—but don't say anything more, Helen; my eyes are full now, and—but I'm half blind. Let me go," and she left the room hastily.

"Poor child," thought Helen, "how can her mother complain of want of sentiment? It seems to me that she has too much."

Madge did not sleep much that night. The few moments of respite which she caught, as it were, from the anxious fever of disturbing thoughts were not passed in rest, but broken by frightful dreams and visions. Two or three times she shrieked aloud. Helen, overhearing her, rushed into the room.

"What is it, Madge dear," she exclaimed, as she held her sobbing friend close to her heart; "what is it, darling, that so disturbs you?"

"Oh! Helen, such a dream as I have had! terrible! terrible!" and she buried her face in her hands, and her whole frame shook with the violence of her grief.

"But it was *only* a dream, dear, and is past now; only one of those sickly, disordered fancies engendered by your nervous state."

"I am not nervous, Helen; have never had occasion to know that I had nerves. Papa always calls me his robust, muscular child."

"But you are nervous now; only see how you tremble."

"No, I am frightened—that dream *seems* so real; even now I can scarcely convince myself that it is untrue. It makes me shudder. Don't go away, Helen; stay awhile longer with me; I am afraid."

"Tell me your dream, Madge; perhaps the mere repetition of it to me will take away your fear; come, tell me, darling."

Thus coaxed into confidence, Madge gathered the bed clothing about her shoulders, and, flinging her rich hair away from her brow and face till it floated down her neck in long, rich masses of half-curls, and taking Helen's hand in one of hers, while the other shaded her eyes from the light, she began to speak, in a quiet tone.

"It was a strange, confused sort of dream. I thought I was in a wild woody place, alone, at night time; there was neither moon nor star-light, yet it was not dark. A sort of blue-grey light served as a lamp to show me the gloom and desolation by which I was surrounded. I can recall the scene perfectly now, and the same vague, indefinable, chilly fear creeps over me that crept over me then, as an old, haggard, witch-like creature emerged from some of the recesses of the woods, and, seizing violently hold of me, bore me, in spite of my cries and prayers, off with her to a horrible-looking den, where she said I properly belonged. 'You are not Madge Vertner,' she said, 'but a dirty, wicked sprite, whom I have at last found, and you shall not leave me again.' I importuned, I begged, I wore my breath out with cries and entreaties, offered her all my father's wealth if she would only release me, but she only laughed the louder, saying that her revenge was at last gloated. At this point I awoke with that scream which roused you. The dream, as I repeat it, Helen, sounds foolish, delusive and dream-like, but to my fancy it had a terrible distinctness, and even now it haunts my memory like a half-reality."

After much soothing, and at Helen's urgent solicitation, she took an anodyne. Madge fell into a sound sleep, which proved a sweet restorer, and the next morning she rose refreshed and in her wonted spirits.

At ten o'clock the carriage was at the door. As Helen wrapped Madge's shawl around her shoulders, she lovingly whispered,

"Dearest, let me go with you. I cannot bear that you should have such distressing excitement and no one near to soothe or comfort you."

"No, Helen, you have not nerve enough; besides, you would be no possible assistance to me. Let me perform my dismal task alone. I am strong to-day as a Hercules. I feel that my nerves can endure anything. Burning rage and scorn are the only feelings I know of now, and they consume in secret. I have an object in this."

"What is it?"

"Not now, dear Helen; perhaps I *may* tell you some time, but certainly not now."

"I'll not urge you further; but promise me one thing, darling— that you will not tax your strength too far."

"I promise," and, kissing her affectionately, Madge jumped into the carriage.

"Henry," said Helen to the coachman, "drive Miss Madge where she directs; watch her well; if she seems much excited or looks sick, urge her to come home."

"Yes, miss, I will," replied the slave, in an obsequious tone, well-pleased with the compliment which Miss Helen's command implied, and, after receiving Madge's order (with very evident surprise), he mounted his box and drove off rapidly through the village to an old out-field about half-a-mile from the town. Here they found already quite a number of people, from the town and country for twenty miles round about, assembled to witness, one would suppose, some great gala sight. Stopping the horses suddenly, Henry descended from the box and, looking into the window, asked,

"How near does you want to go, Miss Madge? Shall I stop on de outside of de crowd or does you want to go a little higher to the post?"

The negro's voice fell upon the last word.

"I suppose we cannot get the carriage any nearer, and may as well stop here."

She sank far back into the carriage and drew her veil closely about her face. Persons were gathering in tens and scores, pressing near to the carriage, and peering curiously in. Madge felt her cheek flush and her eye flash as she was thus rudely and vulgarly stared at.

"Miss Madge," said the driver, as he drew near the window, "Miss Madge, these country folks stares at you so dat it must pester you a good deal; hadn't I better drive you back?"

"No, no," was the hasty, but positive, answer.

Henry turned away disappointed. The fact is, he was mortified and did not like to have one of his mistress's friends seen at such a place. As the farmers' boys and girls passed the carriage and tried to peep in under the drooping silk curtain, he called out to them,

"What's you peepin' so fur? Did you never see quality before? Keep yer eyes to yourself, or I'll fling sand into 'em."

"Never mind it, Henry; let the poor, idle people look at the carriage if it gives them occupation. They have come to see a terrible thing. By and bye they'll have no eyes for me."

"Yes, marm; but, den, I never lets 'em gap 'at sort o' way at Miss Helen or mistress when they goes out to drive. Dese poor whites has to be kep' down, Miss Madge; dey ain't no better dan corn-field niggers."

"Yes, but you would allow corn-field negroes to look at whatever they wished."

"No, marm, I wouldn't; dey has no sort o' bisness looking at quality."

The negro (the slave), be it remembered, is never a democrat in principle. The rule that has oppressed him makes him also wish to oppress others.

Meanwhile the populace—the towns-people and country folks—had been steadily flocking to the field, until a very great crowd had assembled.

Following close behind a band of two or three men—constables or some petty officials—came the prisoners. First, Maria and her husband, then those who had been convicted as accomplices, Rachel bringing up the rear-line. All eyes were fixed upon them.

The officer walking in front waved his baton and cleared away the crowd that pressed so close to the whipping-post. Beside this four-sided post of eight or nine feet in height, with iron clasps on the opposing sides, stood the man hired to do the *law* honor by whipping these wicked negroes. He cracked his whip (which was a long, red cow-skin), as if to try its quality, and, turning to one of the bystanders, said, "It'll do, and will take some of the fire out of them d—d black skins."

"Take off your coat and shirt," was the command of the constable to Peter.

The negro obeyed.

The iron clasps were then fastened upon the wrists and ancles, and an order given to the man to "lay on the whip," which was promptly obeyed. The victim writhed with pain; but no cry escaped his lips. "Nine and thirty lashes upon the bare back, in the presence of witnesses," were given to vindicate the most honorable and Christian law!

Covered with blood, and with a face working with pain, Peter was set free from the post; then followed Maria. At the first lash, she screamed aloud, prayed and begged for mercy; but the crowd of boys only shouted out in reply, "You ought to thought of this when you was runnin' away." Her agony was terrible to witness; and we believe even that heartless and ribald crowd was glad when she was released from the stock. And now every eye was drawn with peculiar, if not anxious, interest upon Rachel. Her step was firm and unfaltering as she drew near the post; but the deadly whiteness of her face, the dark, defiant glitter of her eye and the nervous twitter of her lip proved how deep and terrible was the emotion she sought to conceal.

"Take off the waist of your frock," said the man.

Without a moment's hesitation she removed the bodice, and, with an eye growing fiercer in its expression, stood calm and unmoved. A shudder ran round the crowd when that fair skin was exposed to the coarse and vulgar view. Fathers—hardened workmen though they were—thought, no doubt, of their own daughters, whose skins were scarcely fairer, and could not resist the shudder.

Lash after lash descended upon the quivering flesh; blood flowed at every cut; but the face of the victim was as stern as an iron-mailed soldier's. Except what was natural from the loss of blood, the cheek itself scarcely grew paler; but the eye shone out with a fearful and vengeful light. As the twenty eighth lash descended, a voice from the crowd cried out,

"Hold, you shall not strike the woman another blow."

"Who said that?" asked the man. "I'm the minister of the law; here to do my duty, and I won't be interfered with!"

But Col. Vertner, looking as pale as the poor bleeding victim beside him, stood close to the post. A whispered word to the man, no doubt the promise of pecuniary reward, satisfied that worthy luminary of our most *wise* and virtuous law.

Rachel had been firm—hard, it would seem—until now, when she heard Col. Vertner's voice and saw him standing close beside her; then everything gave way, and she swooned. Andrew Vertner, with a man's heart in his breast, forgot for the moment outward circumstances, and caught the fainting form in his own arms and pillowed that sorrowing head upon his bosom. "Poor, poor girl," were the words that he whispered, as he held her to his heart, in the presence of that jeering crowd, which for the moment was silenced, if not awed.

In a moment there was a buzz of curious wonder as a light, girlish figure made its resolute way through the crowd. Throwing back her veil, she said, in a firm tone,

"Papa, let me assist you."

"Madge!" cried Col. Vertner, in a voice of painful surprise.

"Yes, papa, I am here; but I did not expect to meet you. Bring the woman to the carriage."

"Who brought you here?" he asked.

"I came in Mrs. Mason's carriage, and there I intend to take this poor woman."

"Have you asked permission?"

"Helen is willing."

Just then a negro woman, whom we recognize at once as Hetty, rushed up to the post, crying out,

"Oh, Lord! young miss, here, I'se got some soft cotton and a drop or so of ile for dis poor critter. Give her to me, Mas'er Vartner; I can tote her to de ravine nigh here, and wash dis blood and grease off de poor critter, and den she'll be mightily he'ped up."

Yielding her to Hetty, Col. Vertner and Madge followed. The stream was quite near, and Madge watched the woman as she tenderly washed off the blood stains, and applied oiled cloths to the wounded flesh. Slowly Rachel opened her eyes, glanced round, then closed them with an expression of pain.

"Poor critter, she is more 'an half in a dream now," said Hetty; "poor chile, I'se glad to do even dis much fur you, bekase you'se been kind to me."

In a half-senseless state Rachel was taken to the carriage. Madge ordered the driver to place her upon the most comfortable seat; and, getting in, sat near the sick woman, taking one of those dark hands softly within her own, and gazing with an expression of tender regard into the care-worn, suffering face beside her. Col. Vertner marked this; and if he *had* hitherto loved his daughter, he now worshipped her as an angel whom he had been entertaining unawares.

"My child, God bless you," he said, as he pressed his lip to her brow; "but stay; one word. This poor, half-crazy woman will, no doubt, rave in delirium. You know, Madge, it will not be well for you to heed her. Extend to her the courtesy of not listening, which you would give to a woman of your own color."

"Certainly, papa."

As the carriage drove off, and Col. Vertner turned to remount his horse, he murmured to himself,

"What a child she is!"

But, poor man! he could not be heroic and brave without apologizing for it; so he betook himself again to the crowd, and there explained that the victim was a woman, and her punishment had been too heavy for her strength of constitution; that he was opposed to the use of the whip, &c. But the crowd, though obsequious to him, was a little more astute than he thought; they had heard too much of neighborhood gossip to "swallow," as one man expressed it, "all of the Colonel's statement about pity," &c.

Madge drove rapidly to Mrs. Mason's house.

Drive me to the private entrance, Henry; and now tell one of your house-girls to say to your Miss Helen that I wish to speak to her."

Helen obeyed the summons promptly.

"What is it, Madge?"

"Only see, I have brought Rachel home in an insensible state; I suppose you will not refuse her your house."

"Certainly not. Here, Henry, you assist Lyd to carry her into the little off-room of the left hall."

Very soon after this, Rachel was snugly stored away in a comfortable bed; cordials were administered; and the two friends, Madge and Helen, had the satisfaction of seeing very evident signs of returning consciousness and improvement. Slowly the weary woman opened her eyes, fixed them earnestly on Madge, murmured some inaudible words and closed her eye-lids, as if to sleep.

"How pretty she is, in spite of that painful expression and that wounded flesh," said Helen.

And that night, when talking the matter over with her husband, she was enthusiastic in praise of her friend's brave charity and her many quiet acts of mercy, not the least among which she reckoned this kindness to Rachel.

"Ah, yes," replied Mr. Norton, "Madge Vertner remembers Christ's words, 'Inasmuch as you did it to the least of them, you did it unto me.'"

XXX

The kind attentions of Madge and Helen wrought most favorably on the sufferer. They had the satisfaction of soon seeing her in a soft, sweet sleep.

"Come, now," said Helen, gently, as they watched the quiet, undisturbed breathing of the sleeper, "come, now, Madge; she sleeps well; let us go to our rooms; we will leave the lamp lighted and the little bell on the table, close by her bed, so that she can call for anything she wants."

"Somehow, Helen, I don't feel willing to leave her; besides, I am not sleepy, but I insist upon your going to bed. Leave me here awhile longer."

"Madge," repeated Helen, in a half rebuking tone, "do you think it is right to act thus? Do you know that you are trifling with your health—with your life, *perhaps?* After this intensely exciting day, I think you need rest and calm. Why should you risk yourself longer in this room? Now, I never dissuade you from anything where I think there is a shadow of duty, but I can't think it wise now to neglect warning you."

"Don't say any more, Helen; I shan't sit up long; but do leave me a few minutes here; be sure I'll not forget your warning."

With very evident reluctance, Helen left the room, and Madge seated herself in a chair near the bed. But she was of too restless a temperament to remain long in this quiet sort of way. Going to the window and throwing back the curtain, she looked up and afar at the still and peaceful stars.

"Strange! is it not?" she thought, "that *we* cannot be quiet, orderly and peaceful as those old pale planets. I see the stars move on in their old, accustomed and well-directed course; the flowers are true to their annual comings; everything obeys Law, and is in harmony, except man. Why is this? Ah, me! I am half tired of life. 'Tis hard to feel thus when things might be different. I can't understand why all this pain and trouble should be in the world. The sight I witnessed to-day can never be wiped out of my memory; and here, by the bed-side of this poor sufferer, and with the still stars shining down on me and the cool night-breeze that blows from heaven, fresh upon my brow, I call God to hear my vow, that I never will, by any voluntary act of my own, contribute to the perpetuation of slavery."

"*Amen*" was uttered in a hollow, sepulchral tone, close to her.

She started, half in surprise, half in fright, and saw Rachel sitting upright in the bed.

"What, are you awake? Do you feel better? Has your sleep refreshed you?" and Madge hastily closed the window.

"Yes, I am better, Miss Vertner; that is, these flesh wounds do not pain me so much; but the wounds made on my spirit are not healed, though your gentle attention and kindness have not been without effect."

Rachel passed her hand hastily over her eyes, then drew off very slowly some of the oiled cloths from her wounded arms and back. Shaking her head and smiling scornfully, she muttered,

"Oil and cotton may heal the flesh, but who, who is to pluck the poison from the soul? Let me see" (turning toward Madge and taking the little lamp from the table, she held it close to the young girl's face)—"let me see, Miss Vertner, who you look like. Ah, yes, I see it: slightly, very slightly, like your father; the resemblance is not in the features, but it lives and burns in the expression; there is a battle-axe in your eye; if you mean a thing, you will do it. You are stronger of purpose, more single in soul than your father." Here Madge lost the words, though the woman still muttered to herself.

"My father stood by you in the hour of your painful trial; and when your strength gave way, it was *his* arm that upheld you." Madge said this with some show of pride.

"Aye, yes; his arm *did* uphold me, as you say, but, young lady, it was when that wretch's lash had done its worst, when my strength had oozed and gushed out with my blood. Yes, with my blood! Do you hear *that?* Tell it to your father, as my last message." Her tone had grown very loud, and her eye flashed fiercely; flecks of froth were upon her writhing lip, while she twisted her fingers together as though they had been cords.

"But stay," she continued, in a calmer voice, "you did me a service, and I shall not forget it. If ever I can serve you in any way—and it may not always be beyond my power—be sure I shall, for I am not one to forget a favor, especially such kindness as you have rendered me; and 'tis well for you that your heart prompted you to such goodness, else God only knows what my revenge *might* have prompted me to do. Now, I have double reason for keeping what I know." She shook her head, mournfully and slowly, two or three times, repeating, in a half whisper, "Yes, double reason for it."

Madge was surprised; she did not understand this wild kind of talk, and was about to question the woman, when she remembered her father's injunction, and thought,

"No, I'll not play a spy upon her feverish, delirious raving"; so she resolved to leave the room.

"Rachel," she said, "I am going to my own room now. Is there anything you wish? Won't you drink this? it is a soothing draught, and will do you good."

Rachel drank it, and, pushing her hair back from her brow, she drew Madge Vertner close to her.

"Oh, beautiful child, pure-hearted girl! let me look at you once again; let me hold the lamp so, close to your face; let me examine these temples, these eyes so fine and fiery. I know whence comes their power. Miss Vertner, 'tis well you have been kind to me in this fatal hour, for you have plucked the sting from my revenge, and have saved me the commission of an act I should ever after have regretted. 'Tis well, 'tis very well," she muttered to herself; "and now, child" (as she replaced the lamp upon the stand), "you had better go to bed; do not let me keep you up any longer; I am very much better. Thank you for all your kindness to me. I belong to a despised race, but one that is patient, long-suffering, and, above all, truly grateful. This little act of yours you may not know, you cannot know *now*, what it has bought. Let me ask you, now and here, to be as kind when you can to all of my poor wretched race whom you may meet or find in trouble, and God will bless you." With a tremulous voice and tears flowing unchecked from her eyes, she drew Madge yet closer to her, and, taking that fair young face within her hands, she pressed her lips gently to the brow. Madge Vertner did not withdraw, tears were in her own eyes as she said,

"Good night; try to sleep, good Rachel, and to-morrow you will be really better"; and so she left the room.

Scarcely had the door closed ere Rachel half sprang from the bed and began dressing herself.

"I shall not stay here an hour longer. I shall be off, and the places that have known me shall not know me again for many years, if ever. 'Tis wrong and dangerous for me to remain. I know not that I could again be strong enough to resist the temptation of revenge. That poor fair child, with her winning voice, has softened me. But could she do so again? No, I'll not trust myself."

She was soon ready for her flight, and, stealing noiselessly from the house, started directly for her own cabin. How strange, wan and half weird she looked when gliding through the bare woods, in the pale light of the newly-risen moon! Had any one met her, he would surely have taken her for a witch, "goblin damned," or some sort of unrighteous spirit commissioned for the execution of a deed of horror. At length, after a weary walk, she reached the cabin. Upon the very threshold she paused, overcome by a tumult of feeling, and, sitting down upon the sill, burst into a flood of tears. Pushing open the half-closed door, she peered into the darkened room, and then, with a sad wail, broke out,

"It has been a good home to me. I've had both pain and pleasure here, but I shall never have either again under this roof. Oh, my heart *ought* to be stout, *ought* to be strong, but it is not; it is only weak and bruised as my poor body." And there she sat rocking her form back and forth until her grief had fairly spent itself, when she set to work. Gathering together several articles of clothing and some few valuables and relics, she made up a package, and, about dawn, took leave of her cabin.

"All my furniture, small though it be, my cabin, horse and cow, my poor little handful of goods and effects, I leave for those white people, whom I hate, to do as they please with. I shall have no further use for the things of this world. My bread must be found by the wayside, and my raiment gotten only as chance or circumstance may provide. I've lived out my time—my peace; and now, as I feel the tide of wicked feelings rising high again in my breast, I must be gone at once— God only to care for me!"

We shall not follow her in her long wanderings, through wood and wild, over stream and fell, bog and mire, restless as the Wandering Jew. We must part from her now, not to see her again for some time.

....

The next morning Madge was both surprised and distressed to discover Rachel's flight. When her father called, she related to him all that had passed between herself and the woman.

"Was it not strange, dear papa, for her to leave so suddenly? I feel uneasy about her. She was in no condition to go out. I wonder if she went to her own cabin."

"Very likely, my child. Have you told me all of her talk?"

"Yes, all that I remember."

"I hope you were not frightened by it. 'Twas only the incoherent, meaningless talk of a sick, nervous woman. But come, my dear, my chaise is at the door. Your mamma wishes you to come home."

She thought her father's manner strange and slightly agitated. Going up to him, she passed her arm round his neck and pressed her lips to his brow.

"What is it, papa? What is it that troubles you so? Your countenance is troubled."

"Nothing troubles me, darling; only I fear that you have over-exerted yourself."

"Helen," she said, when she had left the parlor and was arranging her bonnet and shawl—"Helen, papa is not well; something *is* the matter. I wonder if that little kind act of his yesterday to that poor creature has caused people to annoy him in any way. But—psha! he would not care for that. Who are these town's people but a set of idle curs, whose opinions are not worth a farthing?"

Madge did not soon forget the look of anxious, tender solicitude which Helen gave her in reply to this, as she silently folded her to her heart and impressed a kiss upon her slightly-flushed cheek.

XXXI

We are to suppose the flight of weeks and months, the passage of winter, with its winds and snows, and the coming and going of March, April and May, in the interim which marks the last chapter from the present, and to find ourselves now in the middle of the leafy June—the fairest month of all the twelve. Few changes had occurred in the lives of the occupants of Vertner Place, if, indeed, we except a trip to New Orleans, where our little Madge saw the great world of fashionable life as it heaved, bounded and *rollicked* in that most brilliant and dissipated of American cities. She went to the opera, theatre, *bal mosqué* at the St. Charles; drove down the famous shell road; lounged through the mornings in galleries and print shops; dined and supped late; laughed at the beaux and criticized the belles; moved among the brilliant throng, but bore no part in its revelry. At length, after wearying through three months, Mrs. Vertner concluded, to Madge's delight, to return to Kentucky. The tedium of the latter portion of the *soi disant* gay season was enlivened by a visit from Mr. Butler, who had just returned from Havana in time to join the Vertner party and accompany them to Mobile. Those were delightful, sunny afternoons when he and Madge sauntered along the bay, gathering shells and talking poetry. Madge did not say much; *she only listened.* He used, sometimes, while in New Orleans, to drive her, in an open chaise, for miles down the shell road.

When beyond the city, she often took the reins from him and drove for some distance, while he lolled back with a sort of *laissez faire* manner, admiring the small white hands that so dexterously guided the reins. During such hours of sweet, familiar intercourse, who can say what mysterious sympathy grew up between them? Certain it is that the wild eyes of our young heroine now began to grow dreamy beneath their curtain of long, slumbrous-looking lashes, and her cheeks flushed and paled more rapidly than was their wont, while a pretty, peculiar pettishness marked her manner. About this time Helen Norton observed a change in the tone of Madge's letters to her; there was no longer that critical vein, no curt, sententious observations upon the "fashionability," as Madge termed those gay metropolitans; she also missed the light-hearted jest, the witty animadversion or hilarious description. All was toned down, subdued and half solemn, with an occasional mention of Mr. Butler, such as "he says or thinks so."

"I understand and see it all," exclaimed Helen, as she one day folded up a short letter from Madge. "She is engaged, and will not or does not choose to tell me. Well, never mind, I shan't question her about it."

Mr. Butler accompanied the Vertners home; and when Helen first saw him and Madge together, her conjecture was confirmed.

"But, dear Helen," cried Madge, after the first embrace was over, "how pale and thin you look. I really think you should have gone with us to Orleans. The air was so soft and balmy—soft as our May. I wished for you often, particularly when *we* strolled through the orange groves or drove down the shell road."

"Whom do you mean by *we?*" asked Helen, with a smile.

"Oh, nonsense! mamma, papa and all of us," Madge replied, with a blush.

Several days after, when they were alone in Madge's queer little room, and as Helen rested on the sofa, and her friend sat on an ottoman beside her, chafing those now sunken temples, Helen asked,

"And what, Madge, of Mr. Butler? He has come back with you. Why and in what capacity?"

Madge turned away her head; the long lashes drooped till they swept her crimson cheek, and her fingers toyed with the ribbon-lacings of her basque.

"Come, tell me, Mignion," added Helen, coaxingly.

"Well" (in a whisper), "we are engaged; but, dear Helen, don't look at me or speak of it. I am free on every other subject, but this one seems to involve the charm and mystery of my very life, and so changes or seems to change my whole nature that I hug it to and hide it in my heart, almost as if it were a guilty thing; and yet I am not coy, as you know, on other matters; but this strange, new relation that I have entered into appears like a wild, fanciful dream, which a word, a tone may possibly dissolve."

All this was said with an averted face and in a voice subdued to a whisper.

"How you love him, and with so much of romance!" added Helen, very softly.

"Not romance, Helen," Madge replied, as she withdrew her hand from the prolonged clasp of her friend's, "but perhaps fervor; and yet, when we were first engaged, I can't say that I was happy. It seemed that I had parted from my own independence—bartered away the right to myself. Several times I was on the eve of going to Mr. Butler and begging him to release me from the oppressive bond. In those dreary hours of doubting love, Helen, I wished for you, and once actually wrote a long, full letter describing my state of feeling, but did not send it. I had no one to talk to; I dared not go to mamma, for I knew she would condemn it as eccentricity; and so I worked it out alone—a difficult problem, to be sure. I never afterward dared to tell Mr. Butler; for do you know, Helen, I can't think that men understand women!"

"No, they don't; how can they? But my husband seems to know *me* as thoroughly as any one—as thoroughly as I wish him."

"What does he intend doing with your slaves? I thought they were to be freed at once," inquired Madge, in her old, abrupt way, as, without an apology or explanation, she broke off from the main staple of their conversation.

"Oh" (Helen coughed), "they are to be liberated as soon as the affairs of the estate are wound up; but my father's business was left in a dreadfully perplexed condition, and the executors seem fearfully slow in winding it up; but we must bide our time and patiently await results."

"It is a pity you cannot do it at once; for I am sure you must dislike this putting off of a solemn duty; beside—beside"—

She could not finish the sentence; tears choked her utterance.

"Beside," continued Helen, "you were going to say *I* may not live to witness the performance of so just a deed. Don't cry, Madge; I know my fate—know that the sand in my glass is almost run out; but, then, my noble husband, he who first taught us the sin of slavery, will remain to do the work."

"Is there no question of his doing what you wish?"

"Madge" (Helen's cheek flushed), "how can you ask such a question? Who made you and me Abolitionists? Who spoke the first anti-slavery word, uttered the first free thought and liberal sentiment we ever heard? Who but my husband? And now you ask if there is any doubt of his acting out the whole of his idea and performing his duty? Madge, I am surprised."

"Nonsense, Helen, why get excited about such a thing? I have heard papa say that not one in a hundred or even one in a thousand of those talking Abolitionists would *act* out the theory they preach if they could change places with slaveholders; moreover, I heard that the people about here, the villagers and country men, were speaking of Mr. Norton as a suspected person, when some one observed, 'Oh, no, indeed, we have fixed him; as soon as he married Helen Mason, and got negroes of his own, you didn't hear any more of the "sin of slavery." I dare say he calls the institution divine by this time. Don't say anything about him; he is all right on the goose.' Now, I am sure, Helen, you do not wish your husband to be charged in this way with such cruel and selfish inconsistency; do you?"

"I don't like it, Madge; of course ill-natured remarks are never pleasant; but I am by no means as much annoyed as you probably expected; for I know and cannot blame the villagers for speaking thus. They do not understand a mind and heart like Mr. Norton's. He is made on a plane too far above them. But I do not like for you, Madge, my nearest and dearest friend, to doubt him. Be sure everything will be for the best; and the great plan which my husband proposes will be carried out fully and entirely. I would as soon doubt the old, eternal principles of Justice and Truth as distrust him. Unworthy taint or doubt never yet touched his name."

Large tears stood in Madge's clear eyes and lingered lovingly upon the sweeping fringe of brown lashes as she laid her head tenderly upon Helen's shoulder, saying,

"Forgive me if I believe that we are all mortal."

"What do you think, Madge," said Mrs. Vertner, as she entered the room, holding in her hand two fine Bohemian wine-glasses of different color—"what do you think? That beautiful amber glass belonging to my Harlequin set is missing. I am sure Ruth has broken it. This is the first time I have been into the china closet since early last summer, before we went to the Cave. Col. Vertner wishes to have a little card party this evening, and I went in the pantry to get out this set, and I find the handsomest glass missing. It spoils the set, and I am puzzled what to do, for such things can't be replaced in our little good-for-nothing village. Helen, has your mother a set of Bohemian?"

"No, ma'm, I am sorry, but we have nothing of the kind."

"It is too provoking. Nothing goes right in the pantry, china-closet or dining-room since that vile Daniel ran off."

"Why, mamma, I am sure you said you were glad that he was gone, and wished that all the others might follow, as they were only a good-for-nothing, trifling set," observed Madge, with a sly smile.

"So they are, and the bother and pest of my life; but you should not say a word, Madge Vertner; for if it had not been for your impertinent interference, your father would have advertised Daniel, and then we should have had him back. Ruth is very awkward in the dining-room. I believe I'll have her hired out next year, and will hire a boy in her place. I don't think it is proper to have a girl in the dining-room; besides, a woman is never as quick or so good a waiter; but there comes Ruth. I'll attack her with this. She is certainly the most artful creature and ready at a falsehood."

The girl entered, with a broad smile lighting up her countenance, and looking very tidy in her clean apron and head handkerchief.

"When did you break that amber Bohemian glass belonging to this set?" asked Mrs. Vertner, as she held the glasses toward Ruth.

"Me, miss—me, miss—*me—me* never broke dat wine-glass; me never seed it sense I's bin 'tendin' on de dinin'-room an' keepin' de pantry. I'm sure Dan'l must have broke it. Dan'l was *powerful* kereless boy. I hearn 'em say dat he broke more chany and flung it away dan I could shake a broom at. Dan'l was an orful sly'un, miss."

All this was delivered in a rapid tone and with an unflinching, wide-open eye as she stared her mistress full in the face. No lawyer could have excelled her in the readiness and art of lying. Moreover, she had an old grudge against Daniel for running off to Canada without giving her a hint, and now liked to implicate him. Mrs. Vertner looked alternately at Helen and Madge, then at Ruth.

"'Tis de truth dat I speaks, miss; 'pon my soul it is; I could cross my heart to it."

"Helen," asked Mrs. Vertner, "did you ever hear anything quite equal to this? I am sure that girl broke the glass; and though she knows her punishment will be slight, if any, she prefers telling a lie to the truth."

"I hain't told no lie, miss; hope de Lord may kill me if I has."

"Mistress, does you want to know who broke dat 'ar wine-glass tumbler?" exclaimed Pomp, as he rushed in at the open door, looking very "smart" and spry, in a red soldier-jacket with brass buttons, which his Miss Madge had given him.

"I ken tell yer all 'bout it, 'kase I seed 'em."

Ruth turned suddenly round upon the boy.

"'T wasn't me, was it, Pomp? 'twas Dan'l, wasn't it? yer seed him." Then, in a whisper, she said, "I'll give you a bagful of marbles and a gum-ball."

"No, now, Ruth, me ain't gwine to tell a story to miss, not fur two bags o' marbles; but will you (in an undertone) gib me dat feather an' old ridin'-hat you stole from Miss Madge? If yer will, I'll say what yer wants me to."

Before Ruth had time to reply, Mrs. Vertner had taken Pomp by the arm and drawn him away, saying,

"Now, if you dare to tell me a lie, I'll have you taken to the lock-up or sent to the overseer. Come, what do you know about that glass?"

"Well, now, mistress, last summer, when you all was 'way, dat yaller 'ooman, Rachel she call herself, come here one day to see Uncle Peter an' Aunt Polly; and Aunt Polly brung Rachel down here to de dinin'-room, whar Ruth an' Dan was a-sittin', courtin'; dey use to be all time talkin' 'long 'emselves or walkin' 'bout locked arms; an' Dan'l,

he went an' got out some wine an' cake, and dem fine tumblers, jest de
same as you's got in yer hands, an' dey all tuck a glass o' wine and a slice
o' cake. I looked in de winder an' seed 'em, so I axed Dan'l please to
give me some. I thought you wouldn't kere, miss, if I had a little as long
as de rest was a usin' it up. I didn't mean to drink de wine out o' yer
tumbler—no, indeed, miss, I wouldn't do de like of dat. I was gwine to
git my tin cup, an' git de wine in dat; but Dan'l, he jest put his hand out
de winder an' shoved me off, an' said, 'go way, nigger, when yer betters
is eatin' an' drinkin'; but I never went 'way; I jest looked right in at 'em.
Dar dey all sot round—Aunt Polly wid 'em—drinkin' de wine an' eatin'
de cake, an' my mouth jist watered fur it. Every two or three minnits
Dan'l keep sayin' to me, 'go way, Pomp,' but I never minded of him, but
looked right in at 'em. Ruthy had a yaller glass, an' she kept holdin' it
on her fingers, jest like I tops my ball, when she let it fall off and break
to pieces at her feet. Den Dan'l say it didn't make any difference when
he seed Aunt Polly and Ruth so skeered. Dat is de way it got broke,
miss."

"Laws, Pomp, ain't you 'shamed to tell sich an orful lie? Miss, 'fore
Heaven, dar isn't a scrimption of de truth in dat 'ar he has bin a-tellin."

Mrs. Vertner took her purse from her pocket and gave the boy a
dime. Pomp, quite elated at his success, bounded out of the room, after
the "thankee, miss," was said. As he passed Ruth, she shook her fist at
him saying,

"I'll pay you for dis, yet."

"Very well, Ruth, I see you; do you dare put on your impudent
capers where I am?" said Mrs. Vertner; "this is the way you behave
yourselves when I leave home, is it? You are the meanest and most
ungrateful set of negroes that I ever heard of, after all my efforts to
make you religious. Don't I give you time off Sunday afternoons to
go to church? And when clergymen are here and hold prayers, don't
I allow you to come in and kneel down in the corner. Yet you will lie
in this way. Well, I can't blame myself, for I have had you all talked to
by religious men, and I paid thirty dollars toward the building of that
African church; yet this is the reward. Go out, now, Ruth; the overseer
will settle this matter with you."

Of course the girl began to cry, but not to beg; she knew that further remonstrance would be of no avail, so she did as she was commanded.

"Isn't it too bad," said Mrs. Vertner, "that I should be so treated by my servants when I do such a good part by them? Helen, does your mother have so much trouble?"

"She doesn't complain as much as she used to, and, I really think, gets along better; though they do annoy her a great deal. You know she is nervous and weak."

"Mamma," put in Madge, "I do not think it was anything wrong for the servants to have had a little amusement while we were off enjoying ourselves at the Cave. I am sure the wine they drank was never missed; and as for breaking your glass, to be sure it spoils a handsome set, however we can easily replace it when we visit the city; but, dear mamma, I didn't feel exactly right about your giving Pomp a reward for his treachery."

"It was no treachery," said Helen, who was anxious for the exactness of terms.

"Yes, to his race. I never like to have one of the servants tell on the other, and I shall discourage such a thing in Pomp; it looks mean."

"Did you ever hear any one talk so recklessly?" exclaimed Mrs. Vertner. "Why, Madge, what sort of mistress will you make?"

"I never mean to keep slaves."

"Nonsense! you won't sell our old family servants when you are fortunate enough to come into immediate possession of your property."

"No; I'll do something better by them. I'll set them free."

"Ridiculous! Madge, do remember that you are on the verge of womanhood, no longer a child, and don't talk such nonsense. It seems as if your mind did not grow an inch; you talk as a child. But what do you think of Ruth's stealing your riding-hat? Pomp said something about it. Have you missed it?"

"Yes, I lost an old, disused hat; but it was of so little consequence that I never cared to look for it. I am sure Ruth is entirely welcome."

"There, there," cried Mrs. Vertner, "is another evidence how little interest Madge takes in the souls of the negroes. She doesn't appear to understand religious responsibility, and would allow an offence of this kind to pass unnoticed. I take a very different view of it, and hold myself bound before the Lord to make these negroes obey God's law, and not violate the commandments. Our clergyman always said that it was a very beautiful relation, that of master, mistress and slave; and I think so, too, when the slaves are willing, obedient and docile; but mine are so ungrateful."

"Mamma, what have slaves to do with God's written law or the Ten Commandments? They can't read."

"But I send mine alternate weeks to the black Sunday schools, and they have preachers who tell them their duty."

"Poor mamma!" exclaimed Madge, as Mrs. Vertner left the room, "she really thinks so."

"Ah, there is the difficulty," replied Helen; "when people believe an error, they are not willing to open their minds to truth. Our friends act upon a predetermined sentiment, and so they lock up their consciences, and we don't know how to work best with them."

"Well, Helen, I found something the other day that pleased me very much. Papa asked me to overhaul some papers for him and clear out one of his secretary drawers. While I was doing it, I found a little pamphlet; it was a speech of some Northern man of whom I never heard, because I do not read political papers. Well, I began reading it. Of course there was much that I did not understand—reference to old party measures, Congressional enactments, &c.—but there was a charm and spell about the language and spirit that went direct to my heart. The more I read, the more the fascination increased. That man is an earnest, truth-loving, great-souled character. I read the little pamphlet through two or three times, and was so charmed by it that, even as I held it in my hands, the paper itself appeared to magnetize me. I forgot to look for the paper papa wished; and when he came into the library, he found me sitting on the carpet, busily reading this speech; when I showed it to him, he laughed heartily."

"What was the name of the speaker?"

"*William H. Seward.*"

"Oh!"

"Did you ever hear of him?"

"Yes, indeed; from him, I rather suspect, my husband has borrowed some of his strongest arguments. But what did your father say of Mr. Seward?"

"Well, after he had laughed heartily at me, and expressed surprise that I could even understand the speech, I asked him to tell me who and what Mr. Seward was. He represented him as a fine subtle-minded politician of great power; and, to use papa's exact expression, he said, 'Seward can drive the political car like a very steam engine'; he also added that if it were not for a few fanciful notions of philanthropy, he would say that Mr. Seward was as wise as Jefferson and as resolute as Jackson. Then, will he not sometime be our President? I asked. 'Yes,' said papa, 'when people get better; but just now we want wicked craft.' Now, Helen, what do you suppose papa meant? For, pretty soon after he said, 'But, Madge, I do not want you to bother yourself with political speeches. There is another course of reading more suited to your mind.' But he had better let me read what I wish to, for I am not, as you know, much attracted to books of any description."

"Will you let me see that speech?"

"Yes, indeed; I took possession of it, and have it hid away. I am going to find out if he has any others published; and if so, I shall get them all."

Certainly he has, my dear—a whole volume of them. Don't you know all over the country he is regarded as our first public man; the only politician whom the South really fears, for they say he is as wise as he is true; and though Southern politicians have watched him closely and tried to ferret out some flaw in his character, some inconsistency, some short-coming or even social error, yet the whole corps of political detectives could find nothing against him; and so they—even his enemies—pronounce him our *preux chevalier, 'sans peur, sans reproche.'*"

"How delighted I am to hear all this, Helen; but where do you learn so much of these public characters?"

"My husband tells me, and I read newspapers."

"Horrid old things! I couldn't read them," cried Madge, as she sprang to the window. "There, there comes Mr. Butler from his walk. He is beckoning to me, so I must go, dear Helen."

XXXII

Madge began to regain her old habits. She went, as of old, to the quarter to talk with the slaves. Of sunny afternoons, when returned from her ride, she read to Uncle Peter, and ate Aunt Polly's cake; scampered about with Rover; rambled through the poultry yard; and sometimes, with her shot-pouch slung across her shoulder and gun in hand, she went out hunting, always accompanied by Pomp and Rover. Mr. Butler found her a most enchanting companion, one who, from her free habits, made no demand upon his time. When she went, in the evenings, into the parlor, on the verandah, or to the tea-table, she always had some interesting exploit, wild adventure or mad prank with which to amuse him. Then, too, he loved to follow, unobserved by her, when she went to the quarter; and sometimes he listened to her conversation with the slaves, and his heart bounded with delight when he saw the reverent affection with which those poor creatures regarded her, and the little delicate attentions with which they sought to honor her. One would bring her flowers, another fruit, a third cool water; they hung round her, listened with admiring attention to every word she uttered, and rushed with delight to obey her slightest command.

"See," said Mr. Butler, "how the humble and lowly revere her. I have found and won an angel."

As they rode together through the woods or strolled about on moonlit evenings, he began to learn more of her character and disposition, and to appreciate her. Little traits which, from their imperfect association, had been hidden from him, now shone out only to attract and fascinate the more deeply from their partial eclipse.

"Madge," said he one day, as they were rambling through the woods, "give me your hand. What! you will not? How forward and wilful! Ah, there, now, that is sweet and confiding; and as I hold it thus between my palms, let me tell you how constantly you are surprising and pleasing me by some new revelation of your nature."

"Come, now, Mr. Butler," she answered, as she gave him an arch glance from under her broad straw hat, "don't try to flatter me; it doesn't come well from you, and reminds me too strongly of those Macassar-heads I met in New Orleans. They could never speak without a compliment."

"Yes, but you will, darling, let my heart talk to you sometimes, will you not?"

"No, not if your heart says such foolish things."

"You are a little tyrant in your way," he said, as he lightly pressed her hand.

"Oh, pray don't do that, Mr. Butler; you pressed this ring into my finger until it pained me dreadfully."

He laughed heartily, saying,

"Ah, Madge, you are all yourself, entirely *sui generis*. Where else can you find me the young lady who, when her lover, in the enthusiasm of the moment, clasps her hand, would cry out against the pain? 'Tis very funny; but come, darling, don't blush so deeply; I only admire your candor and simplicity, and love you the more. Don't try to be other than you are; the least touch of art would spoil nature's admirable and simple plan."

As if to please him and show her gratitude for his flattering appreciation, she passed her hand lightly through his arm, and looked kindly, lovingly up into his face. Ah, he—hard, stern man as he had been, dry old thinker, searcher after wisdom, companion of musty tomes—was now *young* in feeling again, and happy, as he gazed down into the clear depths of those young eyes, and saw his own image reflected in the heart below!

....

Days and weeks flew on as if by magic; the glorious summer was waning fast; the rich, golden harvest, with its full and plenteous moon, its soft, warm airs, the pleasant songs of the reapers, and the merry-makings of the negroes, had come and gone, and September, with its hazy sunshine and its warm, delicious atmosphere, was upon us. Madge fairly lived in the woods, and Mr. Butler was her constant companion. The very birds seemed to know and greet her with their loveliest songs.

"Ah," said Mr. Butler to her one day, as they sat together in a prettily secluded beechen grove, "I shall often think of these dear American birds when I am in old merry England, and most of all" (he placed his hand upon her head) "I shall sigh for the music of my bird Madge,

> "My bird with the shining head,
> My own dove with the tender eye,"

and he gently laid his hand upon her bright-brown curls, upon which the sunlight, softened by the shadow of the grove, fell with a dim splendor, like a faint aureola; nor was he surprised to see a moisture upon her drooping eyelashes, for he was aware of a certain tender sadness in his tone, which would, of course, affect such a gentle heart as hers. There was a winning grace in her low reply:

"You will come back to us—come back to these American birds and flowers?—to find, I trust, the bird whom you have loved and petted, grown softer and more docile. Then you shall not have such difficulty in training her; she will fly into that pretty cage you have prepared for her, and perch upon the highest seat."

Then, as if ashamed of her boldness, she hid her crimson face in her hands, while he poured out a volley of love-expressions, which we cannot take the liberty of repeating.

....

Mrs. Vertner was delighted with the engagement. Mr. Butler had always been a favorite with her, and we will whisper, *sub rosa,* that she was not sorry at the prospect of having Madge married. True it is that she felt herself disappointed in her child; and seeing that she had no power to change her, she found her heart closed against her; though to

Mrs. Vertner's credit we will say that she struggled hard against this state of feeling. Col. Vertner, however, protested against a speedy marriage; he declared that Madge was too young to think of marriage yet awhile. He had no possible objection to Mr. Butler; indeed, he was the very man of his own choice and election; but the engagement *must* be for three years. "What," he would half angrily exclaim, "give up my child now— let her go off to England, resign her, just when she is most necessary to me? No! no! I am too selfish for that."

"I shall not leave you, dear papa," exclaimed Madge, "if you feel thus. Who will you have to love you, to cheer you when I am gone? I will stay here as long as you wish."

In vain were Mr. Butler's pleadings and Mrs. Vertner's remonstrance. Col. Vertner remained firm, and Madge determined to obey him. The bond of affection between her and her father was not the least weakened by the new relation into which she had entered.

"But," said Mrs. Vertner to her husband, "if Madge marries, it may have a good effect upon her; it will, perhaps, sober her down and make a woman of her. I think your partiality blinds you, Col. Vertner, to her very obvious faults. 'Tis useless for me to call your attention to her utter want of manners and social polish. Madame La V—— of New Orleans said that she really pitied me; and many other ladies of the highest society commented upon Madge's rudeness and want of manners. Indeed, the girl was a constant source of mortification to me last winter. Why, Madame La V—— told me that she actually saw Madge playing with Gen. H——'s dogs and sitting on the floor in the hall of the St. Charles, dressing a doll for some child. I could scarcely believe it, though I don't see why, for that girl does the most outrageous things; and when I questioned her about it, she replied, in her usually impertinent way, 'Well, what is the odds?' I can't see how that girl can be my child. And you, Col. Vertner, never sympathize in my mortification."

The cloud upon her husband's brow deepened, despite the lame attempt he made at a smile, when he said,

"Ah, well, never mind! she is *my* child, and I both love and am proud of her. Her future husband does not seem to share in your disgust; he is almost as proud of her as I am—but hush! here she comes, with a face as fresh and lovely as May roses."

Madge sprang upon her father's knee, and, kissing him on either cheek, exclaimed,

"Only see Rover! Down, sir, down; you don't expect papa will let you get upon his other knee, sir; but it would be funny. May he, papa?"

"Certainly, dear."

"Up, Rover, up, sir, to the seat of honorable affection," and she patted her father's other knee. The dog sprang to the appointed place, and sat bolt upright, just opposite Madge, with his face almost touching hers.

"Isn't it funny, papa?"

"Ridiculous," exclaimed Mrs. Vertner, as she quitted the room in evident disgust.

"Now, papa," continued Madge, "you can't imagine what a fine race Rove and I have had all round, up and down the quarter, and across the lawn."

"Tell me all about it."

"First, we went to Aunt Polly's cabin to carry her a little roll of tea and sugar, which she sent to me for yesterday; she is not well; and Uncle Peter complains of the rheumatism, so I took him a little smoking tobacco, of a quality superior to what he generally uses, also a small bottle of camphor. Well, the old folks were delighted to see me. How very grateful slaves are. Did you ever remark it?"

"Oh, yes."

"I thought both of them would have devoured me with compliments and attentions; though Uncle Peter is half lame, he hobbled up from his seat and brought me out the best chair in the cabin, after first dusting it off with his coat-sleeve, and, as usual, he called me his white-robed angel. It touches my heart to be enthusiastically loved by these poor, sincere hearted creatures; they win me by their artless intensity. But I am forgetting: after that visit Rover and I took a regular scamper, sometimes he distancing me, and then I gaining upon him, passing and almost reaching the goal first, in spite of his four legs. I sprang over that side fence; if it had not been for my flowing skirt, I could have accomplished it with great dexterity. How often I wished for those 'kirtles short' which I wore at the Mammoth Cave."

"What of the Mammoth Cave?" asked Mr. Butler, in a cheery tone, as he entered, pausing in the door way, where a broad patch of quivering sunlight lay, gilding and sparkling all around.

Madge laughingly sprang off her father's knee, and half ran toward Mr. Butler, when suddenly, recollecting herself, she paused and stood blushingly gazing down upon the carpet. As Mr. Butler smilingly approached, and took her hand within his, he said,

"Apropos of the Mammoth Cave, I have just had a letter from an English friend of mine, who has crossed the Atlantic solely to visit America's two greatest curiosities—Niagara and the great Kentucky Cave. The former he saw and admired, and is now sojourning at the Cave, more deeply charmed with its wild and terrible beauty than he was with the softer glory of the great Fall. He, like ourselves, became much interested in Stephen; and now he writes me, in the saddest spirit, of the death of that most extraordinary person."

"Dead!" exclaimed Madge; "Stephen dead!"

"Yes."

"And his freedom not won?"

"I will, with your permission, read you what my friend writes." Mr. Butler glanced toward Col. Vertner.

"Certainly, sir," he replied; "I shall he happy to hear what your friend says."

"Do read at once," exclaimed Madge, in one of those quick, staccato tones which sometimes annoyed Mr. Butler's slower temperament, and for which he often reproved her, both by word and look. This time, however, he said nothing, but began reading, in a quick tone, the following letter:

"DEAR BUTLER: Though the season is fast waning, I am still lingering here, enjoying the 'dolce far niente' which this sweet September atmosphere seems to engender. This Cave is indeed a sort of enchanted spot, and I can almost fancy there is some unseen Egeria, who holds us here in spite of ourselves. Four other young men, like myself, are too much bewitched to get away, though they assure me that business is calling them hence. I have been off on a four days' jaunt since I last wrote you; went to Harrodsburg. What a lovely

and cultivated spot, to be sure! Rambling through that
extensive and well-kept park, one would imagine he was
walking over the finest manorial grounds of our own merry,
happy England! Then, too, I passed down the Kentucky
river to where it empties into the Ohio. It is a stream of
the wildest and most poetic beauty. I am surprised that
one does not read more of it in books of travels; tourists
cannot know of its wonderful attractiveness; it is a sort of
Rhine of the wilderness, without a singer to bring it into
fame. I drove also to a queer place, known about here as
the 'Devil's Hollow,' which is one of the most curiously
beautiful spots I ever remember to have seen. I enjoy
Kentucky more than any of the States I have yet visited; the
people are all warm-hearted, cordial and hospitable, with
a sort of downrightness of assertion, and outrightness of
action, which, though new, are perfectly 'taking' to me.

"That poor guide, Stephen, who always remembered
you with so much grateful pleasure, has at last died. I
was with him when he drew his last breath. They say he
killed himself by over-drinking and dissipation, but I, who
looked deeper into his nature than the mere surface, say,
beyond doubt, he died of a broken spirit. With the most
extraordinary talents, a wild ambition, love of personal
independence, and fineness of soul, he was yet held back
from any attempt to escape by a sort of notion, which
assumed all the austerity of duty, that he was bound to
pay the *thing* who called himself his master—a drivelling
old, double-painted Shylock—the extortionate sum he
demanded. Though I condemned this feeling in Stephen,
I could not speak against it, because, unconsciously, I had
a respect for it. But when day by day I saw this fine-souled
creature dying fast—when I watched him curb the angry
flash of his eye, and rein down his mettlesome spirit—
when I saw how he was spurred onward to a true sense of
manhood, yet held back by a false notion, I could but curse
this hellish slave system, that cost him so many throes of
anguish and *manly* impatience. It drove him to drink, for

in the cup he found slight relief from the wearing torture
of his life. Toward the close he talked more freely with me;
and in those final moments I learned, what I had often
feared, that his burden had been indeed too heavy, and
his yoke too oppressive. Just before his death, taking my
hand within his and kindly thanking me for the few little
services I had rendered him, he said, with an expression of
face which I shall bear with me to the grave, 'I am going,
sir, to a land where my freedom will be secure—a land
fairer than Canada—God's own Canaan, the black man's
only safe home. I shan't want any free papers there, for I
am written down in the Lamb's Book of Life, a man and
not a slave.' Then, throwing out his arms with one of those
graceful motions for which you know he was so remarkable,
he exclaimed, with a passionate fervor, while his eye glowed
and nostril dilated, 'The strength has gone from my arm;
the blood trickles slowly and does not leap as it used to
through these almost dried veins. My limbs have lost their
power; my heart will soon be still, my life over; but my love
for freedom will live when my body shall be stark and cold.'
This struck sadly upon me, Butler, and put me to thinking
more than I had ever done, upon the nature of this
domestic institution. You know, at home I used to laugh
at the Abolitionists and condemn them as a weak-minded,
intermeddling set, who went too far from home with their
philanthropy. After this, I shall not refuse them the helping
hand. One needs to see slavery, to properly hate it."

Folding up the letter, Mr. Butler said,
"There are only a few other allusions, of a purely personal nature
in which you will not be interested."
"Your friend," observed Col. Vertner, "should not have passed
sentence upon our domestic institution from its fatal influence upon
one, and an exceptional character at that. I grant you, Stephen should
not have been a slave; there was too large an infusion of Caucasian
blood in his veins. He was a most remarkable person; and it pained
me to see him in slavery. Your friend, however, should go more among

our people, and watch the practical bearings of this peculiar system of domestic servitude, before he joins that Quixotic tribe of Abolitionists who don't know what or who they are fighting against."

While Mr. Butler was reading the letter, Madge, who was deeply interested in it, crept up softly to his side and leant over toward him, until her long brown curls swept his arm. She formed a very pretty picture indeed; with her head bent forward and face slightly upturned, while the eyes shone forth with a sort of dreamy, lambent earnestness, with lips slightly parted, through which the breath came in quick, gusty sighs.

"But, papa," she inquired, as Col. Vertner paused, "did you not say, the other day, that when we were better, when people—the voters I mean—grew more informed, more virtuous and God-fearing, Mr. Seward would be elected to the Presidency? And is he not an Abolitionist?"

"Not exactly an Abolitionist, my dear, but he is opposed to carrying slaves into our new territories; he does not wish the area of slave ground extended, though he has not eaten of that insane root which turns the brain, and makes a man believe that a negro stands on equal ground with a white man."

"Do you think amalgamation a great wrong to the race?" Mr. Butler naively inquired.

Col. Vertner looked a little uneasy, turned a half shade paler, knit his brows and bit his lip. Mr. Butler was mortified, and stood rebuked—believing that Col. Vertner thought such a question too indecorous to be proposed in the presence of his daughter; so he half blushingly said,

"I beg pardon; Madge is so child-like, and bird-like, that I often forget she is a lady."

Col. Vertner bowed complacently, and the cloud faded quickly from his face as he said,

"Madge, my daughter, haven't you some little household duty to attend to? how is it with Rover and your pets in the quarter?"

"Now, papa, I am not going away; I want to hear you and Mr. Butler talk about amalgamation. What does it mean?"

"Madge, don't let me have to ask you to go out again."

"But, papa, I wish to stay and listen to the conversation; why should I always be sent off just as if I were a child? Now, amalgamation, according to the dictionary, means 'to unite metals.' As you and Mr. Butler apply it, I suppose it means the union of two races, the intermarriage of the negro with the white. Of course that is never done; and yet it does not seem so strange and out of the way, particularly to me, who was nursed by a mulatto woman." Her father looked so utterly worried that Madge felt a saucy pleasure in continuing the conversation. "Now, Mr. Butler," she archly asked, "would you marry a pretty quadroon, an octoroon, or one who had a wee drop, a sprinkling of black blood in her veins? Suppose she was handsome, cultivated, well-bred and refined. Answer me sincerely, frankly."

"The argument, my dear, must be met upon higher ground than that of intermarriage; and yet, since you put the question so directly, I will answer you freely and without reserve. For myself, I have been now so long in America, and so long seen the negro in his degraded and servile state, that almost unconsciously I have imbibed the prevailing prejudice against his race, and am sure I could never be willing to marry a girl with negro blood in her veins; but this does not make it right; it is all a matter of taste."

Col. Vertner strode uneasily up and down the floor, every now and then passing his hand rapidly through his hair, and nervously twitching his under lip.

"You agree with him, papa," exclaimed Madge, "do you not?"

"Of course, of course," he quickly answered; "but, sir" (turning to Mr. Butler), "the negro blood sometimes so finely and cunningly intermingles with the Caucasian that it is difficult for the most acute ethnologist to detect it; indeed, this conjuncture of opposite blood sometimes so harmonizes, as to produce the finest order of female beauty. Go to the coffles, the trading-places, those heart-sickening bazaars of New Orleans, and look on those octoroon girls there daily exhibited, and tell me if Circassia itself can match such beauty; aye, sir, that eighth drop of yellow blood, like a grain of fine gold, seems to gild and make the woman's face more lovely."

His manner had become very much excited, and his feet seemed to plough the floor, as he strode back and forward.

"Papa, papa," exclaimed Madge, springing forward and seizing him by the arm, "what has excited you so? I never heard you speak thus of the negro, and yet I believe what you say; for I saw octoroon and quadroon girls in Orleans, last winter, whose beauty I coveted; and even that poor mulatto woman, Rachel, was as handsome as any one I ever saw; poor creature! Papa, do you remember her appearance at the post?"

"Yes, child; yes," he replied in a low tone; "but never mind about that."

Passing his hand across his brow, he wiped away the large drops of perspiration which had gathered there. Madge still hung fondly on his arm, gazing up into his face with the utmost tenderness and affection. Mr. Butler had not been an unmoved witness of this scene. "Oh," he thought, "Col. Vertner's conscience is not easy on this matter; he begins to see the danger of this blending of races; because, when the white man's eye once becomes fascinated with the beauty of the slave girl, crime and ruin follow." Rousing himself from these reflections, he addressed Col. Vertner in a very placid tone, saying, "Well, sir, seeing, as you must, the enormity and infinity of moral consequence which results from this illicit union of races, may I ask what remedy you propose? For my own part, I should advise that the children and the mother in such cases, be allowed by law to assume the condition of the father."

"Yes, yes," said Col. Vertner, "that would be well, but hardly practicable. I confess I have always disliked to see *white* blood on the auction block or in the coffle."

"I don't like to see *black* there either," said Madge.

"My dear," replied Col. Vertner—

The conversation was here broken in upon by Pomp rushing in, exclaiming, "Miss Madge, Miss Mason's Andrew is out here at the avenue gate, with the carriage; says Mrs. Mason has sent for you, 'kase Miss Helen is sick, and fit to die."

"Then I will go to her at once," exclaimed Madge, and left the room in great haste.

XXXIII

Helen Norton had been stricken down by the rapid development of that most insidious of diseases—consumption—the seeds of which she had borne in her system from her very birth. Madge knew, at the first glance how the case stood, and that her dearest friend's life trembled upon a very hair. The house looked gloomy and cold, as though it participated in the knowledge of the painful secret. Madge felt the death chill, the ominous foreboding fall upon her as she stood on the door-sill. The shutters were closed, the bell muffled, and within persons moved on tip-toe, and never spoke above a whisper. In the darkened hall, she met the doctor, who silently clasped her hand and hastily passed out. The servants moved carefully about with tears in their anxious eyes. Madge asked no questions, but paused a moment in the library to regain her self possession. As she sat there alone, ten thousand happy little incidents and pleasant passages in hers and Helen's life-long intercourse came over her mind and heart. She remembered, with a passionate sadness, how Helen had always sympathized with her, responded in heart and spirit to all her whims, dreams and fancies, and yielded her, alike in joy or sorrow, the most friendly interest; and now, this friend, so tried and true, so near and dear, was about to be taken from her.

"Oh," she thought, "anything but this. How can I live without Helen? Who should I go to with all my little sorrows and troubles? Not to papa, for he would only laugh at them; not to Mr. Butler; he is too cold and dignified. They will have to die out in my own heart. Helen is my only sympathizer. Certainly, God will not take her from me. He will spare me this my great, almost my greatest treasure. I will pray to Him. I will ask for this one blessing to be granted awhile longer to me. I remember mamma and the good old minister both said that I should go to God with my troubles. I will take this one to Him, and if He, indeed, observes the fall of every sparrow, and numbers each hair on my head, He will consider kindly this heavy bolt that is about to crush me. 'Come unto me, ye that are heavy laden, and I will give you rest.'"

She knelt down beside the sofa where she and Helen had so often sat together, and, with streaming eyes, poured out her troubled heart in prayer to Heaven. The very effort gave her relief, for it roused the two strongest powers of her soul—faith and hope. Soon a sweet peace, soft and subduing as summer moonlight, settled over her, and, with calmness, almost resignation, she rose from that moment's communion with God, and went to the chamber of her sick friend.

Pale and wasted, with dark purple lines about her mouth and eyes, features sharply contracted, Helen Norton lay upon her bed of death. The room was darkened. It was Helen's own pretty little chamber, full of happy, familiar associations, but how altered it looked to Madge now! A small table, filled with phials and pill-boxes, was drawn close to the bedside, and near by sat Mr. Norton, his hand resting gently upon his wife's head. Old Milly, the colored nurse, stood near, applying bottles of boiling water to Helen's feet, and everything was so still that Madge heard audibly the ticking of a watch that lay upon the table with the medicine.

Helen moved slightly as Madge approached.

"Is it you, dear Madge?" she murmured in a half whisper.

The sound of that voice made Madge start, it was so fearfully uttered.

"Helen, dear Helen!" and Madge bent down to kiss the purple lips so dried and shrunken.

"Be gentle," said Mr. Norton, "and do not lean over her; she must have all the air this small room affords."

"Oh! don't send her away; let her stay close to me," added Helen, with a fluttering breath.

"Here, Madge, here"; and she took her hand and laid it over her heart. "Do you feel how quickly it beats, dear? Well, the wheel will soon break; a watch of such rapid and irregular motion does not last long. Don't try to conceal your tears, Madge. I know, dear, that your heart aches. Let me rather have a free and open expression of your grief; it will do me no harm and you some good. I am now willing to die. A few months ago, I found it hard to yield a ready assent to God's call; but now I am cheerful and resigned. I have had a very happy life—always surrounded by the dearest and best of friends; and, most of all, highest among God's many great blessings to me do I reckon the possession of such a friend as my husband has been to me." Here she reached out her other hand, which Mr. Norton immediately clasped within his and covered it with kisses. "Only think, John," she added, turning her eyes toward him," into what heavenly paths you have led my footsteps! Who but you taught me to love truth, justice and humanity above all creeds and dogmas? Who but you, dearest and best of husbands, opened my eyes to the great wrong which I was silently encouraging? You took my heart, and, by your plastic hand, moulded it to better uses. I owe you everything, higher honor, truer love, a broader humanity. Oh, John, when you come to follow me and lie upon your death-couch, the remembrance of the good you have done at least to me will be as a lamp to your feet or a star of promise to your closing life. And, Madge, you owe something also to his influence; and when I am gone—which will surely be in a few days—I hope that you and he will be kind friends— talk together of me, and think, if possible, my spirit shall be near you. Do not grieve; think only of me as gone upon a pleasant voyage, whither you shall ere long follow; think how hopefully I shall await your coming on the other side of the line, beyond the shining river. It would have given me pleasure unspeakable to have lived long enough to see the liberation of our slaves; but I cannot be spared so long. Well, God orders all things aright, and I can cheerfully submit; yet I had hoped to be spared that long. I intended that the day of their liberation should be made one of rejoicing and feasting. How proudly and happily my heart would have throbbed as I gazed upon the faces of those whom I had the power to make free! It is a great thing to turn a chattel into a man, or rather to give back to a man his truest right to himself, of which he had before been defrauded; but all this I shall not live to see or feel. Yet, my husband, I am happy to think you will have the right to do it, and in your joy I shall bear a part, though divided from you by the poor limits of a grass-grown grave. Who is that sobbing? Is it you, mammy?" she inquired, turning to the old colored nurse who was weeping violently. "Don't cry, mammy," she continued; "don't cry for me; you shall soon be happy and free. Will you like to be free? Why don't you answer me? Pray don't cry so. Tell me, will you be happy in your freedom?"

With a great effort, and in a voice broken and stifled with tears and sobs, the old negro replied,

"Don't ax me, Miss Hel'n; don't ax me; 'pears like my heart'll break smack in two. I hain't got no thought 'bout freedom now. No, you Lord-blessed-chile, I am jist studyin' 'bout gittin' you well; never mind 'bout us niggers, honey; jist study 'bout yourself, and try to git well. I had heap rayther have you 'an freedom. Laws, Miss Hel'n, don't take on 'bout dese here things, but git yer mind easy, an' de Lord'll fetch it out right. I've done bin to Him wid dis here case, an' I knows He'll spar' you; so don't git yourself weak talkin' 'bout dat."

"But, mammy, that's no answer to my question. Shall you like to be free?"

Wiping her eyes, and brightening her countenance, the negro replied,

"Why, Laws bless yer, honey, freedom is sweet to everybody—it's mighty sweet. 'Pears to me nothin' is half so sweet. I look out in the poultry yard at them 'ar fowls—I looks in the stables at the horses, and in the cuppen at de cows an' dem little skittish calves, an' I see how dem poor dumb critters loves freedom, an' I studies 'bout it to myself, an' I keeps on studyin', an' I think de Lord must 'ave put dis love o' freedom into everything he made. Yes, Miss Hel'n, I'd love to be free; I'd love it for myself; I'd like to die free; but den I studies heap more 'bout my chillen an' gran'-chillen how to have 'em, for dey is young; you have 'em made free, an' I'd stay a slave myself. Oh, Miss Hel'n, it's powerful kind o' you to gib up all dis property, to be willin' to be poor, so as to make yer niggers free; but de Lord Jesus, he takes notice of dis here; He ain't gwine to forgit it either, an' so I don't feel oneasy 'bout yer; yer ain't gwine to suffer, for He'll be lookin' to yer. But, den, I ain't gwine to 'low my boys, great stout fellows, to take dar freedom from you an' not make no return. No, that wouldn't be fa'r. Dey shall work every year, an' pay you so much for 'emselves, an' it'll be a-helpin' yer along. God knows, it's good enuff of you to give 'em dar freedom. Now, Miss Hel'n, I kan't stand dis; 'twill break my heart!" And, with her apron over her face and her body writhing as if in a paroxysm of pain, she rushed out of the room. Pretty soon, however, she returned, with an additional bottle of hot water.

"How is it now, honey, wid yer feet? Oh, dey is gettin' colder; does you feel dis bottle? It's bilin'-hot. How does it feel? don't burn? I's feared it's too hot."

"I don't feel it, mammy."

"Don't feel it, chile! Why, it's bilin'; I kan't keep my hands to it; but here yer poor little foot lies by it an' don't move. Oh, God o' mercy! yer foot is stiff an' cold. Somebody run for de doctor." And again she rushed from the room, no doubt to despatch a messenger for the physician, whom she believed almost capable of restoring the very dead.

"Poor old mammy," said Helen, "she doesn't realize how near I am to death. Be gentle and kind to her, John, for she was always a faithful nurse to me. Oh that I could live to see them all free people!"

"Can't the deeds of manumission be drawn up at once?" asked Madge of Mr. Norton. "What is the hindrance? Why can't she have this pleasure at once? I am sure some exertion should be made to gratify her."

"I wish it were possible," answered Mr. Norton, "but we found the estate in such a complicated and vexed condition that such a thing is utterly impossible for two or three months yet, at the nearest calculation. My dear wife knows how much joy it would afford me to bring her this happiness; but Helen is not going yet; she will get well, she will grow better, when I shall take her to a softer climate; and we shall keep her for many more years."

The dying wife only answered by a long and fervent pressure of the hand.

....

Late that night, near about twelve o'clock, which had been her birth-hour, Helen Norton breathed her last.

Her husband, mother, the doctor and Madge, together with the old colored nurse, were the only persons with her. Softly and gently as a child sinking to sleep she died. Madge held one hand, while the grieved husband firmly clasped the other, as if disputing with death his right to such lovely and precious prey.

"Am I dying, doctor?" she asked, as that good man's hand rested for a moment upon the slow pulse.

"Yes, my child."

"May I use my strength to say good-bye?"

"Better not."

"If it grieves you so, my friends, I will not speak; but do stand near me; let me look into your eyes; let me take with me to my new home the remembrance of your happy faces. Don't let me see them gloomy or unhopeful. I know that is mammy sobbing so piteously: tell her to control her grief or go out of the room, for now I am too weak to bear it."

The doctor motioned to the nurse to leave; but, crouching down upon the floor close to the bed, and clinging to a portion of its drapery, as though it brought her into closer contact with her young mistress, the woman muffled her sobs, and, by a strong effort, controlled her grief.

Mrs. Mason, who was almost as near death as Helen, sat, propped with cushions, in a great chair near the bed, her face concealed amid the pillows, while her grief fretted itself to rest in one of those strange trance like dreams. In spite of Madge's and Mr. Norton's opposition, she had insisted upon being brought into the room and remaining with her daughter; but nature and grief both gave way, and she now slept, while the grim and shadowy monster, with wing unfolded, stole away her dearest treasure.

"Good-bye, dears; good-bye; don't forget—"

The sentence was unfinished, for Helen Mason's breath failed; her spirit had left the body. Madge sank upon her knees, burying her face in her hands. The frantic husband forgot his self-collection, and bewailed his loss in loud words and bitter tears. But poor old mammy was fiercest in the expression of her grief; she tore her turban, wrung her hands and prayed aloud for mercy to fall upon the house. Mrs. Mason was carried from the room in a fainting fit.

XXXIV

Helen Norton lay in her coffin, still and beautiful as one upon whom a sweet and dreamless sleep had fallen. Only in a certain light could the gazer perceive the wasting work of disease, as shown in the purple lines about the eyes and mouth. Loving, friendly hands had decked her for death as for a happy bridal. The long white wrapper, with its silken girdle, gave to her form a fulness which did not properly belong to it even in life. A wreath of white blossoms bound her brow, while a Marie Stuart point of rich lace covered her shining hair, and in her crossed hands was a bouquet of white tea roses, with one large camelia, which Madge had placed there. The coffin was taken into the great parlor, where, but a short time before, she had stood a happy and trusting bride. Madge sat by it all the while—no coaxing could get her away—her hand or arm resting constantly upon the coffin or near the body.

"Dear Helen!" she once said, when she found herself alone with the body, "can't your spirit, somewhere in this vast and peopled space, look down upon me? has it indeed left this dear body? Oh for one word, one half word, to assure me that you have not entirely left me! Will you not, Helen, come back to me at some time? Do you not see or hear me now? What was that?" She started, as she heard a faint, low murmur, very close to her ear. Glancing round, she saw no one; yet she felt the air ripple coolly by her cheek, as if a gentle breath had fanned her.

"Could that be Helen's spirit?" These words Madge uttered aloud. Again she thought, or imagined, as you will, that she heard a faint sigh. Looking anxiously round the room, she satisfied herself that the doors were all fast-closed. Approaching the window, she lifted the heavy curtain drapery to discern if any one was hidden there, then softly opened the doors, but could find no one lurking about. Returning to the head of the coffin, she gently laid her hand upon the cold, white brow of her dead friend, saying, in a slow, solemn voice,

"Dear Helen! I accept the omen."

Beside the coffin she still remained, as the hours of the day wore slowly on. Mr. Butler came and sat beside her. He took her little hand within his own and soothed her with many a kindly-spoken word. As he sat stroking her long, spare fingers, and soothing those acorn nails, he said, in a low tone—for unconsciously one lowers the voice in the presence of death—

"You cannot be well, dear Madge, for I notice a yellowness about the points of your fingers and round your delicate nails, which indicates bile in the blood."

Madge examined her fingers and replied, with a smile,

"I see nothing unusual the matter with my fingers; they are always a little darker than my face; perhaps because I am so much exposed to the sun and seldom wear gloves."

"Why won't you leave this sad scene for a little while? Come and walk with me. Let us have a stroll upon the outskirts of the village. It will do you good; and as I am soon to leave you, I think you ought to gratify me."

She looked up with a pained expression upon her countenance, saying,

"I will go with you, since you ask so earnestly; but it half breaks my heart to leave her. While I am by the coffin, I do not so wholly realize that she is gone, and there is something in those features that brings her heart, her life, her very self, so warmly and closely to me that I cannot bear to tear myself away. You do not know how love, sympathy and intimate association knit us together—welding, as it were, our very hearts."

"Shall I not supply her place?" he tenderly asked.

"You will be to me, perhaps, more than she was—as much at least—but not the same," she honestly answered.

"My little Madge hasn't much enthusiasm; and do you know I fear she only gives me her heart by halves? An Englishman, remember, always makes a jealous lover and husband."

"Jealous—jealous—why do you talk of jealousy? Jealous of whom, of what? Surely not of this piece of cold life-clay that lies so beautiful before us!"

He passed his arm gently round her waist, and imprinted a kiss upon her bent brow. Again Madge heard that ominous sigh, and, starting from his half embrace, she exclaimed,

"What did you hear?"

"Nothing, dear."

"Didn't you hear a sigh—a soft, low, mellow sigh, that seemed to come from the coffin? And yet that still, uncovered face does not look as if a broken breath had disturbed its sleep."

"Madge, Madge, my dear, you are weary and weak; your feelings have been overtaxed. Come with me, away from this sad room, out into the open, fresh air: you will feel better."

Kneeling down by the coffin, Madge pressed her lips long and fervently to the brow and lips of her dead friend, then, giving her hand to Mr. Butler, suffered herself to be led out of the room. Soon after, wrapped in her mantilla and with her jaunty little hat upon her head, she sauntered out of the front door and wandered off in the direction of a beechen wood which skirted the town and had once been a favorite walk of hers and Helen's.

"The air is a little chilly. Are you warmly wrapped?" asked Mr. Butler, as he folded the mantle yet closer about her shoulders.

We shall not follow them in their walk or pause to recount the sad conversation which she and her lover held. Madge felt that her once healthy and exuberant spirits were sinking under the pressure of troubles. But perhaps he to whom she had given her heart now soothed and comforted her with promises and pictures of the future.

....

Mournful indeed it was, after the funeral service (which was performed by the same kind clergyman who had married Helen), to see the family and friends one by one come up to take a last look at her who in life had been so dearly loved. First came the grief-stricken husband and mother; then Madge, leaning on Mr. Butler's arm; following her were Col. and Mrs. Vertner; then the friends and acquaintances of the town and country. Next came the negroes, all neatly dressed, their black and brown faces beaming with a cordial and loving sadness. Mammy's black, rugged face worked with pain as she looked fondly down upon Helen, and great tears fell from her eyes; her lips worked as if words were struggling for utterance. At length she could stand it no longer, and, forgetful of the *decent* solemnities of the scene and place and oblivious of strangers, she burst forth in a long, loud cry of lamentation as some of the other negroes hastily bore her from the room.

"Dar lays one o' God's own angels, what was too good for dis ar airth; so He done tuck her off to Heself."

. . . .

"Dust to dust!" exclaimed the minister as the coffin was let down into the vaulted grave. The friends gathered close—to the very brink. Some threw in flowers, evergreens and sprigs. Madge dropped a large full-blown japonica.

"It was Helen's favorite flower," she said, in a whisper, as she let it fall upon the plated lid of the coffin, "and it shall be my last gift to her."

Slowly, in groups, pairs, or one by one, the mourners, friends and acquaintances turned away from the new-made grave to seek their different homes or pursuits. Hearse, carriage and foot-passenger had retired. Mother, husband, and friend had left the grave. One—only one—remained, and she was the faithful old nurse, Helen's mammy. The sexton and grave-digger still lingered; the latter, with his reversed spade, had smoothed and shaped down the moist earth to a grave form, and now rested upon his mattock, looking anxiously at the old negro, who was seated upon the ground beside the grave, patting it down with her hand, as though she were trying to compose and soothe the sleeper below.

"Well, aunty," said the man, "we all has our time to die; hern has jist come a little sooner than the rest of us; but we's all bound to foller, sometime."

"Yes, yes, I knows it," muttered the woman; "but she was an angel. She was too good for dis airth. I never seed her mad or heard her speak a rough word to anybody. When her ma used to scold her, an' dat she did mighty often, she never spoke back, or seemed de least put out or cross. De Lord jist seed dat she was too good fur down here, an' He done tuck her up yonder, whar she'll w'ar de white robe an' sing de song of de Lamb. I tells you, I knows all 'bout dis dear baby dat sleeps in dis grave. I was her nurse, her mammy, and I knowed her well as my own chile."

She laid her head down upon the grave and threw her arm across it.

"Wal, I s'pose," said the man, "you'll have a fine tombstone to cover her over? Rich folks don't bury like poor ones. In thar lives they live better than poor uns, and so they sleeps grander in thar graves. I s'pose now, because your young mistress was rich, she'll have a big stone with her name on it, a-tellin' everybody how good she was."

"I tells yer," replied the woman, "you ain't got stone clean and white enuff to write her name on. She was de best of de good."

....

Weeks flew by, and Time, that angel of the grief-stricken, brought peace and seeming content, to Helen Norton's widowed husband and bereaved mother. But in Madge's heart she was less a memory than a presence. Once a week she went to that monumental grave with her offering of flowers, which were oftentimes watered with her tears.

Mr. Butler had left for England, and our young heroine had now all her time at her own disposal. At first, sad and listlessly, she resumed her old life. Silk came out from the stall, where she had, no doubt, mourned, in her dumb way, her mistress's change. Rover, with a joyous bark, sprang forth from the kennel to receive Madge's pat of welcome; and, with jibe, joke and yarn, Pomp returned to his old vocation from which erewhile he had been banished. Once again through the autumn woods, with crisp leaves rattling and rustling beneath her horse's hoofs, Madge rushed like a sprite, and again the uplands rang with the echoes of merriment, as Pomp and Rover dashed swiftly after her. Col. Vertner saw with delight the shadow fade from his daughter's brow, and the health bloom burst like a spring rose over her cheek, as she returned to her old pastimes and pleasures. All again was jocund and joyous, and the father fondly hoped that his child would forget that there were such things as death and trouble in the world.

Long, loving letters came from Mr. Butler by every steamer. They were Madge's first love-letters, and with what a curious, half thoughtful, half quizzical, beaming, timid, loving eye she glanced over them, pausing to note every word—reading them not once, but many times a day, then carefully laying them away in a corner of an ornamented portfolio which she had bought for the express purpose. Ah! a girl's first love-letter is the first event in her heart-life. How daintily she handles it—how she guards it from soil or taint, folds it in the same folds, places it in the same envelope, and stores it away with perfumes, even as she keeps the memory of the writer fragrant in the choicest corner of her heart!

Thus days, weeks and months glided onward, to her, chronicled only by some new joy. The weary negroes, the strong, energetic ones, with the idle, lazy, drivelling and discontented of Vertner Place, still plodded on in their usual manner. Miss Madge, like a stray sunbeam, came often to the quarter to "make sunshine in a shady place" for those poor negroes; and of winter evenings, with her book in hand (for now she was herself beginning to like to read), she came, and, taking the central seat in Aunt Polly's cabin, read to those simple, listening creatures, strange, wild stories of the sea or fairy extravaganzas, or those singular and valuable stories of the Old Testament. How earnestly they listened to her, and how eager they were to learn! They plied Madge with questions and oftentimes puzzled her ingenuity for a reply.

We, who know the negro best—have seen him in his dreary slave shamble—have talked with him in his privacy by the dim light of his own cabin fire—know how wildly and intensely he longs for the smallest item of knowledge—how, like a hungry spirit, he stands begging for the very crumbs!

XXXV

"How pleasant everything is!" exclaimed Madge to her father, one day, in the early December, as they sat together, beside a cheerful fire on the library hearth. "Do you know, papa, when I was serious, I was not happy? It tires the heart and patience of one to look into the causes of things. I felt, as my bird and wild woods life seemed to pass away from me, that the world was a very sad place, and I longed to be out of it; but now I feel reconciled to most everything. Our servants" (her voice fell a little) "appear very happy, and I do not hear of any cruelty being practiced in the neighborhood; so nothing grieves me now. Yet I do—"

Her head drooped on her breast, and she twisted her fingers together as was her custom when embarrassed.

"What is it, darling?" asked her father, as he lovingly placed his hand upon her head. But as she did not readily reply, he added,

"We will have another letter from Mr. Butler to-morrow. Ha! how is it with that little fluttering heart? But I think my own Madge is not very much in love. Perhaps she thinks Mr. Butler is too old?"

"Too old, papa! What can you mean? I do not like to have you say I am not much in love. Mr. Butler has all my heart—that is, all which you do not occupy. Since Helen's death, I have felt as if I had more room for him. You know how large a portion of my heart was hers; for I think she understood me better than any one else. At least I never

had to translate or explain myself to her. She read me freely as an old
thummed school book. But for Mr. Butler I have a reverent sort of love
that seems as much a necessity of my soul as prayer. You know, papa, he
is so good, so great and grand. I look up to him. He will be a staff for
me to lean upon, and I shall grow better and wiser. Since I have known
him, I have felt a wonderful quickening of my moral perceptions, and a
healthier tone to my thought. He has been a great help to me."

"It seems, my daughter, that you describe respect, rather than
love. Now, if for Mr. Butler you cherish no warmer feeling than this, I
must urge you to pause, question your heart, investigate, find out the
depth, extent and fervor of this feeling. For you have, my pet, a strong
nature; and if, after a while, after being married to him, you should
discover that there was a power or force in your heart which had not
been moved by him, then would come the moment of awful danger to
you—the moment most fatal to woman's truth and faith."

"If such a discovery should come, sir," answered the girl, with
a strange, unusual dignity, "I should know my duty. No path is too
narrow, too tortuous for a true woman to tread."

Col. Vertner drew her closely to his heart, and heaved a deep sigh
as he held her firmly there. Looking up from his bosom with a crimson
cheek, and shaking back her tangled curls, she said,

"But, papa, don't be mistaken; I do love Mr. Butler with the most
delicious feeling. I tremble when I think of him; and I am sure, out of
all creation, he is the one man intended by God for me; so don't trouble
your dear self about anything of that sort."

The bright flickering fire was the only light in the room, and the
hour was the one just past twilight in the winter, which is always so
sacred and confidential. Madge had talked more freely of Mr. Butler to
her father than was her wont. The geniality of the hour had cheated her
out of her confidence. Ruth came in to close the curtains and light the
lamp, when Madge stole off her father's knee, and, as if to avoid his eye,
in the broader lamp-light, she went to a bookcase and busied herself
there.

"Master, will you and Miss Madge have tea in de library? Mistress
isn't comin' down to-night; she has ordered tea in her chamber."

"Oh, let us have our tea served here, papa; it will be so cosy. You
and I can enjoy a pleasant *téte à téte.*"

"It shall be as you wish, my daughter."

Ruth drew a little round table close to the blazing fire, and brought in the tea and toast, to which Col. Vertner and Madge sat down with delight.

"Isn't it charming, papa? only I don't like to have Ruth standing all the while just behind my chair; it annoys me. Can't I send her away? We have everything we wish; and if I require her, I can ring the bell."

"Certainly, Madge, you shall have everything your own way."

Ruth was no doubt very glad of the chance of a little respite from her usual wearisome attendance upon the table.

"Dear papa!" exclaimed Madge, "how delightful it is for us to be alone. I do love to be with you"—she paused abruptly, for she felt that her feeling was not kind or respectful to her mother. Of late, since our young heroine had begun to use her powers of reflection, she had held herself to quite a rigid account for the manner in which she regarded her mother.

"I ought," thought Madge, "to love mamma above all created persons; but my heart will not warm to her. I am very, very sorry for it, but how can I change my feelings?"

But now, as she sat alone with her father, in the cosy and comfortable little library, she felt how much more sincerely she loved him than her mother, and a pang of conscience rebuked her.

"Come, child, come, little Blossom," broke forth her father, "cheer up; send that care right out of your face; let us have no shadows, no disputes with yourself. Be happy with your father to-night. Shan't we have a little more talk as we sip our tea, and afterward a game of whist?"

"Certainly, papa; but just now a question occurs to me: what do you think Mr. Norton will do with his slaves? You know, Helen expected them to be set free, and Mr. Norton is an Abolitionist."

Col. Vertner laughed heartily, as he replied,

"Yes, yes, he was an Abolitionist, but now he *is* a slaveholder. You see, my dear, there is quite a difference in the relative positions. He will never set those negroes free, and he would be a fool if he did."

"Papa!"—and the half-lifted cup fell from Madge's hand—"papa, what do you mean? You always laugh at everybody's goodness. Now, don't you think Mr. Norton will do what he said, what he taught his wife to believe just and right?"

"He will never set his negroes free."

"I am sure he will; I feel assured of it; and yet I wish he had done so before Helen's death. But I am sure he is sincere in what he professes."

"If he had been sincere in what he said he thought of slavery, I tell you, my child, he would never have married a woman who held slaves. If his conscience had been so tender and sensitive, I tell you, he would have had those negroes manumitted before marrying Helen. But, no; he has calmly enjoyed the fruits of slave labor ever since his marriage, and now tells you, as he told his credulous wife, that the time has not arrived for liberating his slaves. Well, that is exactly my argument. 'Tis quite likely—and I am willing it should be so—that in the progress of years, slavery will be banished from the country; but that time is distant, and he who would now liberate a slave—except in rare and highly exceptional instances—does him a great unkindness and injustice. The negro is not fitted for the experiment of self government. He is a child; he must be thought for, acted for, provided for, just like an infant, and managed according to the discipline of a superior."

"He isn't worked for."

"Neither is the horse."

"Yes, but the negro shows more intelligence than a horse."

"Not a bit; he is naturally lazy and wasteful, and, if left to himself, would pass his whole life either in pleasure or begging. Nothing but the rule and law of a master can make him get along."

"How can you say that, papa? Don't you remember how beautifully our place is always managed when we are away. I have oftentimes heard you say that things went on as well without as with you."

"Because I appointed an overseer."

"He, however, is one of the slaves, and the white men at work upon our public roads always have a superior appointed."

"Yes, yes; but don't bother over that. Now, let us rather, as I first said, have one pleasant evening together."

Madge was not so brilliant or gay as usual. Her father had cast a cloud over her by the expressed doubt of Mr. Norton. True it was that she herself had once implied as much in a conversation with Helen; but that had been so effectually set aside and overcome by the zealous wife, that Madge's confidence was entirely restored. Though she did not again advert to the subject, her thoughts were constantly wandering off from the conversation, so that, after all, they did not have the pleasant, social evening Col. Vertner had wished for. When he kissed her good-night, and brushed back the rich brown hair from her slightly-swelling temples, he said, in a rather serious tone,

"I can't bear to see a shadow on this brow. Madge, look happy, be happy, dear child, or my heart will break. Are you sure that you are happy? There are times when I tremble lest you should not always be so." (Then, in a lower voice, though heard by her) "Retribution must not fall on her. Oh! no; let me have it a thousandfold."

"What do you mean by retribution?" she asked in surprise.

"Nothing, dear—only a foolish fear, born of my over-weaning fondness for you. I only half dread, at times, that the penalty belonging to some of my earlier boyish vices may fall upon you. Providence could punish me in no more fearful way than through you. But don't let my foolish, fond apprehension impress you unhappily. Trouble, sorrow or grief can never come to you, my beautiful summer bird; there is a special angel set to guard you in this life."

"So I have thought, dear papa; but is there not an angel charged with the guardianship of each and every human life?"

"The Catholics believe so, my darling; and, indeed, I see no reason why it may not be true doctrine; certainly it is very poetical, and I can well understand why a fresh, pure-hearted girl like you should be watched over by angels; but for a coarse, rugged, world-weary life like mine, I fear, there are no such pure and heavenly guards."

"Dear papa, I have been afraid of late that you are not quite so happy as you used to be. You are more moody, and strange at times. Has anything gone wrong in your business? Are you about to 'fail,' as people say in the city? Come, tell your child, your wilful but loving Madge, this mystery. Dear papa, you will feel better for the confidence. Unlock your heart for once, and take in my sympathy."

Closer and closer, as if he would draw her into his very heart, the father clasped his child. At that moment a figure—a strange, wild-looking creature—glanced in at one of the windows, from which a portion of the heavy curtain had slipped away. This frightful creature

paused for but a moment—saw that loving embrace—shook a clenched
fist defiantly toward them—then quickly vanished in the thick darkness.

....

Her father's conversation made such an impression upon
Madge that she went, the next day, to Mrs. Mason's, hoping to have a
conversation with Mr. Norton. She found Mrs. Mason very ill, lying
on a sofa, with no other company than the faithful Lydia, who still—as
ever—patiently bore her mistress's complaints, fretfulness and rebukes.
"What a wretched thing," thought Madge, "is a poor ill-tempered,
selfish invalid! with no higher thought than her own headache, cough or
deranged digestion, and no loftier purpose in life than to protect herself
against cold."

"Don't leave that door open," "Give me that tonic," "Don't rock
your chair," "Speak lower—I am very nervous," were the few phrases
that constituted the staple of Mrs. Mason's conversation. Poor Lydia
bore the brunt of her mistress's constant complaining without a word of
defence.

"Ah! Madge," croaked out the invalid, "have you come? Well, I
am glad to see you; nobody comes to see me now that Helen is gone.
Here I lie and suffer out my days without a word of sympathy from
any of my friends and neighbors—no one with me but that awkward,
sleepy, ill-natured, negligent Lyd, who frets me to death."

We will, without intending to contradict Mrs. Mason, state that
every day she had four or five calls from the ladies of the village, and
that she was constantly receiving flowers, preserved fruits and other little
delicacies and luxuries with which favored invalids are blest. Indeed,
her wealth (certainly not her amiability) secured her such attention and
service.

"Only see," said Madge, without heeding such idle complaints,
"what I have brought you," and she produced a small porcelaine jar of
orange marmalade. "I thought you might like this; and then, here is a
pretty little silk tidy, which I have knit you because I knew you were so
fond of such things."

"Yes, they are all very nice; but, then, Madge, you don't do
this for my sake, but because you loved Helen." This was spoken in a
peevish, ill-natured tone, and Madge was too honest and truthful to

contradict it. What but the love she had borne Helen could induce her now to minister, even with these petty trifles, to such a selfish, complaining, unhappy, luxurious valetudinarian?

Finding that no good, profit or pleasure, would result to Mrs. Mason from her visit, Madge cut it very short.

When about to leave, at the front door, with no one near, Lydia stole up to her and whispered,

"Miss Madge, I'd like to say a few words to you."

"Certainly, Lyd."

"But I'm 'feard somebody'll come here: won't yer please to go inter de library? Nobody is in dar."

"Where is Mr. Norton?"

"Eh! ha! he's bin down town dis good while. It's safe in dar, if you'll please to walk in." So saying, she flung the library door wide open, and Madge passed in, followed by the girl.

"Well, Lyd, what is it?" asked Madge, as she seated herself upon the sofa.

The girl stood, half anxious, half inquiring, half hesitating; something was evidently troubling her; yet she doubted the wisdom or safety of entrusting it to another. Again importuned by Madge, she said,

"Miss Madge, did'nt Miss Hel'n say, 'fore she died, that all her black folks was to be free?"

"Certainly."

"So I thought, and so I 'membered," replied the negro, with passionate energy.

"Why did you ask such a question? You surely recollect what your Miss Helen said; besides, Mr. Norton could tell you."

"Dat's it, Miss Madge—dat's it; you see, Mr. Norton ain't gwine to set us free now; he done tole grandmammy dat de law wouldn't let him, an' dat he couldn't do it no how jist yit. Now, Miss Madge, he's done forgot what he promise Miss Hel'n on her dyin' bed; an' I jist b'lieves, when missus dies, dat we'll all be sole down river, or put on de block an' cried off to de highest bidder; dat's what I b'lieves; 'kase Mr. Norton, he is mighty hard to please, an' jist thinks a nigger has got no tire in him. Our people was never drove half so hard as sense Mr. Norton come inter de family; I tells yer, Miss Madge, he jist fairly grinds de work out us. Missus don't know de half; an' alldough she is cross an' hard to please, she never drove so wid de work. An' den, Mr. Norton jist follers round, lookin' after housework, same as he was a woman. I never seed gentlemans do dat way. He is so fussy; things mus' be done jist so" (here she gave a very significant gesture). "Dey tells me all dem Yankees is dat way. I don't like 'em, I tell you. I'd rather work for one o' our own gentlemen, what never interferes with wimmin's work. Miss Madge, an ab'litionist makes a mighty bad master. Why, I hearn Mr. Norton say a nigger turned his stomach. Miss Madge, whar did Mr. Butler come from? hope he ain't a Yankee. Poor Miss Helen, she was too good to know Mr. Norton. If she was 'live now, it would most break her heart. Why, Miss Madge, he don't 'low de men dar reg'lar Saturday arternoons to work for darselves; an' he complains dat we claims too many holidays. Now, we's never bin cut short of our holidays afore. I tell you, Mr. Norton loves de chink; he never gives us any. You know all gentlemen gives dar slaves a little change now an' den, but he never do. Oh, La! dat is his step. I must git out here an' be at work, for he quarrels powerful if he sees us doin' nothin'."

"What does Mrs. Mason say to this?" inquired Madge, indignantly.

"Nothin', Miss Madge, 'cept dat Mr. Norton is a good manager; dat's what she say; but I must be gittin' out here; he is comin'."

Once again at the doorway, Madge was interrupted by the incoming of Mr. Norton, whom she was glad to meet, for she had resolved, if possible, to have a direct understanding of him.

"Well, bonny Madge," he exclaimed, "I am glad to see you."

She extended her hand to him, saying, cordially,

"I have wanted to see you very much, and have at last mustered courage to come and have a long talk."

"Walk into the library, dear; I shall be glad to talk with you on any and every subject."

The air that had been loaded with the heavy sighs and heavier words of the slave girl, was scarcely cool when the bland, polished, but cold-hearted and selfish New-Englander entered. Madge was too much excited to be cautious and approach her subject by slow degrees; she plunged at once into the very deepest of the difficulty.

"I have been waiting and watching, Mr. Norton, for you to fulfil the promise made to Helen, and carry out the noble plan which you first suggested to her, and to me, viz., the duty of slaveholders to manumit their slaves."

The man of rule, measure and method never moved a muscle or quivered a nerve, but sat there firmly gazing at the pale, excited girl.

"I understand all that, Madge," he answered, in a slow, methodical tone—"I understand the hot alarm of an impulsive girl; but you know time is required for the accomplishment of every great work. Rome, my dear young lady, was not built in an hour, and I must have time, care and thought for the carrying out of my design. Reason, philosophy and thought must act in this matter, not impulse and enthusiasm."

"When do you suppose you will see your way clearer than now?"

"I can't say; some time in the course of a few years, perhaps. These poor negroes are very ignorant and degraded. I must prepare them for a life of freedom."

"How? by keeping them still longer in slavery?" she archly inquired.

"For the present, yes," he replied, with a smile, "because slavery to them *now* is not an evil, only a necessary condition, such as any infant must suffer for a while. These people are in their infancy, mere babes, in knowledge of life. I must bear with them patiently and—"

"How marvellously you talk like a native Southerner; but this is not the language you used when I first knew you, Mr. Norton. *Then,* you looked at the *moral* wrong, and found no ready excuses for the toleration of such an evil. There was then no 'paltering in a double sense' with a terrible human wrong. Now, Mr. Norton, my patience with you is exhausted. I have inquired and have learned that you are doing nothing toward the instruction of your slaves, but keeping them ground down in the old working routine. You are only coining their very heart-throbs into money, which I hope will never do you any good. Could Helen Norton see you now, though she loved you once so dearly, I believe she would scorn and hate you, as I do now, for a poor, narrow, money-loving Yankee, who sold his birthright for a miserable mess of pottage"; and with this she swept out of the house, vowing to herself that she would never cross the threshold again.

XXXVI

Madge's time was now solely taken up with her horse, dog and evening visits to the quarter. Time was slipping by sweetly and gently as though it moved on golden sands. Mail day formed the one event of the week, as she constantly looked for a letter from Mr. Butler. Each steamer brought her two or three; but as she lived so far from the sea-board, she did not get them as often as her anxious heart desired. Funny, indeed, it was to see her when she wrote her first letter to him. Sheet after sheet of paper was written over, read and then thrown into the fire. At first she was at a loss how to address him. "Dear Mr. Butler" sounded too formal; "dear friend" was not exactly what she wished to express; and "*mon ami*" seemed too questionable. How very arch she appeared, sitting in the library, with paper spread out before her and pen held loosely in hand, while a queer, odd, perturbed expression stole over her usually free and sunny face. But somehow or other she got through the difficult task, and, after the first one, it was easy enough to write the others.

The great subject of conversation now at "Vertner Place" was the approaching wedding of the young mistress, for at length, in answer to Mr. Butler's earnest solicitations, seconded by Mrs. Vertner's wishes and Madge's timidly-expressed desire, Col. Vertner had consented to allow the marriage to take place some time during the coming summer. They were now beginning to expect Mr. Butler over. Each letter alluded to his return. For he declared that even England, his dear old home, could afford him nothing at all compensating for the delights of America, particularly the jolly and pleasant little "Place" in old Kentucky.

The house was now filled with that greatest of all domestic nuisances, painters, and paperers, and upholsterers. The time was April—that lovely, fitful month, when the woods were all abud and fresh with the tender early green which makes the south-western spring so delightful and charming.

Madge, for whom all these household preparations were going on, seemed to take but little interest in them. "Indeed," she one day exclaimed to her mother, "I don't see any use in all this renovation of the house and furniture. Why can't matters stand as they always have? Let me get married in a quiet, unostentatious manner. I don't like to see the house so torn up. I wish the paperers and painters would be away." To this her mother returned no other answer than to order her off as a silly child who did not understand anything rational. The old negroes worked regularly of nights, of holidays, and during little rare, odd moments, upon baskets and fancy brooms, which they wished to present to Miss Madge on her wedding-day; these were to be kept profoundly secret; so whenever Madge came into the cabins, these articles were carefully hidden away, tucked under beds, or slipped off in old presses or cupboards.

"What are you driving at, Aunt Polly?" asked Madge, one evening, as she entered the cabin, and Aunt Polly began bustling about, pushing something off in a pine box which was used for a sort of cupboard.

"Oh, nuffin, Miss Madge; nuffin at all, only some little fixin' o' mine dat you don't kere to see."

"Now, ain't she an angel?" the old woman continued to Uncle Peter, when Madge left; "she jist give up right away and never axed to see a bit; now, it was jist her right to make us show it to her; but she never axed or said a word arter I tole her 'twas some'in' she warn't to see."

"Yes, she arn't no wise 'quisitive," replied Uncle Peter; "she's a mighty lady person, Miss Madge, she is."

....

Pleasantly, sweetly and brightly as a moonlight dream the days stole on. Madge was happy as ever; the bond which united her and her father seemed to strengthen each and every day. Col. Vertner loved his daughter more and more, and Madge's faith and trust in him increased. Of late she had marked with regret the deepening of a cloud upon his brow, and she feared it was occasioned by the thought of losing her.

"Dear papa," she one day cried, as she entered the library and found him sitting there, with his face buried in his hands, "what is the matter with you? Don't think that I have not observed the gloomy cloud on your brow which you have so vainly tried to conceal from me. Are you distressed at the thought of losing me? Mr. Butler will be reasonable; he will not take me away; we will live here with you."

"No, dear child, no," replied Col. Vertner as he strained his daughter to his heart, "you shall not leave me. I have written to Mr. Butler that I would never give away my daughter, though I would consent to receive a son."

"But what an *old* son!" exclaimed Madge, with a bright smile. "Why, papa, Mr. Butler must be as old as you."

"Don't ever say that to him, dear," replied the thoughtful father. "Oh, my Madge, if trouble should ever come to you—you whom I have so shielded and sheltered from the rude blasts of the world—if it should come, how it will wear you down! You have never been accustomed to rough usage. Should things fail to run smoothly with you, come directly to your father; he will know how to soothe and comfort you. Here in my heart is your home, your asylum. Always love your father, darling, and know that he has meant to do justly, kindly by you. If he has failed, has made a mistake, think he did not mean it, and that his whole life was given to the atonement."

"Papa, what makes you talk so? What could ever happen that would make me blame you? Of late you talk so much in this strain."

"Do I, darling?" he asked, in surprise.

"Yes, and I cannot understand you. Do you ever suppose that I can be ungrateful to you or blame you for aught?"

"No, child, no. I am very foolish and fearful; forgive me; don't heed me; I am an old dotard; my love for you is crazing me."

Mrs. Vertner had grown fonder of her daughter than usual. As the time approached for giving her up to the keeping and love of another,

Madge's virtues and graces shone out to her mother and rendered her of some little consequence in that worthy person's estimation.

Madge now began to count the days that were to elapse before the return of Mr. Butler. A late letter had informed her of the vessel upon which he was about to take passage. Of course she was all anxiety and interest. One day, when she had gone into the woods for a walk—it was now about the middle of May; the woods were green and fresh, a carpet of soft, young grass enamelled with violets and early May flowers, was spread around—she was half lying on an old log under a beautiful beech tree, with a well-read letter of Mr. Butler lying open beside her, and with hat untied and her mantle thrown off, was watching with intense interest the lively movement of a squirrel which was bouncing and hopping from bough to bough, when a rustle and noise near by surprised her.

"Hush! hush!" she exclaimed, in a subdued tone, without turning round, "don't disturb Bunny."

A hand was suddenly and rather rudely laid upon her shoulder. Quickly she turned.

"Who are you?"

There, close to her side, she beheld a wild, weird-looking creature, a woman with torn and ragged dress, hair hanging neglected, matted and tangled over her tawny, sunken cheeks, and a wild, feverish light in her eyes.

"Who are you?" repeated Madge.

Yet the woman did not speak, but, with her hand still resting heavily on Madge's shoulder, she earnestly gazed into her face.

"Who are you?" asked Madge for the third time.

"Who am I? You have forgotten me, Madge Vertner; I know you well enough." There was something harsh in her voice, and Madge thought it expressed revenge or dislike of her. Though undismayed, she asked,

"Whoever you are, and you seem to know me, I hope you are not one who bears any ill will to me. I have wronged no one. Why, then, have you seized me so?"

The woman relaxed her hold, and stepping a little off from Madge, asked, as she parted the long mats of tangled hair,

"Have you forgotten our first place of meeting? or do you remember when and where we parted?"

Madge struggled with a vague sort of memory. It seemed as if she ought to know the woman; there was a tone or a look that she thought lay hid away somewhere in her mind, but which she could not now fully recall. The longer she looked, the more puzzled she became. At length the woman said,

"Rachel!—whipping-post!!—Col. Vertner!!"

These words broke hissingly through her clenched teeth; and then, as if by a lightning flash, the whole past scene came back to her.

"Rachel! poor Rachel! is it indeed you?" Madge sprang forward, attempted to catch the woman by the hand, but she waved her off, saying,

"Don't come near me till I tell you what is on my heart, what I have many times meant to tell you, but could not, for a seal was on my lips; don't come nigh me, I say again."

Her eye was very wild, her cheeks flushed, and her entire manner indicated one mentally deranged.

Madge felt like urging her not to speak, but again the woman waved her off.

"Madge Vertner," she said, "you are not the daughter of Mrs. Vertner, nor yet the legal child of your own father. In your proud veins flows a little of that blood which your mother and the whole white race so despise. You are an octoroon, the child of a quadroon woman, who was a slave; and were it well known who you are, you would be a slave now, owned by your own father and counted as his property."

Though Madge did not believe one word of this, she turned deadly pale, and a greenish light stole over everything. Dizzily she sank down upon the log from which she had previously risen. Immediately Rachel rushed to her side, and caught her in her arms. "I remember the time when you rendered me a generous service, and for that act of kindness I have never forgotten you. Mine and your" (the woman smiled) "race can at least be grateful. Madge Vertner, you have been gently and tenderly reared; had your education and fortune made you proud and haughty—made you rude and overbearing to your father's slaves—I should, God knows, long ago have entered your Eden and poisoned all the flowers of your life. But I found you kind and sympathizing, loved by every one, most of all by your father's slaves. From them I heard the kindest things of you; and in the moment of my own great trouble, you were the one who relieved me. I feel, then, that I owe you a great deal. Yet this secret, which, I doubt not, will pain you, has laid so heavily on my heart that I *must* tell you of it; but now I shall never again speak of it to mortal being, only let it, if possible, increase your sympathy with the race to which you belong by one little drop of yellow blood. I see you are incredulous—perhaps, positively disbelieve me; but push back the hair from your temples; see if they are not darker than other parts of your face; examine the points of your fingers, see the yellowish tint there, and you will recognize the one drop which, in the eye of the whites, corrupts your blood and puts you beyond the pale of refined sympathy.

Like one stupefied, Madge sat listening to the woman. She believed her mad, and yet a thousand doubts forbade her condemning the statement as utterly false. She recalled, in a moment, how often her father had talked of some possible trouble that might come to her—of a wrong he had unwittingly done her; then, too, she remembered her mother's coldness and seeming want of love for her. Doubts, such as these, spite of faith and life-time love, battled for an entrance. A trying moment it was to her then! "What!" she asked herself, "not the true daughter of these parents? Am I a poor alien child, of low birth, with a stain on my name and blood? No, I can't and won't believe it." Then, speaking aloud to Rachel, she said,

"I can't believe you, poor distraught; you are not accountable for what you say; but I forgive you freely the momentary trouble you have caused me, for you have suffered deeply and have been deeply wronged."

"You think me crazy," cried the woman with a wild tone and a fierce eye; "*you* think *me* crazy. God knows I have borne enough in my life to make me so, but I'm not crazy; no, thank God, I have a spark of reason left, though the white people have done little to let me keep it. I only wonder that my very life was not smothered out. Look here, Madge Vertner," and Rachel drew close to our young heroine, took her seat on the same log, and laid her hand on Madge's—"I was not always what I now am. I remember the time when I had friends, and thought I should have always a father's love around me. God knows I never expected to become the thing I am. My father was your father, Andrew Vertner's uncle, so that you see I bear the same blood in my veins and am every way worthy to sit by you. My poor father did everything for me; he had me well educated, and left me money enough to take care of me, with prudence and economy; but your father found me in my quiet Northern home, where he should have left me unmolested; when, however, did a white man and a slaveholder respect virtue or honor in a mulatto? Let it be enough to say that my story is the old story of faith belied, confidence deceived, and a heart broken in its first life. I followed Andrew Vertner as a dog; I lived upon the mere light of his smile; followed him out to this dreary country, and lived quietly for years in that cabin where you first found me. I think him not all a bad man, for there were times when he showed something like genuine feeling and regret for 'the follies,' as he termed them, of his early life. Ah! God! his 'follies' have been mine and your ruin. Though he was married when I first met him, he never told me so. I was promised, at some future time, honorable marriage; and when I came here, I learned, with horror, that a young and lovely slave girl, a beautiful and petted quadroon, belonging to a friend of Col. Vertner's, had also to pay, with her heart's best blood, the price his youthful 'folly' demanded; and you, my child, are the sad fruit of that unhappy love. I have heard Alice (your mother's name) say that when Andrew Vertner first looked down into your eyes, as you lay in the cradle, he struck his breast in an agony of grief, for he knew to what an inheritance you were born; but he swore a fearful oath that he himself would go into slavery rather than let you bear the misery and degradation of such a lot, and well he kept his word. About this time your mother, or she whom you have been taught to regard as your mother—I mean Mrs. Vertner—had put her own babe (a sickly child) out to nurse, and this child soon after died; then your father conceived the plan of putting you in the cradle, and, without acknowledging the death of the other, pass you off as the legitimate child. Of course Alice joyfully agreed to the plan, for she knew it would be for your good. Old Lucy, the nurse, was paid a large bribe to keep the secret. There were only three of us beside your father who understood the secret. I was obliged to be told it, as I knew of the death of the other child, and no deception could be passed upon me. Do you believe me now?"

"I can't say why, but there is something that makes me fear you do not speak altogether falsely. But, oh! say that you have deceived me, have played upon my foolish fears, and I will kneel to you and bless you forever."

Madge had risen from her seat, clasped her hands wildly, and was about to fall upon her knees at the mulatto's feet, when the latter suddenly checked her, and drew out a paper, saying, as she offered it,

"Read that, and satisfy your doubts."

The paper contained a full confession of the fraud which had been practiced upon Mrs. Vertner, with an acknowledgment of the large bribe received by the nurse, and was signed with the cross mark of old Lucy. The confession had been drawn up and written off by Rachel. Madge's eye ran rapidly over the words, then, as if shocked beyond all possible mode of expression, she let the paper fall at her feet. Rachel gathered it hastily up and again concealed it in the folds of her dress.

"I can't understand," said Madge, through her tears, "why, even if this dreadful story be true, you should come to blight all my happiness, to dash the full cup of life just as it was about to be pressed to my lips—I—I who never did you any harm, who strove, even when you were a stranger to me, to do you the little good that laid in my power. How have I warmed in my breast an adder that stings me now—here you are biting at my very heart and poisoning me to death."

Rachel laid her hand upon Madge's shoulder.

"Take it off," cried Madge, starting from her, "I will not have you come near me. You have killed me with these terrible words. But I'll not believe you; you are a poor crazy wretch, whom I should only pity."

"Go, ask your father!"

"Yes, that is what I will do, and he shall prove you a mean, wicked liar," exclaimed Madge, all the passionate fire of her nature returning.

Hastily gathering up her letter and hat, she moved rapidly away; but when a few yards off, at the border of the wood, she could not resist the impulse to turn and look back at her tormentor. There, under the budding trees, with her torn feet crushing the fresh grass, stood the ragged and forlorn woman. All the harshness was gone from her face, only a look of sadness had succeeded, and, with downcast eye and arms drooping wearily at her side, while the tattered garments hung like sackcloth about her form, she looked a very Magdalen. The scene was peaceful and beautiful, for the evening star and the young moon had risen and were softly shining down upon the green May forest. As Madge turned round, and with a quick glance, took in the whole scene, the mournful attitude of the woman, softened by the subduing influences of the hour and scene, touched her heart and made her half forgive the wrong Rachel had done her. She was tempted to turn back and say as much to the woman; but another and a prouder feeling checked her, and she continued her walk in the direction of home.

XXXVII

Col. Vertner sat alone, the next morning, in his library; through the open window stole the fresh, morning breeze, laden with the perfume of roses and laburnums, while a bright ray of early sunlight rippled over the papers and books that were carelessly thrown upon the table. Col. Vertner's face wore an unusually pleased expression; a favorite volume lay open before him, but his eye wandered constantly from the page, as though some pleasant thought dwelt in his mind and monopolized all his attention. This train of fancy, however, was broken by the sudden entrance of Pomp, with the mail-bag.

"Hy, boy," exclaimed the Colonel, "have you much of a budget to-day?"

"Yes, sar, an' it's mighty heavy; dem 'ar letters mus' weigh somethin'," replied the boy as he dashed the leather bag from his shoulder, and drew a long, loud breath, expressive of the exertion which it had cost him to carry so weighty a burden.

"Well, give me the key, and here is a dime for you."

"Thankey, mas'er; turnkey, sar," and the boy fumbled away at his pockets in search of the key. Being a little slow, his master inquired,

"What! you rascal! I trust you have not lost the key of the mail-bag."

"Oh, no, sar, me hain't lost him; he is down here somewhar 'mong my marbles."

Accordingly, a quantity of marbles, twine, wrapping thread, bits of paper, rags, odds and ends, &c., of the "dear knows what," as Aunt Polly styled it, were fished up from those capacious pockets, and among other things the little missing key was at last found.

"Oh, here it am, mas'er; here it am; me think he wasn't lost."

As he looked over the letters, Col. Vertner found quite a number addressed to himself, and one for Madge. The father smiled as his eye conned over that British postmark; and he well knew how happily his daughter's pulse would bound at sight of the well-known writing.

"Go, tell your Miss Madge to come to me, Pomp; I suppose she is out now for a romp with Rover round the lawn."

But before the boy had time to obey the command, the library door was slowly opened and Madge Vertner appeared, looking pale and listless as though she had spent an anxious, troubled night.

"Why, daughter! But what *is* the matter?" exclaimed Col. Vertner, his tone changing from the gay and joyous to the frightened and surprised as soon as he observed her appearance.

"You are not well. Let me reach you a chair."

Madge took the seat and motioned to Pomp to leave the room.

"What is it, daughter?" asked her father with anxiety.

"Let me be still for a moment."

Remembering the letter which had just come for her, Col. Vertner hoped to soothe her with it. Placing it gently in her hand, he said,

"Only see, here is an English letter for you."

Madge started and let it fall from her hands.

Passing his arm round her waist, and stroking her brow tenderly, he sought to beguile her into a happier mood. What is it, my pet? what has disturbed you so? The morning is so beautiful and inviting, I had hoped that it had found you, as it has me, in a cheerful and happy state of mind. Come, come, what is it? Some ugly dream? But read your letter; it will cheer you up. Only see how you have allowed it to fall from your hands. This is not the way you usually greet Mr. Butler's letters."

"Break the seal and read it to me, papa."

This was a singular request, and perfectly inexplicable to Col. Vertner, for Madge generally read her own letters, and on all former occasions had made a great matter of the mere breaking of the seal. Now, however, though much surprised, he obeyed her without further inquiry into the strangeness of her mood.

"And so," he observed, as he refolded the letter after reading it to her, "Mr. Butler will not sail for another month. That is rather provoking."

"It is providential."

"Why so, my darling?"

"Because I have that to say to him which had better, far better, be written than spoken."

An inquiring look was the only answer she received.

"Papa" (Madge paused at each word, as if gasping for breath), "did you ever know a quadroon girl—a slave—by the name—of—*Alice?*"

Col. Vertner let go his daughter's hand and reeled back a few steps, like one suddenly stricken by a severe blow. Madge's eyes were firmly fixed upon him. Leaning eagerly forward, with parted lip and a nervous motion of the fingers of her outstretched hand, she watched every movement of his. Her hope, love and life trembled on the answer.

"Oh, God!" gasped Col. Vertner, "the curse has come at last!"

"Papa"—this time Madge's voice was calm and fearfully cold— "you need not tremble and turn away from me with that dismayed look. I know all."

"Not *all*, child—not all—not half. They cannot have told you how I have suffered, the hell I have carried in my bosom."

"I am the daughter of that quadroon, Alice—not, alas! the honorable child of an honorable marriage. I am here in this house only by courtesy, or rather by means of a base lie and a baser fraud."

Her eye flashed and her lip curled disdainfully as she uttered these words.

"Spare me, my child; spare me. I have tried to atone for that great wrong. Spare me, I beg; don't let curses come from you; but, no, I'll not ask you to spare me; 'tis better that you should curse. I deserve it. Great God, why was I spared for this?"

"*And why was I born to it?*"

A moment of deadly silence ensued. Madge sat in the most moveless, statue-like repose, while her father remained standing over by the window, with his hands clasped to his temples, neither looking toward the other. Such was the change of a few hours. A father and daughter, whose very lives had hitherto seemed blent into one, sat, now, estranged and riven apart, as though a fathomless river flowed between them.

Madge was the first to break the silence.

"You have nothing further to say?" She did not even glance toward him.

Suddenly, as if recollecting himself, and forgetting what his ravings had betrayed, Col. Vertner exclaimed,

"Madge, who have you seen? what witch or sprite, fiend or monster, has been playing upon your credulity. 'Tis all a lie, a base, prepared, premeditated lie. Don't think of it again, my child; but tell me who has dared such villany; tell me, and I will throttle the dastard in his next speech. Come, come, poor panting bird, to your father's heart."

He stretched out his arms to receive her, and advanced a few steps, when she waved him off.

"No, papa; no; another lie will not wipe out this terrible fraud which has been practiced upon me and mamma—I mean *Mrs. Vertner.*"

There was a terrible bitterness in her tone; it cut her father's heart like a sword.

"Don't be sarcastic, Madge, for my poor brain turns round; I am bewildered and grope about like one blind."

"I have seen Rachel, papa, and she has told me all. The proof of the horrible truth laid in her natural sincerity, though I despised and defied her, and hastened home to have you refute it all; something, a voice I could not distrust, deep down in my soul, bade me believe the woman. What ages of pain and torture I lived through last night! How I hoped that peace would break over my soul with the breaking day! But, no, there is no peace for me. I have parted from it with my childhood. Perhaps I have had enough happiness in my early life and should bear this great shame and trouble patiently. Oh that I had been strangled in my cradle and not saved for this bitter moment!"

She pressed her long fingers to her eyes, while tears burst through the partings and rained down upon her lap.

"Oh, Madge, Madge, cry, weep, my child, let the fountain run dry now, but don't scorn your father; love him, cling close to him in spite of this."

Col. Vertner had drawn near her and was about to lay his hand upon her partially-bent head, when she slid softly from the chair, and laid herself down upon the carpet, with her face buried in her hands. He stood over her, gazing down at her prostrate form, with a measureless anguish depicted on his countenance. He dared not speak, but left her to the flow of her own grief. What would he not then have given for the power to recall or wash out "*the follies*" of his youth?

Moments passed like ages, so full were they of bitterness and suspense. After a gust of sighs, moans and tears, Madge Vertner, by virtue of the strength and energy of her nature, commanded herself sufficiently to assume a composed air.

"Papa, since this dreadful news *is* a fact, I shall accept my fate. Forgive me if I have seemed harsh and unkind. It was a great blow, and, coming so suddenly, quite stunned me; but now, as my reason and right-thinking return, I recollect all that I owe to your tenderness and generous consideration. You petted my childhood and loaded my life with blessings. Such atonement as your full-handed generosity and affection could make have been freely made, and it is not for me now to revile and curse—no, no (with tears), rather let me love you the more. Take me, *father and mother*—for you have been both to me—to your heart; let me rest there. I have nothing else left me in the wide world but you, and, as the vine clings close to the sturdy oak, I will twine, clasp and interlace the tendrils of my heart and soul about you." And there, sobbing and moaning like a weary child, she lay upon his breast, with his arms locked closely around her.

But by and bye the fury of the storm spent itself, and, wiping her eyes and composing her manner, she sat down upon the sofa, and asked her father to take the place beside her.

"Papa," she said, after a moment's pause, "tell me something of this Alice—of—my—moth—er." Her lip trembled and tongue faltered on the syllables of the last word.

Mastering himself by a considerable effort, Col. Vertner replied,

"I will tell you all I can; but how am I to begin? where and when?" Suddenly rising from his seat, he paced the room with irregular and uneasy steps. Striking his clenched fists together, he exclaimed,

"What a *thing* is a man bowed with shame in the presence of his own child!"

"Does it pain you so much, dear papa? If so, deny me; but I thought it was best to know *all* now, and then put the subject away forever from our minds. I think, after this, a better relationship will be established between us; and now that I know your secret trouble, I can sympathize the more with you."

"Dear child!" he cried, as he held out his hand toward her. "Already you are unselfishly forgetting yourself, upon whom the heaviest blow falls, and only remembering to pity and sympathize with me. But, Madge," he continued, after a slight pause, "give me, first, a full account of your meeting with Rachel. Ah! I always knew that trouble would come to me through that proud and high-spirited mulatto."

"Papa, she calls herself your cousin, and she told me of fearful wrongs and deceptions which you had practiced upon her."

"Yes, yes; I suppose it is well for you to know it all, and yet it would have been kind to have spared me the humiliation in my child's esteem; but, Madge, dearest and best of children, you will not despise me?"

"Oh, no, indeed," and she sprang to his embrace.

With as few words as possible, and in a seemingly calm tone, she gave him a faithful and minute account of the interview. Several times, when she repeated Rachel's words, he winced and writhed as though he had been put upon the rack. When she had finished, she clasped his hand tightly between hers, and asked,

"Now, papa, tell me of Alice. I cannot yet learn to call her mother, even in thought."

Passing his hand lightly across his eyes, he said,

"Alice, my dear, was a beautiful quadroon girl, of sprightly mind, but utterly without education or any kind of moral instruction, yet a person of the keenest instincts, and more beautiful than any living creature I ever beheld. You, my Madge, have, at times, a certain piquant expression which recalls her to me. She was a slave, owned by a friend of mine, a Mr. La Rue, of New Orleans, who spent his summers on the place adjoining this, and which he then owned, but afterwards sold. Alice was Mrs. La Rue's dressing-maid, a petted upper servant, with many advantages, one of those gay, bird-like creatures to whom slavery had no horror. How happy she was when I first saw her, singing the whole day through! Fascinated as I was by her extraordinary personal beauty, it was a dangerous position that I found myself in—meeting her, as I so often did, in my morning drives and afternoon rambles through the woods, for Alice's duties were light, and most of her time was at her own command. It was not a cold and, as you perhaps think, a willing wrong I did to Alice, for I loved her more than I had ever loved before or shall ever love again; and after your birth, I offered to buy her from La Rue, for the sole purpose of setting her free; but she was a pet of his wife's, and five times her appraised value in ready gold could not secure the purchase. Such was my anxiety that I confessed to her master the relation which she had held to me; but it was of no avail. He would willingly have surrendered her, but his wife's consent could not be obtained. However, he let me have you for a very small consideration; in order to secure this, his wife had to be told the secret, and only then and upon that condition would she give you up. About this time your little half-sister, your mamma's (for you must still call her so) child, who had been put out to nurse with old Lucy, your mammy, died, and I conceived the plan of putting you in her place, and concealing from my wife the fact of the death or the exchange. For a handsome pecuniary consideration the old nurse kept my secret. Of course her freedom was a portion of the bribe; and when she left to find a home in the Northern part of Ohio, I fondly believed that my and your secret was safe; but Rachel has at last betrayed me. I was obliged to tell her of the affair."

"But, papa"—Madge's voice faltered, and she timidly cast her eyes downward—"what induced you to deceive poor Rachel, and decoy her out here, when she was so pure and happy in the North?"

"Don't question me, child, too narrowly or closely; that was one of the mad freaks of my wild and somewhat vicious youth. I have repented of it a thousand times, but repentance came too late."

"She was a lively, graceful creature when I first saw her; and do you remember, that time I met you over at her cabin-door and inquired earnestly who she was, when you put me off by saying that she was a seamstress? Ah, papa, how you deceived me!"

"Yes, but don't recall it now."

After another rather long pause, Col. Vertner asked,

"Madge, darling, you will say nothing of this to your mamma. Spare me disgrace and humiliation before her."

"My first thought was to tell her, for I think it so wrong to let her rest under such a deception, especially as she has never loved me, and it might soothe her heart and conscience to know that I am a poor alien and not her child; but since you ask me not to tell her, and knowing, as I do, how severely she would reproach you, I shall be silent; but of course, papa, you know that I will write to Mr. Butler and inform him of all, as concisely as possible."

"Madge, you do not mean what you say?"

"Of course I do; to act otherwise would be dishonorable."

"Child, you are honor-mad. Why will you blight your own happiness and my proud expectation?"

"Because I believe it to be right. Papa, do you remember Mr. Butler once said, in answer to a question of mine, that he could never marry a girl who had one drop of colored blood in her veins? Knowing this, it would be a cruel wrong in me to marry him without first letting him know who and what I am."

"Oh, God! more trouble is yet to come upon me; Madge, how can you forgive me?"

....

Col. Vertner sought out Rachel and had a sad, strange interview with her. She told him that an impulse, which she could not resist, had urged her back, and, driven desperately, perhaps by love, perhaps by revenge, she had told all to Madge. Seeing her frightful condition, Col. Vertner did not reproach her as severely as he intended, and it may be that in his secret soul he blamed her less than he thought he did. The interview was a strange and by no means pleasant one. The broken down man of power and influence heard words from the lips of a mad woman which placed his character and position in an entirely different light from that in which he had usually contemplated them. They parted with reproach on the one side and recrimination on the other. And the morning after the interview, a party of wood-cutters found the body of a mulatto woman hung by a small rope to the branch of a beech tree. Upon examination, it was identified as Rachel's, and another blow fell upon Col. Vertner's conscience. He, indeed, began to feel that Providence was sending him retribution fast and in large instalments. Madge heard of the suicide with a feeling of poignant regret.

In a brief but dignified letter, she told Mr. Butler of the recent painful discovery which she had made regarding her birth and identity; then, after a few kindly-expressed feelings and recollections of the past, she relinquished all claims of love and duty which she held upon him.

After posting the letter, Madge went about her usual avocations with an apparently light heart. But those, her father and the negroes, who watched her closest, saw that a great change had come over her. Now she was always busy doing something for someone else. She did not ride, or drive, or play so much with Rover, but went about among the neighbors, and the poor, or the sick, hunting up sufferers and rendering them little attentions and services, while all her evenings were spent in the negro cabins, talking with the slaves, reading to them or taking some little delicacy or comfort to such of them as were sick or in trouble. In fact, Madge was trying to fly from memory, trying to live outside the sphere of herself and her own grievances. Affliction always awakes the Christ in us.

Her father marked with anxious interest the lessening bloom of her cheek and the want of elasticity in her step.

"What is it, Madge?" he one day asked; "all your animation appears gone; you step with a heavy, wearisome tread. Are you not well? I must send for the doctor."

"No, don't, papa; I am quite well; only a little languid. Never mind, I'll soon be as strong as ever." Even Mrs. Vertner, who was not wont to heed such matters, observed the change.

"Something had better be done for her," she said to her husband; "the child is weak and ailing, it is plain to see."

Weeks sped on; still no letter from Mr. Butler. Madge eagerly seized the mail-bag when Pomp returned from the village, hastily and nervously examining each letter, hoping to find among them the well-known writing; but disappointment followed disappointment, until her heart grew faint. Perhaps—who shall say?—she hoped, after all, that he would not avail himself of the opportunity which her sensitiveness afforded. Perhaps she thought he had spoken suddenly, ill-advisedly of his prejudice against the race; and, after all, she might be happy. With such tempting and tormenting thoughts, she still watched and waited.

XXXVIII

That heart-sickness which comes from deferred hope pressed all too heavily upon poor Madge, and her health gave way with the failure of her hope. As long as possible she held out a stout resistance, and would not succumb; but as weeks waxed into months, she began to realize that she was, in truth, cast off. Pride put on a haughty look, and tried to affect *the indifferent;* but when was Pride unconquered by Love? Thoughts of the past, dreams of the future, and memories of the ideal and the idol looked mockingly in upon her forced resignation. Poor tired, young heart, with no well-spring at which to quench its burning thirst!

Day by day her step grew weaker, and her cheek paled as though a canker were secretly feeding upon its bloom. Friends and acquaintances marked the change, and artfully traced it back, as is always the case, to some little cold which she had taken. Only the father knew that the fountain of his child's happiness had been sapped by the just penalty due to those *innocent* "follies" of his youth, which young men sometimes jocosely style "sowing wild oats." He remembered, as he clenched his fists, and swore deep oaths against himself, that God's curse sometimes reaches to the second and third generation.

....

"Are these books so very pleasant, dear papa?" inquired Madge, one afternoon, as they sat alone in the library. "I wish I could learn to be fond of them, for they seem to have such a beguiling power. If I could be content to sit and pore over them as you do, I might learn to forget"—

She suddenly caught her breath then added quickly,

"At least, now, when I am so dull and prosy, a good book might wake me up. I remember it was Charles Reade who first gave me any sort of interest in books. And what a great vista of reflection was opened out by that wonderful story, 'Never Too Late to Mend.' I am surprised that everybody who reads it is not moved as I was. That book aroused my sympathy for all kinds of human suffering, and gave me an enlarged view of matters and things, 'institutions,' if you will, by which I was surrounded. How well I recollect the first time I read that story! it was the night that Jack and Milly ran away; and my impulse was to tell you of their flight, when suddenly the book seemed to speak to me, to warn me that if I hindered them, I would but write myself down a very Hawes; and so I kept my own counsels; and that act was like the opening of a window to my mind; light poured in afterwards. Say, papa" (she passed her hand across her eyes), "when will you liberate our slaves? You must believe that it is wrong to hold them thus."

"My child" (he spoke with evident irritation), "our negroes are not yet ready for emancipation; when they are, I shall consider the matter. Were you well and strong, my dear, as you used to be, and as I hope before many months to see you again" (he stroked her hair), "I would talk the matter over with you, and try to explain some of its knotty points; but just now I should prefer to see you in a quiet, unexcited state of mind."

"Believe me, papa, I have sufficient strength to talk on this or any subject; moreover, I am so very much interested in this whole business that I think talking of it will do me more good than harm. Why can't you make some arrangement by which their freedom will be secured? What prevents you from doing it at once? Like Mr. Norton, whom you denounced as an insincere person, you always confront me with that horrid monster, '*the law of my State.*' Now, if the law of my State is the devil's compact, I despise it."

"Madge"—Mrs. Vertner's hand was firmly laid upon Madge's shoulder—"Madge, what do you mean by this irreverence? Your father should not listen to such mad talk. I am ashamed—but, good heavens! how pale you are. See, see, Col. Vertner, she is fainting."

The strong man passed his arm lightly around his daughter's waist, and bore her to the open window. Mrs. Vertner dashed a glass of cold water in the colorless face; and, with a fearful shudder, the girl returned to human consciousness.

"Oh, papa, I feel so strangely, as if all my blood had run out—so weak, like beaten flax; and the air!—I can't breathe."

Again she closed her eyes. The whiteness of her face increased.

"Only see! she swoons again," cried Mrs. Vertner. "Send for the doctor, Col. Vertner; the child will die here without aid."

"I cannot leave her," exclaimed the terrified father, now fully realizing that she was altogether *his* child. "You go, my dear, despatch a servant at once for the physician."

The fact was, Madge had not been well for some time. She had felt, without understanding it, for several months past, a strange, uneasy feeling in the region of the heart, quick flutterings and palpitations, with sometimes strong physical pain. Now she had become a little too much excited in the conversation with her father, and a swoon was the result. The doctor came, looked at her, felt her pulse, asked a good many questions, left a prescription with strict injunction that the medicine be given faithfully every half-hour until he called again.

And so it was for some time. The attack which all had thought slight kept Madge bed-fast for weeks.

Slowly, and oh! how reluctantly! Col. Vertner became aware that his child was sinking rapidly. There was a tight pulling at the chords of his heart, a thick, choking fulness of the throat, and a blindness, as of a night cloud, before his eyes—still, no tears. He ground down his agony, locked up his feelings, and tried to appear as usual before Madge. But the fond and tender daughter marked her father's forced manner with an anxious eye.

One morning, after a feverish, sleepless night, he came into her chamber. She raised herself upon the pillow.

"Come here, papa. Oh, how I *should* miss that morning kiss if it were to fail me," she said. Then, giving him her hand, she added, "But ere long, dear papa, my morning greeting will fail you. Signs came to me, last night, by which I know that I am fast going—signs which I cannot mistake. There were voices calling underneath my window, flappings of strange wings about my bed, and murmurs close to my ears, as though the angels were calling me to come away. I am not afraid to go, papa; and if it were not for you, I believe I should be glad. I leave this life just as it begins to pall. I go with my first disappointment. And when I am gone, fairly gone, papa, fast, deep-buried in the earth, you will write—give me a drink of that water; my throat is thick—there! there! I say, when I *am* dead and buried, you will write to Mr. Butler and tell him of it. Break the news gently to him, papa, without a word of your own grief, and let there be no unkindness."

"Oh, angel-child, can you, do you forgive him? I never can."

"And why not? I pity the little cloud of weakness and pride which for the moment overcame him. You, my dear papa, of all other men, should blame him least. Before he came to this country, I dare say, Mr. Butler had none of this vulgar prejudice against race, or color" (she smiled), "as it is facetiously styled. He learned it in America, with tobacco-spitting and other vulgarities. None of our fine gentlemen would marry a quadroon. Why, then, expect greater magnanimity of an Englishman? No, papa, you have felt the recoil of the gun which you had loaded for another. Bear it patiently, or profit so far by it as to quit the business of slaveholding. Throw your fortune, life and influence into the scale for freedom; and, oh! promise me, before I go, brighten my dying moment, soften my death-pillow by the pledge that you will liberate our slaves; and tell Mr. Norton that my last message to him was to remind, beg, urge him not to trifle with his conscience, to count all earthly possessions of little value when arrayed against justice, truth and human love. Tell him to remember his promise to Helen, and no longer restrain those negroes from their liberty. And, papa, have I your promise?" She pressed his hand warmly. Of course it is needless to state that he gave the promise. How could a father, in such circumstances, do otherwise?

....

Daily, almost hourly, Madge sank rapidly. Her illness was characterized by a sleepy, silent sort of languor. For hours she would lie

in a half trance, with her eyes rigidly fixed upon some flower or figure
on the papered wall; and when asked how she felt, would reply,

"Weary; oh, so weary!"

The doctor said it was a premature worn-out-ness, a failure of
all the physical functions, and that the heart had become partially
benumbed. The negroes came in, as often as they were allowed, to look
at her—each one bringing some little tribute. The baskets and fancy
brooms which they had designed for her wedding presents were now
offered as an amusement for her sick hours. Old Uncle Peter hobbled up
to the house from his cabin, every morning and evening, to see her. She
appeared to enjoy his visits more than any others, for he always talked
to her of the New Jerusalem, and delighted in picturing it as a great
city of golden streets, with a summer's sun always beaming down upon
its palaces of diamond and jasper. The old negro had heard somewhere
of the story in Revelation, and out of such fragments as his memory
afforded had patched up quite a fascinating little picture.

"Oh, Missy Madge," he used to say, that's the right place for sich
as you. Dis here airth ain't good enuff fur ye. Up dar" (indicating with
his cane) "is de place whar de folks is angels, de sky bright, de ground
gold, an' de houses precious stones. Ah! de Lord make a mansion for his
own. He knows dis no fitten place for de angels, an' he only sent you
down here fur a little while. Now he wants you back. Oh, it ain't hard to
go, Miss Madge; it's jist one step over de stile, down a moonlight lane,
an' den de New Jerusalem breaks right on to your sight.

"'Oh, you's gwine home,
Home, home to rest.'"

He broke out singing, in a sweet, plaintive style, a verse or so of a
popular negro hymn, "Home to Canaan." All this had a soothing
influence upon Madge, so that the old negro left her always more
composed than he found her; yet, though he talked to her in this
encouraging manner, those who watched him when he left discovered
that he was always in tears. However, in her presence he restrained his
feelings, painting to her, as a brighter and more experienced intellect
might have done, the heaven to which she was fast hastening. "Cast all
your fears," he was wont to say in his talks with her—"cast all your fears

on Jesus's breast. He's de lamp, de light and de joy what's gwine to lead you through. Oh, think on the cross; see his bleedin' side, de nails in his hands and feet, an' dat orful thirst when dey give him vinegar an' no water. Think, blessed child, what he suffer, and never fear to go right to him. His arms done stretch wide out to you now; all you is got to do is to go straight to him. He stands waitin' an' willin'. I ken most see him now stand on de edge of dat white cloud dat rests so still over yonder, wid de sunlight making it so bright."

Aunt Polly was not allowed to see her often, as she could not control her feelings sufficiently, and always excited Madge. Ruth came dozens of times through the day with flowers, and her great, curious eyes always swimming in tears. To her, Madge bequeathed all her ribbons, old gloves, laces, hats, &c. Though the poor girl was charmed with the finery, this evidence of kindness on the part of her young mistress, at such a time, touched her deeply; and, with her apron thrown over her head, she would rush from the room, crying out,

"Miss Madge, dear, blessed Miss Madge, done broke my heart right in two."

Every morning, Pomp was sent for to tell the news from Silk and Rover; and Madge would smile her old, joyous smile at the boy's narration.

It was amusing, yet touching, one morning, to see the little black-faced, frolic-loving fellow, as he stood close by his mistress's bed, with his shining face lighted up with merriment, in the midst of a long story; while Madge, with her arm poised upon the pillow and her head resting upon her frail, white hands, listened to him, with eagerness and animation written all over her wasted face.

"And Rover?" she asked.

"Oh, him jist whines and grieves 'bout you, Miss Madge; he cries all round dis winder and jumps up on his hind legs, tryin' to get in; he follers every one to de door an' tries to get in arter 'em, but den he is pushed back an' he jist tucks his tail hind his leg and pokes off, lookin' so lonesome like. See, dar he is now, Miss Madge, lookin' in at dat glass door."

And as Madge bent forward from the bed, sure enough there was Rover perched up, looking in at the window, with that wistful gaze which speechless animals some times give.

"Oh, let him in; let him in," exclaimed Madge.

Quickly Rover's fore paws were upon the bed, his tail wagging in delight, and he licking his mistress's outstretched hand.

"Poor fellow, poor fellow," said Madge, "how he has missed me. He looks thin. I am afraid, Pomp, you have not taken good care of him."

The dog seemed wild with delight, and Madge herself appeared to enjoy the meeting nearly as much. As she bent over, caressing the dog, her father entered the room.

"Ah," he cried out, "how natural this looks! My daughter, you will get well; only see how your odd old pets, Pomp and Rover, woo and coax you back to health."

That afternoon Ruth carried her in her arms to the stable to look at Silk.

"Here, Ruth," said Madge, "don't you think you can lift and bear me in your arms to Silk's stall?"

"Yes, indeed, Miss Madge, and I is glad to do it."

"Get me that brown mantilla, and my hat with the black lace fall. There, now, gently, very gently, Ruth! I feel so weak, and as flimsy as unstarched muslin."

Arrived at the stable, she said,

"Put me down upon this painted trough; hold me so, your arm round my waist; there, Ruth, keep your hand firmly there. I feel almost giving way. Poor Silk! pretty, graceful Silk! I have come to tell you good-bye—come to see you for the last time. Never again, oh Silk, shall I spur you through the summer woods. We will never again together see the sun rise, or watch it set beyond the banks of Green river. I'll not mount you again, my pretty Silk." Thus, with her hand on the pony's mane, stroking the long silken threads or patting the high-arched neck of the graceful animal, Madge poured out expressions of affection, and Silk appeared, by her mournful *pose* and a moist sort of eye-light, to give intelligence to what her mistress was saying.

"Take me back, Ruth; take me quickly, and bear me gently, gently, for I am sinking."

Large tears hung on the fringed lids of her eyes, and her fine lip quivered as, leaning forward from the servant's arms, Madge pressed her lips to Silk's bowed neck.

"Oh, Miss Madge! What! you ain't gwine to faint? Oh, please don't," the girl innocently exclaimed.

"Faint—ah, faint forever!" replied Madge, in a languid tone.

When she was again laid upon the bed and her father had administered a cordial, she said,

"Don't you see them, papa? don't you see them just there, at the foot of my bed, here close to the pillow; now there, flying all round about; spirits, with bright eyes and silver wings; they bring me flowers and fruits, and now they float away on soft, white clouds. See! they beckon me to come after. I must go"; and she half rose from the bed, then sank back on the pillow, murmuring, "they have all gone and left me."

Soon after, the doctor came in and felt her pulse. Col. Vertner observed the expression of his face change.

"What is it, doctor?"

The man of science shook his head mournfully. Col. Vertner caught some such words as "God's will be done"; he heard no more, but understood *all*. Taking his stand at the head of the bed, he laid his hand gently upon his child's brow, and remained thus through all the bitter scene.

Mrs. Vertner was sent for. Ruth and the nurse came in also. There, silent, they stood, until the doctor, placing his hand upon the pulse, turned to them, saying, in a low voice,

"All is over."

Then such a shriek went up from the group as seemed to break the ceiling.

But Madge had spoken no more after the vision of the flight of angels. With her eyes and lips firmly closed, she sank to that sweetest of life's sleeps, whose awaking lies on the other side of the blessed river!

....

They buried her with her kindred, in the family graveyard. A white marble shaft—engraved upon which is her name, her age, birth and death—points to the spot where she rests.

In conclusion, we have only to say that in Col. Vertner's heart there was left ever after an unfilled void. Sometimes, it is true, he thought of his promise to his daughter of liberating his slaves, but, then, opposed to that promise were self-interest, love of worldly possessions and a profound belief that holding slaves was an unerring mark of respectability. Besides, his wife and friends and family connections would have laughed at him and derided him as a "negrophilist" (a word the meaning of which, though in current use at the South, we are sorely puzzled to make out), so he continued to put off the promise, saying to himself, as many another has done, "I'll liberate them at my death."

And as for Mr. Norton, he, we learn, was another one of those swift converts to the doctrine of the South, "that God has cursed the negro with perpetual slavery"; so he continued to keep and to add to the number which his wife left him, sowing the seed of iniquity, to reap, at some future day, the whirlwind and the tempest.

If there are those who blame Mr. Norton and Col. Vertner for their temporizing spirit, we only ask them to look into their own hearts and see if they are not also playing with the spirit of Justice and trifling with higher instincts. Col. Vertner and Mr. Norton—wrong and wicked though they be—are yet far less to blame than the law which gives them such irresponsible and cruel power. Let all such as condemn these two men remember to do their part to lessen such unjust power by fighting a good fight and casting a true vote in 1860.

The End

About the Author

Mattie Griffith (c. 1825–1906) was born into a slave-owning family in Owensboro, Kentucky. Orphaned at a young age, she inherited six enslaved people, whom she emancipated after leaving the South and joining the antislavery movement. Over the course of her abolitionist career, she wrote two novels, *Autobiography of a Female Slave* (1856) and *Madge Vertner* (1859–1860). Neither novel earned her fame or monetary success.

In 1866 she married Albert Gallatin Browne, a lawyer and fellow abolitionist. At various times they lived in Cambridge, New York City, and Boston, moving in society circles in each city. In 1869 Griffith served as vice president of the National Woman Suffrage Association.

Accessible Archives utilizes computer technology and a large team of conversion specialists to provide easy access to vast quantities of archived historical information previously available only in microformat, hard copy form or as images.

Diverse primary source materials reflecting broad views across American history and culture have been assembled into comprehensive databases. Developed by dedicated instructors and students of Americana, these databases allow access to the rich store of materials from leading books, newspapers and periodicals then current.

Current Collections

ᐧ **African American Newspapers**

The Christian Recorder (1861–1902)
The Colored American (1837–1841)
Frederick Douglass' Paper (1851–1855; 1859–1863)
Freedom's Journal (1827–1829)
The National Era (1847–1860)
The North Star (1847–1851)
Provincial Freedom (1854–1857)
Weekly Advocate (1837–1837)

ᐧ *Frank Leslie's Weekly*
ᐧ *Godey's Lady's Book*
ᐧ *The Liberator*
ᐧ *The Lily*
ᐧ *History of Woman Suffrage*
ᐧ *National Anti-Slavery Standard*
ᐧ *National Citizen and Ballot Box*
ᐧ *The Pennsylvania Gazette*
ᐧ *The Pennsylvania Newspaper Record: Delaware County*
ᐧ *The Revolution*
ᐧ *Scenes in the Life of Harriet Tubman*
ᐧ *South Carolina Newspapers*
ᐧ *Twelve Years a Slave*
ᐧ *The Virginia Gazette*

ᐧ **American County Histories**

Central
Mid-Atlantic (Parts 1 and 2)
Midwest
New England (Parts 1 and 2)
The Southeast
The Southwest
The West

ᐧ **The Civil War**

Part I: A Newspaper Perspective
Part II: The Soldiers' Perspective
Part III: The Generals' Perspective
Part IV: A Midwestern Perspective
Part V: Iowa's Perspective
Part VI: Northeast Regimental Histories
Part VII: Abraham Lincoln Library Abolitionist Books

ᐧᐧ accessible-archives.com ᐧᐧ

www.ingramcontent.com/pod-product-compliance
Lightning Source LLC
Chambersburg PA
CBHW051629180726
48284CB00006B/1660